The Pain of

Em Jones

CW01064566

This is a work of fiction. Similarities to real people, places, or events are entirely coincidental.

THE PAIN OF AFTER

First edition. June 12, 2024.

Copyright © 2024 Em Jones.

ISBN: 979-8224042746

Written by Em Jones.

Table of Contents

For every young queer child who felt as though they never had a safe space.
safe space.
Welcome home.

Prologue

After

Love and time are the cruelest devices. Most often, working in tandem. One always thinks you have more time than one does. One never stops to appreciate the time one has until it's too late. Until one is left reminiscing and longing for memories long passed. Most will tell you that time heals. It will heal old wounds, and at some point, it won't hurt as much, but no one ever tells you how much time will go by before it stops hurting.

In the beginning, time allows those feelings to fester. It allows those thoughts and longings to continue until one day they consume you. Until one day they consume everything you are. Maybe after a few years you won't cry over a slight memory of the person. Give it a few more and maybe you will smile when you hear their name. Time heals slowly. Almost too slowly to notice.

This is the tale of two girls. Two girls who fell in love hard and fast because neither one of them knew if there would be another day for them. They fell in love because they weren't supposed to be in love. They fell in love because every second they were together was an adrenaline rush neither had felt.

Phoebe Conners and Sydney Garcia. Two complete opposites in every way. Sydney Garcia, her life planned out from the time she was born. Phoebe Conners, the girl no one truly knew. The girl who hid behind thick walls because she didn't want anyone to see what was happening on the other side.

Phoebe Conners and Sydney Garcia. Two girls whose love was doomed from the start.

Part One

Before

From the time I arrived in Auora, I listened to what was taught to me. I stayed as far away as possible. If I saw her walking toward me, I would bolt in the other direction. My father put in a request to the school that we were never put in the same classes. He didn't want an influence like Phoebe Conner's to rub off on me. I was their perfect daughter who had the perfect life ahead of her. I had no room to mess anything up.

For three years I did what my parents told me. I was never in a class with her. I never met her eyes. I would never speak to her. I listened to what I was told. I never strayed. That all broke apart my first day of senior year.

I walked into class that first day, Lindsey Johnson, my best friend since childhood following closely behind me. I froze, Lindsey bumping into me when I saw her. Phoebe Conners. Right there in my class. Right there, twisting an unlit cigarette between her fingers.

"What in the word is she doing here?" I whispered to Lindsey, my heart pounding in my chest as I stood in that doorway. I watched as a smirk found it's way to her face.

I hear Lindsey curse under her breath before she grabs my arm and pulls me out of the doorway.

"After class we will go to the counselors and get your schedule change. Just don't engage."

With that she walked into the class, leaving me standing outside of the classroom looking like a fool. I took a deep breath, straighting my shoulders before walking into the class, quickly scanning each desk for my name while making a point to not look towards her.

When I found my name, I sat down, taking my first breath since walking into that classroom. I looked up, only to find the blue eyes of Phoebe Conners staring at me.

"Well, I was wondering how long it was going to be before you were finally forced to face me," she says.

I stared, my heart quickening in my chest. This couldn't be happening. There was no way we were trapped in the same class and now I had to sit next to her.

"What, did you want one?" she asks, holding out the unlit cigarette in her hands.

My eyes widened, as I tried to wrack my brain to find an rational answer.

"No," was all I managed to squeak out.

She laughed before taking the cigarette out of her mouth and twirling it around her fingers again.

"Relax, it's just clove, nothing that will kill you," she said.

As if the fact they were clove would sway my opinion about her holding a cigarette in the middle of class.

"Oh come on Garcia. Don't tell me you have a stick up your ass like your father," she laughs.

I didn't dignify that with a response. I spent the rest of the class, staring ahead at the board and trying to ignore the feeling of Phoebe's eyes on me. The second the bell rang, I bolted out of the class, leaving Lindsey to catch up with me.

.I stormed through the door to student services, my breath coming out in short pants.

"I need a class change form," I gasped.

The receptionist looked at me with a look of surprise before looking down and grabbing a paper from her desk.

"What class do you need changed?" the receptionist asked.

She slid the form through the small slit between the glass and the desk, and I reached out, snatching it from the desk and digging around my bag for a pencil.

"Career Management and Selection," I answered, looking down at the form.

"I can't do that, Miss. Garcia," the receptionist says.

I look up from the paper, my stomach sinking.

"What do you mean you can't switch that class?" I demanded.

"That class is required for all seniors, so we can't transfer you out," they said.

"There has to be another teacher I can switch to," I pleaded.

"The only teacher who teaches Career Management and Selection at that time is Mrs. Mercer, and looking at your schedule, the class period you have it is the only period you could take it would be 5th period," the receptionist said.

My heart sunk into my chest. I would be stuck in a class with Phoebe Conners for the next four months.

"There's nothing you can do?" I asked one last time.

The receptionist shakes her head, and I slide the class change form back towards her.

"Thanks anyway," I muttered before shrugging my bag back on my shoulder and slowly walking out of class.

Lindsey is waiting as I walk out the door, and by the frown on my face, she already knew I couldn't get the class changed.

"You know, maybe it won't be that big of a deal," Lindey tells me. "It's not as if this is the entire school day, it's one class."

I looked over at her, an incredulous look on my face.

"You're crazy. You are actually insane."

From behind us someone clears their throat. Lindsey and I turn around, smoke hitting our faces as we come face to face with Phoebe Conners. A man stands next to her, a cigarette pressed to his lips as he glares down at us. My hands reach towards my mouth, covering my mouth and nose as to not breathe in the smoke.

Phoebe lets out a laugh, pulling in a puff of smoke.

"You know you odn't have to cover your mouth right? It's not as if the smoke will kill you."

"Actually, second hand smoke is almost as dangerous as if you are smoking yourself," I find myself saying.

There was an amused look on her face as she turned to look at the man next to her.

"Did you hear that, Alexander, all those times you smoke around me is as if I was smoking myself," she laughed before turning back towards us.

Lindsey is staring her down with a look of pure malice on her face.

"Did you need something, Conners?" she demanded.

Phoebe laughs, leaning off the wall and walking towards us. "Conners now, is it?" she asked. "I didn't realize we were on a last-name basis."

"Well, I certainly don't respect you enough to use your first name," Lindsey said, staring Phoebe right in the eyes.

"Oh shit," she laughs. "Didn't know you had it in you."

Alexander put his hand over his mouth to stop laughing. That only made me more annoyed. They thought this was a joke. They thought of my pain and torture as something to laugh about. She, indeed, was diabolical.

As we were standing there, staring at one another, I couldn't help but notice how tall Phoebe was. Lindsey was by no means short, but Phoebe had her beat by at least 3 inches. As she was staring at Lindsey, she glanced at me, and a smile came over her face.

"Just to let you know, because you bolted out of there before you could hear, but Mercer's seating chart is final. Looks like the two of us are going to be seat buddies for the entire semester," she said before turning back towards Alexander. She tossed the cigarette on the cheap tile and stomped on it, Alexander soon following suit.

Lindsey shifted in front of me as if to shield me from Phoebe.

"See you in class seat, buddy," she calls out before turning and walking away, leaving the scent of clove and smoke in her path.

Lindsey and I stood there dumbfounded at the exchange that had just occurred.

"Not going to be a big deal?" I demanded as we watched Phoebe Conners walk away. "Not gonna be a big deal, huh?"

Before

Those first few weeks were a nightmare. However, Phoebe wasn't looking at it the way I did. She was amused, taking every chance she could to tell me just how amusing the situation was. After a few weeks, I stopped become Garcia and was now second hand smoke. That was when she decided she was going to share a fact of the day during every class.

I did everything possible to avoid her, not even looking in her direction. She would give me this this look of smug satisfaction as she shared the most random fact before pulling out another cigarette. She would watch me as she twisted it between her fingers as if waiting for a reaction, but I refused to give in. I knew that if I gave her the satisfaction of a response, she would only keep going, and the last thing I wanted to do was continue these interactions with Phoebe Conners.

"You know, you're not a lot of fun," she said one morning.

I choked out a laugh and turned towards her, anger burning inside of me.

"Is that supposed to be this morning's fact of the day?" I demanded.

Phoebe nodded before holding out the cigarette to me.

"I didn't know if you knew, so I figured it was my job to educate," she answered.

I rolled my eyes, my heart pounding in my chest.

"Fun fact for you Phoebe Conners, you are not as hilarious as you like to pretend you are," I said, turning to look at her. I wanted a reaction from her. I wanted anything to prove that she was an actual human being who had feelings. But Phoebe Conners was not one to give in. Her smile didn't even falter.

"How would you know Garcia? You've avoided me your entire life," she questioned.

"I hear things Conners, everyone in this town does. Everyone knows you have been arrested for public intoxication. You smoke weed until your mind is so messed up that you can't even function without it and make stupid decisions because of it. You self destruct until there is nothing left in your life to be happy about. You destroy everyone near you because you have nothing left in your life you can be happy about."

Anger fills her eyes as she stares at me. The smile disappeared as her hands clenched into fists in her lap. A note of satisfaction rolled through me. I had gotten exactly what I wanted from Phoebe. A reaction. She finally gave me the reaction I wanted.

"You and your dad can go fuck yourselves," she seethed before throwing the cigarette in her bag and looking towards the front of the classroom, avoiding my gaze the rest of class.

Lindsey texted me asking what had just happened and I just shrugged. I knew what I had said was out of line but if this was the only way to get her out of my life, then that is what it took. There was no better way to do that then to make her hate me.

The minute the bell rang, she picked up her bag, threw it over her shoulder, and raced out of class, not even stopping to push her chair in. Everyone stopped to stare past her, but no one had an explanation for what had just happened. I felt guilt start to knaw at me but I swallowed it down. I shouldn't feel bad. I couldn't start to feel bad for her.

"What the hell was that all about in there?" Lindsey asks from her spot next to me.

"I told her she destroys everything and everyone around her," I answered her.

Lindsey smiles, wrapping her arm around my shoulder.

"Don't worry about apologizing. She's been messing with you for weeks; all you did was give it right back. And she's a bitch. You don't need to apologize to a bitch for being a bitch right back," she said.

I wanted to tell her that she was right. I wanted to say that I agreed and didn't feel bad about what I had said, but that guilt continued eating its way through me. What I said shouldn't make me feel this way. I shouldn't feel guilty for telling the truth, but I would have done the same thing Phoebe had if someone had told me that.

My father had always told me there was no shame in telling a wicked person to their face that they were wicked. He said that was the only way the world would progress, but there had to be a line drawn. I had crossed the line of telling a wicked person and completely insulting them.

I promised myself that I would apologize to her. Even if I was going to be staying away from her, I would still tell her what I said was out of line. I could still be civil and apologize without being close to someone.

After

Phoebe Conners had this light to her. A light that drew you in like a moth to a flame. I would later look back on those times when I searched everywhere for her as a beginning to an end. The way I tried going out of way to apologize to her for what I said. Tried to act like I just felt terrible about what I said, but that was not the truth.

From that first day, I was in class with her, I wanted to know Phoebe Conners. Not the Phoebe Conners everyone told you about. Not the druggy. Not the one who smoked a pack of cigarettes daily. Not the one would come to school drunk or stoned at least twice a week. I wanted to know the side of her she hid away from the entire world. I wanted to know why she acted the way she did. I wanted to know what was going on in her life that made her like this. I wanted to know what happens in her head. I wanted to know Phoebe Conners.

My family never did understand my fascination. My eager interest in the girl who soon occupied my every thought. They would whisper that I had gone crazy or that this was just a simple act of teenage rebellion, but it didn't matter what they said, my fascination never changed.

My fascination started with her life. I wanted to know everything. I wanted to know what made her brain tick. What she thought about on a daily basis. What had caused her to be the way that she was.

I should have known that when you spend that much time thinking about someone, you are bound to fall for them. And when I fell, I fell hard. She was everything to me. She became my entire life. She was everything to me. Everything that I loved and held dear. She was my entire world.

Phoebe Conners built walls. She prevented anyone from getting too close because she knew the minute they did. She was going to be the one who had to deal with the loss but when you got close to her. When she let you in, she would never leave you.

Phoebe Conners never left anyone. Once you gained her trust, she was loyal for life. She was never the one to start fights. She was the type of person who would climb through your bedroom window at 1 a.m. just because you said you couldn't sleep. You were never worried about saying the wrong thing. You could scream at her and tell her she was nothing. You could physically ruin her but if she loved you, she would stay.

No matter what, she would stay. She would stay like no one else in her life had stayed for her.

IF YOU ASKED ANYONE, they would tell you everything had started with the death of Phoebe's sister Autumn. She was four years older than Phoebe, and from the moment Phoebe was old enough to walk, the two of them were thick as thieves. Wherever Autumn went, Phoebe was guaranteed not to be far behind.

What many didn't know about were Phoebe and Autumn's parents. Both born trust fund children. You would know it just from looking at them. They met 3 years before having Autumn Conners. 4 years later, there was Phoebe Conners. Genevive Conners wouldn't speak ill against her husband. He was tough, she would tell people when aksed. He expected a lot from their children just as he had been expected a lot of as a child.

Doing your best was not tolerated in the Conners household. You either succeeded or you didn't. There was either winning or losing and losing would result in punishment. Genevieve bought their children their first bottle of concealer when Phoebe turned three. She didn't want anyone to know what harm had been caused by their rash, uncaring father.

Often you would catch Autumn flinching at loud noises or if someone came too close to her. Many thought more sinister things occurred in that house, but there was no way to prove it. It was hard on both of them, but one day it got to be too much for Autumn.

It was Phoebe who had found her the morning of Feburary 16th, the day after Phoebe Conners turned 14. Phoebe would later tell the police it had been her best birthday. There were no fights, no accidents. Just her family being as a normal family would be. She said Autumn seemed more at peace than she had been for years. Pheobe didn't look too much into it. She thought it was just because it was her birthday and a break from the daily fights in the house. Autumn even gave Phoebe her favorite necklace and told Phoebe she just wanted her to have it. Said she wanted to pass on her favorite things to her favorite person. The next morning, she realized why Autumn had been so at peace.

In the cold light of Feburary 16th, under the watchful eye of the snow falling past the windows, Phoebe Conners walked into Autumn Conners bathroom to find Autumn dead in the bathtub, her wrists hanging limply out of the tub.

Phoebe Conners would have liked to say that she didn't remember anything of that day but she would wake up in a cold sweat at dreams of all that red. The red that was staining every tile. The red that clung to every inch of Phoebe Conners as she sat down next to Autumn and held her hand. Held Autumn's cold limp hand because she knew it was her last time she would ever be able to touch her again.

Phoebe didn't call for her parents. She didn't want them to know yet. She wanted one last chance with Autumn. One last time to be there with her sister.

"I didn't cry," she would say. "I just sat there, red staining my pants. Autumn just looked so at peace. So happy with the outcome. I couldn't blame her either. I blamed myself. Maybe if I had been a better sister or acted older so she thought she could talk with me, she would still be here. Police would tell me there were more deep-rooted problems that I couldn't have done anything to help, but that didn't make things feel any better."

When Phoebe finally called for her parents, neither of them came running. Both of them took their time to get into the bathroom. Phoebe couldn't even blame them. If she had known what she was walking into, she would have walked as slowly as possible.

When they got to the room, they both stood in the doorway. Phoebe saw the look of surprise and pain that covered every inch of her mother's face but her father just stood there, no emotion in any of his features.

Neither of them cried when they saw Autumn. Phoebe was scolded by her mother for sitting on the ground and staining her pants. Her father just muttered that he would be calling an ambulance before he left the room. Phoebe's mother tried to get her to stand up and get away from her sister but Phoebe wouldn't do it. She wouldn't leave her sister like this again. She needed to be there for Autumn. She couldn't leave Autumn.

Phoebe didn't start crying until the EMT's tried taking away Autumn's body. Phoebe screamed and tried to wrap herself around Autumn's body. Her father pulled her back, holding her away from her sister as Phoebe screamed. She could have still been alive. No one had checked her pulse. She could have still had a pulse.

Phoebe broke away from her father as the ambulance started to load Autumn in. Phoebe chased after them, trying to get into the ambulance with Autumn. Her mother grabbed her, crushing her into her chest to make it look as though she was hugging her. She wasn't hugging her. She was trying to silence her cries.

Phoebe turned around just in time to see the ambulance drive away with her sister inside. She thought she heard someone screaming as her legs gave out from underneath her. Phoebe wouldn't realize until weeks later that she was the one screaming. She had been the one screaming for her sister. She was the one screaming as if her entire world had just been ripped away from her.

Phoebe's father ripped her from her mothers arms and backhanded her, telling her displays of such emotion had no place in this world and told her to back to her room. Phoebe had debated taking her own life that night. What was left in the world if Autumn was no longer in it? Who was Phoebe without Autumn? Phoebe didn't think she would survive.

At the time, Phoebe didn't think her father had done anything wrong. She had been screaming in front of someone. She had made a fool of herself. After the day Autumn died, Phoebe didn't let anyone know how much it hurt. She didn't cry in front of anyone but at night, if you listened close enough, you would have been able to hear the heartbroken sobs of a girl who had just lost the most important thing to her.

Sometimes you can still hear those cries. If you listen close enough to the whistle of the wind, you can hear the sobs of a girl who had just lost the only thing that had ever mattered to her. I wouldn't advise listening for those cries. You will never be able to forget the sound of them.

Phoebe Conners didn't speak for a year after that. Her parents tried everything they could, but there was nothing they could do except wait. Everyone told her Phoebe would come around, and it would be like nothing had ever happened. She did come around at one point, but it wasn't like they thought.

The Phoebe Conners who followed her sister and did everything her sister did was gone. There was no getting her back. She became the person everyone knew her to be. Cold, abrasive, and uncaring. That's how everyone pictured her, but that just wasn't true. The old Phoebe Conners was still in there. The old Phoebe Conners waited for someone to let her in and let her heal and work through the grief in a way she had never been allowed.

What child should be raised in a house where they are punished for showing feelings? What kind of child should worry about not showing any emotion when they lose one of the most important people to them? That is something a child should never have to worry about. In no world should a child be punished for loving someone enough that they don't know how to live without them once they are gone.

Before

I wish I could say there were someone who occupied my thoughts more than Phoebe Conners, but that would be a lie. For the next two weeks, she refused to talk to me. I would catch her looking every so often, but she offered no snide comments, no joking relations. It was as though she had shut down completely. The few times I ran into her in the hallway, she would turn the other way and refuse to speask. The times I walked by her while she was smoking, she said nothing as I plugged my nose. I didn't care so much about breathing in second-hand smoke anymore- I just wanted some reaction from her, but there was nothing. It was as if I no longer existed to Phoebe Conners.

I realized how ridiculous it sounded to care. I shouldn't have cared about her as much as I did. Everytime I caught myself thinking about her I would scold myself. There was no reason I needed to be thinking of her, and yet she accompanied my every thought. I told myself that I was only thinking about her because I felt bad about what I had said. Once I apologized to her, all of this would go away. It was just the guilt. And yet, when I would walk into class I found myself searching to see if she was in her seat. I would catch myself looking for her in the hallways, or purposefully walking past where she and Alexander would go to smoke, just so I would be able to see her.

We would make eye contact in class everyday as I sat down, but we both would say nothing. A few times I told myself that I was going to apologize. I was just going to walk in there, tell her I was sorry and then never have to speak to her again, but when I walked into class, I could never bring myself to commit to the words. If I saw her in the hallway she would immediately turn the other way, Alexander following closely at her heel. If I saw her at her usual smoking spot she would watch me as I passed as if daring me to speak to her

It was hard to ignore the looks I got from everyone as I walked through the hallway. Somehow it had gotten around school that Miss Sydney Garcia, who went out of her way to stay away from Phoebe Conners, had gotten put into the same class and had done something to tick her off royally. Sometimes, I think Mercer knew as well and found some form of enjoyment from the fact she had us sitting next to each other.

"What if you just write her a note and slide it in her locker?" Lindsey said one day. "Then you don't have to speak to her, and you can just be done with this whole situation."

"It's not going to mean anything if I don't say it to her face Lindsey," I answered.

I kept Phoebe Conners to myself though. I wouldn't speak to anyone other than Lindsey about Phoebe. I knew what my parents would say. I knew my mom would have told me to give up on apologizing. She would say that you didn't apologize unless you meant it and in her mind, I could never be sincere with an apology to Phoebe. My dad would have reminded me of everything Phoebe had done. He would tell me she was a ship on fire. In a matter of time, it was going to burn down and everyone who didn't jump ship would go down with it.

I kept promising myself that after I apologized all of these feelings would go away. I was feeling guilt and that was why I was drawn to her. I felt pulled in her direction because I wanted to apologize. That was it.

I would repeat 'ship on fire' whenever I saw her in the hallway. Whenever I felt like maybe I wasn't just wanting to apologize I would tell myself that she was a ship on fire. I repeated that phrase that it became a mantra to me.

"Ship on fire," I repeatedly whispered to myself when no one was looking. "Ship on fire."

After two weeks of the same process, I walked into class to see Phoebe Conners sitting at a seat halfway across the room. She stared me down as I walked to my seat, moving as slowly as possible to give Mercer the chance to correct me and move me to the seat over by Phoebe. Maybe she had just changed the seating chart. Teachers did that. They would change things around sometimes but Mercer got off on putting us closer together. She lived for the chaos.

But Mercer said nothing. I tried to ignore the flush in my cheeks as I sat down in the seat, still feeling Phoebe's eyes digging into my back. When Mercer began talking, I risked one glance in Phoebe direction.

Bruises. That was all I saw when I looked at Phoebe. On her cheek there was a bruise that took up almost half of her face. You could see the splotches of concelor even from halfway across the room. Her neck had scratch marks that reached all the way up to her jaw. It looked like an animal had gotten to her. I sharply inhaled, causing Phoebe to turn around and stare at me. She didn't hesitate with popping her collar as she saw me staring. She gave me a look that was meant to me malice, but all I saw was exhaustion in her eyes. Exhaustion and pain.

I couldn't focus on anything other than Phoebe Conners for the rest of the class period. Those were not bruises that came with hickeys. Those were not the bruises that came from joking around and falling. Those were the type of bruises that were placed there on purpose. The kind that doesn't go away for a long time. When the bell rang, she bolted up from her seat and ran out, her hand holding her collar to her neck. Lindsey watched as I stared after her, shaking her head.

"Following her won't do you any good if she is not talking to you," she said before walking out of the classroom, leaving me standing there, unsure of who to react.

What do you say to someone when you see something like that? How do you play it off as though it was normal for a person to be covered in bruises? How can you look at someone the same way again? It was none of my business. Every instinct told me not to do anything and let it happen, but I couldn't just sit there and not do anything.

"I have to try," I said to Lindsey as I raced out of the classroom to catch up with Phoebe. I raced through the hallways, not stopping for anyone. I heard curses of disapproval coming from behind me as I ran but couldn't stop. This could be the only chance I ever got to apologize. I chased her out to the parking lot, my back swinging haphazardly as I balanced it on one shoulder. When I finally saw her, she and Alexander got into the car.

"Pheobe," I yelled, every head turning as I steadied myself and walked closer to her car.

"What the fuck," I saw her say to Alexander before stepping out of the car and leaning against it.

"Garcia, to what do I owe this pleasure?" she asked, her arms crossed over her chest.

I froze. I had rehearsed this so many times in my head, but now that I was actually here I was frozen. I didn't know what to say.

"Shit, or get off the second-hand pot smoke," Alexander called from inside the car, a cigarette dangling from his fingertips.

I turned back to look at Phoebe Conners; her arms were crossed across her chest, that smirk covering her face.

"I'm sorry," I blurted out.

Phoebe didn't let any sign of emotion appear on her face. That smirk just stayed there.

"What are you sorry for?" she asks, grabbing a cigarette from her pocket and pressing it to her lips, her other hand hovering over her other pocket as if to decide whether she wanted to light it.

"I'm sorry for what I said a few weeks ago. It was uncalled for, and I had no reason to say such a thing," I answered, nervously fidgeting with my hands.

She looked at Alexander, who was sitting in the car, looking as though he was ready to fun me over with his car.

"Did you ever stop to think that I was not that upset with you?" she asked.

My brain short-circuited. I thought that was the whole reason she moved seats. I thought that was why she avoided me in the hallways, and I couldn't see her walking around anymore.

"But you convinced Mercer to move seats," I said, my voice almost in a whisper. "You avoid me like I'm the plague. You refuse to even look in my direction unless you think I can't see you. That seems like the behaviour of someone who is upset with another."

She laughed and reached into her pocket to grab the lighter. After lighting it and taking a deep puff, she looks down at me. I had never seen such malice in someone's eyes before.

"Don't get me wrong Garcia, I was pissed off at first, but I got over that quickly. I know you have never had to pay for your actions before because of your father. You can't blame someone who doesn't know any better, now can we? The thing is, Sydney Garcia, I just don't like you that much. Don't think I haven't noticed we have not had a single class together for the entire time we have gone to school together. Don't think I don't know the rumors your pig father spreads around about me. Don't stop thinking I care about what he thinks about me. I asked to be moved, not because I was upset with you, but because I couldn't stand being so close to you. So you can take your pity apology and your asshole of a father's opinions about me and shove it up your ass, okay," she says before throwing the cigarette on the ground, stomping on it with her boot, and climbing in the car.

I stood there dumbfounded. I had to jump out of the way to avoid being hit by Alexander as he tore out of the parking lot.

"Great talk Garcia," Phoebe yells out the window of the moving car.

Tears pricked the corners of my eyes, but I swallowed them down. I was not about to let Phoebe Conners be the reason I was crying in the middle of the school's parking lot.

I felt everyone's eyes on me. I had gotten so sick of that feeling. I wanted it gone. I felt someone wrap their arm around me and I looked to see Lindsey. There was no pity in her eyes as she spoke.

"I tried telling you, Syd, nothing good comes from Phoebe Conners," she says before grabbing my arm. "Ship on fire Sydney, ship on fire."

After

Three months after Autumn's death, Phoebe Conners picked up her first cigarette. She found it in her father's office and took it from his desk. She climbed to the roof and lit it with a lighter she found in Autumn's room. She felt sick from the first inhale, but it was the first she had felt anything in 3 months, so she kept going. Her parents thought she was just doing it for attention, and yet attention was the last thing Phoebe Conners wanted. She wanted nothing more than to feel something again. She wanted to go back to when she could close her eyes to see her sister's dead body in that bathdub. She wanted to return to a time when her father didn't touch her.

The first time her father touched her was two days after Autumn's funeral. She remembers him coming into her room late that night and telling her not to make a sound. After that, Phoebe Conners blocked the rest out of her mind. She shut her eyes and tried to pretend like it was not happening. After it was over and her father had left, Phoebe Conners told herself it was all over. He wouldn't do it again. He was just upset because he had lost his daughter and needed to let the emotion out somewhere. She thought it was the only time it would happen. She was wrong. Three days later Phoebe Conners closed her eyes and pretended she wasn't there. Her father told her not to tell anyone, and she was too scared to.

The first time Phoebe Conners cut herself was five months after Autumn's death. She sat there with the knife pressed against the skin on her thigh, tears streaming down her face. All that was in her head was Autumn lying down in that bathtub.

"One swipe against your thigh won't cause any harm," her mind told her. "One quick swipe won't kill you."

From downstairs, she heard the door open to the kitchen, signaling her parents were coming home. Panic filled her mind. She listened to her mother calling her from downstairs. She pressed the knife down into the skin, letting the pain wash over her. She watched as the blood slowly dripped down her thigh. She heard her mother calling her again, and she took the knife away and pressed a tissue to the skin where blood had trickled and wiped the blood away. Without looking at the cut she had made in her skin, she pressed a bandage on it and threw her sweatpants back on.

She walked downstairs, trying to clean up her face and act like everything was normal. At this point, she didn't even know what normal meant. No one even noticed the red stain on her thigh where the cut was.

The first time Phoebe Conners drank was eight months after Autumn died. Her parents had gone to spread Autmn's ashes in Ireland and had left Phoebe home alone. That first night was the hardest. She sat at the kitchen table, an open bottle of whisky, fifteen pill bottles, a pack of clove cigarettes she had bought with Autumn's old fake ID, and her switchblade in front of her. It was her choice. She would be choosing how she died.

She knew she could slip into a painless death and drink until she couldn't see two feet in front of her. She could do even more damage by adding cigarettes to it. She knew it would be painless, she wouldn't even feel a thing, but she didn't deserve that in her eyes. She deserved to die the way Autumn had died. She deserved to feel the same pain Autumn had felt. She knew she could press that switchblade to her wrist, cut, and be done. Go out the same way Autumn did, except this time... This time there would be no one there that cared about her to find her the next morning.

She could swallow a bunch of pills, but there was always the possibility that she would throw them up, and then her plan would be ruined. Phoebe Conners couldn't handle living another day. She wanted to die and she was going to do it tonight.

Her hand was shaking as she reached for the switchblade. Tears threatened to spill as her hand grew closer and closer. She drew her hand back before reaching toward the whisky bottle and chugging as much as possible in one sip.

The whisky burned as it went down, causing her to cough and splutter. She stumbled towards the kitchen to grab water, to try and stop the burning, but fell on the floor before she could. She tried to pick herself up off the ground and walk toward the fridge but stumbled the entire way. She grabbed a cup and filled it as high as possible, ignoring the overflow. With a shaky hand, she pressed it to her lips and took a giant sip, trying to stop the burning. Her head felt like it was swimming as she took another sip. An overwhelming feeling spread throughout her entire body. A feeling that stopped all pain. A feeling that Phoebe Conners was sure would lead to her death.

Phoebe Conners walked closer to the bottle, grabbed it by the neck, and drank as much of it as possible. She didn't want to live through this day. She just wanted the pain to stop. She wanted the missing her sister, the nightmares that plagued her every night, and her father coming into her room every other night. She wanted it all to stop. She was determined to make it stop.

Phoebe Conners didn't remember much from that night. Someone who did remember what happened was Charlie Garcia, the latest appointed police chief. He got a call from the Chadwick house around 9:30 that night. Their youngest son Alexander had gone to the Conners household to check on Phoebe Conners and found her unconscious on the kitchen floor, surrounded by a bottle of Fireball whisky. He called 911 and told them where to find her. When the ambulance arrived, no one was sure what to do in the situation other than bring her to the hospital and do everything they could.

Never before had they seen a 15-year-old try and drink themselves to death. When looking over the kitchen, they found a pack of clove cigarettes, a switchblade, and 15 pill bottles. The whole town knew what had happened to Autumn Conners just a few months prior, but no one expected the other Conner's sister to try and follow so closely behind.

The police tried contacting Phoebe's parents. They expected the usual panic from the parents when they hear that their child had just attempted suicide, but Jonathan Conners didn't sound worried. He told the police he and his wife would be back in a week. They were in the Bahamas.

No one could believe what they had heard. These parents whose children had just tried to commit were staying on their vacation and leaving their child there alone. When Phoebe was told the news she told them she would rather her parents be spreading her sisters ashes then be there with her.

No one told Phoebe Conners where her parents really were. They led her to believe her parents were spreading her sister's ashes, knowing that a 15-year-old as unstable as Phoebe Conners would not be able to handle the truth. No 15 year old, not matter how unstable would have been able to handle that. They were positive she would learn the truth at some point, but they were not going to be the one's who told this child what her parents were doing. Ignorance is bliss, and in this situation, ignorance was livesaving.

That was the first time the police would be called to the Conners household. There would be hundreds of other calls throughout the next three years that would forever maim the

Conners name. This would not be the first time Phoebe Conners would try to commit. This would not be the first time Alexander Chadwick would find Phoebe Conners in her house. This would not be the last time Jonathan Conners refused to be there for his child.

Before

The car ride home with Lindsey was silent. Neither of us said a word. Lindsey had been right and she knew it. I expected to hear the words 'I told you so' at some point during the ride home, but she never said them. Neither of us said anything.

She put the car in park as she pulled into my driveway, and looked out the window. I couldn't bear being in that car anymore. I threw my bag over my shoulder and walked inside, leaving Lindsey sitting in the driveway by herself. I dropped my bag on the ground, walking towards the pantry to get food. After the day I had I just wanted to sit in bed with potato chips and Netflix.

"Sydney, I'm so glad you could finally join us. Please come have a seat," My father says from the living room. I turn to see my entire family, all of them starting at me, sitting in the semicircle of furniture that filled our living room.

I come from a big family. I was the second oldest of 6, meaning that other than school, my other full-time job was babysitter. My older brother Tyler and I were basically unpaid third and fourth parents.

Tyler was older than me by two years and had just dropped out of college. He moved back home with the promise he would look for a job and pay rent. So far, that has not happened yet.

After me came the twins; Christine and Carlise. They were six years younger than me, putting them both in their first year of middle school. After the twins came Adam. Adam was nine, and you hardly ever saw him. He was always either on his Xbox or playing with his friends outside. Then came Cindy.

Cindy was six years old and had never gotten in trouble once in her life. Tyler and I say that after five kids, my parents just thought it was too much work to discipline the last one, so they just gave up.

"Hey, guys, what's going on?" I asked, grabbing the chips from the cupboard and shoving them into my mouth before walking into the living room.

"Syd, come sit down, please. We need to talk," my dad says.

He was still wearing his uniform from work. I slowly went to sit down on the loveseat across from my parents and the rest of my family.

"I thought we should talk about what has been happening at school lately. Mrs, Mercer tells us you have a class with Phoebe Conners, and you two have had an altercation," my dad says.

"We have one class together," I explained. "We used to sit together and we got into an argument. Phoebe convinced Mercer to move her so I don't even sit near her anymore. Honestly it's like we don't even have a class together."

That wasn't at all true. You could have felt Phoebe Conners presence from halfway across the world.

"Syd, we can talk to your counselors and get them to move you. You don't need to stay in a class with her. We know how important your future is to you, and we would hate for one class to ruin all of this," my mom says.

I shake my head again.

"Trust me, I already asked them but this is the only period I have open for this class. It's really not that big of a deal though. I said something that upset her and then apologized for it. There will be no more interaction between the two of us," I told them.

"One apology turns into sympathizing Sydney. You may say it's one apology but what happens if she apologizes to you. You will be forced to interact with her and then it's like the two of you are best friends," My father turns to the rest of my siblings to speak to them. "May this be a lesson to all of you. We do not allow any interaction to begin with those that are not good influences. If you feel uncomfortable at anytime with someone in your class, come to me and we will speak with the school."

"Dad, it was one interaction," I blurted out, every head turning to look at me. "She's eighteen. It's not like she will climb into your room at night and stab you to death in your bed."

Every head turns to look at me. My mom instinctively wraps her arm around Cindy and pulls her closer to her.

"Are we done here?" I ask, turning towards my mother.

She nods slowly as if she can't believe that just happened, and I stand up, muttering a quick "great" under my breath. Everyone is staring at me as I walk away from the living room.

I can feel my father's eyes boring into my back as I walk up the stairs toward my bedroom. I close the door behind me and flop on my bed. I'm too tired for this. After everything that had happened today, that was the last thing I needed.

My father would now be keeping a close eye on me. I knew he would be contacting my teachers at least once a month to see if anything happened between Phoebe and I. Mercer was going to have a field day with this.

I had never once questioned whether or not my father's thoughts on Phoebe were too harsh. After all of the stories he had told us since becoming the police chief, everyone knew to stay away from Phoebe Conners. Not just my family. It seemed the entire town had heard every story there was to know about Phoebe Conners.

My dad was first called to the Conners' house three years ago. He wouldn't tell me exactly why he was called, but after that, there was at least one call a month. He stopped going to the house about a year ago and started sending his officers. He would come back from the office after one of the days when someone was sent to the Conners' house with a grim look on his face and a silence that lingered between the entire family for what felt like weeks. Late at night, I could hear my mom whisper to my dad and ask about what had happened, but he wouldn't tell her much. He would only say that he was thankful for my mother and he was raising their children in a stable environment.

I opened my laptop on my bed, logged onto Netflix, and tried to find anything that could distract me from everything that had happened. Never once in my eighteen years of life did I say something to my parents that could have upset them. When you have as many siblings as I do, you have to set a good example for the rest. You can't let yourself get carried away because the minute one of the youngers sees it, they believe it is okay for them to do it.

I heard the door creak open and saw Cindy standing in the doorway. I closed my laptop and turned to look at where she was standing.

"What's the matter, Cind?" I whispered.

She doesn't say anything. She just jumps into my bed with me and wraps the blankets around her.

"Mommy and Daddy are fighting. I didn't want to hear it anymore," she whispers.

My breath catches in my throat. They were fighting because of me. Cindy was here because of me.

"I'm sorry, Cind," I whispered into her hair. "You can stay with me until Mom and Dad stop fighting."

I held her there, letting her fall asleep on my chest. Right there and then, I promised myself I would never let anyone take me away from my family. I didn't care what Phoebe Conners did, there would never be anything that would take me away from these people. They were my entire. They were the only thing that mattered, and nothing would ever come in between my family.

After

Twelve months after Autumn died, Phoebe Conners climbed to the roof of her house and smoked a pack of cigarettes in her honor. Her parents decided to leave her home and return to Ireland to visit, where they spread her ashes, so now it was just Phoebe Conners by herself. Alexander Chadwick had come over one night after she had drank herself to sleep and hid anything she could hurt herself with. Phoebe had gone into a rage, screaming and throwing things at him until she fell into a heap on the floor crying.

Alexander was the only person who had seen her cry in the past twelve months. Every morning he had come over, handing her coffee and a blueberry bagel with cream cheese. He had started to drive her to school in the mornings and sat with her at lunch. For the first little bit, he didn't say anything. He would just come over, hand her the food and wait for her to get into the car. After about two weeks, he said his first sentence to her. He was the first one to get her to talk in a year.

"Your parents didn't make me do this, just to let you know," he said.

"I know," Phoebe replied.

And just like that, a friendship emerged. Exchanging books, watching cult classics, and smoking together on the roof. At some point, Phoebe Conner's parents mentioned that she wanted less attention since Alexander started coming around. Even though she had never gone into detail, he knew certain things that had

41

happened to her. He noticed when she wore sweaters and long sleeves in the middle of a heat wave. When she stopped wearing shorts, and when she would, she would hold her hands close to her thighs as if to shy anyone away from seeing anything.

Alexander was good at reading between the lines. He knew something was happening behind the scenes, yet he couldn't do anything about it. He felt horrible sitting there doing nothing, just waiting for something bad to happen to her but he had no solid proof to go to the police with.

When Phoebe woke up in the morning, she had the worst hangover of her life. Alexander held her hair back as she threw up and cried on the bathroom floor. He bought her greasy burgers and fries to try and soak up the alcohol and made her drink an entire pot of coffee. After she was sobered up a bit, he drove her back to his house and hid her in his room. His parents didn't like the idea of her coming over to his house, but he knew she couldn't be alone at this time.

Alexander stayed with her through everything. He would come over before school, bringing her food, and would stick around for a few hours after school. Whenever her parents left to go somewhere on vacation, he would come and stay over so she wouldn't be alone. He made her feel something for the first time in a year. He made the void that was left after Autumn died to feel smaller. Calls became less frequent to the Conners' house until 15 months after the death of Autumn.

Alexander came over one Sunday morning to check on Phoebe. Alexander would later say he had never felt panic like that ever before. He felt like he couldn't move. There was Phoebe, lying on the ground with 5 empty pill bottles surrounding her. Alexander ran over towards her, picking her up in his arms and trying to make her throw up the pills she had swallowed. He fought to get her to throw up the pills. He needed them out of her system. Alexander had never felt such relief as she threw up. The pills were out of her system. She was going to be okay. Alexander would never be able to forget how she lay on the ground, sweating and dry heaving to get all the pills out of her body.

After he called the ambulance and they brought her to the hospital, they asked him if there was anyone they could call to come and pick him up. He shook his head, telling them he would stay with Phoebe until she could leave. He slept there for three nights if sleep was the word you could use to describe what he did. He would sleep for two hours before waking up in a panic, immediately looking over to where Phoebe laid.

His parents tried telling him he shouldn't waste his time. They told him he was getting involved in something he had no control over. They kept telling him this was too much for one person to take on and he needed to let some things go. He refused to listen, though. He stayed with her in that hospital room and didn't leave until she did.

Phoebe Conners wouldn't talk to anyone except for Alexander. She didn't want them to call her parents. She didn't want to go home. She was upset with herself. She was convinced she had finally done it this time. She had thought she wasn't going to wake up again. She was convinced that this was the last time. She was finally going to see her sister again.

When she got back home, her parents were waiting for her. They told Alexander they were grateful he was there and he could leave because they could handle it. Alexander was hesitant. He didn't want to leave her there. He didn't know what would happen, but the look on her father's face made it sound like he didn't want to know what would happen. He gave Phoebe a hug and drove away, a nagging feeling of fear growing stronger as he got farther away from the house.

PHOEBE CONNERS WALKED into school the morning after she came home with bruises under her eyes she claimed were just dark circles from lack of sleep, and the white bandages wrapped around her wrists were just from a mishap when cooking. It wasn't a mishap during cooking. She had taken the razor to her wrist again. She did it because he left her alone with her father. It was his fault.

Alexander tried asking her what had happened, trying to find proof of her being harmed by her parents, but she wouldn't speak on it. She kept claiming it was an accident and she was just tired. That was when she got into her first fight.

Those in school felt it was okay to ask her what it had felt like when she tried to kill herself. They asked her if she was upset it didn't work or if she would try again. Alexander would tell them to stop, but that didn't stop the nagging questions. Phoebe thought these were mindless questions. How could she not be upset it didn't work? People didn't try to kill themselves just for the fun of it all. They tried killing themselves because they hated their lives and they hated themselves.

She snapped when Tyler Garica asked if she had just done it for attention. Phoebe Conners lunged at him, tackling him to the ground and punching him. No thought was in her brain other than the fact she had failed. She was still here, and Autumn wasn't. She moved with a blind rage, screaming with every punch. She heard the sickening crunch of bone underneath her fists, but she didn't stop. She kept going, taking out all her anger and frustration on him.

When she was pulled away from him she remembers looking around at all the scared faces, her eyes landing on one. One face that she could recognize from anywhere. It was Sydney Garcia, the sister of Tyler and the daughter of Charlie Garica, the police chief.

She felt so much anger and hatred towards him, and she found herself wishing that it was Sydney who she had just pounded into the ground. In some way, destroying a Garcia would be just like going after Charlie.

Charlie had never done anything to help her. He had seen everything that had happened. He knew Autumn killed herself and yet he never did anything to help her. She blamed him for everything. Every part of this was Charlie's fault.

Phoebe vowed to herself that she wouldn't stop until she could watch the entire Garcia family burn to the ground. She would not stop until Charlie Garica was nothing. Until he had nothing.

Loud voices yelled at her as she was dragged from the scene of the fight towards the principal's office, and when asked why she had done it, why she had physically assaulted someone she had never met, she just shrugged. She told them she just felt like doing it, and would do it again if she had the chance. She was told Tyler Garcia had to go to the hospital to get his nose set because she had broken it that badly but she just answered that he had it coming to him.

Everyone stood there wondering what had just happened. How could a young girl like this be so careless? How could one girl cause this much damage? Everyone knew what had happened to Phoebe in the last year. They knew what happened to Autumn and what that had done to Phoebe, but in their eyes, that was no excuse for what she had done. When they asked her if she would apologize to the child or get suspended, she said she would rather die than apologize. That was the first time Phoebe Conners was suspended.

Phoebe acted as though she wasn't scared, but deep down, she was terrified. She knew what would happen to her when her father found out. She knew the kind of punishment she would receive for her actions.

That night Phoebe Conners closed her eyes and pretended nothing had happened. When her father came to get her, she refused to look him in the eye. She stared out the window of his car as he drove her home, his hand hovering closer toward her thigh with each second. She blocked out her mind, stopped trying to fight, and just lay there.

She was called down for dinner, her mother acting as though nothing was the matter as her father stared at her from across the table. She was looking down at the food, refusing to eat anything.

"You should eat something," her father whispered to her from across the table.

She didn't say anything; she just continued to push the food around the plate.

That was the first meal Phoebe Conners skipped. Her parents never noticed. They just told her she should eat something before her father took her upstairs. She would shut her eyes again and pretend that nothing was happening. She crawled into the corner of her bed when he left and cried. She refused to eat because the only control Phoebe had over her life anymore was her food.

Alexander would begin to notice the lack of food she was eating. He would remember her putting the bagel in her lunchbox and drinking her coffee. He remembered the shakes she would get when holding the coffee cup. She remembered how weak her body was when she was standing. It looked like one breeze would knock her over.

That was when Phoebe Conners collapsed in the middle of class, seventeen months after Autumn died.

Before

When I went to school the next morning, Phoebe Conners was not sitting in class. I kept looking towards the door, wondering if she would walk in at any moment, but there was nothing. She was gone for the entire class. After I left, I went with Lindsey to the parking lot, trying to make it look like I was not actively looking for Phoebe Conners. I watched as Alexander got into the car and drove away, not even waiting for Phoebe.

Lindsey saw that I was watching. She knew who I was looking for. She rolled her eyes, turning away from me without saying anything. She didn't say goodbye as we got into our separate cars. She knew I was doing the exact thing she had told me not to do.

I drove away by myself that day. I had to meet my father at the police department. I was interning under my father to be able to My dad had to pull a few strings to get me the job, but that was a bonus of being the chief's daughter. I had been promised the job of police chief since I was born. My entire life had been planned out. I would get my degree in english at NYU and move back home. I would take the police job and when I retired I would become a writer. That was our compromise. He wanted someone to he trusted and knew could do the job. He wanted the legacy to continue. He did everything he could to ensure I was ready to take over his position. That included being trained the best way possible, so I got the internship without much protest.

I didn't want to walk in there. I didn't want to face my father. I didn't know how tonight was going to go. My dad didn't talk to me after yesterday's conversation. My mom came to tell Cindy and me that dinner was ready, and we all sat in silence while we ate. That was the quietest this house had ever been.

My mom had come in that night and said my dad was just worried about my future. He didn't want me to throw my future away on some whim that deep down Phoebe Conners could be a good person. She told me that no matter what happened, I had to keep my goals in mind and promise her that I would do my best to keep the family dream alive. I told her that nothing was going on between Phoebe and me. Phoebe had made that blatantly clear.

The station was eerily quiet when I walked in. Usually, there were sounds of a printer or walkie talkies going off with codes but there was nothing. Everything was silent. I looked around to see everyone sitting at their desks, but they were staring at the holding cells. I looked at the holding cell to see Phoebe Conners leaning against the wall, her eyes closed. She looked like a mess.

Her hair was in knots down her shoulders, and she had dark circles underneath her eyes. Her hands were shaking as she leaned against the wall, and when I looked over at her, I noticed almost her entire body was shaking. I sucked in a deep breath and walked over to the reception desk.

"What's going on?" I asked Sherry, who was sitting up front.

She looked at me with sympathy, as if my dad had told her what we had talked about yesterday.

"We picked up Ms. Conners on public intoxication, resisting arrest, and assaulting a police officer. Kevin went to pick her up, and she gave him a nasty burn with the cigarette she was smoking. We are waiting for her parents to come to pick her up, but we don't think that will happen anytime soon. We haven't been able to reach them for a few hours now," she explained.

"How long has she been here?" I asked.

"Seven hours," Sherry answered.

I shook my head, thanking Sherry, and walked towards my dad's office. I knocked on the door, waiting for him to give me the go-ahead to come in, and when he did, I walked in and closed the door behind me.

"When was the last time you called her parents?" I asked.

"I'm not sure what you are talking about Sydney," my father answers.

"Phoebe Conners parents, dad. When was the last time you called Phoebe Conners parents?"

My dad runs his hands through his hair and looks up at me. He was giving me that look. The look he gave when he was interrogating someone.

"An hour ago," he replies.

"Did you even try and call Alexander Chadwick. He would come get her faster than her parents would," I said.

"This is why I told you to stay away from her," my father yells. He had never yelled at me. Heads turned from the bullpen as they heard him yelling. I closed the blinds before they could see anything else. "She may seem stable one minute, and then the next, she lashes out like a mad woman."

"I know dad," I answered.

"You must know I do everything I do for your good. If you continue like this, you will end up just like her. Smoking cigarettes and drinking while being hungover at six in the morning," he says. "I say what I say to act in your best interest Sydney. It would do some good for you to remember that."

"Did you see any bruises?" I asked, my voice in a hushed whisper.

"What do you mean bruises?" he demands, his voice clipped and quiet.

"She has bruises sometimes. Her arms, the back of her neck, or her face. I didn't know if you had seen anything," I ask.

He shook his head. "No, we didn't see anything that wasn't self-inflicted," he tells me.

"Well, how do you know if it was self-inflicted? There must be some extremely hard places to self-inflict wounds," I responded.

My dad walks over towards me, placing his hands on my shoulder.

"Trust me, Syd, we did a strip search. We know all of them are self-inflicted," he tries to reassure me.

Strip Search. Those two words echo around my brain. What was the need to do a strip search? There was none. There was no reason anyone needed to look at her like that.

"Did you at least get a female officer to search?" I asked, already fearing the answer. There were only three females in the department; one was Sherry, and the other was me. My dad shakes his head.

"Brian searched. You weren't there and Sherry is a receptionist. She isn't qualified to do the kind of search we needed. We did what we had to do," he states before turning toward the door.

"Did you at least ask her if she consented to one?" I demanded. "Did you at least get her permission?"

My dad runs his hands through his hair in frustration, avoiding my eyes as he answers.

"She doesn't have to consent, Sydney. We needed a strip search, and we were going to get one,"

"She has every right to consent. This is her fourth amendent right. That was illegal search and seizure dad. What you did was illegal. It was against the constitution. You could be sued for this," I yelled.

This wasn't my dad. My dad would never have done this. In no world would my father commit a crime such as this. My body felt frozen as I was looking at him. This wasn't my dad. The man standing in front of me he never would have strip searched someone without their consent.

"I'm questioning her, and then I am going to drive her home," I said not even waiting for a response from him before turning away.

"Sydney, I can't let you do that. You are an intern and not an officer. You are not qualified to question someone."

"Sherrif Garcia," I wouldn't call him dad. He didn't deserve to be called dad. "She is not going to want to talk to a male officer after you sent one to violate her. If I go in there you are more likely to get her to say something,m" I explained.

There was a very slim chance he was going to allow me to do this. A very slim chance he would listen to what I was saying and let me go in there and talk to her.

"Fine," he mutters under his breath and moves to open the door. "But if I am sending you in there, you better come back with some good and compelling information."

"Yes sir, Sherrif Garica, I can do that," I said before opening the door and walking towards the holding cells. As I walked closer, I could see her slowly banging her head against the wall and tapping her fingers on her inner thigh.

"Phoebe Conners," I called out.

She opened her eyes and looked towards me. I felt like I could almost see tears in her eyes, but she blinked, and they went away.

"Did you need something secondhand smoke?" she asks.

I take a deep breath to try to steady myself. I was here to do a job, not let myself get worked up by petty disagreements.

"If you could follow me to the interrogation rooms. We just want to ask a few questions," I said, reaching over to open the door to the holding cell. Phoebe doesn't move from the ground.

"I'm not telling you anything if that's what we are doing," she says.

"I know," I replied. "I just thought you may want to get away from all these officers staring at you."

She looks around at everyone staring her down like she was an animal in a zoo.

Phoebe says nothing as she stands up and walks out of the holding cells.

"Glad you enjoyed the show fuckers," she yells, throwing up her middle finger as she walks down the hallway.

"Jesus Christ," I mutter under my breath, running ahead of her to grab the doorhandle. I held the door as she walks in and sinks into one of the chairs.

"Put your hands on the table, please," I said, holding out a pair of handcuffs.

Phoebe Conners smiles and puts her hands on the table, close to where I could cuff her hands.

"Don't worry, Garica, You're cuffing me. You know I can't do anything when cuffed."

I roll my eyes, trying to ignore the red forming in my cheeks as I cuff her and walk towards the door again. I open it, reaching towards the camera and clicking the button to turn it on. I let the door close behind me, and I look at her. Her hair, the color of a flame was in tight tangles around her shoulders. She had strands sticking in front of her face and clinging to her neck with sweat. Her clothes are thrown back on haphazardly, and I can see a bruise clinging to her collarbone. She has dark circles under her blue eyes and closes them when she thinks I am not looking. She has bruises littering almost every inch of her body. Everything about her seems drained. She looks like it is taking everything inside of her not to fall asleep right then and there. I wonder how long it had been since she had gotten a full night of sleep.

I walk back in to see Phoebe Conners leaning against the chair, her arms stretching out in front of her. I see bruises littering her arm as she stretches.

I sit down across from her as I wait for her to speak.

"Are we going to say anything or just sit here with that camera rolling?" she demands.

I force a smile on my face as she sits there, fidgeting in front of me.

"How long were you drinking last night, Phoebe Conners?" I ask.

A look of anger flashes across her face. She looks as though she is about to start throwing things.

"I told you I am not answering any questions. I just wanted to get away from those fucking pigs," she angrily mutters through her teeth.

"Well, last time I checked, we are in an interrogation room, so that means that I am going to ask you questions. As it is, we are going to have to charge you with resisting arrest, assault of a police officer, underage drinking, and public intoxication. Would you like to add obstruction of justice on that list as well?' I ask.

Her eyes narrow into slits as she glares at me. She looks like she is about to lunge across the table toward me.

"You can't do that Garica. Your dick of a father told me it was my right to remain silent, and that is exactly what I plan on doing."

I leaned across the table, folding my hands together like I had watched my dad do hundreds of times before.

"I believe you fail to understand that I am the police chiefs daughter. I can do whatever I want and charge you with whatever you want and no one is going to do anything because there is nothing they can do, so tell me, do you want obstruction of justice added to your long list of charges?" I answered.

I hated acting like him. I wanted to make her trust me. I wanted to make her believe she could tell me whatever she needed and me sitting here threatening to break the law to get her to confess was the exact opposite of what I wanted to do. My dad would take over if he didn't think there was any progress. I couldn't let her face my dad again. I just wanted to get her out of there.

Phoebe doesn't let her face falter as she leans back in her chair, the handcuffs stopping her from leaning any further.

"I don't think you realize what I have gone through these past 7 hours. So far, I have a killer hangover, and no one is giving me anything that is helping with that; I have been surrounded by 12 police officers with their guns raised, screaming at me to get on the ground, I have been stripped searched by four police officers who sat there and gawked at me as if they had never seen a pair of tits before, my bra and fucking underwear have been taken from me, and I have been left in holding cell while I have been stared at. So excuse me if I don't want to talk about something that number one, I don't even remember, and number two has been attempted to be forced out of me for the past 7 hours," she yells.

Her face softens, her bottom lips quivering as she speaks.

"Please. I just want to go home and forget this shit ever happened."

I wanted to reach over and grab her hand but I knew she would just flinch away. I didn't want to make her any more uncomfortable than she already was.

"I am going to restart the tape, erase everything that has already been said, and then you are going to create some fake story about what happened. We can get you to confess, apologize and then I will drive you home," I whispered as if someone could hear me through the concrete walls.

She nods her head, and I stand up to leave the room. I walk over to the camera and grab the tape from inside, shove it in my pocket, and put in a new one. I watched her through the window as she sat there, trying to control the tears from spilling from her eyes. She looks down at her thighs, and a look of disgust covers her face, and she quickly closes her legs. I press start on the camera again and walk inside, her head snapping up from her thighs to look at me.

"So, Phoebe Conners," I said. "You are being charged with resisting arrest, assault of a police officer, underage drinking, and public intoxication. Is there anything you would like to say?"

She nods, looking towards the camera. "I stole the liquor from my parent's shelf. I took their car and drove somewhere and drank it. I didn't know why I did it but I don't remember much from last night. I am sorry to anyone I hurt by doing this and I can promise this will not happen again," she said.

I nod my head, pressing my hands on the table and standing up. "Thank you, Phoebe Conners."

I walked over towards her, unlocking the handcuffs and opening the door so she could walk through. Her hand goes to her shirt, and she picks it up over her shoulder to try and cover her collarbone.

"Are we done?" she whispers.

I nod, press the button to turn off the camera, and grab the tape from inside. I put my hand on the small of her back, to try and guide her away from the room but she flinches away from my touch. As we walk into the bullpen I sit her down in one of the chairs.

"I am just going to hand this to Sheriff Garcia, and then I can drive you home," I told her.

She slowly nods her head, trying to ignore the stares that are coming from everyone in the room. I walk over toward my dad's office. I knock on his door and wait until he gives me the go ahead and enter the room.

"Did you get anything?" he asks as I walk in.

"Yes, sir, I did," I tell him, reaching out to hand him the tape. "I got the tape and I am going to bring her home."

"Set it on my desk and close the door behind you," he tells me, keeping his head buried in his paperwork. I quickly move to set it down and close the door behind me. As I walk out of his room, everyone is staring at Phoebe, and she sits there staring right back at them as if she is not just in an interrogation room.

"Has no one in this fucking office ever seen a pair of tits before?" she demands. Her hand reaches toward the hem of her shirt, and I lunge toward her.

"Okay, and on that wonderful note, I am going to take you home," I said, careful not to touch her.

"Great, goodbye fuckers," she called as she storms outside. I threw up my hand as a quick apology and chased after her. When I made it outside, she was standing, her hands wrapped around her bare shoulders, trying to preserve any warmth she could.

"Here," I said while holding my jacket towards her.

She grabs it, quickly tossing it over her shoulder. "Thank you," she whispers.

I let her follow me to my car. She opened the passenger side door and slowly slid in, staying at the very edge of the seat before buckling. We remained silent as I drove. She didn't move to turn on the radio, she just sat there with my jacket wrapped around her shoulders, staring out the window.

"What's your address?" I finally asked, breaking the silence.

"Oh, yeah," she mumbles before turning to look toward me. "It's uh..." she trails off.

We stop at a red light, and I turn to look at her. Tears are shining down her face as she tries not to meet my eyes.

"I don't want to go home right now," she whispers, her voice sounding fragile in the dark. I nod, starting to drive again as the light turns green.

"Do you want to go to Alexander's house or do you want to go to mine?" I ask.

She looks over at me with a look of surprise on her face. "Your father would never let me sleep over at your house," she said.

I looked at her, a ghost of a smile hovering over my face.

"Who said he has to know?"

After

Phoebe Conners was diagnosed with anorexia seventeen months after Autumn's death. She remained in the hospital's rehab center for eight weeks before she was sent home again. Her father was the one who came to pick her up, and for the entire car ride home, she sat on the edge of her seat, trying to create a much space between her and her father as possible. She didn't sleep the next two nights. She remembered curling up into a ball on her bed and just sitting there, waiting for something to happen, yet nothing did. For the first time in seventeen months, Phoebe Conners let herself feel safe within her own home. But as many of us know, it is in those moments when we feel the safest that the universe decides to remind us just what it can do.

The first time Phoebe Conners's father laid a hand on her since she had gotten back home was after she dropped the coffee mug she was holding, eighteen months after the death of Autumn. Her hand was shaking as she tried to lift the cup. Even holding a cup like that required more energy than her body had. When her father came and sat next to her, she panicked, and the glass slid out of her hand and crashed on the floor.

She would remember the fear she felt when her father turned around and stared her down as she picked up the pieces from the ground. She would remember the pain as his hand came onto her face and the way tears stung her eyes as he screamed at her. After he left she touched her hand to her cheek and flinched when she felt a bruise forming. That was the beginning of a long cycle that she would soon learn would never end.

PHOEBE CONNERS DIDN'T talk to anyone about what had happened to her for three years. She didn't want anyone to know what happened behind the scenes. She tried to hide it. Tried to hide her fear when someone moved to touch her. Hide her panic when she was standing next to her father. She didn't want anyone to know. She thought that if she told anyone they would leave. She couldn't bear to lose the one person she had. She couldn't handle losing Alexander.

Phoebe Conners used to say forever was subjective. Each and every person is perceived forever as something different. After so much loss, she didn't trust anyone who said they would be there forever. She came to know forever was a ticking time bomb, just waiting for someone to set it off and implode, taking everything she had known out with it.

THE FIRST TIME PHOEBE Conners walked into a church was after one of the nights were she closed her eyes and pretended she didn't exist. She watched as her father listened and sang along with the sermon as if nothing was the matter. As if he had slept in his room for the whole night. She remembered listening to what the priest said. Remembered him telling her that if she liked someone of the same sex, she would go to hell, or if she had sex before marriage, she would die. She would remember the way her father looked at her and winked as if they were in on some inside joke. Phoebe Conners had never wanted to crawl out of her own skin more than when she saw her father look at her like that.

Phoebe went home that morning and locked herself in her room. She grabbed the bible that had been left open on her desk and opened it to the back of the book. She would read through those verses and parables, feeling increasingly sick each second. In her mind she told herself that sick feeling as good. It meant she was changing. She should feel disgusted by the way she had acted before hearing the word. This was how she was supposed to feel.

Often she would find herself flipping through, trying to memorize the verses. Trying as desperately as she could to be a good Christian, the kind God would want her to be. Maybe if she followed God's word, nothing back would happen. Maybe if she knew the most important verses, her father would spend the night in his room. Maybe if she were who God wanted her to be, nothing horrible would ever happen to her.

When her father would come into her room, she would recite verses under her breath to try and make herself feel better. To try and forget what was happening. She would kneel by her bed every night and apologize. She would apologize for making her father do what he did to her. Maybe if she were just less appealing or dressed more modestly, it would all stop. Maybe if she just prayed more it would all be okay.

Phoebe Conners started learning every hymn. She would bring her bible everywhere with her, just trying to find some way she could fix herself. Try to save herself from whatever was going to happen. When it came time for her first confessional, she went in there and told the priest all about her sister, the drinking she had done, the suicide attempts, her father, and everything she had done. She held back tears as she confessed everything she had done.

The priest told her she needed to be more careful about the temptations she brought upon men, blessed her, told her it was all forgiven, and sent her on her way. As Phoebe Conners walked out, she ducked into a bathroom and sobbed. She cried as she lay on the bathroom ground and cried. She tried to whisper the Lord's prayer under her breath, tried reciting verses she had learned to try and remind herself that it was okay. This was just the first step. Soon she would begin to feel better. She just needed to believe more. She just needed to believe in God's plan. She just needed to remind herself that everything that had happened was part of the fantastic plan.

That night was the third time Phoebe Conners tried to kill herself. She would later say she held the lighter up to her bible and burned it, watched as it burned, and went up in flames. As she watched it burn, she realized what she had done. She tried putting out the fire, running into the bathroom, and trying to douse it under water, but it was already beyond repair. That one simple action had ruined months of trying to be so good, ruined everything because she was feeling impulsive.

Tears streamed down her face as she slowly moved a blade over her wrist, watching the blood bubble up on her skin and ran down her arm until it fell onto the bathroom's tile floor. She would later say it was painless. After the initial cut, she felt no pain. Just as soon as the lightheadedness kicked in, she collapsed. Phoebe Conners had finally done it. It had finally worked. She was going to die the same way Autumn died. She was going to see her sister again.

When Phoebe Conners awoke to see the blinding lights, she knew she had failed. Alexander was sitting beside her, holding her hand as if she might break.

"It didn't work," Phoebe whispered loud enough for Alexander to hear.

He shook his head, a sympathetic look on his face. He wasn't sympathetic to the fact she was still alive, no. He was sympathetic to the fact she was so disappointed she was still alive.

Phoebe Conners was so sure it had worked this time. She was convinced that this time it was done. She was so sure she wasn't going to live this time. Alexander would have to hold her down as she screamed, kicking her legs and trying to grab whatever she could find. Alexander had to pry a syringe away, trying to keep her from stabbing it into her neck. He pressed the button to call the nurses and doctors, and twelve of them came running in. Five of them held her down as the others grabbed a sedative. Alexander just stood in the corner, tears threatening to spill as Phoebe screamed. He didn't understand how one person could want to be dead this badly. How could someone want nothing more than to die and do anything within their power to die?

Phoebe Conners would be sedated for two days after that, doctors coming and going while her parents didn't show up once. The hospital told Alexander he could no longer drive her home with Phoebe Conners's parent's permission, and they had to come to get her. He would remember looking into the room one night to see doctors examining bruises and cuts on her thighs. Later they came to ask him if he had ever heard or seen anything suspicious happening in the Conners household, but he just shook his head, saying no. Phoebe had told him many times that if someone came and asked, he was to say no. No one was supposed to know.

He couldn't shake the feelings of guilt he felt after saying no. He knew exactly what was happening, yet he couldn't betray Phoebe's wishes. She had told him that she wanted no one to know and that is what he planned on doing. He wasn't going to be the one to endanger her life anymore. But maybe if he had said something, she wouldn't be hurt. She would have gotten away from her house. Maybe she wouldn't want to die anymore.

After Phoebe Conners was released and sent home, Alexander would notice more bruises. He would stumble through answering when people asked why she was wearing a turtleneck in the dead of summer. People stopped even looking at Phobe Conners, dismissing her as crazy. She could often be seen reciting the Lord's prayer under her breath or looking through her bible in the middle of class. Rumors spread around that she was in a cult, that she slept with the priest and that is where she got her religious beliefs from.

Sometimes Phoebe Conners would see Sydney Garcia in the hallway, and she would be filled with that same rage she was when she smashed her brother's face in, but she would never let that anger take over. She would tell herself to focus on what God said. She would listen to what God was telling her. She felt she could finally be a normal person because she had God there right by her side.

Phoebe was starting to treat Alexander like someone she could fix. Like he was privileged to be in the presence of her. For her birthday that year, all she asked for was another bible, seeing as she burned hers. Her comments started almost in a joking way, but Alexander knew it wasn't. It only escalated from there. Those who loved someone of the same sex. Those who had sex before marriage. They would all be going to hell. Every single one of them would be going to hell.

The Phoebe Conners Alexander knew was gone. She had brainwashsed. There was no one to blame but her father. He wanted control over her and he was going to get it anyway he could. It wasn't enough for him that he had taken her childhood away. It wasn't enough that he had taken her innocence. He wanted to take everything she had left and he would not stop until he had Phoebe Conners to himself for the rest of his life.

Alexander never understood how far it went until Phoebe spent a night at his house. He had heard her pray before she went to sleep that night. She asked if he would like to join and he told her no. He knew she wouldn't have been happy but he wasn't feeding into her delusion. He wasn't about to let her think that all of this okay;.

That morning, Phoebe made him drive her to church so she could speak with a priest. He watched as her leg bounced up and down in the car, her fingers tapping against her forehead as she sat, clutching her bible to her chest.

"Phoebs," he asked her while she stopped at a red light. "What made you start going to church?'

She looked at him, an odd sort of smile on her face as she looked down at the book clutched to her chest.

"My father started taking me every Sunday. It's completely changed my life," she answered.

All he could do was nod. There was no sense in reasoning with her. This was not the Phoebe Conners he had come to love. This Phoebe Conners was someone else entirely. This was someone Alexander had never met before in his life.

He couldn't help but blame himself though. If he had just told the people at the hospital what he thought was going to happen, then maybe this wouldn't have happened. Maybe he wouldn't be driving to a church on a Friday morning before school. He tried telling himself that was ridiculous.

He knew complete control and indoctrination like this doesn't just happen overnight. It takes years for this level of control. Years and years of grooming, control, and helplessness get a person to this point. It wasn't just something that could have gone away overnight. Alexander blamed himself though. If he had just told the police or the doctors what her father had been doing she would be safe. If he had told someone, her father wouldn't have the chance to hurt her anymore.

Alexander refused to walk inside. He didn't want to see her like that. Didn't want to see the result of her father's control. He watched closely as she walked inside. She was walking slowly, taking her time before walking in the church. He sat there, guilt, panic, and regret making him feel nauseous.

Time seemed to pass even slower as she was in that church. He watched the front door, willing Phoebe Conners to come out and realize how stupid this was. To realize that she was being brainwashed. Begging her to understand this is just another way her father can control her.

After half an hour, Alexander was ready to come in and grab her for himself. They were going to be late for school, and he was not going to explain to the teachers he had been late because Phoebe had decided to see a priest early in the morning. When Phoebe Conners did come out, her face was red and puffy as if she had been crying, and her bible was hanging limply by her side. She climbed into the car, not saying a word, and he drove off. He knew better than to ask.

Twenty-four months after Autumn died, Phoebe Conners wholeheartedly believed that everything that happened to her was her fault.

Before

P hoebe Conners stood in the corner of my room and watched as I prepared a place on the floor for her to sleep. I had given her pajamas she could borrow for the night, even though they would likely be way too small on her. After getting changed, she stood in the corner of my room, hugging her body like she was trying to keep herself together. After setting up the sleeping bag and blankets, I looked back at Phoebe.

"You can sit down, you know," I joked. "Nothing in this room is going to hurt you."

She glances around the room before slowly lowering herself on the blankets and pulling her knees to her chest. I had never seen one person look so small before.

"Have you eaten yet today?" I asked.

She shakes her head. "No."

My heart tugs in my chest as I look at her. I couldn't remember a time when she was not practically a stick. Almost three years ago, she had an eating disorder and had to stay in the hospital for weeks. When she finally came back to school, she was sickly looking. Her body would shake from doing the smallest things, even opening her locker took a lot of strength. She improved over time, but I could still see the remnants of disordered eating.

"I'm going to go get you something to eat. I need to turn the light off, or else my parents will come in here. Are you going to be okay with it off?" I questioned.

She didn't say anything, just nodded her head slowly, her arms tightening around herself. I walked over and sat next to her, adding enough space between us so she wouldn't feel uncomfortable. She looked over at me, a soft smile appearing on my face.

"What are you doing?" she asks.

I looked at her, my hand resting in the space between us.

"Just sitting here until you don't need someone," I answered.

She looked away, a twinge of red coming onto her cheeks. Her arms were still wrapped around her as she looked around my room.

"I don't need you here," she said. "I can survive for ten minutes while you go get food."

"I know," I answered. "I just think there are certain times when a person shouldn't be alone."

She rolls her eyes before lying on the ground and staring at my ceiling.

"It seems that your father doesn't share the same philosophies as you, Sydney Garcia," she noted.

I sat, silent. A little while ago, I would have defended him in a heartbeat. I would have said that he was doing everything he could to make sure this town was safe, but after today, I didn't know if there was anything I could defend him for.

"My dad has certain views he likes to uphold," I answered.

Phoebe Conners snorted out a laugh but didn't say anything else. We both sat in an awkward, elongated silence before I stood and walked toward the door.

"I am going to go get you food, and then I will be back," I told her before flipping the lights out and closing the door behind me.

I walked downstairs as quietly as possible, so I didn't wake up any of my younger siblings. My mom was sitting at the dining room table, a pile of bills sitting in front of her.

"Hey, mom," I said, pressing a kiss to the top of her head.

She looks up from the crossword she had been solving.

"Hey, Syd," she said. "What are you doing awake?"

"Homework."

"Your dad told me about today, great work Syd," she told me. I could hear her trying to sound excited, but she just sounded tired.

I sat beside her, trying to force a smile on my face. "Yeah, I learned what I know from watching you with handle all of the monsters in this house," I laughed.

She reached over and grabbed my hand, a look of pride on her face.

I walked around the counter, grabbing a pack of Oreos and a bag of chips from the pantry.

"Hungry?" my mom questions in a laughing tone.

"Starving," I answered, trying to keep my voice steady. I hated lying to her. I felt like she could always see through me.

She watched me as I started my way upstairs, clutching everything to my chest, trying not to let anything fall.

"Goodnight, Mom," I called but didn't wait for a response.

I walked past my siblings' room, stopping to look in Cindy's. She was fast asleep, clutching the stuffed llama she got a few years ago. I smiled, watching as her chest rose and fell. Guilt rose in me. Everything I was doing right now was hurting my family. It was hurting even someone as young as Cindy. I sighed, closing Cindy's door and walking quietly towards my room. I grabbed the doorknob, opening it slowly and closing it behind me, trying not to make too much noise. I flipped the light on to see Phoebe Conners lying down, holding her phone up as if trying to get reception.

"Damn it," she cursed under her breath before turning to look towards me.

I kneeled and dropped the food on the ground near her before moving to sit on my bed. She stared down at the food before looking back up at me.

"These are empty carbs. I can't eat them," she told me.

I had never heard anyone say that before. I could tell she was embarrassed about what she said because she turned her head away, a small red forming on her cheeks.

"It's okay," she finally says. "I'll be fine."

Phoebe didn't look at me as she grabbed the pack of Oreos and opened it, taking a bite out of one and staring down at it. I had never seen anyone look so conflicted about eating something.

"Is everything okay?" I asked her.

She froze for a moment before turning back towards me.

"Oh yeah," she answers. "Everything's good."

With that, she takes two more and shoves them into her mouth. I didn't want to stare at her as she was eating. I didn't want to sit there and watch as she ate for the first time in the day. She was already uncomfortable enough.

I sat there on my phone, trying to make it look like I wasn't paying attention. Both of us

were silent. The only thing I could hear was Phoebe chewing on the floor. When she was finished, she put all the wrappers and packages in the bag of potato chips.

"Is there someplace you want me to put this?" she asked, looking around the room for a trashcan. I pointed to a can underneath my desk, and she stood up and threw everything away before sitting back down.

"Thanks," she whispers, not looking at me.

I didn't know what to say after that. The last time we talked was in an interrogation room; before that, it was in the school parking lot. What was there to say? I knew I shouldn't ask her about what had happened at the police station or what had even led her to get to the police station.

"Why did you ask to bring me here?" she asked suddenly.

"What?" I asked, confused as to where the question came from.

"I have been nothing but a bitch to you since this year started. You have been scared of me since you moved here. What led you to offer me a place to stay at your house? What led you to forget everything that your father has ever told you to do something for me?" she asked quietly.

I don't know how to answer this question. I wasn't thinking about anything other than her when I offered her this. I don't know why I did it other than a morbid curiosity. Phoebe Conners was the only thing on my mind anymore. She occupied every single one of my thoughts.

She was in my mind when I woke up, and she was there when I went to sleep. Phoebe Conners was the object of my fascination. I wanted to know everything about her. I wanted to know everything I could know about her and what had happened to her. I wanted to know everything I was forbidden to know.

"There are times when a person shouldn't be alone. This is one of those times. I couldn't let myself bring you someplace you didn't want to go. I offered to have you stay here because I wanted to make sure you knew you were safe," I answered, looking her in the eye.

Pieces of her hair were hanging in front of her face, and she moved it behind her head, letting me see her entire face clearly. I felt like the air was knocked out of me. I had always known she was beautiful but somehow that beauty had multiplied under the shining light of the moon.

It was no doubt to anyone who saw her that she was striking but when you looked into her eyes, honestly, look at her. She took gorgeous to a new level. Her eyes, even in the dim light, shone brightly. The deep blue seemed as deep as the deepest depths of the ocean. Her hair, as fiery red as her personality, was hanging down halfway down her back; wavy at the end, but tangled. Her slim fingers, indents from where rings had been worn over the years, with chipped black nail polish on each finger.

"You're not what I thought you would be, Sydney Garica," she says, a sly smile appearing on her face.

As I look down at my lap, my face turns a shade of deep red.

"And what did you think I would be like, Phoebe Conners?" I wondered.

"Well, Garcia, this is your fact of the day. What did you think I thought about you?"

I smiled, looking down at her from my bed. God, she was so beautiful.

"Well, I know how people see me. I know they think I'm just a younger version of my father. A young narc," I answered. "People think I'm crazy because of how I dress or how much caffeine I drink."

She smiled, and everything inside of me melted. I tried telling myself that this was Phoebe Conners. This was not someone I could fall for, but her smile was permanently imprinted in my mind. I will never be able to forget it.

"In some aspects, you are right. I thought you were going to be just like your father, and in some ways, you were," she tells me.

I faltered, a shock covering my face, but she just laughed when she saw it.

"You didn't think I noticed that in our tiny-ass school, we never had a class together? I knew what you were doing, Garcia. I know what people say about me. When you walked in on that first day, I thought you would walk right back out when you saw me, but you didn't. I expected you not to be in class the next day, but you were. You surprised me, Garcia. I didn't think you had it in you."

I felt guilty, but not in the way I expected to feel guilty. I felt terrible, not at the fact that she had noticed, but at the fact that I had done it in the first place. I had been overreacting for so many years. My parents had done everything in their power to ensure that I was never in a class with her. I had let them because I believed that my future would be ruined if I got anywhere near her, my future would be ruined.

"You came around though, Garica," she whispers. When I looked back down at her, she was looking at me with pride in her eyes. I took pride in what I wasn't sure about, but I wanted to make her feel that so I could see it more often.

"I came around in what way?" I asked her. I just wanted to hear her voice again.

"You don't seem to hate me anymore. You did something to upset me, and you came and apologized. You drove me to your place and gave me food, which is something you would never have done- even a week ago," she tells me. "Change is good for you, Garica. I can see it. I can feel that somewhere deep inside you, something has changed."

She didn't say anything else as she laid down, and I followed suit, figuring that was a signal that the conversation was over, but I didn't sleep. I couldn't sleep. I couldn't sleep because Phoebe Conners was *right there*. She was right there, close enough to reach out and touch but far enough away that I knew no matter how hard I tried to reach her, I never would.

At that moment, I had made up my mind. At that moment, I knew that no matter what happened in this life, I would make sure Phoebe was in it. I didn't care what I had to do. I wanted Phoebe Conners to be in my life for as long as I was able to live it.

After

Phoebe Conners would step into a church for the last time thirty months after Autumn died. Her father had driven her there one morning when it was just the two of them. For some reason, she was excited. She was ready to show her father how good she had been with her worship. Maybe he would be proud of her and stay in his room that night.

But after that last time, she refused to go inside. She walked out of church that day with tears streaming down her face. She had tried to get away from her father, but she couldn't. She had bruises covering her entire body. She felt as though she had been run over by a truck.

She never wanted to go into that place again. The next Sunday, when her father tried getting her into the car, she locked herself in her bedroom and cried with her head in her hands as she listened to him pound on the door, screaming at her to open it. She was terrified that his fist would come through that door and he would be able to get to her, but he finally gave up and went without her. Since that day, her father punished her every Sunday when she refused to go, but she wouldn't do it. She would not go inside that church.

She had stopped talking to Alexander. He had told her that she needed to get her ego in check and realize she was not as important as she might seem. One day when she was hiding in her room, she heard a car pull up outside her window. She panicked, thinking her father was coming back to get her, but it was Alexander's car.

A wave of relief flushed over her, and she ran downstairs into his arms when she saw him. He held her face into his shoulder as she cried. He stood there and let her cry. Alexander insisted on driving her back to his house. He told her she was not to go home and into that house until her father came hacking down his door with an ax. She agreed, wanting nothing more than to get away from that man and everything he had done with him.

Thirty-three months after Autumn's death, Phoebe Conners went to her first party. She hadn't been invited, but she had heard about it and wanted to do anything that would show her what it was like to be a normal person. After that night, she went to any party she caught wind of. She was never invited, and never knew those who were throwing it but she was at every single one.

Overdrinking became a weekly tradition. Half the time, she didn't remember how she got home the night of the party, but she would always wake up in her bed. There was something about drinking alone but surrounded by hundreds of strangers. Something about the solitude kept her coming back night after night.,

Thirty-four months and 12 days after Autumn's death, Phoebe Conners kissed her first girl. She didn't remember why she did it or even remember how it started, but she did remember the feeling. She remembers the pure exhilaration as her hand tangled in the girl's cropped black hair. The way her lips melded together with whatever the girl's name was. The way her tongue felt in the girl's mouth. The feeling of pure freedom. That was the part she chose to remember.

Something in the back of her mind told her this was wrong. She was going to hell for this. She was going to burn forever for this action. But if this was wrong, why did it feel so incredible? If what she was doing was wrong, why did God let her kiss this girl? Why did he not just smite her out of the air? At that moment, she stopped caring. The lines between right and wrong blurred into one intoxicating, cherry-flavored blur.

Phoebe remembers stumbling into a wall as she was kissing the girl. The girl reached her hand underneath her shirt to cup her boob, she would remember the slight feeling of discomfort that filled her, but she tried to ignore it. She just went back to kissing the girl. The girl tugged Phoebe's shirt over her head. Phoebe would remember how the shirt got caught on her nose and then lost in her hair, but the girl didn't care. She was starting to get annoyed at the girl trying to take her shirt off. All she wanted to do was kiss her. She knew what was coming next, but she wanted to kiss her.

The last straw was when she felt the girl's fingers slip into her underwear and press onto the top of her clit. She drew back as if she had just been stung, the girl's hand getting caught in her pants. Phoebe wanted nothing more than to get away from her at that moment. The girl grumbled with annoyance as she got her hand out of Phoebe's pants, and Phoebe scrambled to get her shirt. The girl walked away, still grumbling angrily under her breath as Phoebe was pressed against the wall. Phoebe tried to shove down the feeling of discomfort and focus on the feeling of giddiness she felt after what she had just done.

Phoebe Conners had kissed a girl, and she liked it. She kissed a girl and was not smited off of the Earth. Everything she knew was telling her how wrong it was, but she couldn't ignore the feeling of that girl's tongue in her mouth. The taste of her cherry chapstick as she was pressed against that wall.

She ran outside, grabbing her phone to call Alexander to tell him to come to pick her up. She stood there and waited until Alexander showed up. She remembered feeling giddy as she walked towards his car when he finally did get there. This was the happiest she had felt in years. For the first time since Autumn died, she felt joy. Her heart was still pounding from the memory of kissing that girl. Her lips still tingled, and she reached up to touch them as Alexander drove.

"I have to do something before we go home," she told him with a sly smile. "And I need your help."

Alexander took the steering wheel in his hands, preparing for whatever she needed.

"I need you to drive me to the church," she yelled, already getting high off the pure adrenaline running through her body. Alexander felt a wave of panic wash over his body as he looked at her, but this time she didn't look like she did the last time.

Phoebe Conners wasn't anxiously tapping her fingers against her forehead or bouncing her leg; she sat at the edge of her seat, looking ready and prepared. She had a look in her eyes as if she knew what she was doing. As if this was the first time she had ever had a taste of freedom.

When they pulled into the church parking lot, she turned to look at Alexander.

"Keep the car running, and follow me inside. I think it's time we hold a bonfire," she said, a look of pure glee covering her entire face.

ALEXANDER HAD NEVER seen Phoebe Conners like this. Phoebe ran around in an adrenaline-filled rampage, grabbing every Bible, every hymn book, and every envelope asking for a tithe from the pews she could fit in her arms. She would run back out of the church before running back in to grab more. She would not stop until she had every single one. They ran out of the church, Phoebe shouting with glee with her hands full of stolen articles. Alexander sat in the driver's seat, watching as Phoebe rolled down the window and screamed and laughed out the window, letting her hand hang out the window with her middle finger raised.

They drove into the woods behind Phoebe Conner's house until they found a clearing. Alexander's car looked as though it had been mauled by a wild animal with the amount of scratches, but he didn't care.

Phoebe jumped out of the car, dragging logs over to make a big circle. She meticulously set up a ring of the books as Alexander watched. She took the lighter inside her pocket and pressed a cigarette to her mouth. She handed one to Alexander and happily obliged. They sat there momentarily, letting the cigarette smoke fill their lungs before Phoebe held the lighter to Alexander.

"Would you like to do the honor, kind sir?" she asked, a smile taking up her entire face. Alexander reaches into his pocket and grabs his lighter. "I think this is the kind of thing that takes two people," he smiles.

Alexander never forgets the joy and freedom that covered Phoebe Conner's face. He would never forget the sound of her laugh, something he had only heard a few times through the three years of their friendship. She grabbed his hand and danced around the woods, watching as the books rose in flames. They watched until every one was burned to ashes, smoking, and dancing until it was over. After they finished, they sat on the hood of the car and drank a beer, just talking as if they had never talked before.

"I kissed a girl tonight," Phoebe said at one point, the words slurring together.

Alexander looked over at her in shock. He couldn't believe this was the same Phoebe Conners he had been seeing in the past year. Tonight he was seeing a whole other side of her. A side that just needed a chance to be let out.

"It should have felt wrong, right?" she answered. "I should have hated and felt wrong for doing it, but I didn't. It was the best thing I have ever done."

Alexander didn't know what to say. He had his best friend back. This was not the same Phoebe Conners who told him he was going to hell just a few months ago for not attending church. This was Phoebe Conners, the one he remembered from before this. He didn't know how his silence would be perceived. I didn't know what she would think since he was so quiet.

"She tried going further," she whispered.

Alexander reached over and laid his hand over hers. She looked up at him, a look of understanding on her face. She didn't flinch at the touch for the first time since he had met her.

"What did you do?" he asked.

She shook her head, still not moving her hand away.

"I couldn't do it," she mumbled. "I froze. I pulled away. She was pissed."

He wrapped his arm around her shoulder, letting her lean against him.

"Is it your father?" he asked, almost silent.

She shook her head. "For the first time, I wasn't thinking of him. When I was kissing her, the only thing I thought about was how good she tasted or how amazing it felt to be pressed against a wall. I wasn't thinking of him when she took my shirt off. I wasn't thinking of him when she pressed a finger to my clit. I wasn't thinking about him at all. All I could think about was how uncomfortable I felt when she did. I finally couldn't take it anymore. I pulled away, and she left upset."

Her head was still resting on his shoulder, but she wasn't looking at him. She was staring off into the trees, listening to the ruffle of the leaves from the breeze.

"I don't know, Phoebe. I wish I said I had an answer, but I don't." he tells her.

She didn't say anything for a moment, just stared straight ahead.

"In some way, do you think this is his fault?" she asks.

She didn't even need to clarify who she was talking about. Alexander already knew. Her voice was low when she spoke, almost as if he would be able to hear them from the middle of the woods.

"I don't know, Phoebe," he muttered. "I don't know."

FROM THAT DAY FORWARD, nothing could separate Phoebe and Alexander. Phoebe could spend less time at home because she always had Alexander. For the first time, Alexander saw a side of Phoebe that would laugh and smile every day. She would laugh. She would make jokes. She would come up with witty comebacks and then smile at them herself. He had never felt better than when he was finally seeing her happy. She was happy.

After a long party that night, Alexander got a call from Phoebe. She sounded drunk as she begged him to get her early. Alexander knew something had happened. She would not be asked to leave a party early if everything went right.

When he got to the house, he knew his suspicions were correct. Phoebe was sitting on the front steps, halfway asleep, with her head resting on the banister. He walked over to help her up, knowing she could not walk by herself. She groaned when she felt him picking her up but didn't say anything as he carried her to the car.

Alexander wanted to be upset with her for drinking this much. He wanted to be pissed off and scream that she needed to be safer because he would not always be there to bail her ass out, but he just couldn't do it. He couldn't bring himself to yell at her like that.

Phoebe was silent on the way back to Alexander's house. She said nothing as he drove. When he parked the car and got out, he went around to help Phoebe as she struggled to try and get out of the car by herself.

"Do you ever wonder why he does this to me?" Phoebe asked suddenly as Alexander was carrying her up the stairs.

His heart stopped when she asked this. There was no good answer. Of course, he had often questioned why her father did what he did, but there was no real explanation. Nothing he could tell her would give her a reason for her father doing these things to her.

"I found a journal of Autumns," she said, her words slurring together. "She wrote all about what happened to her. He did the same thing to her. He hurt her in the same way he hurt me."

Alexander walked Phoebe over to the bed so he could look her in the eyes and talk to her about what she had just said.

"He did the same thing to Autumn, Alex. That's why she killed herself. He is the reason I don't have a sister anymore."

He sat beside her on the bed, kissing her head and rubbing his hand on her back. That was the first time she had ever called him Alex. In the most fucked up situation, that was the first time she had named him Alex.

"I'm so sorry, Phoebs," he whispers into her hair. There was nothing else he could say in this situation.

"I want to kill him, Alex," she told him, her voice void of emotion. "I want to make him suffer like he has made me suffer. Like he made Autumn suffer."

"I know," Alexander answered.

The pair sat together, Phoebe's head on his shoulder as she fell asleep and Alexander rubbing her back. There was nothing he could do now but sit with her and let her know that she wasn't alone. No matter how bad things got, he would always be with her.

Before

I didn't sleep at all that night. I couldn't sleep when Phoebe Conners was right there. I kept my eyes on her all night. I told myself it was because I wanted to make sure she was okay, but she would have been okay whether or not I turned my back. She was peaceful when she was asleep. She was somehow even more beautiful asleep than she was awake.

She had this serene look, a calm I had never seen her have before. She didn't move much but she snored. She never stopped snoring the entire night. She didn't turn away from me though. She continued to sleep on her left side, facing right towards me. A couple of times, I thought she had woken up, but when I looked away, as not to make it obvious I was looking, she settled back down into the blankets and fell asleep.

I couldn't take my eyes away from her. How was this the same person screaming at an entire police department only a few hours before? How was this the same person I had been warned away from for years?

I watched as the light filtered through the blinds in the morning, and I watched how the early morning sun rays danced on her hair. I looked away when I saw her eyes slowly blinking open. I turned around, hoping she wasn't awake enough to hear me shifting.

"Good morning," she whispers.

Well crap. I turned to look at her, trying to ignore how every part of my brain noticed every single feature of her.

"Morning," I mumbled, trying to make my voice sound groggy.

She paused for a moment before smiling and looking back at me.

"It seems as though your entire family is awake," she tells me.

I hadn't noticed it before, but when you listened closely, you could hear my entire family, all 7 of them singing off-key to Dean Martin. She sat there together, smiling for a moment at the noise downstairs.

"How are you going to get me out?" she asked.

"Crap," I muttered before bolting out of bed. "I didn't even think of that."

She laughed before walking over to the window, grabbing the latch at the bottom.

"You distract your family, I'll climb out, and then you can drive me home," she said.

I nodded, moving to open the door but snapped around.

"I am on the second floor; what the frick are you thinking," I whispered and yelled.

Phoebe laughed, putting her hand on her mouth to try and cover up her laugh. "The word you are looking for is Fuck, my dear Garcia, and why do ye have so little faith?" she said.

I stared at her, not able to comprehend what was happening.

"Come on, Sydney, just trust me. I have my ways," she told me.

I shook my head before walking out the door and down the stairs, just trying to trust Phoebe and her psychotic plan.

TYLER TURNED TO LOOK at the stairs as I walked downstairs and called out to me.

"Look who is finally awake," he yelled.

I nodded and shuffled towards the table. It was too early for this, and I was too worried about someone seeing Phoebe scaling the side of the wall of whatever she was doing.

"How'd you sleep, Syd?" he asked me.

I threw a thumbs up, not wanting to tell him that I hadn't slept at all, before taking a long sip of coffee from my mom's cup. She smacked my hand away, but I had already drunk half her cup.

"Perra," my mom mutters, and I smack her on the shoulder before I notice what is happening outside the window. My eyes involuntarily widen when my dad sees me looking out the window, and he turns to look. Phoebe Conners was currently scaling down the wall, a look of deep concentration in her eyes. She winked when she saw me looking before jumping down on the ground.

"So, dad, how was work yesterday?" I blurted out, trying to do anything to distract him from Phoebe Conners outside the window.

He turned to look at me, a smile appearing on his face. He loved talking about what he did at work and spent hours telling my younger siblings stories.

"Nothing as interesting as what you did earlier, my little crime fighter," he said, a smile appearing on his face.

I tried to force a smile on my face but failed, shoving pancakes into my mouth to hide the fact that I wasn't smiling. I didn't waste any time eating or shoveling down the pancakes like they were nothing before getting up and throwing my plate in the sink.

"Where are you off to in such a hurry?" my mom asks, my entire family staring at me.

I swallowed, trying to come up with a convincing lie. Again with the lying. It was going to become a habit if I kept going.

"Lindsey and I are meeting this morning to discuss plans for the upcoming Astronomy Club meeting," I said, not waiting for a response before grabbing the keys and ducking out of the house, starting my car. I wanted to get out of there as quickly as possible so my parents couldn't look out the window and see Phoebe in my car.

"What's up fucker," I hear someone yell from the back seat.

I jumped, turning around to see Phoebe Conners sitting on the backseat floor.

"Jesus Christ," I yelled, my hands jerking the wheel.

Phoebe just laughs as I try desperately to steady the car and get it back on the road. Phoebe moved up to the front seat, climbed over the center console, and settled in the seat.

"I wanted to see if you would curse if I caught you by surprise," she said, a devilish smile on her face.

I frowned, turning away from her to pay attention to the road.

"You couldn't think of a better time to do that then when I was driving? Besides, I don't curse," I told her.

"Keep hanging out with me, Garcia, and we could change that," she replies.

She looks at me, smirking, before leaning back in the seat and taking a deep breath. She rolls down the window and sticks her arm out, letting the air run through her fingers. It took everything inside of me not to look over. Not to direct my full attention toward Phoebe Conners. Not to look at her hair that was running in the wind. Not to pay too much attention to the sound of her laugh as her hair flew in her face. Not to look at her calloused and yet soft hands. Not to look at the smile on her face as she stuck her head out the window.

God, that laugh. It was the most perfect sound in the world. I would do anything to hear her laugh like that.

I didn't realize I was death-gripping the steering wheel until she looked towards me and laughed.

"Lighten up, Garcia," she said. "There is no car in sight."

I took a deep breath, trying to ignore the feeling of her eyes boring into the side of my face. I relaxed my hands before pulling into the 7/11 parking lot.

"What are we doing?" she asks, looking at me with a look of sheer horror.

I smiled, unbuckling my seat belt and grabbing my phone from the center console.

"I don't know about you, but I don't have enough caffeine today, and I can't promise I am not going to drive into a head-on collision," I told her, walking towards the door.

I hear her curse under her breath before she jumps out of the car, following me into the 7/11. I walked over to the coffee, dumping as much cream, sugar and ice into it as possible.

"What in the actual hell are you drinking?" Phoebe demanded. I turned to see her staring wide-eyed at the drink in my hand.

I looked back at her, a confused look on my face.

"What are you talking about?" I asked. "It's coffee."

She looked at me, a wholly horrified look on her face.

"That's not coffee," she said.

I looked down at the coffee, a smile on my face.

"Oh, please tell me you are not one of those who insist that the only real coffee is black coffee," I joked.

She narrowed her eyes, looking at me as if I was psychotic.

"That is the only real coffee," she answered.

I rolled my eyes, walking away from the coffee, calling over my shoulder. "Spare me the debate, Conners. Just get something that will make you less obnoxious.

I didn't look back to see her reaction, but 2 minutes later, she was standing by my side in line, holding a cup of black coffee. She was carrying it with one hand, her other tucked at her side. I watched as her eyes roamed behind the counter where the cigarettes and cigars were stashed.

"Don't even think about it. My courtesy only extends towards buying you coffee, not cigarettes," I told her.

She nods her head, looking away and down at her hands. "Don't bother. I'm trying to quit," she tells me quietly. Her hands are shaking, and I look out of my eye to see her messing with something in the pocket. When it was our turn she put her coffee cup down and looks back down at the floor as if to distract herself from what was happening behind the counter.

"Just this?" the cashier asks.

I nod, waiting as they scan it before sliding my phone in front of the card reader and picking up the two drinks.

"Thank you," I say, but I don't wait for a response. Phoebe is bolting out ahead of me, racing towards the car and standing by it, trying to stop her shaking hands.

"Here," I told her, handing her the coffee, and I watched as she took a giant sip, wincing as the heat reached her mouth. When she swallows it, she grimaces before getting into the car, clutching the coffee cup like it was her lifeline.

I didn't want to ask. I didn't want to make it seem like I was prying into her life, so I stayed silent, letting the awkwardness of the silence wash over us.

"You can just drop me off at my house," she tells me, grabbing my phone and putting the directions in.

"Okay," I answered.

For the rest of the car ride, we just sat there together, not saying anything as I drove. When I finally pulled into her driveway, her hand hesitated to open the door knob, and before she did, she turned to me.

"Thank you, Garcia. I know I was kind of a mess, so the fact you dealt with that means a lot," she told me, holding out her hand as if to touch my shoulder before retracting it.

"Yeah, of course," I answered, trying to keep the blush from forming. "Anytime you need a ride, just call me."

She shifts in her seat uncomfortably. "Alexander is going to be gone next week, and I can't drive. Would you mind giving me a ride?" she asks.

I was so taken aback by this. I meant what I had said about driving her, but I didn't expect her to take me up on the offer so soon.

"Yeah, of course," I answered. I held out my hand for her phone, and she looked at my hand like it was an alien from another dimension. "Let me give you my phone number to let you know when I'm on my way."

She hands me her phone, and I put my number in quickly. I handed it back to her, and she slid it into her pocket before grabbing the handle and walking out of the car.

"Thanks, Garcia," she said, a small smile forming.

I couldn't help the smile on my face as I watched her walk up the stairs and into the house. A week. One more week of this. At least one more week of Phoebe Conners.

After

I t occurred to me when writing all of this down that many would think this was biased. People would read this and say I didn't give the other side of the story, or I needed to talk to people who were not close with Phoebe Conners. I would like to confirm that this account is biased. As I was writing this, I spoke with the people that truly mattered. I talked to the people who knew her the best. I spoke to people who would never judge her for things out of her control. I spoke to the people that were there with her through everything.

Many will also believe I am exaggerating. They will think this is a work of fiction and not something that genuinely happened. Many will ask how a father could truly do such heinous crimes and feel no regret for them. They will ask why a mother didn't do anything, despite knowing what was happening. They will ask why a friend never told anyone, even though he had a good idea of what was happening. They will ask why someone like me would write everything down instead of telling someone.

I, however, believe the real question is why don't people think others can commit such atrocities. When someone murders someone, you hear they couldn't believe that person could do such a thing. There could be undeniable signs, yet you will never hear from people that they knew that person was capable of it. People are always looking to see the good in each other, but sometimes there is no good. In the case of Phoebe Conners's father, there was no good in that man. In the case of my father, the thirst for power trumped that good. People will do whatever they can to get ahead, even trampling others in the process.

What was there to do that would help her? Phoebe Conners hated showing weakness around other people. She spent her entire life around people who would use those weaknesses to attack her. Phoebe Conners just wanted to have an everyday life. She just wanted to be loved the way a child deserved to be loved. In no world should a child have to fight to be loved. Never should a child worry about doing something that would make them unlovable. In no world should a child endure punishment just because they made a mistake.

Many people like to shake their heads at what happens in the world. They will shield their child's eyes, and tell them to look away from the ugly of this world, but what they don't understand is you can't always hide that ugly. What happens when they are forced the face the ugly after being sheltered from it for their entire lives?

I like to think I could have done something more, been something more if I had been shown what the world truly could be. You spend your entire life looking for the good in the world, trying to find the good that was promised to you. But what happens when you don't see that good? Or what happens when you do? What happens when you find the good, and you know that it was the good you were meant to find, and they leave? When that good leaves, and you are left in darkness again?

I held the good. I kissed her, and I was there for her on some of the darkest nights, but even a flame dies at some point. It's only a matter of where and when.

Phoebe Conners was like a flame. When she burned bright, god she burned. Everyone who came to know her, the real her became a moth, a moth attracted to the gorgeous yet dangerous flame. But once a flame is done burning, it's done. It doesn't matter how much extra fuel you add to that flame; after it's gone, you are never getting the same flame again. All you could do was strike a match and light a new one.

I didn't want to replace Phoebe Conners, and the truth was I didn't think I ever could. There was not a day that passed that Phoebe Conners was not in my mind. There was not a morning I woke up that I didn't remember the mornings I woke up next to her. Phoebe Conners imprinted herself on every part of your mind. Every aspect of your entire life.

There is so much every single person could learn from Phoebe Conners. Something that, in every aspect of life, people could remember her. Phoebe Conners was a fighter. She fought with everything left in her until there wasn't a fight left in her. She never let anything that happened to her stand in the way of who she was or what she wanted. She kept going, pushing through those times when she didn't think she could fight until she won. She triumphed in that fight and came out just a bit stronger on the other end.

I have been asked what I think Phoebe Conners would have been like if Autumn had never died. If her father had not been the man he was, I still don't know how to answer this question. Maybe if she hadn't lost her sister I would still be able to hold her. If her father were a good man and didn't hurt her, maybe she would still be here, but if nothing had happened to her, would I have had her in the first place? Would I have been able to hold Phoebe Conners in my arms and kiss her? Would I have been able to spend my nights, my mornings, and my days with Phoebe Conners?

I can't speak on who Phoebe Conners would have been if she had a better childhood. If she had a genuine family, I do know what she was like when she was here. If she had a better childhood, would she believe in forever? Would she have believed in life? Would she have tried to find the good in the world, or would she have been like me? Would she have tried for so long before realizing that interest is so few and far between? Or would she have been the good to someone else? Would she have held someone else and told them they were her forever?

I don't know who she would have been, and I can't speak for the maybe's, but I can speak for the truth. I can tell you that Phoebe Conners was beautiful and unique and deserved much more than this world had to offer. Her soul was one of the kindest and most gentle things I had ever seen. I can tell you she was a beacon of light to everyone that truly knew her, and I can tell you she was misunderstood. I can tell you so much about the Phoebe Conners my heart chose to love. The one that occupied my every thought and the one who will stay with me forever. I could tell you everything about who Phoebe Conners chose to be and how she was too stunning for this world. I can tell you she was that flame.

It burns bright at first, but in the end, the candle burns out, and that flame is gone forever.

Before

It was hard to come up with a convincing lie as I drove Phoebe to school every day. I didn't tell my parents that I was taking Phoebe to school. Whenever they asked why Lindsey wasn't picking me up, I told them some total white lie about something with her community service or a project for the Astronomy Club. By the end of the week, I was clean out of lies.

I didn't tell Lindsey either. As far as she knew, I was driving myself to school because I had to pick up my siblings from school afterward. It was true enough. I had to pick them up many times before, so it wasn't a far stretch, but I could tell Lindsey suspected something. I would notice her waiting at the door for me into school, and then when I did, she would look all around me as if waiting for Phoebe to materialize out of thin air. Lindsey would ask me about her, but I would play dumb. I told her about the police station, and that was it.

When I pulled into Phoebe Conners's driveway on Friday, I pulled out my phone and texted her that I was waiting for her. I didn't want to honk the horn so as not to wake up her family, but after 20 minutes, I lightly pressed the horn to try and alert her. I jumped at it, even though I knew it was coming, but Phoebe didn't come out.

My heart was pounding in my chest as I slowly took the keys out of the ignition and walked up to the front door, trying to calm my racing heart. As soon as I hit the front porch, I could tell something was wrong. I panicked. I didn't want to eavesdrop on what was happening inside. Phoebe was inside, and there was no telling what was happening.

"Will you just fuck off?" I heard Phoebe scream from inside, her voice sounding at a point of hysteria.

I heard something smash, and my breath caught in my throat. My hands were shaking as I stood there debating breaking down that door.

"You don't talk to me like that," a deeper voice.

The other voice came her father. That I was sure of.

"I'll say whatever the fuck I want, whenever the fuck I want," she growled, the words coming out in less of a screaming tone but more fearful as if she was scared of him.

I didn't hear anything for the next few seconds; the silence was almost as terrifying as the screaming a second ago. I didn't know what to do. Did I just stay here, or did I run in there, trying to stop whatever was happening from happening? I needed to get her out of there. I needed to go in there and get her away from him before he does something. Before he hurts her again.

"You don't remember what I told you, do you?" I heard her father yell from inside.

Phoebe didn't say anything.

"No, one talks to me like that," he told her.

I would never be able to get the sound of his hand hitting her face. Even through the door, I was able to hear it. The sound of the crack of bone that I would later learn was her nose. It was one of the sickening sounds I had ever heard. I gagged, my brain replaying the crunch of bone repeatedly.

I couldn't take it anymore. I couldn't just sit here and listen as this was happening. I raise my fist towards the door, knocking twice before calling out.

"Hey Phoebe, we will be late if we don't leave now," I yelled through the door.

I didn't hear anything after that. I took a step back, not wanting to know what would happen next. The door flew open, and Phoebe came running out, her backpack haphazardly tossed over her shoulder. She ran out to the car, jumped in, and slammed the door shut. Not looking into her house, I followed her to the car, jumped in, and started the car, driving away without even looking behind me. I didn't even want the chance of seeing her father.

I drove far past the school. I went outside of town and as far as I could get until I felt the need to stop. My heart was pounding in my chest. I felt sick to my stomach as I drove. I was convinced I was going to vomit. He had hit her. He had hit her right across the face and said nothing about it. When I finally did pull over, I looked over to Phoebe, who was staring at me with wide eyes and blood gushing out of her crooked nose. She said nothing as I frantically reached over to grab tissues from the glove compartment. I handed her the box, unable to look her in the eyes. I hear her wince as she puts the tissue to her face, making me want to vomit even more.

She doesn't say anything, either. She just sits there, holding the tissues to her nose as she looks straight ahead.

"He hit you," I muttered, more to myself than anyone. I was so surprised I didn't know what to do.

"No, he didn't," she answered, grabbing another tissue to stop the bleeding from her broken nose. I heard her groan of pain the minute it touched her nose.

"Phoebe, he hit you," I turned to her and said. "He hit you, and he broke your nose."

She shook her head, starting to look angry with me.

"No, he didn't. He didn't hit me, and he didn't break my nose," she answers in an eerily calm voice.

I scanned her up and down to see if anything was wrong with her. Why was she defending him like this? Did she get a concussion? Did he hit her so hard that she had permanent brain damage? Could a punch to the face cause amnesia?

"Then what do you call this, Phoebe?" I demanded, gesturing to her face. "If he didn't hit you, how did you break your nose? How is your nose currently gushing blood?"

"I fell," she answers quietly.

I couldn't contain the look on my face. Did she fall? What the fuck did she mean she fell.

"Pheobe Conners, you did not fucking fall," I yelled.

She looked at me, a complete and utter shock on her face.

"You just cursed," she said, a smile appearing on her face.

I rolled my eyes, frustrated and annoyed at her while also at the same time being scared for her. Being so scared that this was what she lived with. He hit her. I heard as he punched her in the face. I listened to the crack of the bone as her nose broke. I heard everything, and yet here she was, denying that she had been hit, denying that he had broken her nose. Denying it, just to protect him.

"Why are you protecting him, Phoebe?' I whispered, almost too scared to ask.

"I'm not defending someone who didn't do anything wrong," she replied.

I went to say something else, to argue with her another time, before she turned away, crossing her arms over her chest and looking out the window.

"Just drive me to fucking school," she demanded. "I don't want to deal with this right now."

THE DRIVE TO SCHOOL was silent. I didn't even know what to say. I just kept turning over in my head everything that had happened. I didn't sign up for this. I didn't ask to be thrown in the middle of this. I didn't ask to have to help someone set their nose so it could heal again. I didn't want any of this, and yet at the same time, I couldn't leave her there. I couldn't just see her again. She was in my life, and I couldn't lose her now. I had her in my grasp. I had here right here. I couldn't just walk out and never see her again.

Besides, maybe I had heard wrong, and maybe I had overreacted. Maybe she did fall, and that sound of broken glass was just her knocking over a vase or something. I didn't need to assume what had happened when there could have been hundreds of things that could have happened. There was no reason to jump to conclusions about what had happened.

My dad had always told me to trust my first instinct. Whether that be for math problems or police work. I always needed to trust my gut before my first instinct was typically the right one. At the same time, he told me I couldn't jump to conclusions. He told me I had to make an educated guess about what was happening and try to deduce the problem from there. I didn't know what to believe.

Of course, I wanted to believe that Phoebe Conners had a good family, a loving one that wouldn't hurt anyone. I wanted to believe that nothing bad had happened because it was easier to live in a world where nothing bad ever happened. To live in a world where everything was perfect, and everyone was good. If only I knew how wrong I could be.

I DIDN'T SEE PHOEBE for almost an entire week after that. It was just like it was before. She avoided me, and me doing everything I could to ensure I ran into her somewhere. It wasn't until six and a half days after the incident.

It was late, past 10:30, and Lindsey and I were sitting on the couch watching some random bad animal horror movie we had found online for free. Neither of us was paying too much attention;

instead, we were sitting on our phones, doomscrolling and sending each other the worst of said doomscrolling.

I heard a knock on the door but didn't think anything of it. Lindsey looked towards the door but shrugged, turning towards me and saying. "It's probably just the wind." It wasn't until the next, more frantic knock that I decided to open the door.

Phoebe Conners was standing on my doorstep, drenched in the rain, with mascara running down her face. Her hair was soaking wet, and her clothes were hanging lopsided on her body. She had bruises covering her shoulders, neck, and face. A black eye was slowly starting to form under her left eye.

"Phoebe," I whispered before she let out a heartbreaking sob, sinking to the porch floor. Lindsey came running as I immediately sat next to her, wrapping my arms around her shoulders and pulling her towards me.

"Shh," I whispered in her ear. "It's okay, Phoebe. I got you."

I sat there holding her, feeling Lindsey's eyes boring into my back.

"I'm going to get your dad," she muttered frantically.

I looked up at her like she was crazy.

"Are you crazy?" I demanded.

She looked at me with a concerned look before closing the door behind her and sitting on the porch next to me.

I sat there stroking her hair and whispering in her ear. She sat there, sobbing into my shoulder, clutching onto me as if I was the one thing grounding her to the Earth. I don't know how long we sat there together. I just held her and whispered reassurances in her ear, trying anything I could do to calm her down. I didn't know what had happened. I had a pretty good idea, but I wasn't going to pry. Phoebe needed time by herself. She needed time to process.

When we finally got her inside, I sat her down in the bathroom, cleaning the mascara, cuts, and bruises on her face. She stared blankly ahead, her voice void of emotion.

"Have you ever been to church, Sydney Garcia?" she asked me suddenly, the cloth I was using halting as I looked at her. My family was not the religious type. We went to church on a few holidays when I was younger and had fewer siblings, but now it was much work to get us all ready.

"I haven't been in years, but I used to," I answered, cleaning her bruises again.

She looked me in the eyes, no emotion coloring her features.

"Whatever you do, Sydney Garcia, don't let yourself be consumed by something just to justify what is happening in your life," she said.

She didn't say anything else. I just stared straight ahead as I finished cleaning her up. I tossed her sweatshirt and sweatpants and gave her some privacy. Lindsey was standing in the corner of my room; her arms crossed over her chest.

"What the fuck is going on, Syd?" she demands. Before answering her, I looked towards the bathroom door to ensure Phoebe was still behind the closed doors.

"I don't know what is going on, Lin, but something isn't right," I told her, twisting my fingers in my lap.

She threw her arms up in exasperation, staring me down. "You're damn right; something isn't right. Phoebe Conners showed up at your house in the middle of the night looking as though she just got into a fucking bar fight."

I grabbed her hands to steady her. If I didn't stop her, she would continue ranting until she was blue in the face.

"Listen, Lindsey; I lied to you. Last week I drove Phoebe to school last week because she needed a ride. I didn't have to pick up the twins. I heard something I shouldn't have on Friday, and we argued. Something is happening between her and her dad," I whispered.

"I can't fucking believe you, Sydney," she says. I had never heard such anger in her voice before. "So you lied to me for Phoebe Conners? You decided to ditch me, for Phoebe fucking Conners?"

There was no reason other than my infatuation with Phoebe Conners. I wanted to find some way she would understand. I wanted to do anything so she would see my side of the story and why I did it. How could I, though? There was no rational explanation for me lying to her to drive Phoebe.

"I'm sorry, Lindsey," was all I could say.

She didn't say anything as she brushed past me and down the stairs. That went really fucking well. I heard the door open, and I turned away from the stairway to see Phoebe standing in front of the door, the bright LED lights from the bathroom illuminating her face.

"How did you know it was my father?" she whispers.

I walked over towards her, but she flinched away. I took another step back, giving her enough space.

"I heard your argument last week. I knew it had to be him again."

She nodded, not saying anything, before sitting on the floor, wrapping her arms around herself again.

"I'm sorry," she mumbles, her eyes filled with tears again. "I didn't mean to barge in, but I didn't have anywhere else to go."

I take a step towards her, and I can see how hard she is trying not to flinch away, but she doesn't

"This house will always be open to you when you need it," I told her.

Phoebe laughs an unfeeling laugh, void of anything but pure pain.

"I have a feeling your father would say a different thing," she told me.

I guided her into my room, so we were not standing in the middle of the hallway. She went right to her position in the corner of my room. I watch as she sinks against the wall, her head thrown back and her eyes closed.

"Did your dad throw you out?" I asked.

"He couldn't survive two days without me," she answers.

Neither of us said anything. Phoebe just sat there with her eyes closed, her head resting against the wall, and I was desperately trying to think of the next thing to say.

"I'm sorry," Phoebe says finally. "I shouldn't be dragging you into this."

I sit down next to her on the wall. She looked over at me, a faint smile playing on her lips.

"You are not dragging me into anything, Phoebe Conners. I willingly drove you to school. I willingly let you into the house tonight. I do this because, despite everything, I care about you."

If I could have frozen time at that moment, I would have. The way she looked at me, that smile on her face. The way her blue eyes shone with the light of the moon that was peeking through the window. The way her red hair fell perfectly in front of her face.

"Despite everything," she whispers. "I care about you too, Garcia."

PHOEBE CONNERS SLEPT in my bed that night. We watched TV when she fell asleep, her head resting on my shoulder. I wrapped my arms around her, sinking farther into the bed. That was the best night's sleep I had gotten in a while. The feeling of her weight on my chest and her snores put me to sleep. This felt right in some way. Like I was meant to be here. At this moment, it was

Phoebe and me. Phoebe and I. There was absolutely nothing that could tear us away from each other.

After

The first time Phoebe Conners yelled back at her father was 36 months after Autumn died. She later said it was like she snapped. She couldn't take the pain, the abuse, and the hurt anymore. She remembered the feeling of the vase in her hand as she threw it at his head. She would scream at him, calling him a fucking pervert and a little bitch. He would run to grab her, but she would get away for the first time in her life. She felt exhilarated, knowing that she could get away from her father for the first time since Autumn died.

She ran through the woods, the wind racing through her hair. She ignored the pain in her feet as the sticks and rocks hit her bare feet. She stopped when her foot caught on a rock and she fell, landing harshly on her wrist. That was one of the worst pains she had ever felt, but she didn't cry out. Phoebe Conners didn't show pain. She just sat there momentarily, looking at her wrist hanging limply.

She looked all around her, not recognizing her surroundings. She had run so far into the woods that she didn't even know where she was. She dragged herself off the leaf ridden ground and started walking in the direction she thought was back home. The farther she walked, the most lost she seemed. She didn't recognize anything until she came upon a box sitting on a log. She had seen that box before. She knew exactly what that box was. She walked closer, fearing the worst. She prayed it wasn't what she thought it was. When she came upon it, she didn't even need to open the box.

Phoebe covered her mouth in horror when she saw the picture of Autumn on top of the box.

Her parents had lied to her. They had told her they would spread Autumn's ashes in Ireland, but they just left them here. She sat on the log next to what was left of Autumn as she hugged her knees. Her wrist was screaming but she couldn't be bothered to care. This was all she had of her sister now. She had this one box. Despite knowing Autumn deserved to be in a better place, Phoebe Conners couldn't move it. She couldn't bring herself to take Autumn away and move her somewhere else. She had been here for 36 months. It was too late to go and take her somewhere else.

From time to time, Phoebe Conners would come to stand in the woods with Autumn and talk to her about everything. She would tell her about the girl she kissed, her feelings, and how she knew she didn't want to have sex. She would tell her everything their father would do. Autumn was the first person she had ever told about her father, about what he had done to her. The things she never wanted to tell anyone because if she did, then they became true. Then those memories were real, and she would have to face them.

If she told anyone about those moments when she shut her eyes and pretended she didn't exist, then that would mean she would be forced to face them. When things got hard, or she didn't think she could handle the hard times, she would start talking to Autumn as if she was sitting next to her. Talking to Autumn made her feel less alone and like someone out there understood what she had to deal with.

Dealing with everything was so much easier when she was talking to Autumn. Autumn wasn't even there, but it was like Phoebe Conners had her sister again. She never told anyone about Autumn, not even Alexander. It was like her own secret. That was until she walked back into the woods after a particularly hard day. She walked into the clearing where Autumn was, only to find her father sitting on the log. There was no box next to him. She looked at the ground to see it splintered into hundreds of pieces.

There was nothing she could say. Phoebe ran towards the box, trying to do anything to put it back together, anything to not lose her sister again. His hand grabbed her forearm and hauled her to her feet. Phoebe Conners shut her eyes and did anything she could to forget what was happening. When it was done, she sat in the woods, tears filling her eyes as she stared at Autumn's ashes. That was the first time Phoebe Conners would remember everything that happened in detail. The first time she would sit there and let herself cry. Let herself feel upset about what her father did. She sat there and let herself feel bad for herself.

Phoebe Conners didn't talk to her sister after that. It felt like Autumn had seen the side she would rather have tucked away. She was weak in front of Autumn and couldn't do that again. She stopped laughing. She stopped making jokes and laughing at said jokes when anyone else made them. Alexander noticed a change, but he didn't say anything. Alexander noticed a difference, but he didn't say anything.

He had learned to be thankful for the things that did happen. Phoebe Conners had started to let Alexander in. She started to show him things she had never shown him before and wasn't worried about looking weak in front of him. He was with her constantly, never wanting her to be alone. He was filled with worry when he wasn't with her, just imagining the things happening. She would sleep over at his house if anything happened, and he wouldn't get any sleep that night.

Alexander was there for her through everything, never wanting her to face anything alone. He would remember nights when he would stay on the phone with her all night, not wanting anything to happen when he wasn't there. Everyone told him it wasn't his job. His parents would say he was taking on too much and needed to develop boundaries. He tried explaining that he had boundaries and the most important person in his life was Phoebe Conners, but no one would understand. All they saw was a child trying too hard to be everything for someone with no one.

When something happened, he tried not to blame himself. She tried not to think that maybe she would have been okay if he were there or with her. Phoebe had told him multiple times it wasn't his fault, but he couldn't stop thinking it was. He wanted nothing more than to have Phoebe safe and away from everything horrible. There was no way he could shield her from it all, though. Nothing he could do would take away all of her pain. That would erase the years of abuse and violence she had started to think of as normal. He was one person, and the entire world was stacked against him. It seemed the odds were never in his favor. He was destined to lose.

Before

Phoebe was gone the next morning when I woke up, leaving me to question if I had dreamt the whole thing. I looked around my room, desperately searching for any sign of her, but there was nothing. The clothes I had given her were not on the floor, and all the washcloths I had left on the counter to wash the next day were thrown in the hamper. That was the only sign that Phoebe Conners was even here last night.

It didn't matter how many times I saw her, I was left with more questions by the time she left. How did she have this power to disappear? The ability to act as though she had never even existed. How could she erase every part of herself in a matter of moments? How did she find a way to worm herself into my mind? Why had she not left yet?

As with the past month, Phoebe Conners consumed my every thought. I wanted to know her entire life. I wanted to know the inner workings of her mind. I wanted to know what caused her to run here last night. I wanted to know how often she had run to some other place to escape whatever she was running from. I wanted to know how many times she had been hurt and by whom. Who gave her the reason to run? What else had happened to her at the hands of this person? Who else had those hand hurt?

My parents started to notice my distant behavior. They gave me questioning looks for the entirety of breakfast as I picked around my food with my fork. I couldn't get Phoebe out of my mind.

"Is everything okay, Syd?" my dad asked as we cleaned the dishes at the sink, his hand resting on my shoulder.

I nodded, turning to look at him. I knew he didn't believe me. He was my dad. He knew when something was the matter.

"Are you sure?" he asked again.

I nodded again. "I just didn't sleep well last night," I answered.

He smiled, satisfied with my answer, before returning to the sink to finish the dishes. I tried to distract myself. I watched tv with Cindy. I played board games with Adam, but I couldn't think of anything but Phoebe Conners. Carlise had a soccer game today, so I stayed home when the entire family went to see it. I told them I was going to take a nap.

I waved as I watched the car drive out of the driveway. I watched as it went down the street and around the curve before I bolted inside, grabbing my keys off the chain and racing towards the car. I wasn't paying as much attention as I should have been as I was driving; I was just focused on getting to Phoebe Conners's house as quickly as possible.

I froze when I pulled into her long, winding driveway. Why in the world was I here? I hadn't planned what I was going to say. I had no idea what I would even say. How could you tell someone you couldn't stop thinking about them and wanted nothing more than to know them for the rest of your life? The answer is you can't. There is no way to say that.

I parked my car far enough away from the house that you couldn't see it from the window before walking the rest of the way to her front door. I took a deep breath before knocking on the door. No one answered. I stood there, debating on whether to knock again or just wait. My heart was racing a million miles an hour, and I couldn't think straight.

I knocked again, more loudly this time, before the door swung open, and a small, paper-thin middle-aged woman opened the door.

"Did you need something?" she demanded, staring down at me even though she was smaller than me.

"Yes," I answered, trying to stop the shaking of my hands. "I was here to see Phoebe Conners."

A look of surprise passed her face as she turned to look behind her before she ushered me in. She quickly closes the door behind me before walking in front of me and gesturing to the foyer. There were two staircases on either side and a big balcony in the middle.

"I have to say, Phoebe doesn't get many visitors besides that Chadwick boy," she says hurriedly, almost pushing me up the stairs as she moves. "It is a pleasant surprise to see she has a new friend."

I clear my throat uncomfortably. "Yeah, friends," I answer, unsure how to explain to her why I was there.

I couldn't even keep track of the number of stairs I had walked up. I was almost out of breath as we got to the top, but the woman I assumed was Phoebe's mom continued chatting as she walked. We finally reached a long hallway that was almost entirely dark. A scone hanging off the wall illuminated the hallway, but that was it.

"Damn girl," her mom whispered. "I told her to turn the lights on.

When we finally reached the end of the hallway, her mom knocked on her door before barging in. I first noticed the smoke that traveled out of the door as she opened it. I coughed, waving my hand in front of my nose as I tried to get the smell of clove out of my face.

"Phoebe Conners!" her mom yells as she looks at Phoebe leaning out the window and blowing the smoke out.

Phoebe scrambles to shut the window and put out her cigarette before her mother can grab it. Her mom doesn't say anything else, just frowns with tight lips before slamming the door behind her as she walks. Phoebe turns to look at me, an embarrassed smile on her face.

"So you've met Genevieve," she says, her voice tight in her chest.

I nod my head, my heart pounding in my chest and my hands shaking. I shouldn't be here. I should have just stayed home and taken a nap like I told my parents I was going to. There was absolutely no reason for me to be in her room right now.

She looks at me, an indiscernible emotion in her eyes. I had no idea what she was thinking. I watched as she slowly walked closer to me, like a hunter stalking prey.

"I thought you were trying to quit," I said, desperately trying anything to lighten the mood. Phoebe stared down at me,

"Why are you here, Sydney Garcia?" she asked, coming face to face and staring down at me.

I didn't know what to say. What did I want to say? I wanted to ask why she seemed so hot and cold around me. One minute she was joking and acting as though she actually cared about someone or something other than herself, and then the next minute, she was standoffish and was trying to stay away from anything and everyone. She would disappear for days and then come back and act as if nothing mattered. The first time she agreed to talk to me was when she was arrested and was screaming at everyone in the station.

"I'm confused by you, Phoebe Conners," I finally said.

She looked at me with a questioning look before moving to sit on her bed. She smiles.

"Oh, trust me, Sydney Garica, I am confused by myself as well."

I rolled my eyes and started to pace. "Half the time it's like you don't even want to be seen with me and then the other half, you joke around and show up at my house in the middle of the night. I don't need to know what is happening to you, and if you don't feel comfortable sharing, that is fine, but I can't be the person you ignore and then come to when you need something," I told her.

Her eyes darken when I mentioned last night. She wasn't wearing my clothes anymore, but she still had those dark circles underneath her eyes as she looked away from me.

"Garica, I don't know to explain this to you in a way that would make sense," she whispers.

I moved to sit next to her on her bed, leaving space between us. "Then just start talking," I replied, giving her a soft smile.

"I don't have an explanation for it," she told me. "It's as if I can't control myself. I hurt everyone around me because I couldn't control what happened during those little outbursts, so instead of hurting the people I love, whenever I felt at my worst, I walked away. I leave. I go somewhere I know I can't hurt anyone. During those times, I lost my sense of self and tried to end things. I try to fight it, but sometimes I can't. I feel like nothing will help. I try stopping and reasoning with myself, but it won't work. It feels as though nothing with work."

I didn't know how to answer. No one says anything; we just sit there in silence together. I see her door nudge open, and I look as I see a tiny, furry, fat little body wriggling its way through the door and jumping onto the bed. A small corgi lays down on Phoebe Conners's lap, and a smile appears as she buries her nose in the dog's fur.

"Who is this?" I asked, watching as she runs her fingers through the dog's fur.

"Atlas," she answered, picking him up and hugging him to her chest. "My parents got him after Autumn died. They thought he would help me get out there more."

I smiled, reaching my hand over for Atlas to sniff, and he licked my hand before sinking into Phoebe's lap. She turns to look at me, concern filling her features.

"I don't know why you need to be close to me. I can tell you that if you decide to be around me, things may not end well. Those who are around me get dragged down with me. If you don't want to deal with everything that comes with me, you can just walk out right now, and I won't judge you. I come with a lot of emotional baggage. I wouldn't blame you if you wanted to leave," she tells me.

Without hesitation, I reach over, thread my fingers with her, and look her in the eyes.

"I am not going anywhere, Phoebe Conners,"

After

There will always be people who don't fully understand why you love them as much as you do. They can't comprehend that someone will always be there for them, no matter what happens. They find it hard to trust after years of having that trust broken so many times. It takes a lot of repeating and reiterating how much you genuinely love them; even sometimes, that isn't enough.

That was Phoebe Conners. She put up this wall around herself and wouldn't let herself be hurt by empty promises and fake love, but deep down, she was scared. She was scared to get hurt. She couldn't handle being broken and bleeding in front of someone she trusted. She used to say that people don't like a mess. They don't like things that confuse them or challenge their train of thought. They didn't think what they didn't already know and know well.

No matter how many times you told her you loved her. No matter how often you explained to her that you were never going anywhere, she still had this little voice telling her that you would leave. Most people would get annoyed with having to repeat themselves as many times, but once I saw that look on her face. The look of awe and security in the idea that someone would be there for her no matter what was worth everything.

Doctors would later try to describe a multitude of disorders to try and explain why she did what she did. They would try to say that if she had only been taking this medication or getting treatment for this disorder, she might have lived longer. It seemed that they always wanted answers. They wanted answers for why they had failed Phoebe and Autumn Conners. The truth was that no one had cared enough about them in life and now they were gone, people wanted a reason. They wanted a reason people had never been there for the Conners siblings. They wanted answers to why their father had done what he had done. They wanted answers to everything.

Home should be a place children go to feel safe to feel sheltered from the woes and the dangers of the outside world. Children should never feel safer on the street than inside their own homes. Never should a child have to go somewhere else to feel comfortable. Never should they ever have to worry about what may happen to them when they are sleeping or who they will find with them when they wake up.

People don't like seeing the truth about things that they find difficult. They hate understanding something that they were not taught from a young age. Most people who knew of Phoebe Conners, not honestly know her, would think she was a freak, that she was just someone who went off the deep end at a young age and couldn't recover. Never would anyone take the time to think there was something else going on.

Phoebe Conners used to love Virginia Woolf. Anytime she was having a bad day, or something seemed too hard, she would whisper quotes she used to memorize. Autumn had taught Phoebe her favorite, the one she used to whisper first before any other one.

"On the outskirts of every agony sits some observant fellow who points," she would whisper.

Phoebe Conners would learn many more throughout the years of her life. She would teach some to Autumn, and Autumn would teach some to her. It became comforting to her whenever she had a rough day. Anyone who came close to Phoebe Conners would leave knowing a quote.

That was the last thing Phoebe Conners would ever say to anyone. She called Alexander her previous night. She would stay quiet on the other end of the line before she whispered.

"I feel we can't go through another of those terrible times,"

That was the last time Alexander would hear from Phoebe Conners. It was the last words he would hear from someone he had spent so much of his life loving and protecting. Alexander often wonders if Phoebe Conners knew this time she was succeeding. Maybe that is why she had video called him. Maybe that is why he was forced to watch as his best friend took a knife to her wrists.

He doesn't like to think about what he could have done if he had only gotten there faster or called someone to get there. Maybe he would have gotten there on time if he had put gas in his car before going home the night before. Maybe he could have gotten there faster if he had just run.

Alexander moved away after Phoebe Conners died. He couldn't stay in a place that held so many memories of her. Everywhere he went, he was plagued with thoughts of Phoebe Conners, so instead of facing them, he ran. He went to a place they had never talked about going together, just to try and find someplace that wasn't so filled with Phoebe Conners. It didn't work as well as I thought. There was no place he could go that wouldn't remind him of Phoebe Conners. She was everywhere.

That was what it was like when you loved someone like Phoebe Conners. It didn't matter what it was. You were always going to find parts of her in everything. You could just be drinking coffee and remember how she clutched her coffee in the morning as if it was the only thing keeping her alive. You would be walking down the street and smell a cigarette, and suddenly your would be on her roof, falling asleep on her chest, and you would smell the way she always smelled faintly of cigarettes.

Phoebe Conners was always there. There was never anyway to get away from her. She was just *always* there.

Before

I walked into school the following day and found Phoebe waiting at my locker. She smiled at me, leaning against it, her backpack tossed on the ground next to her. A smile appeared on her face as I walked over toward her. When I get to my locker, she holds out a muffin to me.

"What's this for?" I asked, smiling before setting my backpack in my locker, and grabbing the books I needed.

"I don't eat breakfast so I thought I would bring you this since I don't think I have ever seen you eat something that isn't an energy drink or some form of candy," she told me.

"Hey," I demanded, acting insulted. "I eat things other than candy. Candy just tastes better than anything else."

Phoebe laughs, drawing the attention of everyone near us. I could hear the whispers, a few whispering about the freak, and the others saying something along the lines of "blink twice if you need help, Sydney,"

Phoebe threw up her middle finger behind her before closing my locker and moving to stand next to me. I looked to where she stood next to me as I ignored the looks from all around us.

"Don't you have class?" I asked.

She laughed, shaking her head as if I had said something completely crazy.

"None of my classes are requirements anymore other than career management. It's basically up to whenever I feel like going to class," she answers.

We make it to my class, still talking until I cut her off.

"Hate to do this Conners, but I actually have a required class to go too," I said.

She throws her hand over her heart, frowning as she takes a step back. "You wound me Garcia," she retorted.

I laughed, walking into my class without saying anything.

When I walked into Mercer's class that afternoon, Phoebe was sitting in the seat next to mine again. The entire class, I tried to pay attention. I tried to listen to what Mercer was saying about Adam Smith or whatever she was talking about, but with Phoebe so close to me, it was hard. With Phoebe sitting right there, close enough for me to touch yet so far away, I couldn't focus on anything else. If looks could kill, then Phoebe Conners would have been dead on the floor.

She caught me staring out of the corner of her eye and she laughed silently under her breath, reaching over and squeezing my hand. My heart raced at the contact, but too soon was her warmth gone and I was left sitting there, my mind on nothing else than Phoebe Conners. I could see the looks Mercer was giving me, but I didn't care. I could feel the looks from all of my classmates but I didn't look back at them. I stayed, staring straight ahead and occasionally at Phoebe.

When the bell rang, Phoebe didn't sprint out of the classroom. She stood behind and waited for me before walking out of the classroom. We didn't say anything as we walked, we just walked, seemingly agreeing on where we would be going as we did. That was until Phoebe saw something at the end of the hall that caused her to freeze. I don't think I have ever seen someone look as terrified as she did. Her breaths were coming in deep gulps as she stood there. I looked down the hall, to see if I could see anything and froze as well.

It was unmistakably Jonathan Conners. Phoebe's father. He was shaking hands, smiling and laughing with the principal.

"Phoebe," I whispered, but she flinched away, her hands shaking as she leaned away from me.

"I have to go," she whispered before taking off in the other direction. I didn't know whether or not to chase after her. I just stood there, staring at her father as he walked down the hallway towards me.

I was panicking as he made eye contact and drew near to me. The last time I had seen him he was shoving Phoebe into a wall, and now here he was, in a pressed suit and tie looking like the picture of wealth and luxury.

"Sydney Garcia, I presume," he said when he got close to me.

I didn't know what to say. I just nodded, my hands feeling clammy as I twisted my fingers.

"I heard you stopped by to see Phoebe the other day. I'm glad Phoebe has a friend coming over," he told me.

"Yes, sir," I stuttered, silently cursing myself for my voice stuttering as much as it did.

He smiled a smile that I could tell was meant to be reassuring, but did nothing but send a chill down my spine.

"Do you have any idea where my daughter is?" he asks, turning to look around as if Phoebe would be hiding behind the crowd of students that were flocking the hallways.

I shook my head, trying to stand up straight and look him straight in the eye. "I don't know sir. I haven't seen her since the bell rang," I answered. "Now, if you will excuse me, I can't just sit here all day chatting. I have somewhere I have to be."

I tried to ignore the feeling of satisfaction that I felt as I pushed past him and walked towards the parking lot. I didn't allow myself to turn around to see the look on his face, but it gave me pleasure to know I had turned him down, that I hadn't answered his question.

I had taken the one thing he loved more than anything else in the world. The power to make anyone, do anything he wanted, maybe if only for a moment.

After

When you write about someones life, people expect only the facts. The undisputables. Things that no matter who you ask, they are going to say the same thing. If there is an unknown fact, as more often than not there is, they want different theories on what happened. They don't want feelings. They want multiple people's takes and ideas on what happened. Well, I'm only giving you two. And those two are the only ones that matter.

I was asked when writing if I would be talking to Phoebe Conners father, seeing as though he would be the only one who truly knew what had happened to her. The answer to that question is a resounding no. Never will I give him any more attention that he already has gotten. When you hear about murder cases, or serial killers you hear about the killer more than the victims. People forget that the victims are the only reason that killer is labeled a killer. Phoebe Conners and Autumn Conners are the victims in this story. All those two wanted was a normal life, and both were robbed.

They are not here to tell their stories anymore. They were the victims of years of abuse and neglect at the hands of Johnathon Conners. Phoebe Conners used to say she couldn't see herself living longer than her sister. In her mind, Autumn had so much more to live for than Phoebe, so there was no way Autumn got to live less than Phoebe. Autumn was good. She was there for everyone always, and never let her own problems get in the way. Despite everything she was going through, she was always there for Phoebe.

Phoebe Conners thought of herself as selfish. In her mind worrying over what was happening at her own house prevented her from being there for anyone else. If you asked Phoebe she was a taker. She took everything from everyone around her until there was nothing left to take. She took Alexander's time, thoughts and years of his life. He was always around her. Always with her in case something bad happened to her. She couldn't understand that Alexander did not see this as an obligation. He cared about her, that's why he was always there. She looked at herself as if she was just like her father. She took and took from every single person around her until the only thing she had left to take was herself.

Phoebe Conners didn't see herself the way the people around her saw her. Those who were around her, truly loved her for every part of her. We didn't pick and choose the parts to love. We didn't look at her and decide to love certain aspects of her. Once you loved her, there was no stopping loving her.

However, there was no convincing her that she was loved. There was nothing you could say that would convince her that you loved her, and were not just sticking around because of feelings of obligation. When we stayed, it was because there was nothing, on this planet that could have driven us away.

I wrote this, to hold the correct person accountable for what had happened. I couldn't let him get away with it anymore. I wrote this to give Phoebe and Autumn Conners some peace.

Before

I didn't go to the police station when I left school that day. I drove right to Phoebe's house, trying to think of any place she could possibly be within those massive four walls. Alexander was still at school so she wouldn't have been at his house, she wouldn't have been at mine, so that only left here. The house and the massive 6 mile property they owned.

I found a car parked near the woods, and assuming it was Phoebe who had parked it there, I followed the footsteps. I kept calling out for her name, texting, checking for cell service and calling when I did get any service. There was no answer to any of it.

I don't know how far I walked. You never realize how completely out of shape you are until you are walking through a dense forest and are huffing and puffing, to the point of near exhaustion. I finally got to a clearing, and in the middle of it sat Phoebe. She was sitting in the middle of the log, her legs pulled up to her chest and her face buried in her knees. Limply, hanging in her hand was a pocket knife, opened, with the sharp edge of the blade covered in the remnants of blood. Phoebe's blood.

"Phoebe!" I had screamed, racing over and grabbing her wrist, holding it up to the light. There were thin streaks but the bleeding had stopped. She was looking up at me from where her head was tucked into her knees, her eyes void of tears. She stared at me as I inspected her wrists. There were thin, ugly, angry scars covering her arm, but others seemed more methodical, as if she wasn't shaking when she pressed the knife to her skin. Like she understood exactly what she was doing when she did it. She doesn't say anything, just stares at me.

"Phoebe," I whisper, before she throws herself in my arms.

I held her as she cried, as the sobs wracked her bodies as she hugged my midsection. I pulled her halfway into my lap, letting her cry into my stomach.

"I'm so sorry," she sobbed into my stomach.

I ran my fingers through her hair. "It's okay," I whispered. "It's okay.

The knife fell out of her hands and onto the ground, a soft thud echoing from the rotting leaves and branches.

"I saw him, and I didn't know what to do so I ran," she cries. "How pathetic is that. That I can't even face my own father?"

She sat up know, wiping her tears and backing away from me.

"It's not pathetic," I whispered.

She whirls around, glaring at me. "Don't lie to me Garcia," she yells. "It's absolutely pathetic. I see my father once and I go running. I bet you don't go running in the other direction whenever you go see your own father."

I walk slowly over towards her, trying to keep her calm.

"Phoebe, my father is different from your's," I told her.

She laughs before looking at me.

"You want to know what my father does huh? My father fucking rapes me. He rarely spends the night in his own room anymore." she growled. A look of panic flashes over her face as if she couldn't believe what she had just said.

"Oh my god," she whispers underneath her breath before collapsing to the ground.

I walk over to her, grab her hand and pull her up to her feet.

"I won't say anything," I whispered. "If you don't want me to say anything, then I won't."

I felt like I couldn't breathe. This went against everything my internal signals were telling me. I could do something. I should do something. I could tell my dad, and he could bring in Phoebe's father for questioning. I just want to do something that would help.

"Please, Sydney. You have to promise not to tell anyone. You can't tell Alexander, Lindsey and especially not your dad. No one can know. He'll kill me if someone finds out," she begs.

I nod my head, unsure of what to say.

"I need you to say you promise Sydney," she asks, her hand coming to rest on my jawline.

"I promise," I mumble.

That was enough for her. She turned away, grabbed the knife from the ground, and pocketed it. She starts to walk back towards her house, when I call after her.

"Phoebe, wait," I call, watching as she turns around. "I need you to do something for me."

She nods, not saying anything.

"I know you don't want me to tell anyone, and I can agree to do that, but I need you to talk to me. I need you to let me write down what you want to tell me, but you need to let me have some documentation if anything ever happens to you," I said.

She violently shook her head, her hands messing with the knife at her side.

"No," she mutters.

"Phoebe, please you have to listen to me," I try and tell her but she looks away.

"Sydney, I can't," she tells me.

I walk over, and grab her hands. She shyly looks me in the eyes, and I put my hand on her cheek, tilting her face so she is looking me directly in the eyes. Her cheeks turn slightly red, which does nothing to calm my pounding heart.

"You can't keep dealing with this yourself. If you keep this bottled up, and are only going to struggle even more. Please, just tell me what happened, to you. Let me write it down. If not for my sake, then for yours.

She looks as though she is about to bolt. Like she wants nothing more than to run away and never see me okay.

"Okay," she mutters under her breath.

"Okay," I breathed, pulling her head into my shoulder. I just wanted to hold her. I needed to remind myself that she here. She was okay. That was all that mattered. Phoebe was here. Phoebe was safe.

I walked her back to my car, letting her get in before me. I wasn't letting her stay in that house that night. I drove her back to my house that night, the two of us spent the night in my room again. She laid next to me, her head on my chest as we watched tv on my laptop. My hand is wrapped around her waist as the two of us laid there together.

Everything felt right in this moment. There was nothing wrong in the world when Phoebe Conners was laying here next to me. She made everything alright.

Part 2

After

The minute I could could I moved away to NYU. I wanted to leave Indiana and Phoebe behind. I needed to put it behind me. Leave it in the past. I couldn't do that if I stayed in Indiana.

I went to all of my classes. I did all of my work. I let myself pretend I wasn't that girl from Indiana. It was easier when no one knew what had happened here. I was no longer the girl who held her girlfriend as she died. I was no longer the girl who had broken all of her fathers wishes and destroyed her future for a girl who killed herself only a few months later. When I was in New York, I was Sydney Garcia. That was all I was.

No matter how hard I tried though, I couldn't get Sydney out of my mind. She was just always there. She refused to leave. The dreams were the worst part though. They would start out with just the two of us. It would just be Phoebe and I and then she would start bleeding. She would be screaming my name and I would try running. I would run but I wouldn't get anywhere. She stayed the same distance away.

I would wake up in a cold sweat everynight, screaming her name. I had gone through 4 at this point. None of them could handle the screams. They couldn't handle the midnight calls from Indiana that I would ignore. After the fourth one left, I hadn't gotten another roommate. At this point housing knew the same thing would happen with the next one.

No matter how hard I tried, I couldn't escape Phoebe Conners. At the end of the first year, I knew I couldn't stay here anymore. I couldn't keep running from my past. In some way, I needed to find a way to bring peace to Phoebe Conners. I needed to do anything to get her out of my head.

MOVING BACK TO INDIANA was one of the hardest thing I have ever done. Everything there reminded me of her. I would look at the trees and remember how happy she got in the fall. The way her hair perfectly matched the fiery leaves that had fallen from the trees. Nothing had changed since I had left. Everything still had Phoebe's touch on it.

I wouldn't go anywhere I had ever been with Phoebe. If I had to drive past it I would look so far ahead of the road that is wasn't even in my peripheral vision. I couldn't bear seeing anything else Phoebe Conners had left her mark on. I avoided anyplace I might run into her father. I was afraid that if I saw Jonathan Conners I would kill him on the spot.

When I first approached my father about my concerns he thought I was crazy. I told him everything Phoebe had told me and yet he just shrugged off everything I told him. He passed it off as nothing more than a grieving girlfriend trying to find anybody to take her pain out on. I begged him for months to simply listen to me.

I got Alexander to tell him everything and yet he still passed it off. We were just two people who had lost someone important to them. Of course we would try anything to get her death pinned on something other than suicide.

It wasn't until my father found the document on my laptop with everything Phoebe had told me that he finally agreed to listen. Everything I had told him happened. Everything I spent months demanding he listen too was right there. Everything Phoebe's father had done to her. It was right there on that document. Right there in front of his eyes.

He didn't apologize. Just said he had found the document and was willing to look into the case.He never once said he should have trusted me and not just passed me off as a grieving person refusing to believe their loved one commited suicide. I knew she commited suicide. There wasn't any doubt in my mind that Phoebe Conners had committed suicide, but there was a reason. There was a reason she killed herself and it wasn't just because she had been arrested multiple times and hated her life.

It took many more months to be able to get everyone in the department on board. No one was willing to believe that Phoebe Conners, the Phoebe Conners who had been brought in hundreds of times over the years for various counts of a public intoxication, underage drinking and public indecency. None of them could imagine her father assaulting her was the reason behind her behaviour.

I had to file for a year off from NYU. The office didn't even have to ask why. They knew exactly why I couldn't come back. I had people reach out to me, asking why I hadn't come back and when I was going to show up, but I didn't answer a single one. I wasn't going to let New York become Indiana. I wasn't going to live in a place where I was nothing but the girl who's girlfriend killed herself.

Alexander and I erased any other part of our life but this case. We filed hundreds of freedom of information acts to try and get any police files on Phoebe and Jonathan Conners. We tried finding Jonathan Conners credit card statements. Anything to try and get some form of tangible evidence something had happened. We both knew the only way we would ever find some proof of anything was if we got hospital records. If we could prove that Jonathan Conners had abused his wife and children, we had a least the beginnings of a case.

I refused to forget anything about Phoebe. I wanted to be able to remember the good things that happened between Phoebe and I. I wanted to remember the times the two of us had together before she died. I didn't want to think of Phoebe and picture her dead in the hospital.

Alexander never liked talking about the memories. He had dedicated himself to the case, only talking about the things he had noticed from the years of being around Phoebe, but he wouldn't mention anything about the good memories he had of her.

I was the only one now. The only one desperately trying not to forget a single detail of Phoebe Conners. I never wanted to forget the way her mouth crinkled at the sides when she smiled, the way her hair would fall in front of her face when she threw her head back to laugh, and how her bright blue eyes looked when she was staring up at the moon. The way her fingers would trace the page before she would turn it to move on to the next one. I didn't want to forget a single thing about Phoebe Conners.

My father tried to hide the bad things people said about me. I heard him telling my mother one night that I was already weak enough. He didn't want anything to hurt me any more. I was angry at him for hiding everything from me at first but I knew he was right. I had tried being strong for so long. I told myself I would just hold on for one more day. A new day started and I told myself one day again. One day and everything would be okay.

I knew my father was right. I knew he was doing the right thing in trying not to let me hear all of the bad things. He couldn't hide them all though. I knew there were those who though I was crazy. People would come up to me and tell me such. There were others who thought I was doing the right thing. There was no in between. The worst were the people who thought made everything up. The people who truly believed I was so in love with Phoebe Conners that I would have done anything to find a reason she had killed herself. Most of those who believed that were police officers my father had put on the case.

No matter how hard anyone tried, there was no way they could shield me from all of the criticism that was brought my way. All I had in this life anymore as hope though. If I could just bring myself to hope. Tell myself they would come to believe me at some point. This was just a temporary measure. Everyone is prone to skeptism at everything they hear, and this case wouldn't change that.

It was day in and day out of telling myself that. Weeks and weeks of promising that it was only one more day and that in time, they would come to believe me. There is only so many times one can tell themselves the same things over and over again before they start not to believe it themselves. I had tried for months. Months of demanding that someone listen to me. Months of begging my father to even begin to trust me before he began to put weight onto my words.

I had been yelled at that I was crazy. I had been told by the police officers to give up because nothing was going to come of this case. My own mother had asked me if I had made everything up in my mind. Alexander wouldn't even talk to her about anything other than the evidence for the case. For the first time in my life, I was truly alone.

I wanted there to be a day when I could look in the mirror and not hate myself for letting what happened to Phoebe happen. I wanted there to be a time in my life where I didn't wake up and have my immediate thought be the fact that Phoebe Conners was gone. I wanted a day when Alexander didn't pretend that Phoebe Conenrs hadn't even existed. I wanted a day when I could finally look at myself and say that I had done something for Phoebe and Autumn Conners. I just wanted a day when I tell Phoebe everything was okay. At this point, I didn't know if that day would ever come.

IT WAS 2 AM WHEN I got a call from my father saying they had brought Jonathan Conners into custody. I immediately ran to get Alexander, telling him we would be leaving in 10 minutes. Even 10 minutes felt too long. They had Jonathan Conners. They had brought him into custody. They would have finally charged him with something. They wouldn't have brought him in if they couldn't charge him with anything.

There was not a single traffic sign that was followed as we drove to the station. My heart grew tighter in my chest as we got closer and closer. It had been months. Months of hard work and desperation and they had finally brought him in. They had finally charged him with something.

I stood there next to my father as he looked into the interrogation room where Jonathan Conners sat. I hated how much he looked like Phoebe. When I looked at him all I could see was Phoebe, but not the Phoebe I had fallen in love with. The Phoebe Conners everyone else had known. The Phoebe Conners this man had made her to be.

In that moment, I wanted nothing more than to watch him burn. As he was sitting the same interrogation room I had seen Phoebe in many times before, I wanted to punish him for everything he had ever done to Phoebe. I wanted him to feel the same pain she felt when she cried at night. I wanted him to suffer for the years of suffering he had made Phoebe endure.

"Let me go in there," I finally said to my father.

He looked down, shock coating his features.

"Absolutely not Sydney," my father says.

"I need to go in there. He won't listen to anyone else."

"How do you ever know he is going to listen to you?"

"I knew Phoebe. I was in love with Phoebe. He will take the chance to destroy everyone and what better person to destroy than the one who loved his daughter?" I whispered.

My father didn't say anything. He just stood there staring in at where Jonathan Conners sat.

"If I don't think anything is happening, I am pulling you out. You can't afford any more hurt Sydney. I'm not letting him hurt you anymore," my father finally answers.

"He's already taken what I loved most from me, what else could he take?"

I would never forget the way Jonathan Conners looked at me as I walked into that room. I had never seen a smile like that appear on a mans face. Jonathan Conners had just found the next thing to destroy.

"Sydney Garcia, I didn't think I would be seeing you again," he says. "I trust you slept well?"

I didn't say anything, just sat across the table staring at him.

"I was sleeping quite pleasantly until your buffoons broke in and dragged me here."

"Mr. Conners, I would like to be able to say it brings me no great pleasure seeing you here, that would be incorrect. Seeing you handcuffed to the table brings me the greatest joy I have felt since Phoebe died, but you would know that. You would know the pain I felt when Phoebe died. You would know the damage that did to Alexander. You knew all of that,"

Jonathan sat across from me, a soft smile playing at his features.

"Sydney Garcia, you are not the only one who has been mourning my dear daughters death. Of course it would have hurt you and Alexander as well."

Would you like to know what I think Mr. Conners?" I asked, standing up to circle the room.

"What is circulating in your mind Miss Garcia?" he replied.

"I think you haven't slept well since Phoebe Conners died. You've had no way to relieve your stress since your daughters died and you can't bring yourself to touch your wife like that. You needed to touch your daughters before you were able to fall asleep. Now that you don't have either of them, there is no way for you to relieve your stress."

Jonathan Conners didn't falter.

"I never touched either of my daughters," he said.

"You can keep telling yourself that. You can tell every police officer in this department, but I knew your daughter a hell of a lot better than you knew her. I know the pain you caused her. I know she hated herself because of you. I know she wanted nothing more than to forget the feeling of your hands on her skin. I can pretty much guarantee Autumn felt the same. She wanted nothing to do with you. She wanted to protect Phoebe from you, but she couldn't handle it anymore. She left you, and at first you were upset until you remembered you had another child. A child Autumn had never let you touch.

Your wife didn't do anything. How could she? When you were beating her into submission. You made sure she wasn't able to do anything because you would beat her into agreeing. She knew what was happening the entire time, but couldn't do anything," I screamed.

My father would tell me off later for not keeping my composure. I would never get him to confess when I was screaming like a mad woman but I hated seeing him sitting here. Hated seeing him be right here when Phoebe wasn't. I hated that he got a second chance at life when Phoebe didn't. I hated seeing him sit here and act as though he had never done anything to hurt Phoebe and Autumn when we both knew that was far from the truth.

"I may have hit my wife, but I never touched my children like that."

I didn't wait until he had even finished his sentence before I stormed out, letting the door slam shut behind me. I didn't stop to speak with my father. I just brushed past him. I heard him calling my name but I didn't stop. I wouldn't let him see me fall apart.

I didn't let myself cry until I got into the car. My heart was pounding in my chest as I cried. I cried because Phoebe wasn't here anymore. I cried because I now was the one who had to fight for her. I cried because I had made Phobe Conners my entire life and because of this I was here. I cried because I hadn't done anything to save her. I cried because this would never end. I cried because it didn't matter what I said, Jonathan Conners would always be believed because he was a man with mone and I was just a girl who had lost everything. I cried because no matter what I said, Jonathan Conners word would be taken with more weight than mine ever could.

6 MONTHS AFTER THE initial confession, Jonathan Conners would be convicted of domestic abuse. He was sentenced to 5 years in prison with the possiblitly of parole after two. 5 years for over 20 years of domestic abuse towards his wife. 5 years for over 18 years of abuse towards his children.

Jonathan Conners was not given any charges for rape. Rape was never once brought up in his trial.

Before

I learned to live with the looks. I learned to ignore the stares and the whispers that came with living with the two of us being associated with each other. The whispers never did die down, but over time they became easier to live with.

I would sneak Phoebe into my house at night, just so she wouldn't have to be in her house. We would lay together in bed, her head resting on my chest as I ran my fingers through her hair as she talked. Our conversations never truly held any substance. Never before had I gotten less sleep, but felt as good as I did.

Lindsey still refused to speak wth me. No matter how hard I tried, she would walk away and pretend as though I didn't exist. She had stopped coming to astronomy club meetings, and would take the long way to school just so she wouldn't have to drive past my house. I tried everything to get her to talk to me, even going as far as to corner her in the hallways, but she would always find a way to dodge me everytime.

It became harder and harder to come up with a convincing lie as to why Lindsey was never around anymore for my parents. They started to realize how little Lindsey was over. They noticed the dark circles under my eyes or the small dents in the bushes from where Phoebe had climbed out of my window and missed a step to the ground. I would hear my mother walking slowly past my bedroom every night, stopping just long enough to press her ear to the door to listen for any voices.

Whenever my mom came along, I would press my hand over Phoebe's mouth to try and keep her from saying anything. When my parents questioned me as to why Lindsey wasn't coming around anymore, I would tell them the same thing everytime. I wasn't getting rid of this chance. I had finally gotten to know her. Phoebe Conners had finally let me in. I wasn't going to leave her because I had promised her I was always going to be there and I was not about to leave her now.

There were nights when Phoebe would tell me everything. She told me everything that had happened to her since she was a child. Told me what happened after Autumn died. I never wrote anything down as she was speaking. I always waited for the next day. Sometimes it was intense, and painful. Sometimes it was the 2 of us sitting there and crying. Her for the memories and me for the pain and the loss of innocence Phoebe had suffered at the hands of her father.

There was one night when I was sitting on my bed, typing everything she had told me the previous night when I heard a knock at the window. When I opened the window, Phoebe climbed in, not waiting for me to help her in.

"I have spent my entire life wondering if I was broken. I thought my father had ruined my chances at ever having a normal life but the more I thought about it, the more I realized I have never felt sexual attraction before in my life."

"I convinced myself that I was broken and something could fix me. There had to be something that could fix me I mean what kind of person just doesn't want sex? What type of person just doesn't feel anything about sex? I couldn't seem to understand that this was just something about who I was," she tells me.

My heart was pounding in my chest as she stood in front of me.

"There first time I ever felt anything was when I kissed a girl. I let her push me up against a wall and kiss me until I couldn't feel my own lips. And then I let the next one, and the next one after that do the same," she whispers.

My heart catches in my throat when she says then. I felt like everything inside of me was exploding.

"You know Garica, I kissed all those girls, and yet I never left feeling like I wanted something with them."

My throat was dry. I couldn't think. The only thing in my mind was Phoebe Conners.

"Not once did you ever want to have a relationship?" I whispered.

She shook her head. "Not once. Not before I met you."

Those words send me spiraling. I had rehearsed this happening so many times and yet when I was actually in the situation, I had no idea what to say.

"What kind of relationship do you want with me?" I asked, my voice coming out in a low husk.

She reaches over and grabs my face in her hands. My breath catches in my throat. We had been closer together than this before but it was never like this. Never had it been like this.

"I want to kiss you until I can't feel my lips, and then I want to kiss you even more. I want to kiss you until it physically hurts to, and even then I wouldn't stop," she mutters, her face dangerous close to mine.

I don't waste a second. I pressed my lips to her, testing the waters before diving in deeper. She pulls me closer, her lips working in tandem with mine. I rest my hands on her waist, desperately trying to hold her there. This all felt like a dream. As if I was going to wake up and this would all be gone.

When we break away for air, her forehead comes to rest on mine. She gasps in breaths, a smile on her face.

"You know, I think staying here tonight sounds a hell of a lot better then going home," she whispers.

I nod, a smile covering my face, pulling her hips towards mine and stealing another kiss.

"I'm glad you said something because I was going to suggest the same thing," I replied.

We were silent as we laid there in the bed together. I feel the ends of her hair tickling my shoulder and I move to play with it. Never in my life have I felt more content. I never wanted to be anywhere else but here. I don't want to ever leave right here. I want to freeze time, freeze it so Phoebe Conners and I are always lying here together.

Her cheek comes to rest on the top of my head and she buries her face in my hair. For the first time, the silence between us isn't awkward. It feels full, like there is nothing to say at the moment. There are no words that need to be spoken. Nothing that needs to be said. The only thing we need is each other at this moment. The only thing I need is to hold her. Feel her hands on my skin as she falls asleep next to me. We were both content. There was no place we would rather be right now than in each other's arms.

In that moment, I question who could ever think of Phoebe Conners the way the entire world does. She was nothing like the addict everyone described her as. She wasn't the psychopath who had been arrested 10 times before. No, Phoebe Conners was the girl who was misunderstood. The girl who was holding me like I was the last thing on earth. The girl who snores when she sleeps. I wanted nothing more than to be in this moment with her. To stay here for the rest of eternity.

"I hope I stay with you forever," I whispered under my breath, trying not to wake her up.

"Don't you know Sydney," I hear her say, her voice muddled by the grip sleep had on her. "Forever is subjective. It never means the same to everyone."

SNEAKING HER OUT IN the mornings was never an easy task. It required a lot of distraction and trust that Phoebe would be able to scale the wall down outside my window and hide in my car until I could leave. This morning I woke up to the feeling of Phoebe tracing her hand up and down my arm.

"Morning," she whispers, pressing a kiss to my shoulder before sitting up, her hair cascading down her back like a waterfall of bright red fire.

I groaned, sitting up and rubbing my eyes. There would never be a better sight that Phoebe Conners when I woke up. I would have stayed in that bed forever if I could but we both knew we couldn't. At some point my family would come looking for me and they would freak out if they saw Phoebe.

She opens the window starting to climb out before running back towards me, grabbing my face and pulling me in for a kiss. I let out a startled squeak before kissing her back. She pulls away smiling before starting to climb out the window, leaving me standing in the middle of my room, my fingers feeling my lips where she was only 10 seconds ago.

I snuck downstairs as quietly as possible and started preparing coffee for both Phoebe and I. I didn't even hear my father come in. He was still in his uniform from yesterday, and he looked like he hadn't slept all day. He didn't say anything as he walked towards me and grabbed the coffee pot from my hands, not even bothering to get a mug but just drinking it from the pot. I winced, sliding him a cup from the cupboard.

"Morning dad," I said, trying to sneak past him and out the door.

He grabs my arm, pulling me in for a hug, looking over my shoulder towards the outside. Fear spikes in my heart and I let him go, trying to turn him away from the window. Out of the corner of my eye I see a bush move as Phoebe Conners jumps out of it and runs to hide behind my car. He cranes his neck to look outside again but there was nothing out there. He stares down at me, confusion filling his face.

"I thought I heard you talking to someone last night," he told me, holding my gaze.

My heart pounds in my chest, and I start to panic. We were not being that loud, and even if we were there was no way he could have known it was Phoebe. We were being too careful for that.

"I was watching a movie last night," I answered, trying to keep my voice steady.

He nods his head as if this answers all his questions before pressing a kiss to my forehead and walking back towards the cup of coffee on the counter.

I don't even wait to say goodbye. I race outside, unlocking the car and slamming the door behind me. Phoebe is laying down in the backseat and I speed away, my heart pounding in my chest as I do.

"What is going on?" she asks, as I am white knuckling the steering wheel.

"He heard us last night," I replied quietly.

I hear her suck in a deep breath before cursing under her breath. "Shit,"

We were both so sure we were being careful last night. It only took one time for our entire lives to unravel. This could have been that one time. We had to be more cautious. We had to be quieter. I wasn't going to stop sneaking her into the house but we would just have to be more careful about it. Careful. Just more careful.

We sat in silence as I drove, the silence only breaking after I parked in the school parking lot.

"I should just stay home tonight," she says.

I start to shake my head, reaching over and grabbing her hands. For maybe the first time, she doesn't flinch away from my touch.

"I can't let you do that Phoebe."

Both of us knew that was going to happen if she stayed home that night. She hadn't slept at her own house in a month. She had been safe at mine. He had not laid his hands on her in over a month. We both knew at some point we wouldn't be able to stop it when he did it again, but I wouldn't let him have the chance to. I would not let him touch her again.

She looked at me, staring into my eyes.

"It's okay," she whispered, as if he could hear her in the car. "I can handle it."

I didn't want her alone with him. She hadn't been hurt by him in a month. She had been safe. I promised that I would protect her. How was I supposed to protect her if I wasn't there? How could I protect her if I sent her back home?

"No, I'm not letting you be alone with him," I finally said, tears filling my eyes. "I don't want that monster to touch you."

Her hand comes to rest on my cheek, and I resist the urge to lean into her touch.

"It's okay Sydney. It's one night. I can handle one night."

"Let me stay the night," I murmured.

A look of shock appears on her face. I had never asked to stay over at her house, it was always her coming to mine. Maybe if I were there, nothing would happen. Maybe I could save her.

"You would do that?" she asks.

"Of course," I answer, finally allowing myself to lean into her touch.

She moves forwards, slowly placing her lips on mine. She pulls away before I am able to reciprocate, and she holds my face in her hands.

"You are a wonder, Sydney Garcia. You never stop surprising me."

I DIDN'T EVEN TRY TO sit next to Lindsey in homeroom anymore. I had ditched our old lunch table to eat in my car with Phoebe. When I was with Phoebe, it was easier to forget my best friend hated me but when she wasn't there, I became painfully aware of the way she hated me.

It was like I didn't even exist. For our entire friendship I had lied to her once, and I lied because I knew she would react the same way she was currently reacting. I couldn't handle it anymore. I wasn't going to let her give me the cold shoulder when I didn't tell her because I knew I was going to get this reaction. If she wanted to act like a child then she could, but for once in my fucking life, I was going to speak my mind.

I kept a close eye on her during our last period and when she tried to race out of the classroom I chased after her. Phoebe followed in close pursuit, as I kept on Lindsey's heel. She knew I was chasing her, but when she sped up, I followed.

"Lindsey, what the hell is the matter with you?" I demanded, cornering her at her car.

She wheels around, anger flashing in her eyes.

"Were you going to tell me you were dating Phoebe Conners, or were you just going to keep fucking around like it affects no one else?" she demands.

"What the hell are you talking about Lindsey?" I answered, trying to keep a straight face.

"Don't play fucking dumb with me, Sydney. I saw you kissing her this morning in the parking lot. Don't act as though you haven't changed. I don't know who you are anymore. You are driving your own car every day, you just cursed. Did you really think I wouldn't notice?" she demands.

"It's not like you have put in the time to notice since apparently you haven't even looked in my direction in the past month," I yelled.

"You fucking ditched me the last time I was with you for Phoebe. So don't even start acting like this is my fault."

"She showed up in the middle of the night, in the pouring rain in no car. What the fuck was I supposed to do. It's not my fault you're just a judgemental bitch," I screamed.

A look of surprise registers on her face. She didn't say anything for a moment, just staring at me, her eyes flicking back and forth from Phoebe to me.

"Who are you? I don't know you because whatever this is that is standing in front of me is not Sydney Garica," Lindsey whispers, her eyes filling with tears.

"Lindsey!" I call out. I felt Phoebe's hand come to rest on my shoulder. I lean into her touch, my eyes filling with tears.

Lindsey turns around, her eyes coming to rest on Phoebe and I.

"Don't bother Sydney. I see who is more important now."

After

After the trial, I went to the state prison everyday to try and get him to talk. There would be days when his lawyers said he was in no position and other days when I was waved right through. There was never any pattern to the times he agreed to talk.

His story was never altered each time I spoke with him. There was nothing anyone could say that would get him to admit sexually assaulting his children. It became easier to believe him than think anything against him. His story never changed. It was the same everytime. Someone who was guilty would have a changing story. Someone who was guilty wouldn't be able to keep up these pretenses for as long as he had.

Alexander refused to go anywhere near that prison. He wanted nothing to do with Jonathan Conners and no one could blame him. No one except for me. He had faced him hundreds of times before. He had been there for Phoebe when she was alive. So why was he refusing to be there for her in death.

It was different to Alexander. He told me that seeing him in prison would only make it more real. Seeing him in there meant that Phoebe was truly gone and he wasn't even behind bars for what he did to Phoebe. I told him it had been real since she killed herself. Alexander would end the conversation after that.

I woke up one morning in our shared apartment to find Alexander gone. He couldn't handle the arguments. He couldn't handle the constant reminders of Phobe Conners. He couldn't handle the life he had been leaving. Alexander changed his number and deleted his social media accounts. He wiped his entire existence off the planet.

The days never felt lonelier than after Alexander left. The one person I had that actually believed me was gone. The only person who was willingly doing anything on this case had left. It was just me now. There was no one left that actually believed me. The only two that ever did were now gone. One was dead, and the other might as well be dead with how he disappeared.

There is something so isolating about losing everyone. I had made Phoebe Conners my entire life and when she died, I didn't know what to do with myself. When I started working on this case if felt as though I didn't have to give her up just yet. I was still able to keep a piece of her with me. With Alexander gone, there was less of Phoebe Conners around. It seemed the only memories I had of her now were the one's I would rather forget. I had survived this long without Phoebe, but everyday felt harder. Everyday felt like there were more parts of her slipping away. Everyday Phoebe Conenrs felt farther and farther away.

Lindsey tried coming around again. She would try and get me walk away from the case and go back to college. She tried getting me to live a normal life outside of Phoebe Conners. She stopped when she realized I was a lost cause. She couldn't handle the case. She didn't understand why I was still so involved with Phoebe Conners despite the fact that she was dead. She had hoped that after Phoebe died she would get friend back. She would get the same Sydney Garcia she had before Phoebe Conners. What she didn't understand was the fact that part of me was dead and gone.

Lindsey never understood that losing someone like that wasn't something you could get over in time. There was no way she could understand that feeling until she lost someone like that. To Lindsey, Phoebe Conners was nothing more than a fling. Something I did to defy her parents and make them upset. She couldn't understand how someone could feel genuine love for Phoebe. She would never understand that I loved Phoebe Conners more than I had loved anything else in the world.

Lindsey gave up after a few months. My father stopped giving me new information on the case. Jonathan Conners lawyers stopped letting me speak with him. Alexander was gone. I had nothing left. There was nothing I could do for Phoebe. There was nothing left for me.

I moved back to New York 6 months after Jonathan Conners was convicted. He had been given 5 years. 5 years with the chance of parole for the years of abuse Genevieve, Autumn and Phoebe Conners endured. There was only so much one could take.

I had fought for so long. Fought for someone to believe me. I had spent over a year, screaming and fighting for anyone to listen to me. I couldn't fight anymore. I was so sick of fighting. I left Indiana, vowing I would never come back. I wanted nothing more than to forget that Phoebe Conners ever existed. She returned to the place where she had never been anything other than Sydney Garia. Sydney Garcia. Not the girl who held her girlfriend as she died. Not the girl who had found her girlfriend on the kitchen floor. Not the girl who sat at her dead girlfriends grave for hours after her death. I was nothing but Sydney Garcia and that I what I needed.

It worked for a short amount of time. I made friends, went to parties, and made out with girls, but Phoebe was always in the back of her mind. She was always there. Always at the corner of my mind. In my dreams, she was there. In my dreams, I got to hold her, laugh with her and feel her presence. But when I woke up it was all gone. It wasn't real. It would never be real again.

I tried so hard to forget. Tried so hard to erase Phoebe Conners from my mind. Tried to pretend that Phoebe Conners had never existed. She was just a figment of my imagination. She wasn't real. Phoebe Conners had never truly existed. She never did leave my dreams though. I could feel her at night. Feel her right before I felt asleep. I could hear her whispering that everything was going to be okay. It was when I dreamed that she was right there with me, promising me that she was right there with me. It was at night when I truly believed I could have her again.

During the day however, Phoebe Conners didnt exist to me. I deleted every document I could. The documents I had spent years of my life on. Everytime I deleted a document, I felt another part of me dying inside, but I relished that feeling. That feeling was good because it meant that I was leaving her behind. I was moving on with my life.

I couldn't bring myself to get rid of all of it. I printed every picture before deleting them. I printed everything Phoebe had told me. The documents where Phoebe told me everything that had happened to her. I printed it out and then deleted it off of my laptop, making sure I went to my trash and clearing out my trash, effectively deleting Phoebe Conners from my life.

I kept telling herself to burn the pictures. To get rid of all the memories. If I kept them then she would forever be in my life. I couldn't bring myself to get throw them away. I couldn't bring myself to destroy them. I shoved them into a box instead. When my parents came down for Christmas I gave them the box and told them to put it wherever they want.

Without the constant reminders and the photos and pictures it was easy to pretend that nothing had ever happened. When I was around other people I was Sydney Garcia the English and Psychology major. Everyone started to forget I had taken a year off. It was easy for them to forget. Easy for them to forget. They didn't have to live with the constant reminders.

Everyone had heard of Phoebe Conners at this point. Man made of old American money Jonathan Conners was arrested for domestic abuse and was under suspiscion of sexually assaulting his children. They knew of his children Autumn and Phoebe Conners who both killed themselves at 19. They knew Phoebe Conners girlfriend had come forward and accused Jonathan Conners of sexually assaulting his children. This was the kind of case that was eaten up in the news cycle for a few weeks and then everyone forgot about it.

It was easy for the world to cast their eyes down and say they couldn't believe someone would do this to their own child. It was easier for them to look at her father as a monster who had been apprehended then believe there were others out there like that. They were perfectly content to look at the news, comment on how sad it was and then move on with their lives.

I couldn't do that. I couldn't just seal Phoebe off in the dark recesses of my mind and pretend she didn't exist. It was different when you had lived through it. It was different when you dreamed of her every night. It was different when you woke up to an empty bed every morning and remembered the times you didn't wake up alone. It was different when others around you chose to forget she had ever existed and you were still permanently branded with the marks she left.

My parents made me go see a therapist. They told me getting everything in the open would help. They said I couldn't grieve alone anymore. I couldn't put this upon myself anymore. Well I tried talking. I tried speaking with someone about Phoebe but nothing any therapist could say would help.

Nothing they could say would take away the dreams I had of her every night. The therapists could talk as much as they wanted, but they would never be able to make me forget what if felt like when I held her as she died. Or when I watched as they pulled that sheet over her body.

Putting it out in the open didn't make it seem anymore real. It would always be real. I had to live with the fact Phoebe killed herself. I had to dream of her every night. It would never be more real then when I woke up in the mornings and expected her to be there.

Talking about Phoebe Conners promised she would never leave. Talking gave her more room in my mind. Talking allowed her to grow and fester. Talking meant there was nothing I could do that would get her out of my mind. Talking meant I would never be able to fall asleep without her being there. Talking meant Phoebe Conners was there as long as I lived.

MY THIRD YEAR AT NYU I got my own apartment off campus. Finally living off campus meant Atlas could come and live with me. I had put it off for as long as possible but Mrs. Conners told me that if I didn't come and get him he was going to the shelter. Phoebe would have killed me if he was sent away, so after moving into the apartment I drove back to Indiana to get Atlas.

I stayed with my parents for that night. They tried getting me to go out to dinner with them, or go into town to celebrate me being home for the first time in over a year. I wouldn't go out though. I told them I was here to get Atlas and after that I would be leaving. I knew my mother was disappointed. She wanted to spend the few moments her daughter was back home but I wasn't about to leave that house. I wasn't leaving until the next morning.

I had never seen anything more excited to see a human being than Atlas was to see me. When Geniveve handed him to me, he immediately started licking my face. I felt his short stubby tail whacking my shins. For the first time since Phoebe died, I smiled. A real, true smile.

Atlas was good on the entire drive home. He fell asleep in the passenger seat and just stayed asleep the entire drive. He was even more excited when we got into the parking lot of the apartment.

He raced in front of me, pulling on his leash to get into the apartment. When I opened the door and dropped the leash, he started running. Running from door to door as if expecting Phoebe to race through one of them.

He was more than confused, sniffing around the apartment and staring at me with those puppy dog eyes like he had no idea where he was. It was understandable after moving 763 miles from Indiana to New York City. He had lived with Phoebe's mother until now. Sydney would stop in to visit and see him, but he could never live with her in her dorm rooms.

After searching through every single one of the rooms, he came to sit on my lap. I didn't think a dog could cry before that, but after hearing those whimpers I knew he was crying. Atlas had thought Phoebe was going to be here.

After three years, Atlas had hoped he would see her again. After three years, he still held onto faith that wherever he went, there was a chance she would be there too. There would never be a time when he would ever stop expecting her to be there. He would never fully understand that she was dead and gone. Atlas would still hold onto hope and be disappointed at every turn.

There was no way I could explain to him she was never coming back. Never any way of me telling him that Phoebe was never coming back. I grabbed one of Phoebe's old sweatshirts I had shoved in the back of his closet and let him cuddle up to it. I left him sitting on that couch as I left.

I went to a church that night. I was probably the farthest thing from religious but there was nothing else I could do. I needed to get Phoebe out of my mind. I couldn't live anymore with Phoebe living in my mind. I wanted to be able to be those people who are able to sit there watching the news and say what happened with the Conners family. I wanted that life. I wanted to be those people. I wanted a life without Phoebe Conners.

The church was quiet as I walked in. A few candles were lit on the walls, casting a dim light on the pews. I sat down in a pew close to the back, a statue of Mary looking down at me from the front of the church. I didn't know what to do. I didn't know if I should start with a prayer to the heavens above or whatever figure was listening to me.

"I don't know if there is anyone out there listening, and I don't know if anyone even cares, but I need help. I need something to help me because I can't keep doing this. I can't keep holding on to something that is never coming back. I can't keep thinking of Phoebe Conners. Phoebe, if you are listening, please stop. Please make it go away. Please, I can't think of anything else except for you. I can't think about the fact I quit on you. I was so close, and I gave up. You are in my every waking thought, I dream of you, and I can't get you out of my fucking mind.

I can't stop remembering how you smelled when we lay in bed together—the faint smell of cloves and tobacco. I can't stop thinking of your dimples whenever you smiled. I can't stop thinking about the cadence of your voice. The way you said everything, like you were about to tell a joke. I can't stop thinking about the way your laugh sounded. I can't stop thinking of the way you snored when you slept. I can't stop thinking of you, Phoebe.

Please, let me go. Please make this all stop because I hurt again every time I think of you. Every time I think of you, I only remember the pain of hearing that flatline. I can't stop picturing them pulling the sheet over your body. I can't stop hearing them announce the time of death. I thought I heard you screaming, Phoebe. I thought I heard you screaming and crying, but other times I thought that was me. I never got to say goodbye to you, Phoebe. I never got to say I loved you one last time or feel your hand in mine. I never got to tell you that you were strong and deserving of the entire world. There are so many things that I let stay unsaid. So many things that now I wish I could go back and tell you,"

The only thing I could hear was the sounds of my sobs echoing throughout the deserted church.

"Please, Phoebe," I whispered. "Please let me go."

ATLAS WAS STILL COVERED in Phoebe's sweatshirt when I got home, but he was sleeping with one of his toys. We grabbed as many as I could before leaving but I hadn't seen this one before. I sat next to him and Atlas moved his head just enough that he hit the toy. I expected a squeaker, but I heard something completely different. It was her voice. I had heard her voice.

"Hey Atlas, I love you and miss you, buddy. I'll see you as soon as possible. I love you, my little man!" I heard Phoebe's voice say from the toy.

That was the first time I had heard Phoebe Conners's voice in 3 years. Atlas looked down at the toy before digging his head into it again. Her voice played again. The same message. The same voice. I was the one who pressed the button again after it ended. There it was again. There was her voice.

I sat there with Atlas in my lap, listening to that message repeatedly. Everytime it stopped I would start it again. It was Phoebe's voice. This was all I had left of her. The first time I had heard her voice in 3 years. In this toy for Atlas. Atlas looked up at me, sadness coating his eyes. He had come here expecting Phoebe to be with Sydney, yet she wasn't here. It was just us now. Phoebe was never coming back.

"I miss her too." "I know, buddy," I whispered, holding that little toy in my hands like it was my lifeline. Like it was the only thing keeping me grounded.

Before

I lied to my parents and told them I would be at Lindsey's for an unplugged study session. I knew they wouldn't question anything. They were just happy I was talking with Lindsey again.

I drove as slowly as possible to the Conners' house. I wanted to be there for Phoebe. I wanted to stay the night to make sure she was safe, but something about the house terrified me. The memories of bad times that clung to the walls. A constant reminder of all that Phoebe had endured.

I drove down their winding driveway. I parked at the edge of the woods, walking up to the house. I was glued to my phone, texting her that I was there. I was expecting her to be waiting outside for me, but when I got to the front of the house, there was no one waiting out there.

Phoebe didn't respond to my next few texts. I called, but all I heard was a few rings and then her voicemail message. I texted her again. I called again. Each time there was no response. I started to walk around the side of the house, trying to control my pounding heart.

There were no lights on in the house. It was as if no one was there. My mind immediately went to the worst. What was happening in there that she wasn't answering her phone? I called again, and when she didn't answer, I called again. I left her a frantic voicemail after a frantic voicemail. When she didn't answer, I pounded on the door, screaming her name and demanding to be let in. No one answered.

I raced around to the backyard, trying to see if I could see her, but there was nothing. I couldn't help the tears that were streaming down my face. I raced up to the back door, pounding and screaming her name. Something was happening in there, and I couldn't get in. She was being hurt in there, and I couldn't help her.

I felt a hand on my shoulder and wheeled around, coming face to face with Phoebe Conners. I looked her up and down, making sure she was okay. All I could hear was the pounding of my heart in my ears as I saw her mouth form my name. My hand went to her face to make sure she was there. When I was able to reassure myself that she was in fact real and in front of me, I punched her shoulder.

"I can't tell if I want to punch you or hug you, you fucker," I yelled before pulling her in for a hug, crying into her shoulder.

She wraps her arms around my waist, holding me to her whispering repeatedly. "I'm sorry. I'm so sorry."

She smelled of cigarette smoke and faintly of alcohol. I pulled back, hungrily pressing my lips to hers to kiss her. My hand comes around her neck, pulling her towards me as one of hers goes to my hair.

We stand there together, just drinking in each other's presence. She pulls back first, smiling down at me.

"I thought he had hurt you," I whispered, as if her father was around to hear us.

She shook her head before jerking her head up towards the roof. "I was up there. He was looking for me, so I ran."

A wave of relief washed over me. She had escaped. She was okay. He hadn't hurt her. He hadn't touched her. She was right here, and she was okay.

"I'm proud of you. You ran. You escaped. You're okay," I mumbled, more to myself than her. She looks down at me, nodding her head before looking at the roof.

"Speaking of the roof, I have a surprise for you," she tells me, smirking as I look up.

I CLIMBED MORE STAIRS just to get to the roof than I think I have ever climbed in my entire life. I was out of breath by the 3rd flight, and by the 10th, I thought I was about to die. Phoebe walked in front of me, not even breaking a sweat. When we finally got to the roof, and she opened the door, I plopped my ass down and started gasping for air. She looked as if she was trying to hold back a laugh as I was gulping down air as I had just been underwater for 10 minutes.

"You're an asshole," I said in between gasps, making her laugh. I reached over to swat her but let my hand fall limply by my side out of sheer lack of energy.

When I can finally stand up I look out at the roof and suck in a breath. There are fairy lights strung up all around the roof. Underneath those are piles and blankets with a telescope at the edge.

"What-" I start.

"I was hoping we could count this as our first official date." she cuts me off before I finish. I look at her, smiling before wrapping my arms around her.

"This is beautiful. Thank you," I whispered.

I looked out one more time before turning to her.

"Why the telescope?" I asked.

Her face turns bright red, and she walks over to it, messing with a few knobs.

"I heard that you were part of an astronomy club at school, so I thought that maybe you would want to look out at the stars and things like that," she told me, a sheepish look on her face.

I try to hold in a laugh for as long as possible, but I can't hold it anymore after a while. Phoebe was looking at me as if I was insane and I doubled over in laughter.

"The astronomy club I run is just for zodiac signs and stuff. We play it off as though we are talking about stars and space when we actually talking about horoscopes and what season we are in," I tell her.

She doesn't say anything, she just stares at me.

"What?" she finally asks, which makes me laugh even more.

Her face darkens in color as she sat there staring at me. When I finished laughing she reaches under the pile of blankets, and pulled out a bag of chips and an unopened pack of Oreos.

"I thought it was only fitting that we kick off this date with the first meal I ever ate with you," she grinned.

"You call this a meal?" I shoot back.

"Apparently you do Garcia since this is in fact the first thing you ever fed me."

I laugh, reaching for and grabbing an Oreo before sitting down. She lays down next to me, her hand brushing mine. I lean into her, letting my head rest on her shoulder. Phoebe points up to a star with her hand holding an Oreo. I looked up, trying to see what she was pointing to, struggling to see over the oreo she was holding.

"Look of there Garica, that right there," she tells me. "Is the Big Dipper. Right near it over... There is the Little Dipper. The ones that look like a big pan and a little pan."

I looked up to where she was pointing but saw a clump of stars. For being in a fake astronomy club, I knew nothing about constellations.

I sit and listen as Phoebe points out other constellations, listening to her talk. The lilt in her voice makes her sound so animated and excited, even if she could have been talking about the most boring thing in the world. She didn't talk too fast or even too slow. It was a perfect speed. She would speed up and slow down with each story on how the constellations came to be. I stared at her as she talked.

I looked at the was her, wondering how one person could be as stunning as

she was. The way her eyes shined in the starlight creating this reflection of the stars as she stared up at them. The way her hair was falling her back in soft curls. She moved her hands when she talked. That was one thing I had never noticed before. I couldn't take my eyes off her as she spoke.

She sits up, staring at the stars when she is finally finished.

"Where did you learn so much about constellations?" I asked.

She turned towards me, a slightly sad smile on her face before she answered. "Well, Sydney Garcia, before there was your fake little astronomy club, a little someone named Autumn Conners started a real one, and as the younger sister of the sole member and president of the club, she needed someone to talk about the stars with, so that person became me."

For the first time she had ever talked about her sister, she didn't get teary-eyed, or upset when she talked about her. It was like she was reminiscing on good times instead of being upset that they would never happen again. I didn't know whether or not to keep asking questions about Autumn. I didn't know if I should continue to push or let her talk about things on her terms.

She never spoke about Autumn; when she did it was to discuss her father. She never wanted even to speak her name. Something scared a person when they found their sister dead in their bathroom. Phoebe didn't like thinking about it. She didn't like thinking that for years before her father did something to her, he was doing the same thing to Autumn.

Phoebe doesn't say anything else. She just continues staring at the stars. She points at a string of 3 stars. She sees one constellation, and a smile comes to her face.

"See that one, Syd?" she asks. Syd. That was the first time she had ever called me that. Hearing her use a nickname for me made it more real. "That one is Orion's belt. He was a hunter. My grandfather told me when I was a child that after he died if I saw that sign, then it meant he was there looking out for me. It only comes out in the winter months, but whenever I see it, I can't help but think of him."

I smile, sitting up and resting my head on her shoulder. She kisses the top of my head as I lean against her. Everything about her felt right. It felt like we had been doing this forever. Like we had always been here together.

> We sit together, her telling stories of the constellations
> and her extended family

when she was a kid and me about my crazy family with thousands of kids. She said her father had never touched her like that before Autumn died. He hit her a few times, but he had never laid his hands on her like that. She said she had a normal life. Some kids got spanked and she got smacked. She told me her childhood was completely normal. I didn't have the heart to tell her nothing about what he did was normal.

I fell asleep lying there like that that night. Her head was on my chest and my hand in her hair. I listened to the soft sound of her snores and knew there was no place I would rather be than right here with her. Forever...

After

Phoebe Conners's body was exhumed three years, seven months, and 23 days since she died. After allegations that Jonathan Conners might have paid off the coroner, Genvieve Conners agreed to have the body exhumned to put an end to the whispers. The whispers would not end with this though. They would only grow.

Those weeks leading up to the examination I walked around in a fog. When I closed my eyes, all I could imagine was seeing her cold dead face staring back at me from the coffin. I stopped even trying to sleep. I didn't want to have to see her like that.

I went to classes until the day she was exhumed. The morning the report was given, I didn't want to get out of bed. I just wanted to close my eyes and pretend as though I wasn't waking up every morning with the knowledge that the woman I loved was dead and there was nothing I could do that would bring her back.

When I was finally able to bring myself to stand up, I walked right over to the couch, pulling Atlas into my lap and holding him close to me. I hadn't turned on the tv in over a week. I knew the minute I did, Phoebe would be the only thing on my mind. I grabbed the remote from where it laid on the side table, my hand shaking as I pressed the button and turned on the TV.

The minute I heard the click of the TV, a reporter filled the screen. She was standing there, offering play by play of the case before this. I didn't need to listen. Not when I had lived through it.

A knock sounded at the door as the reporter continued talking. Atlas looked over at me expectantly as the knocking persisted but I didn't even move to answer. Whoever it was would come back if they really needed me. The knocking at the door persisted.

"Sydney?" I heard a voice call from behind the door. I knew that voice. Fucking Kerian.

The door opened and I heard her footsteps pounding down the hallway.

"Sydney are you okay?" she asks again.

Atlas leaps off of my lap and runs towards her. I slowly stood up, casting one last glance to the TV before walking towards Kerian. I don't even have the chance to say anything before she is throwing her arms around me and pulling me into her chest.

"I didn't want you to have to be alone for this," she whispers.

Tears well up in my eyes but I swallow them down. I needed to find a way to get her out of her. I couldn't let her see whatever they were going to find. I couldn't let her see me like this.

"I don't care what you say Sydney, I am not leaving. This isn't something one should go through alone."

The minute I felt the first tear spill out of my eyes, I couldn't stop the rest of them from spilling over. Kerian held me as I sobbed, Atlas at our feet and that blasted reporter's voice coming through the TV.

Kerian walked us towards the couch and sat down, holding my head to her chest. We both sat there in silence as we watched the coroner walk into frame. My heart was pounding in my chest as I watched him open the file in front of him and begin to read.

"After careful examination, there is not enough left of Phoebe Conners body to give any definite answers. Based on what is left, we can say that most of the damage to the bones are not able to be self inflicted. We can say by the way the few bones have healed give us the assumption that the bones were broken by a blunt object.

No human has the force to inflict the damage done to the bones to themselves.

However, at this time we are not able to give any definitive conclusions based on the state of composition. If you have any more questions please direct them towards Mr. Fitzgerald."

"Based on rate of composition." I knew this shouldn't hit me as hard as it did. After three years there was going to be composition that happened, but the thought of her lying in that ground, her body falling apart with time made my stomach turn.

I didn't realize how tightly I had been clutching Kerian until I have to pull away. My stomach was reeling, threatening to lose everything inside of it at any time. Kerian lets me go and races after me as I stumble down the hallway and into the bathroom. The minute I lean over the toilet, her hands reach to hold my hair back as I lose everything in my system.

Her hand moved up and down my back as her other one held my hair as I dry heaved. There was nothing left for my body to rid of, but I couldn't get the image of her decaying body out of my mind. Would her hair still be there? When they opened up that casket did they still see threads of red coming from her skull or was it laying dead next to her. Could they still see her hands? Were the callouses that covered her palms still there? Those hands that I had held so many times. Were they still the same as they were before? Or was there nothing left but the memory of what they once were. Of what she once was.

"It's okay Sydney," Kerian whispers as I sit back onto the bathroom floor, my head moving into my hands. "It's all going to be okay."

I knew what she was trying to do but that was a lie. Nothing would ever be okay because Phoebe wasn't here. More and more of her slipped away by the minute. As time went on, it would take more and more of her until there was nothing left of her but the memories of what she once was.

None of this was okay. It wasn't okay that Phoebe had to be taken out of the ground because the original coroner didn't do his job the way he should. It wasn't okay that I had to sit here and listen to them say there was nothing they could prove definitively because there wasn't enough left of her to be able to say exactly what happened. It wasn't okay that I was still living this fucking hell.

Something in me shifted as I laid on that bathroom floor. I couldn't stay in New York. I couldn't stay here when everything was happening back in indiana. I couldn't be here when Phoebe was there. I couldn't stay now that I finally had a dog in the fight.

THAT NEXT DAY I COULDN'T escape the stares. They followed me everywhere as I walked throughout campus. I hadn't even wanted to go to classes that day. I wanted nothing more than to stay home and pretend as if this had never happened, but I couldn't. I needed to tell my processors I would be completing all of my work online. They deserved more than just a measly email.

None of them asked any questions. They understood. They knew what had happened. They all promised me they would post everything online and that was the end. The stares only increased as I walked through the campus back towards the apartment. I tired to ignore them. Tried to act like I didn't feel the seering eyes on my back as I walked past them.

The news stayed on in the apartment all day. Atlas hovered in the doorway as I packed. I hadn't even told my parents I was coming home, but I needed to be ready. I needed to go home. I shoved everything I would need into my car and let Atlas sit in the passenger seat. A lump appeared in my throat as I picked up my phone to call my parents.

I never thought I was going to be going back there. I had sworn to myself I would never go back to Indiana and yet here I was. I had given up a year ago. I had walked away from the case. I told myself it was better if I forgot everything but I couldn't do it anymore. Phoebe needed me. I wasn't going to let her down anymore.

I took a deep breath and pressed call.

"Sydney, how are you doing?" my father says when he answers. I could hear the fear in his voice. He was treading on ice. He didn't want to say anything that would upset me.

"I'm coming home. Let's fucking finish this."

I MET MY DAD IN DRIVEWAY to drop my car off. Before I was even given the chance to walk inside before my father started the car and drove us to the Indiana State Penitentiary. My mother had met us there and took Atlas back home as my dad drove us. I knew he wanted to say something. He wanted to promise me that everything was going to be okay but we both knew that wasn't true.

My hands were shaking in my lap as we got closer and closer. I was about to face Jonathan Conners for the first time in a year and a half. I was about to look the man who destroyed everything I loved.

My heart was pounding as I looked at the tall building looming in front of me. He was in there. Jonathan Conners was in there. That wasn't enough of a punishment. This building wouldn't give him everything he deserved. He got to live while Phoebe was dead. He got to survive when Phoebe was in the ground.

"Are you going to be okay, Syd," my father asks from beside me.

I hated that word. I hated it when people asked me if I was going to be okay. I would never be okay again. Phoebe was dead. They had dug her body out of the ground because her father was a complete dick. This entire situation would never be okay. I had lost the only person I loved and he was here able to keep living. It didn't matter if this case was solved. It didn't matter if I was finally able to bring peace to Phoebe. As long as Jonathan Conners was alive, I woudl never be okay.

I feel something in my hands and I look down, seeing the box I had shoved every memory of Phoebe into.

"I thought you might want this. A reminder of why you are here," my father says.

I didn't even open the lid to the box before shoving it back into his hands.

"I came here to speak with Jonathan Conners and ot do that I need to be in a rational state of mind," I told him. "Give it back to me later today, and I'll take it, but I can't have it with me."

My shoulder were held high as I walked through that hallway. My father followed behind me, letting me take the front. A guard posted himself out of the door and I walked in after the buzzer sounded.

I didn't expect the first time I saw Jonathan Conners I would be filled with the anger I felt. There was not a single part of me that was scared or nervous, no. I was pissed. He was sitting here while Phoebe didn't even have the luxury of being laid to rest in the ground. He looked healthy. He looked fucking healthy when Phoebe was being dug up from the ground. He didn't deserve to be fed three meals everyday. He didn't deserve to see the light of day. Nothing he got he had ever deserved.

"Miss Garica, it's nice to see you again," Jonathan says.

His hands were chained to the table but he lifted them up in a slight wave. This only infuriated me more.

"I'll be honest with you Sydney after I heard you moved back to New York, I never thought I would see you again."

"You know why I am here Conners," I seethed.

"Oh yes Sydney Garcia you are here for the same reason everyone else has been this past week. I am so sick of answering this question. There is only so many times one can say the same thing over and over again."

"Conners it doesn't matter to me how many times you have answered the question, you are going to say the same thing to me. Expect I'm not going to take your bullshit. I know whatever you have been telling everyone else is not the truth. We both know your sentence here is a mere blip of what you would have gotten if everyone knew what you had done to your children. So why don't we save time and you tell me the answer right now and I will decide if you are bullshitting me."

Jonathan looks across the table at me with a smirk.

"Sydney Garcia, I truly do admire your commitment to the life of my daughter but I can assure you I never did touch her like that. What I don't think you understand Sydney Garcia, you may think you knew my daughter but I can assure you, you didn't. You may think that you know everything about my daughter but in truth you know nothing about her and who she really was. My daughter was a whore. She would fuck any single person that came her way. I was honestly surprised when she didn't fuck you.

Phoebe was one trainwreck after another. She would make problems out of absolutely nothing. Did you think I wanted to have to discipline her the way I did? Did you think I enjoyed seeing my own blodd in pain? I didn't, but if I didn't, then no one else was going to. In the end my efforts were in vain. She got the attention she so desperately wanted by killing herself. She got what she wanted and there was nothing I could have done to stop her."

I wanted to reach across the table and strangle him. She was not a whore. This was Phoebe Conners. Phoebe who hated sex. Phoebe who had never had a sexual urge in her life. Phoebe Conners who wasn't given any attention. Phoebe Conners who put up walls around herself because he couldn't bear to let anyone know what had happened to her.

He wasn't talking about the same Phoebe Conners. This was the Phoebe Conners everyone else had known. This was the Phoebe Conners she wanted to make herself look like because the truth was too much of a weight to carry. This wasn't the Phoebe Conners I had fallen asleep next to at night. This wasn't the same Phoebe Conners who I had held as she cried. That wasn't Phoebe Conners.

"How do you explain the state of her bones then Jonathan? Those wounds could not have been self inflicted. They were done with a blunt force object, one that was likely very heavy. Do you have anything to say that would give proper reasoning as to why her bones were broken in that way?" I demanded.

"She had a lot of people in her life Ms. Garcia. I don't know every single person that came through our house. There is no guarantee that it was me who created those injuries. They may have not been self inflicted, but there is no evidence that it was me who created those wounds," Jonathan Conners laughs. "This is all circumstantial evidence Ms. Garcia. None of it will ever hold up in court."

My heart was pounding in my chest as I leaned in closer. I could feel his breath on my face as I looked him in the eyes.

"You can continue lying for as long as you want Jonathan Conners but I want you to understand there is nothing tht will stop me. I don't care how long it takes me, but I am not leaving until I can be assured your sentence will be a hell of a lot longer than 5 years," I growled.

Conners smiles and leans back in his chair.

"Sydney Garcia I watched you walk away from this case a year a half ago. I find it very hand to believe there is nothing that will take you away from this case. I believe that once things get hard again; once you begin to look back into the case you will walk away again. It wouldn't take much that will take you away from this case. It happened to Mr. Chadwick and it is only a matter of time before it happens to you again."

"Mr Conners, I held your daughter as she cried because of what you had done ot her. I stood in the bathroom as she took a shower just to make sure she didn't scrub off her skin off because she wanted nothing more than to get every trace of you off of her. I was the one who found her in the woods. I was the one who held her and promised her everything was going to be okay when she broke her sobreity streak after you hurt her. I was the one who did that. Not you. I am not going anywhere until I could be assured you will never see the light of day again. Forgive me if I will anything in my fucking power to destroy everything you have."

I didn't give him a chance to say anything else. I didn't want to see the smirk on his face. I stormed out of the room, letting the door slam behind me.

"Let's go," I called out to my dad, not stopping to wait for him.

I had a job to do and I would be damned if I was going to let him get in the way of that.

MY ENTIRE FAMILY WAS waiting by the door when I got home. My mother didn't waste a second before pulling me towards her.

"I've missed you mi amor," my mother whispers.

"I've missed you to mama," I answered, small tears welling in my eyes.

When she finally let me go I got a look at my family. All of them had gotten so much bigger since the last time I had been home. There were times when it didn't seem as long as I thought it was but seeing them here, I knew it had been just as long as it felt. 3 and a half years. I hadn't been back home in three and a half years.

Cindy was 9 years old. The twins had just started high school. Adam was in middle school, and Tyler was engaged. I had missed all of them growing up. I had missed some of the most formative years for them. I knew it wouldn't be the last time either. I had no idea how long this case was going to last but I knew this would not be the last thing that I missed.

I might be home but there would be hundreds of more things I would miss. I wouldn't be the sister they wanted. I would never be able to be there for everything but after all that I missed, I was going to try my hardest to be there for the family.

I hadn't realized how much I missed the mundanity of my family. The sound of my mother singing off key to Dean Martin while cooking dinner. My father teaching the youngers to play chess as they sat at the table waiting for dinner to be ready. When dinner was ready we all sat down in the same places at the table as we had when I was in school. It was as if nothing changed.

When I went to my room nothing had changed. Everything was in the exact same place as it had been before I left. I slowly flicked on the lamp, walking slowly around the room looking at everything. It looked the exact same as it did when I was in high school.

I stopped when I saw the pictures of Phoebe on the desk. Before I left from New York I

had knocked down all of the frames. I didn't want to see anything that would remind me of Phoebe. All of the pictures were placed up on the desk. I picked one up, holding it in my hands as I traced the outline of Phoebe. Her bright red hair blending together with the oranges of the sunset. You could see a small part of her face sticking out from her hair but you could see her smile.

That smile. I hadn't seen that smile in years. I set the picture down and grabbed the one right next to it. My lips were pressed to her check as she smiled into the camera. That damn smile. She was there. She was happy.

It hadn't realized how much easier it was to hold onto the bad memories than the good ones. I had been surrounded by so many bad memories of her that it almost seemed as though those were the only one's we had when we were happy. There were times when we laughed together. There were times when I felt nothing but love. I loved her and when you loved someone and you lost them it was hard to remember anything other than the fact you lost them.

For the rest of the time I was here for this case I wanted to remember the times when the two of us were happy. I wanted to be able to leave that prison and think of something other than what Jonathan Conners did to her. I wanted to be able to think about the nights on her roof when we watched the sunset, or when I fell asleep on her shoulder as she told me about the constellations.

I didn't want to focus on the bad anymore. I didn't want to keep thinking about the worst humanity had to offer. I wanted to remember Phoebe as the first girl I fell in love with. I want to remember her for the free spirit she was. I want to remember her the way I saw her when she alive.

MY FATHER WOKE ME UP the next morning and told me we had an appointment with a potential lawyer. Over breakfast he told this lawyer had reached out to him after hearing about the case. He was willing to discuss the case but he didn't want to speak with us before I was on board. The second I called my father he reached out to the lawyer and told him I was on board and we needed to set up a meeting.

Before I left the table my father handed me the box he had tried giving me yesterday.

"Don't forget who you are doing this for Sydney. This isn't about me. This isn't about and it's not about Jonathan Conners. You are doing this because you loved her. You are doing all of this because she died when she didn't have to. Never forget that."

I held the box in my hands as I walked upstairs. I didn't want to open it. The box held some of the best but the worst memories. I wanted to remember the good memories of her but this box was filled with some of the worst memories as well. Despite everything my mind was telling me to do, I opened the box.

The first thing that was inside was the document I had printed. Everything Phoebe had ever told me was right here. I could hear my heart in my ears as I looked thorugh every picture. So many memories tht I had just tucked in the back of my brain. Memories I had told myself I would rather forget than have to deal with.

I reached up, wiping a tear from my cheek as a laugh escaped. My father was right. This wasn't for me. This wasn't for him. This wasn't for Joanthan Conners. This was about Phoebe Conners. This was about Phoebe and Autumn. This was about two girls whose lives had been taken too quickly. Lives of two girls who had no other choice but to leave to protect themsevles from the monster that haunted their every living moment.

When I left for New York, I had forgotten who I fought for. I had acted as though I was the only one effected by Phoebe's death but my struggles paled in comparison to her own. I may have to live in this world without Phoebe but at least I got to live. I got to continue my life. I got to wake up in the morning and know that today was going to be a new day. Phoebe didn't have that luxury anymore. She wasn't able to wake up and start a new day. She wasn't able to close her eyes and leave the world for a moment.

This was bigger than me. This was bigger than my pain. I was here to bring peace to Phoebe and Autumn Conners. I was here to make sure that if this happened to anyone else then they would be able to tell someone. They would be able to find a safer place where they wouldn't be hurt anymore.n I was here to make sure they were believed.

"MISS GARICA, IT'S WONDERFUL to finally meet you," the man sitting in front of me said.

He had introduced himself as Alastair Reno of Reno and McCoulough. My father had told me he was one of the most high profile attorneys in the state and Reno was willing to take our case free of charge. All I had to do was meet with him and discuss the inside and out of the case and decide if I was willing to have him as my lawyer.

"Thank you for meeting with us Mr. Reno."

"Oh please Miss Garica, call me Reno. If we are going to be working together we must trust each other enough to not use formalities," Reno tells me.

I liked him already.

"I understand you want to talk about the case," I said, grabbing the document from next to me.

"I would like to discuss Phoebe Conners first if that is all right Miss Garica. I have heard about the case from the news and from others in the town but I would like to know who Phoebe Conners was too you. That will give me a better understand of the case than any police file ever could.

In that moment it didn't matter what else Reno said. He was hired. Just from those three simple sentences I knew he cared more than anyone else we hired. Before everything he asked about Phoebe. He wanted to know the real Phoebe. Not the stories that went around. He wanted to know the Phoebe I knew.

"Phoebe loved harder and fiercer than anyone I have ever known. She put up this wall but once you were able to break that wall down she loved you forever. She never once blamed the world for her problems. She had every right to be upset and blame the world for everything bad that had ever happened but she didn't. She knew whose fault it was. She knew her father was the one who was blame for everything.

She loved the snow. The one time I saw it with her she ran outside as quickly as she could, not even bothering to put shoes on, and just spun around. She said she loved the feeling of fresh fallen snow on her face. She loved constellations. She learned everything she knew from her sister and would answer any question you asked. She was obsessed with the classics. Books such as Pride and Prejudice and The Portrait of Dorian Gray. She had read them all so many times she could recite them.

Phoebe was always convinced someone was going to leave her. It didn't matter how many times you told her that you loved her or that she was the greatest thing that had ever happened to you, somewhere in the back of her mind there was that voice saying all of those words were lies. In the end, she didn't think there was anyone out there who cared enough to miss her if she left."

I hear the scratching of pen on paper as I finish. Reno looks up at me and nods, setting his pad of paper down.

"I've looked over some of the documents Sydney Garcia and I have no doubt in my mind Jonathan Conners assaulted his children, but the issue that arises is in convincing other people. Jonathan Conners comes from a long line of influential Americans and he has the money of one. The truth is that he will be able to pay a much better lawyer than I, and that lawyer will be able to turn everything you say against you. We can win this case Miss. Garica, but it is going to take more commitment than you have ever had in your entire life. There are nights you will get no sleep. There will be days when you are faced with the worst humankind has to offer. If you do not wish to go any further we can end this discussion now and you can continue on with your life. So, Miss Garcia, do you wish to continue?"

"Let's send this motherfucker to hell."

Before

When I woke up I didn't feel Phoebe anywhere. I moved my hand all around to see if she was just sitting up but I didn't feel her. I sat up immediatly, scanning the roof. My eyes fell on her curled into the corner of the roof, her hands shaking at her side. She wasn't looking at me. Her eyes had this faraway look in her eyes. I had never seen her look this scared before.

"Phoebe," I whispered, fearing for the worst.

I watched as her eyes found mine. No look of recognition came across her face when she saw me. She just started at me, a blank look in her eyes. I stood up, walking slowly towards her. Phoebe didn't move as I moved closer.

I had slept through everything. I had been right here and yet I did nothing. I could have helped. I could have stopped him but no. I just slept through the entire thing. It happened so close to me, yet I didn't do anything. I hadn't even noticed.

"I'm sorry," she whispers finally.

"It's not your fault Phoebs," I whispered.

She flinched, at the nickname, turning away and starting. A cigarette dangled from her fingers, but it wasn't lit.

"I'm so sorry," I mumbled, taking slow steps toward her. She didn't try and stop me. She didn't ask me to stay away or even hold out her hand. She just stared at me as I walked closer. I sat beside her, not touching but lying my hand between the two of us.

"Why do you stay here, Sydney?" she asks suddenly, not looking at me. "You know what would happen, and yet you chose to stay. Why?"

"I don't leave those I care about when they need me most. You've had Alexander for years, but one person it's enough. And when you care about someone enough you don't leave. It doesn't matter how messy things get. You stay. I stay here because I don't see you as a project. I see you as Phoebe, and Phoebe is the only thing I need you to be."

Phoebe reached over and grabbed my hand, resting her head on my shoulder.

"I don't need you to be perfect. I don't need you never to make mistakes. I just need you to know that who you are is enough. I need you to know that I will always be here no matter what you do, Phoebe Conners. There is absolutely nothing that will ever drive me away from you. I need you to know that you deserve everything," I whispered.

I felt her squeeze my hand, but she didn't say anything. She just stared straight ahead but never let go of my hand.

We sat there together, not speaking but just soaking in each other presence. At this moment, I knew she needed me just as much as I needed her. We were there at that moment. At that time, we needed nothing else. I was her rock. I would stay there forever if she just said the word. I was here for her. I would always be her rock.

I DIDN'T WANT TO GO home that afternoon. I wanted to stay there with Phoebe. I wanted to be there for her, but she told me I needed to get home to my family before they started suspecting things. I understood what she meant, but at that moment, I could not care less whether my family found anything out. I just wanted to be there with her.

I stalled as long as possible, doing anything I could to make sure I could spend the most time with her, but she eventually made me leave. She told me if I stayed longer than things were only going to get worse. I didn't want to leave. I wanted to stay and protect her from the world, but if I did, it would only worsen. I couldn't have that for her, so I left.

I drove home slowly that day, wanting to stay as far away from home as possible. I knew my family would be there, and it was only a matter of time before they figured everything out, and once they did, I was done for. I worried every day, knowing that each day Phoebe and I got closer was another day that I was walking on thin ice around my parents. I told myself I would be willing to sacrifice it for Phoebe but I was scared. Scared that I was going to lose my entire family. Scared the most important people in my life would leave me.

When I walked inside I saw Christine sitting on the counter eating from a bag of goldfish while Tyler stared at his phone. Neither of them looked up when I came into the room.

"Hello, my siblings who are ignoring me," I said, reaching over and grabbing a handful of goldfish from the bag and jerking my hand away before she could smack my hand.

"Hey!" she yelled as she stared me down. She rolled her eyes, finishing the bag and throwing it away. I looked back at her as I ate each one as slowly as possible. I could feel Tylers eyes on me but I didn't look up.

"Where were you last night, Syd?" Tyler finally asks.

"I was spending the night at Lindsey's," I told him, staring at him as he watched me. I had never seen that look in his eyes before. It was the same look Lindsey had when I had lied to her about Pheobe. It was hurt, betrayal, and, most of all, anger.

"Christine, go upstairs for a minute, please," Tyler says. My heart was pounding in my chest as he protested with Christine about going upstairs. When she finally went back upstairs, he put his phone down and stared at me from the other side of the counter.

"Where were you last night, Sydney, don't bother bullshitting me," he growls.

"I told you," I answered. "I was over at Lindsey's. We were studying.

He stood up from the table, stalking closer to me. In that moment he looked more like dad then I had

"Dad heard Phoebe Conner's voice the other night. He wanted me to keep an eye on you. Last night you were not with Lindsey because Lindsey came over here asking for you. She told us everything about Sydney. I didn't think it would be at all possible for you to be this stupid," he yells.

Oh, I was fucking screwed. My father would hire a tail. It didn't matter where I went, there would be a police officer following me. If my parents knew then so would half of the town. My entire life would be ruined.

"I really wanted to believe you wouldn't be this fucking stupid Sydney and yet here we are? You know what she has done. You know who she is and yet you still decided to fuck around with her?"

Tyler had never believed what my father said about Sydney until a few years ago. He thought it would be hilarious to ask what it felt like to fail at suicide. She had pounded his ass. It didn't take much after that for him to believe everything that had been said about her.

"Phoebe isn't what you think she is," I yelled back.

"God Phoebe, you really think no one has ever thought that before. This is Phoebe Conners we are talking about. Pull your head out of your ass and realize she is an egotistical psycopath," he yells.

"Do you even hear yourself right now Tyler. You realize you sound just like dad right? You hate her because you asked an invasive question and she kicked your ass. You don't know half of what she has been through in life so I'm sorry if I gave her a chance when you and the rest of this family are dicks," I screamed.

Tyler yelled after me but I didn't pay attention as I stormed away. This entire family could go fuck themselves for all I cared. I did one thing they didn't like and all of a sudden my brother was up my ass about it? Fuck that shit.

My anger took to a new level when I stood in front of my room. There was no door on the hinges. Everything was torn off the shelves, drawers, and even my closet. Everything was on the floor. I scoured every inch of my room, trying to find anything missing, finally concluding they had taken my laptop. I stormed down the stairs, ready to fight everyone in my family.

"What the fuck happened in my room," I demanded, running downstairs only to find my entire family walking in the door.

"Sydney Garcia," my mother gasps under her breath, but my dad cuts her off.

"Sydney, we need to talk," he tells me. "Kids, go upstairs, your mother and I need to talk with Sydney," my dad tells my siblings.

At this point, they knew not to protest. They knew that tone in my father's voice. It was easier not to say anything than to argue with them. I heard them whisper as they trounced up the stairs. My parents said nothing until they heard every door close.

"Sydney, is there something you would like to tell us?" my mom asks softly.

I knew what they were doing. It was the same method they had used since I was a child. My mom would be the one to empathize and say she wasn't mad, while my dad would be the one to start questioning me like I was in an interrogation.

"Nothing you don't already know," I muttered under my breath, and I could hear my mother's sigh. My dad looked at me like I had a death wish.

"You sure, Sydney?" he asks. "Because I can think of many things off the top of my head."

I stand up, staring them both down. "You know what, I am so sorry that I am not a total douchebag and gave someone another chance. I'm sorry I kissed her and liked it. I'm sorry I kissed her many more times after that. I am sorry I snuck her into the house, so she didn't have to be at her fucked up house. I am so fucking sorry that I found the good in her when none of you would even give her the chance," I yelled.

"We have talked about her, Sydney. You knew to stay away from her, and yet you didn't. How do you think that made us feel?" my mom asked.

I knew she was trying to play nice. I knew she wanted to have a rational discussion but I couldn't do it. I couldn't sit there as they tried getting me to apologize when there was nothing I felt sorry about.

"What about the fact dad forced a strip search without consent? How about dad locking her up in a holding cell for 7 hours? I would think that you would know better, but you do not. And how about you, mom? The last time we saw Phoebe in public, you covered Cindy's eyes like she was going to catch some disease. There is nothing wrong with her. If anything, there is something wrong with you," I shouted.

"Sydney we are your family. Right now the person I see standing in front of me is not my daughter," my father yells.

Those words stung but I didn't let that stop me.

"Are you saying that to me? Dad, you forced a strip search on her with a male officer. Mom, you act as though she is the fucking devil incarnate. Both of you taught me to be open-minded and kind to everyone, but I guess everyone doesn't include Phoebe Conners."

"Go to your room Sydney," my mother whispers.

I opened my mouth. I was about to protest. I was about to say no.

"Now," she yelled, her hand pointing towards the staircase.

She had just yelled at me. My mother yelled at me. I didn't protest. I just trudged up the stairs. I went to slam my door, just for an extra measure, before remembering they had taken the door away from me. They didn't even trust me enough to give me a fucking door.

I leaned against the back wall of my closet, tears crowding in my eyes. Everything was silent in the house for a while. There was no noise. None of my younger siblings were running around playing. My mother was not loudly playing music while she made dinner.

I heard a knocking on the doorframe, and Cindy walked in, looking sheepish.

"Hey, Cindy," I whispered, holding my arms out before she climbed into them. She rested her head on my shoulder, letting me hold her on my lap.

"Why were mommy and daddy yelling at you?" she asks, looking up at me with tear-filled

I smiled softly, wiping away the tears from her eyes and pressing my forehead against hers.

"Mommy and daddy don't approve my girlfriend," I responded.

"Is your girlfriend Phoebe Conners?" she mumbles.

I nod, and she smiles at me with her wide, toothless grin.

"I always thought she was pretty," she whispers.

I lean against the wall, setting her down next to her before moving more toward her ear.

"You want to know a secret?" I whisper.

She nods her head excitedly and leans her ear close to mine.

"I always thought she was pretty too,"

She laughs, smacking her hand over her mouth to control her laughter.

"Why don't mommy and daddy like her?" she asked.

"Well, Phoebe's parents are not nice, making her look bad. Mommy and Daddy don't know that her parents are mean people, so they assume Phoebe is just as mean.."

"Phoebe is not mean," Cindy protests. "She smiled at me the last time she saw me in the store."

I laughed, picturing Phoebe waving at Cindy and my mom's horrified look when she saw it.

"Are you and daddy going to say sorry?" she asked me suddenly.

"I don't know," I answered. "I don't know, Cindy."

I wish I had an answer for her. I wish I could say anything that would give her some peace, but there was nothing. I knew there would not be any peace between my parents until I left Phoebe. When I did that, they would be willing to trust me again, but I had made a promise. I promised her I would not leave her. I promised I would be there through the good and the bad, and I intended to keep that promise.

I spent so much of my life scared of her, not wanting to be anywhere near her. If only I could go back and tell my former self that she would be one of the best parts of it now. The younger me wouldn't believe it. She would think I was crazy, but the older me knew I wasn't. I loved her.

I loved Phoebe Conners and would love her until my heart stopped beating and my lungs gave out. I would love her until my last dying breath, and even then, I would continue loving her. There was nothing she could do that would drive me away from her.

After

I heard from my father that Johnathan Conners spoke with his lawyer after our initial meeting. He had been advised not to speak to my team again. I still went everyday, trying to get him to talk everyday but he never did. After the third week I was taken off the list of people who could visit Jonathan Conners. There was no way I could try and get in to talk with him. The only thing I could do was hope Reno was able to come up with an agreement with Jonathans.

I stayed at home until school started again. I had wanted to stay but Reno advised me against it. He said I would be flying back to Indiana twice a month at no cost to the family and we would do the bulk of our work then. In the meantime, he wanted me to go back to school and get my education. I needed to be the poster child he told me. I needed to look perfect for the media. If I could picture myself as the perfect student, the perfect daughter. The perfect grieving girlfriend.

Reno was there to send me off. He wanted the publicity of a lawyer sending his client back to college in the middle of a high profile case. He had gotten the publicity he wanted. We were met with massive amounts of camera crews outside the airport. I hadn't wanted to take a plane but Reno said it would be better, so I put Atlas in a carrier and deathgripped the handle as we went through TSA.

The plane ride back to New York was a living hell. It seemed as though every single person had watched the news right before that plane ride and knew exactly who I was. I just held Atlas's carrier to my chest and prayed for everything to be over. Kerian was waiting for me as I landed.

"I'm glad you're back Sydney," she told me, grabbing me and pulling me in for a hug.

I didn't take me anytime before I wrapped my arms around her, burying my face in her shoulder.

"I'm glad I'm back to Kerian. More than you could ever know."

That first week back I got more stares than I had before I left. I tried to ignore the whispers as I walked into a room, but my professors pulling me aside at the end of every class didn't help. I knew not to be annoyed at them. I was lucky I they were willing to be as flexible as they were. It wasn't their fault I was flying twice a month to Indiana and back. It wasn't there fault I had meetings and calls with Reno and the legal team. They didn't have to accomodate but they didn't even bat an eye when they recieved an email detailing everything from Reno.

I tried reaching out to Alexander a few times after coming back to New York. Reno thought it would be a good idea if we got one more person to testify in our favor. I tried telling him that Alexander hadn't responded to me in 3 years but he made me promise him to try and reach out. I called the same number I had for three years and I got the same message saying this number was no longer in use.

When I told Reno Alexander hadn't responded he told me to try and contact Phoebe's mother. This time it was my father who told him that she wouldn't testify against her husband. Jonathan Conners had been given 5 years. If the case didn't go to trial until he got out or if he got parole and he knew she was testifying against him he would do whatever he could to silence her.

After that Reno finally understood I was the only one left who was willing to do something. I was the only one who knew the truth and was willing to do something about it. Reno decided to focus on getting my story down. He told me with whatever free time I had I was to write down whatever I could remember about those months with Phoebe. Rewrite everything she told me. Put it all down somewhere. Reno was convinced I would remember more things if I began to recall everything I wrote down.

So I set to writing down everything I knew. Everything I had been telling people for years. Everything that no one had believed. I felt like I was screaming into a void. No one could hear me, or no one cared to listen. I had told this story hundreds of times already. I had written everything down already and yet here I was doing it again. I tried telling myself it was part of the process. It was part of the process to rewrite everything. It was part of the process to hear the same things from Reno over and over again. It was part of the process to feel as though you were going insane. It was part of the process. It was all part of the process.

The year passed and there was nothing. Nothing new came from the case and Jonathan Conners spent another year alive in prison. Another year closer to being released. I continued going back and forth from Indiana and New York as I went into my fourth and final year at NYU until Reno told me the publicity started going south. People were starting to notice I was going back and forth from New York on a weekly basis. Many began wondering if I was as dedicated to my education as Reno had made it look. Some even went as far as to question whether or not I even went to NYU.

With the news sites running rampant, Reno grounded me. Now we were working all of our problems out through the phone or on video calls. There was no point in even going back to Indiana. Reno hadn't been able to negotiate anything with Jonathan's lawyers. Alexander wasn't back and Phoebe's mother refused to go anywhere in public now. Even if the publicity was bad, Reno would have grounded me anyway.

Weeks dragged on into months and there was nothing. The stares stopped over time, but the comments never did. The people coming up to me when I was walking to class or those in my apartment building seeing me in the elevator and telling me how sorry they were for my loss. Apologizing for what had happened and asking me how someone could do something so terrible. It never does become easier to watch people try and act as though they actually care. After losing someone, you learn very quickly that during a tragedy, it's almost as though people want to feel that pain somehow. They want to be able to insert themselves somewhere into the problem and act as though they were there the entire time.

They want people to be able to look at them and listen as they yell that they were there too. They felt that loss as well. There were times when I wanted to scream at people. I wanted to tell them they weren't there for her any second of their lives so they had no right to claim they were there for her now. Screaming wouldn't do anything though.

Screaming would never make someone understand I was the only one there. Screaming would never let them feel the pain of holding someone and loving them and then watching as the life drained out of them. Screaming wouldn't bring anyone to understand the pain you felt ripping through your chest as you watched the only person you have ever loved be lowered into the ground. The way it felt as though you were being stabbed as you watched dirt being carelessly thrown onto the mahogany casket. Those were moments you would only understand once you experienced them yourself.

JONATHAN CONNERS FILED for his first appeal in October of the next year. His appeal went to court on Phoebe's birthday. His lawyer had pushed it through last minte, giving me 2 hours to get to Indiana from New York after Reno called. I didn't even wait until I got a ticket to leave. I called the airline and conferenced Reno in. I had never moved through an airport so quickly in my life.

When I arrived to the courthouse, the judge was just walking in. I could feel everyone staring at me as I sat down next to Reno, but I was looking at Jonathan Conners. He still looked healthy. Not a hair out of place on his head. Here he was filing for an appeal when he had gotten the easy way out. He was charged with 5 years and yet here he was filing for parole.

I watched as he told the jury he had only confessed because he felt pressured by me and the police department. He had been coerced into a confession. He had never hurt his family and he never would. I watched as he told everyone he would never have touched his child like that. I sat there and watched until it was my turn to go up to the witness stand.

I had been told to hold back huring his initial sentencing. I was told that he wasn't being charged with anything relating to sexual assault so there was no reason for me to bring it up. I wasn't going to hold back this time. I was tired of watching him sit here and try to play the victim. I was tired of watching as he acted as though he had never done anything. I was tired of screaming the same story and no one ever listening.

"I held Phoebe as she cried after her father touched her. I had sleepless night after night, making sure she wasn't going to hurt herself. I was the one who patched her up when he hit her. I was the one who wiped off the blood when he broke her nose for the seventh time. I stood there next to her as she stared at the spot where Johnathan Conners scattered Autumn Conners's ashes around the woods. I was the one who sat there holding her hand when she took her last breath.

I was the one at her funeral. I was laying flowers on her grave every day. I cleaned all the graffiti from her headstone because people felt the need to write the things they said. I was the one who was there for her when no one else was, including her father. Jonathan Conners was the reason I was there. Jonathan Conners is the reason Phoebe Conners is not here right now. Because of everything he did to her, she is not here right now. He deserves to rot in hell for the rest of his life. He hurt everyone close to him, even his wife. If you can even call him a man, this man should never see the light of day."

I couldn't bring myself to look Jonathan Conners in the eye as I spoke. I had looked in those eyes enough times to know what I was going to see.

"Parole denied," the judge said.

Jonathan Conners tried for parole three times and everytime, I did the same thing. I would give the same testimony. I wouldn't look him in the eyes and after hearing the judge say parole denied I would walk back to my car and leave.

When I drove home from the parole trials I didn't play any music. I would stare straight ahead of me and try to forget why I was there. I had therapists tell me my level of dissociation was't safe. They were worried at some point I would dissociate to the point where I forgot that Phoebe was dead in the first place. They were worried it would lead to a psychotic break, but I dissociated because there were times when I couldn't handle the truth. Everytime I came back to Indiana I knew exactly what I was getting myself into and yet everytime I come back.

I never went to visit Phoebe. I never went anywhere else other than my parents house and the airport. I would talk with Reno over the phone each night and then go back home. After the last trial though, I couldn't bring myself to go home. My father would be there celebrating the little win. My mother would congratulate me and tell me this was just one big step. Reno would call me later and tell me we kept a guilty man in jail and I should be proud of that.

I couldn't be proud of it though, because he wasn't behind bars for what he deserved to be behind bars for. He hadn't been charged in sexually assaulting his children. He had been given a measly five years for spousal abuse. We may have prevented his parole but it didn't matter because 2 years later he was just going to get out anyway. In 2 years people would be able to put the fact he abused his children behind him and just accept him again. There would be no repercussions for his actions. He would be out and a free man.

It wasn't fair to Phoebe and Autumn. It wasn't fair to those children who closed their eyes at night and prayed to God he wouldn't come in and touch them. It wasn't fair to the girls who cried themselves to sleep because they were so scared of their own father. It wasn't fair to the girls who believed they had no way out of it unless they died.

I didn't go home that day. I just drove. I drove until I was out of the town. I drove until the thought of the trial and Jonathan Conners was far behind me. I drove until it was pitch black outside. I drove until I could see the faint outline of the cemetery lights surrounding the paths to the tombstones.

I sat in the car for a moment, debating on whether or not I was crazy. I hadn't seen Phoebe since I moved out. I hadn't gone back to visit her since this entire trial started and yet here I was 45 minutes after her father was just denied parole for the most miniscule charges that could have possibly been brought against him. I wasn't there to bring her good news. I wasn't here to tell her everything was going to be okay and I finally did what I promised her, but I needed to speak with her again. I needed her to understand that I was not about to stop until he never even had the thought of another parole hearing.

I walked slowly over to the back where Phoebe was buried. There was a tombstone right next to her's detailing Autumns name. I had been the one to buy Autumns headstone. The two of them deserved to be next to each other.

"Hey, Phoebe," I whispered, sitting down on what was left of the grass. After they had dug up the casket, it was going to take awhile for the grass to grow back. Looking down at that ground made me think of all the times I had come here when there wasn't even a headstone to detail her life. The times before I gave up.

"Atlas is doing well. I'm doing well. It would have been better if you were here with me. I'm sorry I didn't come for a while. I couldn't bring myself to be back here. I just couldn't seem to handle coming back. I couldn't bring myself to face everything here. I couldn't bring myself to face you.

God, why can I not get you out of my head? I know that I am here and I'm doing this for you, but I should be able to think about something else in this world. You are in my every waking thought. You are in my dreams. You are in everything I do, and I can't get you out of my mind. I know that is what I promised you I would do but what happens after this is all over? What happens when all of this is over? What happens when I am supposed to move on and live without you once again?

I can't lose you again. I can't live my life without you again. I can't be expected to just move on and find someone else. In a way, I don't want this to end because I will have nothing left when it does end. You will be nothing but a memory. A memory that, over time, fades until your name is no longer anything more than a whisper in the back of my mind. I don't want ever to have to wake up without you in my mind. I don't want to go another day where you are not there with me,"

I felt as though her tombstone in front of me was just a mocking reminder that I was talking to nothing. I had never allowed myself to look at the words before. Never let myself be hurt by them, but as I was sitting there, I let myself look.

"Phoebe Conners, loved daughter, taken too soon,"

Seven words. The tiniest little description to sum up an entire lifetime. Seven words to describe Phoebe Conners. She was more than just seven words fucking words, but how could you sum up an entire person on a piece of marble? How could just a few words describe how her laugh sounded when she threw her head back? How could just a few words describe how her hair shined when the sun hit it just right? How could just a few words properly describe how deep her eyes were and how easy it was to get lost in them?

You couldn't. That was the answer. Nothing Phoebe ever would be able to be summed up by just a few words. She was complex. Nothing about her was linear. The fear that she felt for her and the love she had learned to give her. People will always remember her differently, but Sydney chooses to hold on to all those memories. Sydney could choose to remember the things that made her fall in love with Phoebe in the first place.

"Phoebs, I hope you know I will never stop fighting for you. I will make sure everyone in this world knows the truth because you, Phoebe Conners, deserved the entire world,"

I felt my phone vibrate in my pocket but I ignored it. It was probably my mother asking when I was coming home or Reno wanting to discuss the case. It stopped for a moment, and then started again. When I pulled my phone out of my pocket. It wasn't my mother or Reno. All the caller ID said was "unknown number"

I was sure it was a spam call, and there was no reason to answer spam calls, and yet I felt this tug inside of me to answer. Against my better judgement I pressed answer.

"Hello?" I said.

"Is this Sydney Garcia?" I heard a girl on the other end ask.

"Yes this is Sydney."

"My name is Carson Keller. I saw on TV you are representing the Jonathan Conners case."

It was just another reporter asking for questions. Reno had told me they were going to be calling me but I never expected this many, and this soon after the case.

"Yes, well I am not making statements to the press at this time so thank you but no comment," I said as I took the phone away from my ear too hang up.

"No," I heard Carson yell from the other line. "Please, I haven't said anything about this in 15 years and I need to speak with someone about it. My name is Carson Keller and I was best friends wth Autumn Conners. 15 years ago Jonathan Conners raped me and made me swear not to tell anyone or he would kill Autumn and I."

Before

My door was still off the hinges when I woke up the next morning. The floor was still filled with the items that had been put away only 12 hours before. It took me half an hour to find clothes that didn't look like I had slept in them and even then, I couldn't get the few wrinkles out of the fabric. When I made it downstairs, my father was leaning against the countertop. Neither of us said anything.

I continued my morning as if he wasn't there. I kept telling myself to ignore the feeling of his eyes on my back as I got ready. I scolded myself for thinking about our argument yesterday. I yelled at myself for wondering what he thought of me now. I couldn't give two fucks about what he thought of me. I didn't care what the rest of the family thought about me.

There was nothing this family could do that would tear me apart from Phoebe Conners. They would scratch and claw until there was nothing left of the two of us, but I wasn't going to let them do that. In a matter of time, they would come around, I told myself. Once they saw what I saw in her. Once they saw why I cared about her as much as I did, they would understand. They would finally stop trying to cut her out of my life when they knew the truth.

I heard a car horn honk, and I saw Phoebe leaning halfway across the dashboard to honk the horn. Alexander was smacking her hand and trying to get her away from the horn, but she kept pressing it. I saw my father pursing his lips out of the corner of my eye but I ran outside before he could say anything.

I raced towards her, an immense feeling of comfort falling over me as I saw her flame red hair across the driveway. Before I could open the car door, she grabbed my arms and pulled me into a kiss, wrapping her fingers around my wrist. I let out a surprised sigh before kissing her back, my hand resting on the passenger side door. I could almost see my father watching as I kissed her in the middle of the road, but I didn't care. When we finally broke apart, she smiled at me, not saying a word as I climbed into the back seat.

I didn't let myself look backward at my house as we drove away. My whole family would be up because of how many times that horn was blasted but I couldn't care less. I had Phoebe. Phoebe was here and that was all that mattered.

"If you guys will stick your tongues down each other's throats, please do it when I am not around. I just ate breakfast, and I don't feel like losing everything I just ate on the recently upholstered seats," he groans.

Phoebe laughs, lightly shoving him, which causes the car to jerk on the road a bit.

"Oh poor Alexander. I will make sure the next time I kiss my girlfriend, I am locked away in a nicely ventilated closet, away from the peering eyes of the heteronormative society," she exaggerated as she leaned her head out of the car.

"Fuck off, Pheobe," he grumbles under his breath, but that just causes both of us to laugh even more. I watched as she took a deep breath in and breathed out, letting her hair fly all around her in the wind. Her eyes are closed as she leans farther out of the car, letting her arms dangle out. She had stretched the seat belt as far as it would let her.

This was the Phoebe I loved seeing. She looked carefree as if there was nothing that could hurt her. As if she could have been there for her entire life. A car careens past us and honks its horn at Phoebe. She sits up, opening her eyes before standing up and raising her middle finger.

"Fuck off, douchewagon," she screams after them before sitting back down. "God, I fucking hate people sometimes," she mutters.

She turns to look in the backseat, a smile covers her face when we meet eyes.

"Hello Sydney Garcia. How are you on this fine December morning?" she asks.

Thoughts of my parents and the argument filled my head but I pushed them back. I didn't want to think about that. I wanted to be here with Phoebe. Here in this moment with no one but Phoebe Conners.

"Splendid," I answered her.

I will never forget the smile on her face as I answered. That smile was full of every unspoken word between us. That smile made me feel like I was going to explode. That smile was the reason for my existence.

We pull into the school parking lot, and Alexander gets out, tossing the keys to Phoebe.

"Just lock up when you are done," he says before shouldering his bag and walking towards the school.

"Is Alexander Chadwick entrusting me with his car?" Phoebe calls after him.

Alexander doesn't look back, but throws up his middle finger as he continues walking towards the doors. Phoebe laughs, clutching her midsection. I couldn't help but laugh with her. All of this felt right. For the first time in my life I didn't feel like I was missing something. As I was laughing, I felt Phoebe's lips catch mine. I immediately melted. This is where I wanted to be. Right here in this moment. I wrapped my arms around her waist, pulling her closer to me.

Fuck everyone. Fuck everyone who stood there, marveling at us as if we were on display at a museum. Fuck my parents, who couldn't handle the fact that I could see past the prejudice they had built into their minds. Fuck Phoebe's father, who has done unspeakable things to her. Fuck the entire world.

When I pulled away, from the corner of my eyes, I could see Lindsey staring at you from the corner of my eyes. My heart clenched in my throat at the thought. We hadn't talked since the fight. I knew she had come over to the house the other day and wouldn't know that she had started a full-on screaming match between my family, but she did know what she was doing when she told my family about Phoebe. She knew what she was doing.

Phoebe saw Lindsey staring over at us from the car. She turned towards me, noticing the way I was staring right back. She wraps her arm around my shoulder, starting to walk me towards school.

"Ignore her," she whispers. "She doesn't matter anymore."

Phoebe insisted on dropping me off during the first period. Before we entered the classroom, she wrapped me in her arms and pressed her face into my hair.

"It's going to be okay," she whispers. "Just ignore the stares. They don't matter."

I nodded, pulling away and pecking her lips.

"Thank you," I whispered.

I walked in and sat down, trying to ignore everyone staring at me. Lindsey came in a few minutes later but didn't even look at me as she sat down. We had asked for seats next to each other at the beginning of the year. I think both of us were regretting that now.

I tried to ignore the stares and whispers during class. I would notice Lindsey looking at me from the corner of her eyes, but when I turned to look at her, she would immediately turn away, her face turning bright red. I didn't hear a word the teacher said that entire class. It was like I wasn't even there.

When the bell rang, I watched as Lindsey picked up her bag and rushed out of the classroom. I sat there, waiting for everyone to file out of the classroom. I waited until the last moment before walking out of that classroom. The bell rang, and I still was not in my next class. I didn't want to go. Lindsey would be there too. I knew that if I kept on in this hallway, someone would find me, getting me into even more trouble than I was in the first place.

I walked into the nearest bathroom, tears pounding at the back of my eyes. I yelled at myself for thinking about my family. They didn't matter. Lindsey didn't matter. Who cared what others thought of me? All I needed was Phoebe. If I had Phoebe then everything would be okay.

The thoughts of my family wouldn't leave my mind as I dropped my bag on the stall floor and locked the door behind me before leaning against the door and closing my eyes. In the span of 3 months, everything in my life had changed. I had lost my parents. I had lost my best friend. I had lost my family. And I had gained someone that I never thought would be in my life in the first place.

"Sydney," I hear someone call from outside the door. A soft knock follows the voice, but I don't open the door.

"Sydney," I hear the voice call again. "I can see your shoes from underneath the door. Come out and talk to me, Syd."

I open the stall door to see Phoebe standing with her hand raised as if to knock again. I can see the concern filling her eyes as she looks at me.

"Syd," she whispered before I collapsed into her arms. She buried my head in her shoulder as I cried.

"I'm so sorry," she whispered while stroking my hair.

"You shouldn't be the one apologizing Syd," she whispers. "It's my fault you are in this situation in the first place."

"It's not your fault," I reassured. "It's my family's fault. It's Lindsey's fault. It's this entire godforsaken world's fault."

My mind kept telling me to pull myself together. I was acting weak and the world would eat weak alive., but Phoebe kept holding me to her. She didn't pull away. She didn't call me weak. She just held me. I picked up my head, and she pressed her forehead to mine.

"You are worth everything Sydney Garcia. No matter what anyone says," she whispers. "I don't know exactly what happened and I don't need to know. I just think you don't get told that enough."

A laugh breaks through the tears and I pull her face towards mine, capturing her lips in a kiss. I felt her sink into me as I placed my hand on her cheek.

"Syd?" I asked after pulling away.

Her face turns bright red as she looks away from me.

"Just thought it fit," she answered.

"Okay, Phoebs."

She pulls away from me, a look of mock horror on her face.

"Absolutely not."

"I think it fits quite well."

Phoebe pulled me towards her with a smile and pressed her lips to mine. I wrapped my arms around her neck as she pulled me closer to her.

"Fact of the day, you are worth so much more than you know," Phoebe whispers in between kisses.

I pressed my face into her shoulder, trying to hide the smile covering my face. I feel Phoebe reach down and when I look up I see her holding my backpack.

"Now you, Sydney Garcia, are going back to class because I am certain that if you skip any more of class, your father will come and have my head," she says, handing me my stuff and wrapping her arm around my shoulder.

"Are you sure he won't have your head either way?" I asked.

She looks over at me, a smile on her face. "No," she answered.

Phoebe walked me towards class, squeezing my hand as she walked out of the classroom towards where I presumed her next class was. All the eyes are on me as I sit down at my desk and try to pay attention to the front of the classroom. Trying everything not to think about Lindsey, Phoebe, my father, or my mother. Trying not to think about anything other than what the teacher was talking about.

I had lost the people in my life that used to matter. The person in my life that I used to love more than anything, but now that person was Phoebe. Phoebe was the most important person in my life. Phoebe Conners was everything. She was all I needed now. I could survive in this world if all I had were Phoebe.

After

"Carson, will you tell Reno exactly what you told me?" I asked.

I had never seen a person look so scared. Carson Keller was sitting in front of us at the kitchen table in the house. Reno was in front of her, his hands resting on the notepad in front of him.

"It's okay Carson. We are here to listen."

She gulped, looking as though she was swallowing tears.

"I was 13 years old and it was the first time I slept over at Autumn's house. She had tried putting off a sleepover for as long as possible but I had ambushed her. She couldn't say no if I just showed up to her house. Everything was going well until we had finished our movie and were trying to fall asleep. We weren't being quiet, both of us laughing hysterically when I heard the door open to her room. A look of fear came over her eyes and when I turned around I saw her father standing there.

I'll never forget the look in his eyes as he looked down at the two of us. Even after all of these years, I still don't know how to describe it. I heard Autumn begging him to leave them alone and she promised him she would do whatever he wanted if he just left but before she could get him out he jumped on me. I remember starting to scream and Autumn pleading with him to stop while trying to pull him off of me but he slapped her and said if she kept screaming he was going to kill us both.

I tried fighting him off but I couldn't. He reached down and pulled up my nightgown, and that's where everything goes dark. I remember after he finished with me, he tossed me aside and did the same thing to Autumn except she didn't try to fight him off. She just let him do that to her like she was used to it. All I remember her saying was 'Don't wake Phoebe. She doesn't need to see this.' I remember tasting my tears as I begged him to let her go, but he couldn't hear me. I don't even know if I was saying anything. When he was done with Autumn, he grabbed both of us and said that if we were to tell anyone he would kill the both of us.

I didn't want anything to happen to Autumn, let alone myself, so I kept quiet. I never even told my parents. When I came home from the sleepover I told them I was never going back. I burst into tears as they tried to understand what had happened, but I wouldn't say anything. I didn't want anything to happen to Autumn.

We moved away a few years later and I never contacted her again. I didn't even know she had died until I saw you go on tv and say her and her sister had killed themselves. That was when I knew I had to call you. I knew I needed to say something because Autumn couldn't be hurt anymore and these feelings of guilt over not saying anything will go away."

Her leg was bouncing up and down beneath the table and her hands were shaking. I reached over, grabbing her hand as her other one reached up to wipe the tears off of her cheeks.

"Thank you Carson. We can't even begin to tell you how instrumental this was for the case," I whispered.

"This feeling will go away right? The guilt over not saying anything because I haven't slept in months because her dying had to be my fault. If I had said something maybe Autumn and Phoebe would have been taken away from that house. If I had said something maybe the both of them would still be alive," Carson trembled.

"You didn't do anything wrong Carson. If you had said something he would more than likely have killed Autumn and you. If you had said something, you wouldn't be here now to say it," I answered.

"But this feeling goes away right? This feeling of guilt will go away over time and I won't feel it anymore?"

"I can't promise you that. The guilt lessens overtime but it will never completely go away. I can still feel it and it's been 4 years but I can promise you that speaking up was the best thing for you to do. Speaking up was the right thing to do, but you stayed safe, which is the most important thing," I replied.

I heard the scratching of Reno's pen against the paper and when I looked over at him, he gave me a reassuring nod.

"Do you know if this happened to anyone else? Did you hear of this happening to any other of Autumn's friends?" I asked her.

Carson shook her head. "No. I've never asked if this happened to anyone else."

"That's okay. We didn't expect you to. We just needed to ask in case anything if you knew anything," I responded.

Reno looks up from his paper and folds his hands together on the table.

"Miss Keller, your information here will give us a case, but in order to get him tried for the crime he committed against you, you have to be willing to file a report to the police. Is that something you would be willing to do?' Reno asks her.

Carson nods her head. "I will do whatever it takes. I just want him gone."

A smile appeared on my face and I reached over and grabbed her other hand in mine.

"Carson I made this same promise to Phoebe a long time ago but I promise you this now. I will stop at nothing to get you the justice that you deserve. What happened to you as a child wasn't fair. None of this now is fair, but we have the power now to set things straight. As you agree not to give up, I won't give up."

Carson lets out a tearful laugh and takes her hand away from mine to wipe her tears.

"I promise. I promise to fight just as hard as you have."

"Then it's settled," Reno says. "Tomorrow morning we will go down to the police station and file another report against Jonathan Conners. Tomorrow, the next part of our mission starts."

RENO DROVE THE THREE of us to the police station the next morning. Carson's leg was bouncing and her hands were shaking in her lap. I could hear her sharp inhales of breath and her counting under her breath.

"My therapist told me to count whenever I get nervous. She said it would ground me and remind me everything was okay," Carson mutters under her breath.

"I get it," I replied. "I was told the same thing after Phoebe died."

Carson offers a small smile but looks right back down at her hands.

"How did Phoebe die?" she blurts out. "I mean I know she commited suicide but how? Was it the same way Autumn did? Did she feel any pain? Was she at peace when she died?"

"Phoebe died in the same way Autumn did, yes. I found her in her kitchen after she slit her wrists. The doctor told me she wouldn't feel anything other than the initial sting of the cut. I've thought about all of this before. I've wondered if she felt anything or if it was just like falling asleep. It didn't matter what the doctors said, those thoughts kept me up at night. There are still sometimes when they do," I answered.

The only memories I have of Phoebe are when she was a young child. She was four years younger than Autumn so you would always expect her to be that sibling who always tries to tag along with the older one. You always expected the older one to get upset about it, but Autumn never did. If Phoebe wanted to come along, Phoebe came along. The two of them were so close. It never even dawned on me what would happen to Phoebe after Autumn died," Carson lamented.

"Phoebe wasn't the same as she was before Autumn died. Everyone thought she was a completely different person but she really wasn't. You just had to dig deep inside and that child that desperately wanted to be set free," I answered.

Carson looks over at me and smiles. "You really loved her didn't you?"

"Yeah, I did," I replied. "To this day I love her. I don't think there is anything that could change that."

We rode the rest of the way in silence. When Reno pulled into the police station, I heard Carson begin to count under her breath. I reached over and grabbed her hand, giving it a reassuring squeeze.

"It will be okay. I'll be right there with you."

She nods her head, taking a deep breath and then letting it out. "Okay. Let's do this."

I walked into the station in front of her, letting Reno walk behind her. I could hear her counting underneath her breath as her fingers tapped against the side of her leg. My father met us at the door and directed us to his office. Reno closed the door behind him as my father closed all of the shades. When he was finished he sat down across the table from Carson, Reno and I.

"Thank you for coming Ms. Keller. It is my understanding you need to file a report against Jonathan Conners?" my father asks.

Carson nods her head. "Yes," she turns to look at me. I nod my head, encouraging her to continue. She turns back towards my father, her hands twisting together in her lap.

"15 years ago Jonathan Conners raped me at a sleepover," she whispers.

I hear my father typing as he nods his head. "Could you please state in detail how the events of that night transpired?"

Carson looked at me, and I squeezed her hand.

"It's okay," I whispered. "Just tell him the same thing that you told us."

Carson recounted the events of that night, in the same perfect detail she had told us the day before. My father's fingers moved against the keys on his keyboard as he wrote down everything Carson told him. When Carson was finished the room was silent except for the sound of the keyboard as my father typed. When he finished, he looked up from underneath his glasses at us.

My father looks towards me, a grim smile on his face. "This might be a stretch Miss, Keller, but do you still have the clothes you wore when he raped you? Even if it has been washed, there is still a good chance the DNA is still there. If we can prove the DNA is still there, there would be a stronger case."

Carson nods her head. "I do. I never washed them. They are in the back of my closet."

My heart skips a beat in my chest. DNA evidence. There could be DNA evidence that would prove what he did. We could find DNA evidence on Phoebe's clothes. We could do this. We could win this.

"If you would not mind bringing them into the department and we will give them over to our analysis unit," my father says. "I will make sure this case is expedited and we will find any evidence that remains on the clothing. That is the same for you as well Ms. Garcia. Try and remember what Phoebe Conners was wearing on a night she was raped. There might be a chance there could still be DNA on the clothing."

A smile covers my face as I nod.

"Thank you Miss. Keller. We will file this in the system and inform you of any updates."

Carson begins to stand but Reno stays seated. When Carson notices him not moving, she moves to sit back down.

"Actually Sheriff Garcia, I would like to represent Miss. Keller in her case. We would like to add her charge to the current charges against Joanthan Conners and bring them to court together."

My father looks up at me, a faint smile playing at his features.

"When we have updates about all of the charges, I will let you all know. In the meantime, continue working building your case. I would like to keep Jonathan Conners behind bars for as long as possible," my father says.

Reno stands up, reaching his hand out for my father to shake. When he does, we begin our procession out of the station, filing in the same order that we had coming in. me in the font, and Reno in the back with Carson in between the both of us.

When we got outside and out of view of the station, Carson raced towards me and wrapped her arms around my shoulders.

"Thank you. Thank you Sydney Garcia. Thank you."

I wrapped my arms around her, letting her rest her head on my shoulder.

"No, thank you Carson Keller. You just brought this case back to life."

Carson, Reno and I spent the next week going over the case before I was to fly back to New York. Reno made me promise that I would answer texts and calls so we could keep in contact. He was going to try to obtain permission to go through Phoebe's house to find any of the clothing but there hadn't been any progress so far. Mrs. Conners was firm in her belief that her husband had never done anything. She didn't want there to be a chance she would be proven wrong.

While Reno was fighting with Mrs. Conners, Carson had dropped her clothes off and agreed to save my number in her phone. I told her to reach out to me if there was anything that she needed at all. Even if it seemed like the most miniscule thing, I made her promise me that she would reach out. I couldn't lose contact with her. Not after everything we had done. Not after everything we had fought for.

After a week of classes, Reno scheduled more television interviews and more news sources to go on so I was never without the case. He made me agree to post online and answer any reporters that emailed me. I would speak to anyone on campus about the case. If there was a second of my life that I wasn't spending thinking about Phoebe before going back to Indiana, there wasn't anymore.

I answered calls from Reno every night. Anytime Carson would text me I would answer. I put my best front forward and presented myself in the best way possible. I was a dedicated student, a grieving girlfriend and a confident plaintiff in a court case.

The parts I hated the most were the tv interviews. I would always answer the same questions over and over again, but everytime I would be asked the same questions I was asked the previous week. Reno told me I needed to keep doing them. Bring more awareness to the case. Let people know who I was and why I was fighting for Phoebe. I did what he told me. I answered every question with grace and poise but inside I was dying every time.

After 2 months of the same interviews, with the same channels, Reno finally got me on a high profile news network right in New York City. It wasn't far away from campus and I would only be going on once on Saturday morning. The morning of the interview I woke up and walked over to the station before 2 am. I sat in the green room as they did outfit and wardrobe, my phone went off. A notification from the calendar. It was Phoebe's birthday.

She would have been 23 this year. I knew Reno did this for a reason. He scheduled the day for Phoebe's birthday to garner more sympathy but my heart fell in my chest when I saw the notification. I reminded myself to focus. I had a story to tell. I needed to get more people on our side for the case. I needed to be able to do this without a thought of Phoebe's birthday.

My knee bounced up and down as I waited in the green room for my signal to go on. I had done this before. I had done this well before. Push it into the dark recesses of your mind and forget everything except for the case. Leave the emotions behind. Leave the memories other than the ones you spoke about. Don't let anything distract you. Follow the script you have said a thousand times before. And most of all, do not let anyone know the pain you feel because they will eat you alive if they know the pain.

I heard a knock sound from the door and I stood up, taking a deep breath and walking towards the door to open it. It was my time to go on. There was always a person who knocked on the door to let you go in. I opened the door, expecting an assistant to come and get me, only to find Alexander standing with his hand raising up to the door as if to knock again.

"Sydney," he whispered, his voice coming out choked and quiet.

I didn't say anything. There wasn't anything I could say. He was there. Alexander was there three years later. Alexander who had left three fucking years ago and here he was at a news station before I was set to go on and talk about the case he abandoned.

"Sydney I just want to talk about everything. Please," Alexander pleads.

I tried to answer but nothing came out. I wanted to scream at him. I wanted to know why he had been gone for three years. I wanted to demand why he had just fucking left and hadn't come back. I wanted to scream at him to leave and let me go on with my life the way I had been for the last three fucking years but nothing would come out.

"Sydney, please say something," Alexander begged.

"I can't talk about this now," I finally answered. I didn't even recognize my own voice. I didn't even wait for an assistant to come and tell me it was time for me to go on stage, I just pushed past Alexander, trying desperately to stop the shaking of my hands. I could hear his footsteps behind me as he pleaded for me to listen to him but I didn't turn around.

Don't get distracted. Don't let them see your fear. Don't let them know how hard this is for you. Focus. Stay fucking focused.

I heard the anchors cut to commercial and an assistant gave me a signal off stage to walk on. I took a deep breath before walking onto the stage, settling into the seat and hiding my hands in my lap. They couldn't see how badly I was shaking. I couldn't let anyone know how shaken I was.

When the commercial ended I plastered a smile on my face and turned to look at the camera, waving as I had been trained. I listened as the anchors announced my name and welcomed me to the show. It all sounded so far away.

I answered their questions. I said things respectfully like I had been trained. I did everything perfectly. There were no hiccups. I didn't falter. I did everything just like I had been taught. Reno would call me later with nothing but good things to say.

"For the first time in 3 years, Alexander Chadwick has agreed to an interview, and he is there today. We will welcome Alexander Chadwick back after the break,"

My heart pounded in my chest as I heard the anchor say those words. No. They couldn't bring him on. They couldn't let him speak. He didn't know anything. He hadn't been here for three years. He left. He had left and now he shows up for the first time in three years and he was getting up on national television.

I refused to turn my head as Alexander walked onto the set and sat in the chair next to me.

"Sydney," he starts, quietly enough that no one else could hear him.

"Don't, Alexander," I interrupted. "Just don't."

I didn't say anything as the commercial break ended and the anchor introduced Alexander. Alexander moved in his chair closer to me but I leaned farther away from him.

"You were Phoebe Conners's best friend for years. How has it been without her?" the anchor asks.

Alexander had no fucking right to answer that question. He had left her. Left this case. Left the fight. He had no right to talk about what it has been like without her.

"I can't say it's been easy," he answers. "When someone is there for the formative years of your life, and then you have to try and learn to go about your daily life without them, it's something that takes adjusting."

Alexander didn't have to live with the constant reminders of her. He didn't have to travel back and forth between Indiana and New York. He didn't have to fight just to be able to talk with Jonathan Conners. He didn't have to walk Carson into the police station as she filed a report against Conners because he sexually assaulted her when she was 13. He wasn't here for any of that.

"Everyone knows the story of Phoebe Conners at this point, but what is the truth behind what happened between the two of you?" the anchor asks him.

Alexander looks over at me and for the first time, I meet his eyes. I didn't know what she was insinuating but this was the first time she had ever asked something like this.

"They were nothing more than friends," I answered for him.

"Sydney, I know you believe that, but I think you should let Alexander answer that question for himself," the anchor says.

Alexander doesn't look over at her as he answers her question. "We were nothing more than friends," he whispers.

The anchor looks between Alexander the two of us, a smile on her face. I was shaking even more. I wanted to leave. I didn't want to answer these questions anymore. I didn't want to sit here with Alexander anymore. I just wanted to fucking leave.

"Sydney, did you ever truly believe there was nothing going on? Did you really believe someone that was close to another person wouldn't be sleeping with them? I mean, it's easy enough to lie about being gay and no one would expect anything," the anchor said.

Fuck this. Fuck having to justify Phoebe's queerness. Fuck having to explain that a male and female could be friends without being together. I was tired. Tired of having to tell everyone that Phoebe was queer. Tired of having everyone doubt her. It didn't matter what Phoebe had done. Phoebe could have spent all of her time with a girl. She could kiss a girl. She could have married a girl and people would still try and question whether or not she was queer.

"I don't know what the fuck you think you are getting at here, but whatever point you are trying to make is not going to work," I seethed. "Phoebe Conners did not lie about her sexuality and knew what she was from when she was a young child. Phoebe and Alexander were best friends, and that was all. Alexander was there for her when no one else was. If you think that my pain and what I had to go to was bad, then think about what Alexander had to see. Alexander saved her life more times than anyone could even imagine. He was able to save her, but I wasn't, so if you think you are proving anything by what you are saying. I would suggest you stop before you get ahead but seeing as though you have already pushed this far enough I have to say this interview is over."

Silence followed as I finished. I could almost hear my friends back at NYU screaming as they watched. They had asked before how I dealt with all of the questions and told me at some point I needed to put a stop to all of them.

"Are we done here?" I demanded

When the anchor said yes, I ripped the mic off and stormed off stage. I didn't wait to see who was following me. I didn't take the time to look behind me to see who was following me. I just walked down that hallway, tears threatening to spill from my eyes. I had been doing this for three years. I had been doing everything by myself for three years and now Alexander thinks he can show up and ruin everything I had worked for. I was done. I was done with these fucking questions. I was done with having to justify everything I had been doing. I was just so done.

I slammed the door behind me, sinking down into the chair in front of the table. I didn't even bother to pay attention to what order I was putting things in. I just shoved them in my bag so I could leave. I heard a knock at the door. I didn't move to open it. I knew it was Alexander.

"Step the fuck away from that door Alexander," I yelled, continuing to shove my things in my bag.

"Sydney, please will you just hear me out?" he yells.

"You know Alexander," I yelled, whipping the door open. "I cried over you leaving for almost two weeks. You were gone and I had no one left that believed me. And after you left, I left too because even I couldn't handle the constant reminders, but you know what I did? I came back. I walked the fuck back here, and I started to get the job done. You can't even say that, Alexander, because you were willing to give up. You changed every form of contact. You moved away. I've tried reaching out so many times and you know what happened? Nothing. Nothing fucking happened because you couldn't be bothered enough to stay."

"I'm so sorry," Alexander whispers.

"You don't get to be sorry, Alexander. You abandoned me three years ago. You abandoned Phoebe 3 years ago. You gave up, Alexander. You gave up on me. You gave up on yourself and Phoebe.

"Sydney, please," Alexander begged. "Please just hear me out."

"Alexander, I do not want to hear it," I screamed. "You probably don't even know that one of Autumn's old friends contacted me. She was assaulted by Phoebe's father 15 years ago. She has agreed to join the case. She's back in Indiana with Reno, who is our lawyer who has taken on the case."

"I... I didn't know."

"No, of course you didn't because you left. You don't know what it has been like these past three years. I have done everything humanly possible for Phoebe, when you did absolutely nothing. When things got hard, you left. I have been here, fighting for Phoebe and Autumn, for three years. I worked for so long to be able to be here to share everything, and now here you are, showing up and acting like you know exactly what it has been like. I wake up everyday knowing that Jonathan Conners is still alive. You haven't been here for three goddamn years, and now you show up as though nothing is the matter. There is a lot I am upset with you about but you showing up here again after three years is the icing on top of this shit cake. You stopped fighting. You left Phoebe, you left Autumn, and you left me."

The tears finally caught up to me now. The years of frustration and anger came pouring out.

"Sydney, I am so sorry," Alexander whispers. " I couldn't live because Phoebe was dead and gone. I couldn't handle the fact that we were fighting for Phoebe's salvation because she was now gone, and she couldn't do it herself. My entire life was always Phoebe Conners, but now she is gone. Now I am living a life without Pheobe Conners. I left, and I know I messed up, but please. I can't lose the one thing I still have connected with her. Please. I will never be able to forgive myself for what happened but I can't lose you. I can't lose Phoebe."

"Alexander, just get out. Please, just get out," I whispered, my voice coming out hushed.

"Please. Please let me stay here and fight. Let me help fight this," Alexander begs.

"How can I be sure you won't leave again Alexander? You said you wouldn't leave once and we both know what happened then. What happens when things get hard again? Are you going to leave again? Are you actually going to stay and fight because I can promise you that things are a lot harder now than they were three years ago. So what happens when you can't handle it this time? Are you going to leave again?" I demanded.

"I won't leave this time. I've regretted my decision for these three years and I can promise you I won't leave again," he whispers, tears falling down his cheeks.

Something inside of me wanted to tell him no. I wanted to send him away and not let him get anywhere near this case ever again. I wanted to scream at him more and demand to know what gave him the right to show up here. I wanted him to know how much it hurt when he left. I wanted him to know the pain I had felt for three years.

"Find someplace to stay while you are here. I'm letting you stay and help. Prove to me that you are in this for real this time. Show me you are going to stay, and maybe I can think of forgiving you," I answered.

"Thank you, Sydney. Thank you," he whispers.

Before

Phoebe was never short of interesting ways she could find her way into my room at night. There wasn't a night she didn't spend with me, the both of us falling asleep together and then I would sneak her out the next morning. She would leave my room the same way every morning. I would go and distract my parents while Phoebe scaled the side of the wall and tried not to crush the bushes. On the days when Alexander wasn't picking us up I would drive the two of us to school, Phoebe hiding in my backseat until we got out of sight of the house.

In the afternoons I would go to work with my father as if nothing was different. None of the officers ever brought up Phoebe and Phoebe was never brought in. I felt like rubbing it in my father's face. Look at what had happened in just a few short months. Look at the difference in Phoebe, but I knew that wouldn't make any difference. This was my father we were talking about. He didn't see anything he didn't want to.

And still Phoebe would sneak into my room every night and I would sneak her out. At nights we would lay together, her head resting on my chest and me running my hands through her hair. We never talked about the day. I was always able to tell when she had a bad day. I could see it in her eyes. I could when the usual light in her eyes dimmed.

Everything became routine. I would wake up and sneak Phoebe out. Drive Phoebe too school. Eat lunch with Phoebe. Say goodbye to Phoebe before going to work. Eat dinner as a family. Sneak Phoebe into my room. Fall asleep with Phoebe.

It was routine. Everything was normal. If my family was going to treat everything like it was normal, then so was I.

FOR A LITTLE WHILE I would try to corner Lindsey after class but in the end it wasn't worth it. It didn't matter what I told, she would hate Phoebe just the same. There was nothing I could do that would make her understand, so I gave up trying. There was no reason for me to put in an effort when she would rather pretend I didn't exist.

My favorite moments were the drives with Alexander and Phoebe. Whether it was just to school or if we just drove around town to burn gas and spend less time at home, they were the moments when everything felt right in the world. Alexander took turns picking the music to listen to as Phoebe grumbled that she never got the chance to choose. Everytime we were in Alexander's car Phoebe would take the chance to remind me of how old and dysfunctional my car was when Alexander's was brand new and could actually run. I tried not to pay any mind to her comments. It didn't matter how many times I explained to her that my car was a Garcia family tradition passed down from Garcia to Garcia. This car wasn't going anywhere anytime soon. Phoebe would just roll her eyes and tell me I needed a new car if I didn't want to die because ofcatastrophic engine failure.

It was the three of us against the world. No matter what happened with my family or with Lindsey, I knew I had the two of them to be there. Never before in my life did I ever think the only people who were by my side would be Phoebe Conners and Alexander Chadwick but here we were

Life with Phoebe Conners became my new normal. For what felt like the first time in my life, I didn't feel like I was missing something. I was Phoebe's and Phoebe was mine. It didn't matter what anyone else in the world thought about us because as long as we had each other, everything was going to be okay. There was nothing that would ever tear us apart.

PHOEBE DIDN'T SHOW up at my house for five days. She didn't answer any texts or calls. I waited every morning to see if she needed a ride. I kept my ringer on, hoping everytime I got a text or a call it was Phoebe. It was like she had dropped off the face of the earth. Alexander told me this was just something that happened sometimes. Phoebe woudl disappear for a short amount of time but she would always come back. There hadn't been a time when she hadn't come back yet.

I couldn't explain any of this to my parents. I couldn't explain why everytime my phone went off I raced to grab it as if my life depended on it. I couldn't explain to them why I was sleeping worse a nights and waited by the door every morning. Even if I tried they wouldn't understand. My father would tell me this was just what Phoebe Conners did. He would use this as a reason for me to stay away from her.

Each day I got more and more worried. Every day I called more times. Every second she was gone another part of my brain was convinced she was never coming back. I had made up my mind that if I hadn't heard from her by the end of the fifth day I was going to her house. If I didn't see her or if she didn't answer any calls or texts then I was just going to make sure she was alright. I pulled into the driveway that afternoon convinced that I was going to be racing over too Phoebe's house when I saw her leaning against my garage.

My mind was racing as I got out of the car. I was moving slowly as if she would disappear if I moved any closer. The closer and closer I got to her, the more real all of this became. This was real. Phoebe was here for the first time in five days.

"Where have you been?" I demanded. This wasn't the best way to start off the conversation and I knew that, I was just so worried. So terribly worried.

"I've been home, Sydney," she answers, her voice sounding just as cold as mine did.

"If you were home, why have I not seen you for five days, Phoebe?" I asked. "Why have you not answered any calls? Why have I gotten no texts, emails, or others that reassure me that you are okay?"

"My phone was turned off; I'm sorry," she answered.

"Don't fucking lie to me Phoebe. I thought we ended that a long time ago," I scoffed.

Her gaze turns steely as she stared down at me. "I came here willingly to see you, and I get attacked for it? I went out of my way to come and see you, and yet here you are yelling at me. I don't have to tell you where I have been because it's none of your fucking business so how about you stop asking me questions and actually try and pretend you are happy to see me?"

"Phoebe, you have been gone for five days! I screamed. Do you even understand how many times I looked at my phone desperately wishing for you to call me back? Do you have any idea what it was like to not know where you are. You could have been dead in a fucking ditch and I wouldn't have known."

She looks taken aback as she stands there. She steps away from me, tears forming in her eyes. I walk closer to her as if to grab her hands, but she backs away again.

"I'm so sorry, Syd. I'm so fucking sorry," she whispers before breaking down.

I run over to her, holding her to me as she cries into my chest.

"Shhh, it's okay, Phoebs," I whisper. "It's not your fault. It's okay. I forgive you. We don't have to argue about this anymore. You're here and that's the only thing that matters."

I didn't care if my entire family saw me. I didn't care what they would say. I needed to be here with her. She needed me and I needed her. I held her there and reassured myself that she was safe. It had been the longest give days of my life but she was here.

PHOEBE'S BIRTHDAY WAS two weeks after that first incident. She hadn't even told me it was the day, but when I got into the car, Alexander demanded to know why I had yet to say happy birthday. Phoebe looked ready to strangle Alexander, but she didn't say anything. I wished her a happy birthday in the car, but once we got out and Alexander threw the keys to us, I wrapped my arms around her neck, pressing a kiss to her lips.

"Happy birthday Phoebs," I whispered.

She didn't say anything. She looked down at me, nothing but sadness in her eyes.

"What's the matter?" I asked.

"Autumn was 18 when she died. I'm officially 19. I lived longer than Autumn," she whispered. Her voice was void of any emotion.

I reached up to tuck a piece of hair behind her ear, but she didn't move. She was stuck in her mind.

"I'm sorry, Phoebe," I whispered. I wasn't sure what else to say.

"I never thought I would live past her, but here I am. I'm officially older than she ever will be," Phoebe says.

I didn't know what to do. There was nothing I could say that would make her feel better. Nothing I could say would take away the sting of her knowing she had officially outlived her sister.

"Let's just go inside," she tells me. "I'm going to be okay. Let me just go about my day and forget about it."

I wanted to tell her no. I wanted to tell her that she was allowed to feel what she needed to feel but she had also survived for 19 years. She had lived for 19 years on this planet when god knows her situation was worse than anyone else had it.

But I couldn't make her want to do anything she didn't want to do though. I knew not to say anything. I knew not to do anything that would upset her today. I wanted her to stay. I didn't want her to go anywhere. I didn't want her to disappear from me again. I needed her to stay.

PHOEBE BROUGHT ME TO the woods that night. She sat down on a log, staring down at the ground. I sat there next to her, my hand resting on her thigh.

"Autumn's ashes were left on this log a while back. I would sit with her when I found them, just telling her about everything. It almost felt like I had my sister back again," Phoebe finally tells me.

I turned and looked at her. She had tears gathering in her eyes as she continued staring at the ground.

"What happened to them Phoebe?" I asked. I was almost too scared ask.

"My father found out I knew where she was. He met in the woods one night," she says. "I begged him. I begged him to leave her ashes alone. I begged him to let her rest, but I watched as he opened up that urn and dumped her on the ground."

Her voice was gaining volume as she sat there. Tears were spilling down her face as she continued to speak.

"I sat there and watched as he dumped her ashes on the ground, and then he ruined me on this log," she yelled.

Tears streamed down her face as she turned to me. I had never seen one person look so broken.

"That was my sister. He dumped what was left with her on the ground and did exactly what drove her to kill herself. She killed herself because of him, and I tried Sydney. God, I tried, but it never worked. I am not supposed to be. I was not supposed to outlive her. She was the good one. She should be the one here right now. She was the one who had something worth living for, not me."

Phoebe wasn't looking at me. She was pacing in the woods, her hands tangled in her hair.

"I couldn't keep her alive, Sydney," she screamed. I couldn't keep her alive, yet I am still alive."

I stood up slowly and started walking towards her. She looked like she wanted to step back but just stood there. I kept walking towards her until I was standing in front of her. I grabbed her hands, holding them tightly. She was just staring at her hands in front of her.

"You are meant to be here, Phoebe. You are supposed to be here. It's awful what happened to Autumn and we both know that, but you couldn't have done anything. You were a child. A young child. There was nothing you could have done that would have changed the course of anything."

She looked at me like she doubted everything I was saying.

"You may not have had something to live for back then, but you have something to live for now. You have me. You have Alexander. You're so close, Phoebe. Stay. Graduate and go to college with me. Live the life you wanted when you were a child. You can do this, Phoebe. You can have the life you wanted. You can live the life Autumn wanted you to have."

In a way, this was me begging for her to stay. It was begging her to be here for me. It was selfish, and I knew that, but I needed her to stay here with me. I needed her in my life.

"I never had any plans for my life," Phoebe whispered. "My plans died with Autumn."

After

Afer three weeks of Alexander staying in a motel I let him stay in our guest bedroom. My entire family avoided him like the plague those first few weeks of him staying. They wanted nothing to do with him. My father had demanded to know why I had let him stay when he had given up. There was no rational explanation for what I did and I often found myself questioning my own decisions that had led to this point but all I knew was that I needed him to be close.

I couldn't keep calling Alexander in the middle of the night when Reno called to discuss the case. I couldn't drive over to the motel to pick him up every morning. I didn't care what he had done anymore, that was shoved far back in my mind. I needed everything to be easier. I did what I did for the ease of it all.

My parents started coming around to Alexander after a little while. All it took was Cindy to strike up a conversation and my parents were convinced he was god sent. I warned all of them he could leave at any time. I wanted to be able to trust him. I wanted to believe that he wouldn't leave but I kept those three years in the back of my mind. I promised myself I wouldn't expect him to stay. I had expected that last time and I knew how that ended last time.

My family was much more trusting of Alexander than I was. They would ask him about the times he spent with Phoebe or what his favorite memories were and he would tell them. It dawned on me as they were talking that this was the first time Alexander had ever willingly talked about Phoebe. Every time before he would shut himself away. Pretend the two of them were never friends, but for the first time, he would smile when someone asked him about the memories. He would laugh when my parents would bring up something the two of us had done together. For the first time, he didn't shut himself away.

It didn't pass over me the irony of how only in death they had accepted Phoebe into the family. Only after Phoebe's death did they begin to understand why Sydney fell in love with her in the first place. Instead of my father telling stories to the family about what Phoebe had done when she had been brought into the station he would sit and listen to Alexander and I talk about our favorite memories. Alexander would talk about the nights they spent together but laughing together.

I had my family back. After years of fighting for it, I had exactly what I wanted. Everything I wanted except for one thing. I didn't have Phoebe. This was the life I dreamed for when I had Phoebe and I had only gotten it when she was gone. I had everything I wanted, just a few years too late.

WE GOT A CALL FROM Reno two months after my interview with Alexander. Jonathan Conners had seen it and wanted to speak with the two of us. He had just been told about the new charge against him from Carson and was willing to speak with us. I couldn't believe it. For the first time in over a year, I was going to speak to Jonathan Conners.

We had been fighting for years to have this opportunity. I had screamed and I had begged. I had gone on national television and talked to everyone about Phoebe. I had helped Carson file and charge against Jonathan Conners for his assault on her 15 years ago.

This was a major break. This could help us win the case and I wasn't going to do anything to jeopardize that.

When I told Alexander about Jonathan Conners he seemed reserved at first. He asked if speaking with him was the best thing for the case at the moment. I tried explaining to him what speaking with Jonathan could do after the new charges brought by Carson. Alexander only agreed to speak with Jonathan Conners after Reno stated the importance of all of us going together.

When the day came for us to meet with Jonathan, I tried to explain to Alexander just what speaking with Jonathan in that prison would do. The way I sucked the life out of you the minute you walked in. The way you knew at this moment you were surrounded by people who would do the exact same thing that Jonathan Conners had done and feel no remorse.

I knew Alexander was thinking that the minute we walked in there we would get a confession. All it would take was us telling Jonathan Conners that we knew what he did to Carson and he would say everything he had done to Phoebe and Autumn. I didn't have the heart to tell him that was the furthest possible thing from the truth.

NO MATTER HOW MANY times you enter that prison, the feeling of dread never changes. You felt it as soon as you walked in. Felt the over pouring of complete and utter terror as you were led through the hallways. I knew Alexander felt it as well as we followed the guards through the halls.

I had told him before we left the car that you don't look anywhere else but in front of you. It doesn't matter what sounds are going on around you, you stare straight ahead and pretend you weren't even there. Alexander walked beside me, his hand gripping mine. I didn't even notice when he grabbed it, but he held onto my hand as if I was the only thing that.

It was times like these when you couldn't reassure a person that everything was going to be okay. Alexander hadn't spoken to Jonathan Conners in over three years. He hadn't been at the trial when Jonathan was arrested. He hadn't had to testify against him. He had spent so many years surrounded by Jonathan Conners but once a person left it became a lot harder to come back.

My breath caught in my throat when I saw Jonathan Conners through the glass. He hadn't changed much in those three years. His hair had more gray in it than it had before but he was still as clean shaven as ever. Alexander's hand went limp in mine and when I looked over at him, tears were crowding his eyes.

"The bastard hasn't been suffering. He hasn't had any repercussions for what he did. This is just a pit stop on this way to being free."

I squeezed his hand, Alexander turning to look at me.

"Trust me Alexander, I've been pissed about this for a long time but this is the first step. We go in there and we talk to him and we could get him to say something, anything that we could possibly use against him and it's another step closer towards the endgame," I whispered.

"It's not fair. It's not fucking fair that he gets to sit here and have this perfect life when Phoebe is dead. It's not fair he gets to live when Phoebe killed herself because of him," Alexander whispers.

"I get it Alexander. If there is anyone in this world that understands it, it is me, but standing here and being upset and talking about how unfair it is, isn't doing shit. It wasn't fair what happened to Phoebe and we both know that. We both know that both Phoebe and Autumn deserve to be alive but they aren't. We have a chance to bring this case into more light. We have a chance to get this case expedited. So we can sit here being pissed off and cursing the universe, or we can actually go in there and take the fucker down. You can make the choice right now. You either stay out here and watch as I am in there, or you actually come in there with me and face him like I know you have wanted to for three years."

Alexander's features tighten as he stares straight ahead at Jonathan.

"I'm going in."

I nodded towards the guards, one of them pressing the button to open the door. Alexander squeezed my hand one last time before the door opened and we walked in.

"Oh well this is a pleasant surprise. I didn't know if you would actually come back to speak with me after you met with Carson Keeler," Jonathan states.

"On the contrary Jonathan. We came here because of Carson Keeler," I answered, sitting down across from him and opening the file Reno had given us. "We are giving you this one chance to come clean. If you give us the names of any other girls you might have hurt, we are willing to lower the sentence from life without the chance of parole to life with the chance of parole. We are offering the same sentence to a guilty confession," I finished.

"You're a smart girl Sydney Garcia. It would seem Carson Keeler coming forward at this moment would be perfect timing would it not?" he questions. "One would think it is almost too perfect."

I said nothing, sliding over a copy of the official statement from Carson.

"We both know why we are here, Jonathan," I leaned forward in my chair. "And we both know Carson coming forward wasn't a fluke. With Carson Keeler's confession we have reason to believe there may be more girls out there that you sexually assaulted. If you give us the names right now, of anyone else, Mr. Chadwick and I can leave and we won't bother you again, but if you keep silent, and if you don't give us any more names then I can promise that the minute another girl comes forward, you will expect to see us again. I can assure you that the minute you have another charge brought against you, you will be seeing us within a few days, despite what your lawyer suggests for you."

Jonathan doesn't respond. His eyes travel over towards Alexander and a smile appears on his face.

"Hello, Alexander Chadwick," he says. "After you left I didn't expect to be seeing you again, and yet here you are, back on the case. Tell me Mr. Chadwick, what brought you to return? What was it that finally brought you back?"

Alexander looks towards me as if asking for permission to speak and when I nod my head answers.

"I saw the news of what happened to Phoebe. What you did to Phoebe."

Jonathan smiles, leaning forward in his chair and grabbing the copy of Carson's confession.

"And what did I do Alexander? You've accused me of a lot during the time we have known each other, but what is it that I did this time that brought you back?" Jonathan inquires.

"You destroyed her. Inside and out you ruined her. I had the chance to say something when she was still alive and I didn't, but now, nothing is going to stop me. Those bones, the broken and shattered bones that were Phoebe are destroyed because of you. They may not have been able to make any definitive answers but we all know what happened. You raped her. You beat her. You took everything she loved and destroyed it. I made a mistake walking away three years ago. I couldn't handle hte truth so I left, but now, there is nothing that will stop me from fighting until you never see the light of day."

I tried not to wince when Alexander said rape. Phoebe had hated it. Hated having to say that she was a victim of rape, or that her father had raped her. I hated the word as well. I hated the picture it painted. I hated picturing Phoebe as a victim of the word. She would have hated it. Hated everyone looking at her as one, but there wasn't any way I could avoid it any more. She was a victim of rape. That was just the truth. Reno and I could avoid the word as much as we wanted but Jonathan raped Autumn, Phoebe and Carson. That was just the truth of it.

Jonathan turned back towards me, his smile only widening.

"You don't like that word do you Sydney? The word rape. You know, Phoebe didn't like it either. She used to flinch away any time anyone said it. Neither did Autumn. Autumn used to tell any one who asked it elicited the same reaction from everyone, no matter if you have been raped or not. Why don't you like the word Sydney Garcia? What is it about the word 'rape' that brings you discomfort?"

Hearing him say Phoebe's name sent chills down my spine. I hate the way it sounded in his mouth. The way he enunciated each and every syllable.

"I don't like the image it paints. I don't like thinking of it happening to Phoebe. I don't like the idea of it happening to anyone," I answered.

"A word only holds power if you let it," Jonathan stated.

"Mr. Conners, I told you I couldn't handle the truth but do you know what truth I couldn't handle?" Alexander asked him. Jonathan rips his eyes away from me and settles on Alexander. "The truth that you were allowed to carry on no matter what happened to Phoebe. No one cared about what happened to Phoebe. When she died they said she had it coming and it was only a matter of time before she did. No one even batted an eye at the allegations against you. They didn't want to believe that the man with the big house and even bigger bank account would have done something like that.

In truth, Phoebe had been the only person that mattered in my life for so long that when she was gone, I didn't know how to live without her. I left because knowing that you were still alive, and knowing that you are allowed to walk the earth when Phoebe was dead rocked me to my core. I came back though because I saw how hard Sydney was trying. I saw everything she was doing for Phoebe and I knew that she couldn't be the only one.

I know Phoebe wasn't the only one you hurt. I know Carson isn't the only person outside of your family that you assaulted. If it were up to me, you would be placed in front of a firing squad just for what you did to Phoebe, but that can't happen so I have to settle by sitting right here and getting the information out of you. I do this because this is what Phoebe would have wanted me to do. I do this, because there are other people out there like Phoebe and Autumn and Carson who deserve to be able to live their lives knowing the person who took away everything sacred to them is still out there. I came back because I loved Phoebe Conners and I will do whatever it takes to make sure she and everyone else never has to live with the same fear she did ever again."

If Jonathan's hands weren't chained to the table, he would have started clapping

"That was quite a proud statement Alexander Chadwick. One might think you had practiced that before you walked in here. Is that what you did?"

"You're wasting our time Jonathan Conners," I finally recovered. "Tell us right now if there are any names that we don't know or refuse to give us the information and we leave."

Jonathan leans back, letting out a sigh.

"You two aren't much fun are you? One would think you would allow me some entertainment after being stuck in this place for so long. Well if you are not going to provide me with proper human interaction I will just end this right now. There are no other names. I never touched my children or Carson Keeler," Jonathan finished.

I grabbed the file from Jonathan's hands and stood up.

"Thank you Mr. Conners. Our deal is officially rescinded. You can expect to be hearing from us again very soon," I said, letting Alexander follow me out the door.

When I heard the click of the lock sound I turned towards Alexander.

"You made it through your first meeting with Jonathan Conners. Now we have work to do."

I WAITED UNTIL THAT night to cry. I didn't want to let Alexander see me break down. I needed to stay strong for him because if I wasn't strong, then there was no promise he would be either. I talked with Alexander and Reno about what was said. Reno had me promise him that I was okay and then we went our separate ways. Reno went home and Alexander started his drive to DC for a meeting the next day.

I ate dinner with my family, smiling and promising them that I was okay. I promised them I had done this before and it didn't affect me the same way it used to. I played with Cindy, letting her beat me in whatever we did. I watched tv with my parents after the younger kids went to bed. My father cast wary glances towards me but I made sure I reassured him I was okay every time. I waited until everyone was asleep before I cried.

I cried harder than I had cried in months. Tears ripped down my face as I choked down sobs. Everyone told you that when someone died, it would take time to get over the initial pain.

Things would hurt for a few years and over time they would lessen, but whoever said that was the dumbest fuck to walk the earth.

Whoever said that had the chance to move on. Whoever said that would have been able to leave and live a life that wasn't just the person they lost. I didn't have that luxury. I lived every single day with the memories of the worst that happened to Phoebe. When I cried, I cried over the moments I never got with her. I cried over the broken promise to stay together forever. I cried for the memories we had together but would never have again. I cried because I had planned my entire life around Phoebe Conners, just for that plan to be ripped out from underneath me, but I would mostly cry because Phoebe never got the life she deserved.

Phoebe deserved to have been loved and felt love. She had deserved parents who put bandages over her cuts and held her when she woke up with a nightmare. She deserved a life where she didn't feel like her only escape was death. Phoebe deserved everything and yet she was given nothing. She saw the worst that humanity had to offer. She had been dealt the worst hand and the only way she could get out of it had been to die.

Before

I begged Phoebe to stay with me that night. She tried arguing at first, telling me she needed to leave so she wouldn't upset my family. I told her that her safety was more important that what my family was worried about. She couldn't go home. She couldn't be around her family. I just needed to make sure that she was safe. I needed to make sure she stayed.

My hand rested on her knee as I drove down the road. She was staring out the window but wasn't tense under my touch. She was watching everything that was happening. When we pulled into my driveway, I got out, opened the door, walked to Phoebe's door, and opened it. I didn't say anything as she stepped out of the car. She didn't take more than two steps before she collapsed into my arms.

I felt her melt into my arms as I held her close.

"You deserve to be happy, Phoebe Conners," I whispered. "You deserve to have a life where you are happy, Phoebe. You deserve everything."

She didn't respond, just held onto my arm as if I was the only thing grounding her to this earth.

I held her in my arms like she was the last thing in the world. I never wanted to let her go. I wanted to hold her here, promise her that everything would be okay and that it would just be the two of us for the rest of forever.

I heard a car pull up behind us, and I knew my mother was home. Phoebe pulled away, a look of panic in her eyes.

"I should go," she whispered, trying to pull farther away from me.

"It's okay," I whispered, grabbing her hands.

"Sydney, your family."

"My family can go fuck themselves," I answered.

"Syd, I don't want to be the reason your family doesn't trust you," she tells me.

I heard the car doors slam, and my mother released a sharp gasp behind me. Phoebe tried to take another step back, but I kept holding her hands.

"My family has done nothing but talk bad about you for four years, Phoebe. I don't want to hide anymore. I don't want to be told we can't be together just because they don't like you. I can't promise that you will ever win my parent's approval, but I can promise you that no matter what, I will never care about what they say about you," I told her.

Her eyes dart back and forth between me and the reflection of my family on the windshield. I thought for a moment she was going to pull away. I thought she was going too demand I drive her home. My heart pounded in my chest at the thought of having her go back to her house. She wasn't safe there. I couldn't make sure that she was safe. I couldn't make sure everything was okay.

"Okay," Phoebe breathes. "I'll stay here. I'll stay with you. I won't go anywhere."

I released a sigh, moving to rest my head on her forehead. I felt her breath on my face as she rested her hands on my face. I felt a tug at my pants and broke apart, looking down to see Cindy staring up at the two of us, her mouth agape. Phoebe's face flames as she looks down at Cindy.

"Why is Phoebe here?" she asks, pointing her finger at her.

Phoebe kneels down, tucking her hair behind her ears as she gets on Cindy's level.

"Well hello Cindy Garcia," she says, holding out her hand. "It is wonderful to finally meet you."

Cindy reaches out and grabs Phoebe's hand, violently shaking it. Phoebe laughs, a smile that reaches her eyes covering her face. It had been so long since I had seen that smile.

"Cindy, meet Phoebe Conners, my girlfriend. Phoebe meets Cindy, my youngest and most annoying sibling," I said.

Cindy lets go of Phoebe's hand and turns towards me.

"Hey!" she yells.

Phoebe's smile never falters. "Well, it is a pleasure to meet you, Cindy Garcia. And I know you are not the most annoying Garcia sibling; remember, I'm dating Syd."

Now it was my turn to shout, "hey!" as Cindy laughed and gaped at Phoebe.

"You're funny," Cindy laughs.

The door opens, and I turn to see my mother standing in the doorway.

"Cindy, come on, let's get inside," she says. I knew what she was trying to say, and Phoebe did too.

"No," Cindy yells, holding her hands for Phoebe to take her. "I want to stay here with Phoebe."

Phoebe's smile drops for a moment and her hand comes to rest on Cindy's head. Cindy was the first in my family to think about talking to her, but Phoebe knew she couldn't. She couldn't say anything else to Cindy without my mother running out of the door to drag Cindy inside. Phoebe grabs Cindy's hand and holds it like it is something that would break if she let it go.

"Go on inside, Cindy. I'll see you again soon, okay," she says.

She looks over at me, a sad look on her face.

"Go on to mom Cindy," I said. "Better not to make her mad."

Cindy takes a few steps towards my mom before running back and wrapping her arms around Phoebe's legs.

"Bye, Phoebe," she says. "You better come back at some point."

Phoebe bends down, wrapping her arms around Cindy before shooing her away towards my mom. My mom hurriedly rushes her inside as Phoebe looks towards me.

I grab her face in my hands and press my lips to her, kissing her gently. She sighs into my mouth, pulling me towards her and resting her nose on mine as she kisses me. She pulls away, resting her forehead on mine before letting out a long exhale.

"You're a part of my life Pheobe. They can't always shelter themselves away from you forever," I whispered.

She doesn't say anything, just pulls my face towards her and kisses me again, steady like the last one, but with a sense of urgency on her lips. I held her close. Pulled her closer and closer until there wasn't an inch of space between us. She was okay. She was here. Nothing could hurt her here. Nothing would take her away from me here.

I walked Phoebe inside, the two of us sitting on the couch together. Her head rested on my shoulder as we sat, the tv on in front of us. I could feel my parents standing behind us in the kitchen. My mother's nails were tapping against the kitchen counter, pausing every so often when my father would put his hand over her's.

"I can feel you guys staring at us," I called behind me once. My mother's tapping stopped for a few moments but resumed a little while later.

As we sat there, Phoebe's breathing evened out as she fell asleep on my shoulder. Her hand was wrapped around mine, her breathing matched with mine in a steady rhythm. My parents whispered as they stood in the kitchen, only stopping when one of my siblings would come down and ask them something.

We went upstairs when my mother called everyone down for dinner. She didn't even bother to question if we would be joining them for dinner. I held Phoebe's hand in mine as we walked towards my room, never once letting go. Her hand only left mine when I went to give her a change of clothes she left with me for her to change. When she had changed, she laid on my bed, her head in my lap as I ran my fingers through her hair. We didn't say anything to each other. Neither of us needed to.

The only time I left her was to go downstairs and get the food I had ordered. Before I could sneak back upstairs, my mother cornered me.

"Sydney, why did you bring her here?" my mother demanded. "How could you put your family in danger like this?"

My hands were shaking as I turned towards her. I wasn't putting my family in danger. There was nothing about anything that was happening that was dangerous.

"Phoebe disappeared for two weeks. I didn't see her or hear from her once. I was terrified she was dead. I brought her here because I can't lose her. I need to protect her. I need to make sure she is here because I love her and I can't lose her," I responded.

My mother reeled back, her eyes widening.

"Did you just say you loved her?" she trembled.

I didn't even realize I had. I loved her. I loved Phoebe Conners. I had never said it before. Never told it to her. Never even let myself ponder it, but I knew at that moment that I loved her. God I loved her so much.

I didn't have time to answer before Phoebe walked down the stairs, her hand hovering over the banister. My mother's eyes widened even more, her facing turning a bright shade of red as she stumbled a few steps back. If Phoebe noticed my mother's actions, she didn't let it show.

Phoebe stood tall and proud, staring right back at my mom. Nothing remained of the girl who had crumpled in my arms a few hours ago. This was the Phoebe Conners she presented herself as everyday.

"Did the food get here, Sydney?" Phoebe asks, her voice not faltering once.

I nodded, smiling up at her.

"You just so happened to come down at the perfect moment. I was just about to bring it up."

"Perfect," Phoebe smiles. "I'm starving."

I laugh, reaching down to grab the food.

"I'll follow you up."

"Sydney get her the fuck out of the house right now," my mother blurts out, her face red and her hands shaking.

Both Phoebe and I wheel around, staring down at her.

"No," I answered.

I watched as my father ran over, immediately going to stand in front of my mother as if we were going to attack each other.

"What did you say?" my father demands.

"I told her no," I responded. "I'm telling you that she is not going anywhere. It's her birthday and I am going to let her stay here. She is going to stay the night and most of tomorrow morning. You are going to let us be and not break into my room in the middle of the night like I know you have been doing the past few nights. You are going to sit downstairs and forget she is even here. You are going to treat her like an actual human being. Is that understood?"

By the way, they looked at me; you would have thought I had shot them. My father says nothing. He just stares at me from across the counter.

When they didn't respond I turned back towards the stairs, tightening my grip on the bag of food to stop my hands from shaking. I didn't look back as they watched me walk back up the stairs. Phoebe walked in front of her, closing the door behind me after I walked in. She grabbed the bag from my hand and threw it on my desk. Before I could protest, her lips met mine and she pulled me towards her. I let out a gasp of surprise but wrapped my arms around her shoulders, slotting her body into mine.

"I love you more than the entire world Sydney Garcia," she whispers as she pulls away.

I looked up at her. Her swollen lips covered in a smile.

"I love you too Phoebe Conners," I responded, pulling her into another kiss.

THE LIGHT STREAMED through the window as I woke up. I felt someone's eyes on me, as I slowly opened my eyes. Phoebe was staring up at me from her spot on my chest, a sweet smile covering her face.

"Good morning Sydney Garcia," Phoebe whispers, her hands reaching up to trace my face.

"Morning," I answered, grabbing her hand and pressing a kiss to her open palm.

We laid together, both of us soaking in each other's presence. Her hand traced the features on my face, letting me kiss her fingers whenever they lingered on my lips. I don't know how long we laid there together. It didn't truly matter. Here, it was just the two of us. None of the world's judgemental whispers or looks. None of the biases or assumptions. It was just the two of us together.

When we went downstairs my family wasn't anywhere to be seen. I looked at the clock on the oven to see it was 11 am. I made the both of us waffles and set them down at the table. We sat there and ate, laughing at each other's jokes.

I couldn't help but notice the mundanity of the scene. Phoebe and I, sitting at a table together and eating breakfast. I could see myself doing this for the rest of my life. I was sitting here with the girl I loved. I loved her and she loved me. I was in love with Phoebe Conners. That was a sentence I never thought I would utter.

We lingered for as long as possible, neither of us wanting to leave the little bubble we had put around ourselves. Once we left the house, that bubble was broken. I could assure her safety here. I could make sure nothing bad happened to her here but once we left this house, I couldn't protect her like that. When we finally accepted that the two of us couldn't stay here forever, we got into the car so I could drive her home.

After four tries of closing the door and a long string of curse words, Phoebe was finally able to get the door closed.

"I swear to god, Sydney, you have to get this car fixed," she grumbled, grabbing the seatbelt and quickly slinging it across her so she could buckle it without having to worry about it locking up on her.

"This car works fine, thank you very much," I answered, smiling over at her.

I drove away, my hand lingering on her thigh as I did. Phoebe was leaning her head against the window, looking at the sun setting over the woods by the road.

"I never think about how beautiful it is here," Phoebe mutters. "I've never thought of anything other than wanting to get out of here."

I looked over towards her, white knuckle gripping the steering wheel to keep it steady.

"Would you ever come back after you leave?" I asked.

Phoebe shakes her head, keeping her eyes on the woods.

"I've never wanted anything more than to be away from the constant reminders of this town. I always dreamed of leaving, but after Autumn died, I never saw myself living past her. I just stopped seeing anything past Autumn." she whispers.

I tried paying attention to the road, tried keeping my attention on what needed it the most, but Phoebe being next to me made it near impossible.

"You know, you're not unlike Autumn yourself, Phoebe," I said.

Phoebe turned to look at me; there were no tears in her eyes. When I looked past the tears crowding her eyes, all I saw in her eyes was pure disbelief

"I'm the exact opposite of everything Autumn was. Autumn loved everything. She saw good in everyone. She used to tell me that there was good in everyone, but after everything, I don't think there is any good in this world."

"Phoebe, you may think you are this horrible person, but when I look at you, I don't see a horrible person. I see a young woman who is the most loving and caring person. I see a woman who has everything to live for if she lets herself be happy. I see the woman I would spend the rest of my life with in a heartbeat because she is the best thing that has ever happened in my life," I answered.

Phoebe didn't say anything; she stared straight ahead at the road in front of us. She reached over and grabbed my hand, squeezing it like it was her lifeline. When I got to her house, I made sure I drove even slower than I was on the roads.

"It's been five years Sydney," she whispers.

For a moment, I wanted to ask her what had been five years, but when I saw how she was looking at the house, I knew. It had been five years since 14-year-old Phoebe Conners walked into the bathroom and found her sister dead in the bathtub. It had been five years since Phoebe Conners had lost the most important person in her life. Autumn Conners had committed suicide the day after Phoebe Conners birthday.

I pulled her into me over the center console. She was silent, her arms wrapped around me, but I could hear the faintest sounds of crying. When she pulled away, her face was covered in tears.

"I can't sleep in this house alone anymore, Sydney," she whispers. "I can't do it. I can't let him touch me again. I can't do it Sydney. I can't fucking do it."

"I'm not going anywhere, Phoebe," I told her. "I'm never leaving you again."

We walked slowly inside. It felt like we were on a death march. Like I was walking into my execution. It was dark, making it nearly impossible to see anything. Her parents were nowhere to be found. She led me up the massive stairs, me getting out of breath, not even halfway up, and she walked as though it was no big deal. I could see the tension in her shoulders as she walked. Whenever she got to a hallway, she stopped, checking all around before heading back up. When we did get to her bedroom, she walked as quickly as possible before closing the door behind her after ushering me in. She flicked off the lights, quickly moving to turn on her flashlight and walking over towards her desk.

She grabbed a lighter, quickly lighting one of the candles before setting it down on the desk and grabbing a remote from her desk. When she pressed the button, thousands of fairy lights lit up every corner of her room. It was still dark but light enough to see her standing there.

"Autumn always wanted fairy lights," she says. "I never much cared for them but couldn't help but put them up after she was gone."

I didn't know what to say. I knew there was nothing I could say that would make this better. Nothing I could do would take away the pain of her losing Autumn. All I could do was be here, hold her, and let her cry when she needed to.

"My parents are going to call me down for dinner sometime. There is an extra spot at the table next to me. Please just ignore anything my family says if they are not explicitly talking to you. Father isn't saying anything to you unless it's something that would offend you. I just need you there with me. I just need you sitting next to me."

I walk towards her, wrapping my pinky around hers and holding our entwined fingers up to our faces.

"This is my promise, Phoebe Conners. I will not leave your side. I will be with you for as long as you want me here."

She smiled a real, genuine smile for the first time in a while. She pressed her lips to the side of her hand, and I did the same.

"You never fail to amaze me, Sydney Garcia," she whispers.

A bell rang in the distance, and I felt her body tense up. I didn't let go of her pinky as I put my hand down and pressed a kiss to the side of her head.

"You can do this," I told her. "I'm going to be here the whole time. You can do this."

Phoebe nodded, walking towards the door and pulling it open the door. She walked steadily down the stairs and into the dining room, leaving me to follow closely. Her parents were already sitting at the table, her father at the head and her mother beside him. Phoebe sat down on the father's other side, leading me to sit right next to her. I could feel the eyes glued on me, but Phoebe didn't turn. She sits with her hands in her lap, staring at the plate.

"Phoebe, I didn't know a guest would be joining us today," her mother says, staring down at me. She tried smiling at me, maybe to reassure me or intimidate me, but whatever she was trying to do, it sure was not working.

I could feel her father's eyes digging into the side of my head as I sat next to her at that table. I looked over at him, meeting his eyes and not breaking the gaze. He kept looking at me, expecting me to break eye contact, but I didn't. I wasn't about to let his intimidation work.

"Phoebe, I truly don't think today is the day to have someone over. On the anniversary of your sister's death, I think this is a time for family," her father tells her.

Phoebe looks up at him finally, a look of indignation on her face.

"Sydney stays. It would not be very kind of us if we were to kick our guest out of dinner now, would we?" she says.

Phoebe looked at her father as if daring him to answer. Daring him to disagree with him. Mr. Conners does not say anything; he just stares down at her before putting his hands on his lap. Both of them will fight against one another.

"I think we should take this time to thank the Lord for our meal and our ability to gather here today to honor our dearly parted daughter, Autumn Conners," Mr. Conners says, his hands folding together as he extends his head towards the sky.

I reached over, wrapping my pinky around hers. Neither of us closed our eyes, but we looked toward the ground. I wanted to make it look as though we were praying; I would never speak words of praise to the same god as this man worshiped. I brought her hand to my mouth, pressing a kiss to the top of her hand.

When Mr. Conners was finished, he raised his eyes, but I didn't let go of her finger. She grabbed the fork closest to her plate and slowly took a bite before wincing. I squeezed her hand again, trying desperately to do anything that would calm her down. No one said anything for the longest time. Everyone just kept eating slowly. Phoebe keeps glancing back and forth between her mother and father as if waiting for the explosion to happen. Waiting for the words that would ruin everything to come out of their mouths.

Phoebe's mother keeps looking at her husband from the corner of her eye. She wasn't looking like she wanted him to say something, no. The look in her eyes was nothing but pure fear. She was scared of what he would do. I had seen that look enough times in Pheobe to know exactly what it was.

He said nothing. He kept staring down at his plate and eating, so I didn't say anything. I was not going to be the one to start a conversation like this. The sooner Phoebe and I got out here, the better.

I watched from the corner of my eye as her father set down his fork and looked up at me.

"So Sydney, where did you meet my Phoebe?" he asks.

The words 'my Phoebe sent a shiver down my spine.

"We sit next to each other in class," I answered, looking him in the eyes. I was not about to let him intimidate me. He was not going to take Phoebe from me.

"It's nice that Phoebe has a friend other than that Chadwick boy. I'm glad she finally has a female influence in her life," he says before taking another bite of his food.

I watched as Phoebe's mother curled into herself. Phoebe doesn't look at her father as he says this, just stares down at her shaking hands. It looked like she was trying to do anything to act as though she didn't exist. I kept my hand on top of hers, lightly tracing words onto her hand. When she had finally choked down her food, she placed her napkin on the table in a nice folded manner and looked towards her mother.

"Mother, is there any way Sydney and I can be excused?" she asks.

Her mother looks over at Mr. Conners, and when he nods, she looks back towards us. "Yes, Phoebe dear," she tells her.

Phoebe slowly stood up from the table and pushed in her chair. I followed her motions and followed her right out the door. As we left, I could feel her father's eyes pinned on my back. She walked up the stairs the same way she had when she had walked down them, but this time she kept going past her bedroom. She didn't stop until she got to the top of the staircase. She opened the hatch door at the top, boosting herself up before grabbing my hand and pulling me up.

She lifted me into the air, pulling me up onto the roof, and once I got up, she closed the door behind her. Her hand goes to her pocket bringing out her lighter. I watched as she flicked it open and shut, her other hand shaking at her side. Phoebe turns to look at me, tears filling her eyes. I held out my arms, starting to walk closer towards her. She doesn't wait a second before throwing the lighter to the ground and racing towards me.

By the time she was in my arms, the tears were running down her face. I had never heard her cry like this before. Long choking sobs. Heartbreaking sobs.

"It's okay Phoebe. It's okay," I whispered.

She shakes her head into my shoulder. "It's not fucking okay Sydney. None of this is fucking okay."

She pulls away, starting to pace around the roof.

"None of this is fucking okay Sydney. You saw him down there. You heard what he called me. Autumn died 9 years ago and he can't even grieve without needing me. You saw the way my mother looked at me. She knows. She knows and she won't do anything because she is scared of her own husband. She lets him touch me. Let's him do whatever he wants because she is scared of losing her safety net."

"It's okay Phoebe," I whispered. My heart was pounding. She was screaming and we were on top of the roof. Anyone could hear us. Anyone could hear what she said. "We'll get out of here. You and I will get out of this town and get away from everything here and never look back. We can leave and never look back. We can live the life we both want, without ever coming back here."

Phoebe wheels around, her eyes darkening. "You don't get it Sydney. You don't fucking get it."

"Then explain it to me Phoebe."

"I was never supposed to outlive Autumn. I'm not supposed to be here. She was the one who had everything to live for. Autumn and I planned on leaving this place together and finally taking back control of my life but I don't get that now. I'm not ever leaving this town alive. I'm not going anywhere. There is nothing for me too live for. The only thing I had to live for before was knowing that Autumn and I were going to leave. But I don't even get that now. I don't fucking get that now. I'm either going to kill myself, or die old and cathargic like everyone else who lives in this fucking place. I'm never having a life outside of here."

Her words rang through my head. Nothing to live for. Phoebe Conners having nothing to live for. I had led myself to believe that I was enough. I was enough. She just couldn't think about it right now. It was the fifth anniversary of her sister's death. I couldn't expect her to be thinking rationally.

"Your silence says a lot more than you could ever say Sydney. I know you think I'm just not in the right state of mind to be talking as though I have nothing to live for. I love you Sydney. God, Sydney Garcia I love you, but you have to understand that what we have isn't enough for me to live. You can find someone else. Someone better than me and I know that. I know you will be happier with someone else, but right now, I just want to be able to hold you. You are the only reason I am still here Sydney but you have to know that what we have, the love I have for you, isn't enough for me to want to live."

After

I had dreaded the day for weeks. We all knew the weight that day held, but none of us talked about it. Maybe if we just didn't acknowledge that day it wouldn't come. But no amount of time spend pretending not to remember that day, it still came with the full force it had the 5 years before it..

Reno told Alexander and I we needed to take the day off. The case would be there the next day. Alexander agreed, telling everyone they needed to take proper time to process what had happened six years ago but I fought as hard as I could. I didn't want the day off. I didn't want to have to wake up knowing that I was going to be alone on this day. I wanted to keep working. I wanted to have that reminder to myself that a end was in sight.

Carson was the last vote that counted towards whether or not we would work or not. She agreed with Reno and Alexander that we needed some kind of day off. A day to grieve everything we had lost. Alexander made me promise I wouldn't look at the case during that day.

"You need a day to process everything," he told me. "There has not been a day in the past year you have not thought about this case. Let today be that day. Give yourself time time to grieve what you lost. Give yourself the space you need."

I didn't want the day to process. I knew what I would feel. It would be the same thing I have felt every year before. It didn't matter that she had died six years ago, this day would never hurt any less than it did the day I found her on that kitchen floor.

Despite what Alexander said, I didn't need a day to process my feelings. I didn't need a day to think about what I felt about Phoebe being gone. I felt that pain every day.

I didn't sleep that night. I couldn't sleep when I knew that when midnight hit it would only be a matter of a few hours before she had died. Six years. Six years since I had broken down the door to the Conners home and found Phoebe on the floor. Six fucking years since I heard the sound of that flatline and watched as they dragged the sheet over her body. The pain today wasn't any different than it had been when I first lost her. The stabbing pain. The feeling of your chest constricting, and the feeling of numbness that edged at your soul. You could never quite grab onto that numbness. No matter how much you wanted to reach out and snatch it; no matter how much you wanted to feel nothing at all, it was always hidden in the deepest corners. Never for you to feel. Never for you to escape to.

The sun wasn't shining that morning. It was almost impossible to tell that any time had passed from the night. My bed had never felt more uncomfortable. When I stood up, my body felt heavy. I heard my family downstairs. Music playing and the children yelling at each other. This was a normal day for them. They didn't hurt like this on this day. They would be able to live today as if nothing had happened, because to them, nothing did.

I heard a whimper come from behind me. I turned to see Atlas looking towards me, his eyes wide and sad. Even he knew. Tears choked up in my throat as I looked towards him. I sat next to him on the bed, pressing my face into his fur.

"I know bud," I whispered, my voice sounding foreign to my own ears. "I miss her too bud. I miss her too."

Atlas trailed behind me as I walked downstairs. I could see the photographs on the wall from the corner of my eyes. I wouldn't let myself look at them. Wouldn't let myself relive those memories with her. She was gone. She's been gone for six years. No picture was going to change that.

The noise quieted as I got to the bottom of the stairs. I could feel their eyes on me. They were waiting to guage my reaction. They wanted to know what they need to say. If there was anything they could say that would make everything feel better. I wasn't going to let them know how much it hurt. This day was a typical day for them. They didn't need to feel the same pain that I did.

I sat with them as they ate breakfast, Atlas lounging on my feet. I laughed along with their jokes. I ignored the side eyes I recieved when they thought I wasn't paying attention. I didn't let it show. I didn't let them know how badly it felt. I wasn't going to bring them down with me. I wouldn't do it.

My family stayed for as long as possible, but they couldn't say forever. Everyone had to go their separate ways and I was left at the house with both of my parents. I wanted to go back up to my room. Didn't want to ever leave it, but my parents were there. They needed to believe everything was okay, so I stayed on the couch. I held Atlas close to me and just laid there. I couldn't bring myself to turn anything on. It would just have been background noise anyway.

My parents didnm't leave the kitchen for hours. They just stood there, whispering to each other. I couldn't hear anything they were saying, but I knew it was about me. I knew they wanted me to talk about things. Talk through the feelings with someone else, but I didnm't want to have to acknowledge it. Acknowledging it would only make it worse.

My parents let me sit there for two hours. I would feel their eyes on me, when they thought I couldn't tell. Six years ago tomorrow, I would have been doing the same thing. Laying on the couch, not moving, the pain overwhelming. The feeling of not being able to breathe. The grief a heavy weight on your chest.

"Today won't just disappear if you don't think about it, Sydney," I hear my father all from behind me.

I sit up, the simple action taking so much energy out of me. Something inside of me wanted to scream at him. To tell him he had no idea what it felt like to wake up and know that the person you loved was gone. He was able to wake up and go to sleep with the woman he loved next to him and that I didn't have that luxury anymore.

But it wasn't his fault that she was gone. It wasn't his fault it had been six years since I had screamed and begged for her to wake up. It wasn't his fault the person he loved was still alive, just like it wasn't my fault that Phoebe wasn't.

My father walks into the living, sitting next to me on the couch. He looks like he wants to reach over and envelope me in a hug. He wants to promise me that everything was going to be okay, but even he knew he couldn't promise that.

"You can't pretend like today is a normal day. It will only make things worse," he whispers.

The tears fill my throat, feeling as though they were choking me.

"It's been six years," I finally managed to choke out. "Six years and yet it still hurts so fucking much."

My father moves closer to me, letting me rest my head on his shoulder.

"I know sweetheart," he whispers. "That pain really won't ever go away."

Tears slipped past my eyes as he spoke. I wanted that pain to go away. I wanted the pain of today to just disappear. I wanted the pain of knowing she was gone to go away. I didn't want to have her appear in my mind and have it feel as though the breath had been knocked out of me.

"When was the last time you visited her grave?" my father asks.

I knew I hadn't been back since the last parole hearing. I would love to say that I just hadn't had time or I hadn't thought about it but I couldn't. I couldn't bring myself to go and see her. I couldn't bring myself to look at that tombstone knowing the words etched into the marble would never be able to sum up who Phoebe was. I didn't want to see the reminder that she was dead in front of me.

"I'm not saying it will fix things, but it might help to go and see her. It's been awhile and I think there are a lot of things you two need to catch up on," my father ended.

I knew he was right. I needed to go. I needed to see her, but I couldn't. I couldn't look at that headstone and act as though it wasn't there. I couldn't speak to her as if she was standing right in front of me instead of buried 6 feet underneath me.

"It might help mija," my mother calls from the kitchen.

Maybe it would help. Maybe it wouldn't. Maybe it would only make everything worse. Maybe I would get there and see that inscription on the grave and want nothing more than to tear it down piece by piece until there was nothing left that would ever show Phoebe Conners had been on this earth in the first place. Maybe nothing would happen at all. Maybe I would go and sit there and just talk, and I would feel better about the day. There was no way of knowing unless I tried.

"I'll go," I whispered.

Everything inside of me told me not to go. My body fought against me as I moved too get ready. I kept telling myself to do one more thing. Just put your shirt on and then you can be done. Just put on your socks and then your done. Just get through the day...

There is nothing you can do that will prepare yourself for going to see the person you loved most in the world in the ground. There is nothing you can do to prepare yourself for having to come to terms with knowing the love of your life has been gone for six years. Nothing to prevent you from seeing her cold, lifeless body whenever you close your eyes. Nothing will ever get rid of the past six years of anger and pain.

My father asked if I wanted him to go with me. He wanted to make sure I was going to be okay driving but I reassured him I was going to be fine. I promised him that I would be home before nine, hugged my mother and left. It felt as though my body had finally realized there was nothing it could do to stop the plan that was in motion. I knew I couldn't show up to her grave empty handed. She deserved more than that.

No tears escaped my eyes as I drove. Crying wouldn't bring her back. Crying wouldn't erase what the day was. I knew the way to get the flowers. I had done this simple routine so many times before I went to New York that I didn't even need to even think about the steps. I wanted to just grab the first bouquet I saw and call it a day, but I couldn't bring myself to do that to her. It had been so long since I had done anything for her. So long since I had brought her these flowers. She at least deserved ones that she would have loved.

I spent 20 minutes trying to find the perfect bouquet. One that was not too colorful but had hints of green and pink. Both colors she would have wanted when she was still here. I walked back towards the front of the store, not even bothering to go through the self checkout. I carefully set down the flowers on the belt.

"These are beautiful," the cashier says, smiling as she scanned them. "Someone special must be getting these for them to be so pretty."

I didn't even try to force a smile on my face. Explaining it would have taken too long. I didn't want to have to see the look of sympathy on her face as she tried to apologize for my loss. Apologizes wouldn't do anything though. Apologizes wouldn't bring her back.

I set the flowers down next to me as carefully as possible, as if I was setting a piece of Phoebe herself down on the seat. My mind was elsewhere as I drove to the cemetery. I had memorized the turns and curves a long time ago.

Six years. I couldn't understand how it had been six years. It felt like I had held her in my arms yesterday and yet at the same, it felt like it had been so much longer. There were weeks that had felt as long as years. Seconds that felt like hours because she wasn't there. Everything I had done in the past six years was for her. My entire life had been Phoebe Conners for so long. It was hard to remember a time before her.

As the memories came flooding back, I wanted nothing more than to cry. I wanted to scream and demand to know why she left me. I wanted to cry with the frustration and anger of being left behind after she had promised me she would stay but I couldn't bring myself to.

I didn't have the strength.

I STOOD IN FRONT OF the headstone, the cold granite staring back up at me. I leaned down, placing the flowers in the vase at the base of her grave. They were long enough to cover the words that were carved into the granite.

The world was quiet all around me. I sat down in front of her grave, the ground cold beneath me. The brightness of the flowers were a cruel contrast to the gray of the world around me. I envied those who were able to sit in front of a headstone and remember the life that person lived. That granite in the ground not only held the body of Phoebe, it also held the girl I once was. The girl that didn't close herself off to those she loved. The girl who wasn't scared to get hurt. The girl who didn't fear being alone. The girl who risked everything for love. That girl died and was buried right there with Phoebe.

I had been here so many times before and yet, I didn't know what to say. It was easier six years ago. I would tell her everything that had happened at school, or what my plans were for college. Now, it felt I had said everything that needed to be said. She couldn't hear me. That stone wasn't her. She wasn't physically here. She never would be again.

Alexander would want me to talk to her. To tell her everything that had been happening in our lives. Give her good news about the case, but no news about the case was good news. Carson being assaulted wasn't good news. Examiners digging up Phoebe's body and not being able to make a definite decision about what had happened wasn't a good thing. There wasn't a single thing about this case that was a good thing. It seemed foolish that we would have ever thought of it that way.

Though, no matter how foolish it was, I listened to Alexander. I listened to what my father told me to do. I ignored everything my mind was telling me, and I began talking.

"Hey Phoebe, it's me. It's been a while. I never meant for it to be this long, but you know how things get sometimes," I whispered. My voice was quiet, as if I was worried about disturbing the dead that surrounded me. "It's been six years, Phoebe. Six years since the last time I kissed you. 6 years since the last time I saw your face. I remind myself of what it was like to kiss you. I make myself remember what it was like to hold because I am terrified that if I don't torture myself with the memories, they will begin to slip away. That you will start to slip away. And I can't lose you. Not again."

I felt the trail of tears down my face before I even realized I was crying. I reached up, not wiping the tears off of my cheeks but feeling the wet against my skin. Something in me broke.

I couldn't stop the sob that racked it's way through my body. The tears choked me, making it feel impossible to breathe. I wanted to scream. Wanted to let every emotion I hadn't been able to show in the past six years come pouring out of me at once.

I had never let her see me like this. In our relationship, I was the strong one. I was the shoulder she came to cry on. I was the rock who promised her that everything would be okay. I wasn't a strong enough rock for myself. I couldn't blindly promise myself that everything was going to be okay. Not like I did with Phoebe. Not like my family did to me.

"I don't know if I'm alive without the pain. The pain serves as a reminder. It promises me that no matter how much this hurts, no matter how difficult things get that I am still living. I don't remember how to live without the pain.

You know, it doesn't matter what happens in this trial. You won't ever know what we did to help you. This trial could go either way and you wouldn't know, and yet if this trial goes wrong. If we lose, I won't know what to do with myself. I made you a promise six years ago. I promised you that no matter what, I would make sure that he paid for what he did to you. For what he did to your family. But now, it's not just your family. It's Carson. It's every single person who hasn't come forward yet.

I have spent so fucking long fighting over this. So long just trying to figure out how to live my life without you in it. Trying to figure out how to live knowing what he did to you and the fact that I couldn't save you. This case became the one thing I held onto. The one thing I told myself would make everything all right. If this doesn't work I don't know what I will do with myself.

You aren't weak for leaving. Sometimes I think you made the right decision throwing in the towel when you did. I wish I could do that everyday but I promised you, and I can't go breaking my promise now.

I am making a new promise now. I am promising you that he is going to suffer for what he did to you. He is going to feel pain just as you did. I am going to make sure there is not a second that goes by that he is not going to be suffering. He will burn in hell if it is the last thing i do.

I love you. Fucking hell I love you more than anything else. I don't hate you for dying. I don't hate you for how you died. I know sometimes it might seem like I do, but I promise that I don't. I can't say that it would have hurt less if you had died another way. I can't say I would have rathered you die any other way because I don't know what it feels like to lose you that way.

I can say that I know how it has felt to wake up every morning the past six years and know you died because you felt there wasn't anything left on this earth that was worth staying around for. I know how it feels to go about my day knowing that no one else knows what it feels to lose you like that.

Maybe it would have hurt less if didn't take your own life. Maybe it would have given me more closure to know you didn't die willingly, but I don't think it would change anything. Because at the end of the day, you are still gone, and I still wake up alone.

Alexander once asked me how I handled it all. How I was able to wake up every morning and know that I was building a case against a man who took the person that mattered most to me. How I am able to talk with him as if he isn't the reason you aren't here. I didn't know how to answer him. I couldn't tell him the truth. The truth that I don't handle it.

I want to kick and scream every single time I hear him say your name. I want to kill him with my own bare hands every time he looks me in the eyes. I go home and I cry because I know that nothing I do will ever bring you back. Getting your father charged will not resserect you. No matter what happens in this case, you will still be dead, and I will still have to figure out how to live a life without you.

I live with the constant reminders of you. I live with them because if I don't have them, then I don't know what I have. If I can't remember the way you held my hand in Alexander's car on the way to school, or the way you would smile at me across the halls, then what will I remember?

I can feel parts of you slipping away from me. Small moments that I can't quite put my finger on anymore. If I am losing those memories now, what am I not going to remember a few years from now? Will I not remember the way your eyes looked in the morning? Or the way your jeans perfectly fit your body? What will I not be able to remember in the next few years? What memories will slip away from me? Will I know they are missing? Will I notice there is something missing in my life, or will the memory just fade without me ever looking back?

If I lose those, I will have nothing left of you. This case, this headstone with it's awful fucking inscription is all I have left of you. I can't lose those. I can't lose those memories. I can't lose you. God, I can't fucking lose you.

I used to want so much from this world. Now if I could hear you say I love you one more time, I would want nothing else. If I could just hear those words one last time. If I could just hear your voice, maybe things would get easier. Maybe I wouldn't doubt every single move I have taken in the past six years. Maybe I would believe in myself again. Maybe I would believe in others again.

It's cruel. Cruel that the one thing I want more than anything in the world is something that can't happen. I can't hear those words again. I can't hold you. I can't feel your lips on mine as a promise that we would figure everything out. It doesn't work that like that. I will never get that again."

I reached out, placing my hand on her headstone, feeling the cold engraving of the words that have haunted me for six years.

"I don't want to let you go. I want to be able to remember everything, but I can't do this anymore. I can't keep holding onto to dreams that won't ever come true. I can't keep begging the world to give me something it never will. After this case is over, I'm moving on with my life Phoebe. I'm going to find someone who will love me. Someone who wonm't leave me. I know that's not fair to you, but it's not fair to me to keep holding on like this.

I love you Phoebe Conners, a part of me always will, but I can't keep going on like this. After this case is over and the trial is finished, I am going to let you go. I am going to try and find the person I was before you. You have changed me in ways that I can't erase, but I need to get some part of me back. I need to find her again. I need to be able to live a life without you.

I hope you can forgive me. I know it's not fair to you. You didn't choose to haunt me in the way that you do, but at the end of this trial, I am stopping it."

My hands rest on the ground, pushing me up from the cold ground. The world around me is silent as I look down at the flowers.

"I love you Phoebe. I always will. Nothing will ever change that.

I let myself have one last look at her headstone before I let. This one headstone that signified 19 years of someones life. That was the only piece of her that remained on this earth. I reached down, pressing my fingers to the engraving of her name. I traced the letters with my finger one last time before walking back to the car, feeling like I had just left another piece of me there with her.

I OPENED THE FRONT door to my parents standing in the foyer. They waited for me to say something. For me to say anything that would show them that I was okay. That was all it took for me to break down again.

I collapsed into my mother's arms, letting her hold me as I cried into her shoulder. She held me as I let go of every emotion that had held me hostage, rubbing my back and whispering into my hair that everything was going to be okay. She let me go when my phone rang, assured me everything was going to be okay one more time and then set out into the kitchen.

I didn't even check to see who was calling before answering the phone.

"Hello?" I asked.

"Hey Sydney," Alexander says from the other end. "How are you doing?"

Being alright never meant the same to everyone did it? All right could mean that I was simply alive to him. It could mean that I had gotten through the day without any tears. You never know exactly what the other person means by okay.

"I'm okay," I answered.

I hear a sigh come from the other end. "It hasn't been easy for you either has it?" he whispers, his voice weak.

"No, it hasn't," I whispered.

"I really don't want to be by myself right now. I know I told you it would be best if we spent the day with ourselves and let ourselves grieve but i'm sick of grieving right now so would you like to come over and get some food? Just sit here and talk maybe?"

I wanted to tell him no. He was the reason I had spent the entire day sitting at Phoebe's grave. He was the one who said I needed to be able to grieve everything I had lost. I shouldn't have to come over when he decides he has had enough of being sad for the day.

I couldn't do that to him though. Today was hard for the both of us. We were the only two people who knew what if felt to lose Phoebe Conners. We were the only ones who knew what it was like to grieve the way we did. I might have been upset with him, but the truth was that neither of us should be alone. We needed to be with each other. With the only other person who knew what it was like to love and lose her.

"Okay."

THE WORLD WAS DARK around me as I drove to Alexander's. The roads a ghost town. Not a single sound. There was not a single soul haunting the road as I drove. Alexander met me outside of the apartment complex. He wraps his arms around me before I could even close the car door.

"I'm sorry," he mutters. "I'm sorry for expecting you to be alone today. I'm sorry for calling you only when I couldn't handle it anymore."

I wrapped my arms around his shoulders, letting him collapse against me.

"You thought you could handle it. We all overestimate ourselves at some points. What matters now is that you called. That we are both here."

He doesn't speak as he walks me up to his apartment. Boxes litter the every inch of the floor as I walk further in.

"I couldn't bring myself to unpack anything," he whispers.

I walked towards the only open box, reaching in and grabbing the book on the very top. It was then I understood why he couldn't bring himself to unpack anything else. Phoebe's favorite writer.

"It was one of Phoebe's," I hear Alexander say. I pick up my head to look up at him. "I took this copy from her house at the reception after her funeral. Only would Phoebe's parents serve food for their friends after their daughters funeral and have the audacity to call it a reception."

I nodded my head, reaching into the box to grab another. It was another Virginia Woolf.

"Where do you want these?" I asked.

Alexander looks over towards me, a small smile covering his features.

"That bookshelf over there," he tells me.

The two of us didn't speak a word the rest of the night other than to ask where something went. We spent three hours unpacking every box and putting everything away. When we were done, Alexander walks me into the kitchen where a long forgotten container of takeout sat waiting.

"I figured it was only right to order Phoebe's favorite," he tells me.

I smiled, grabbing the nearest fork and taking a bite, wincing at the cold noodles. Alexander laughs, the first real laugh I had heard the entire day and grabs the container from me.

"I was going to suggest heating it up first."

I nodded, sputtering as I ry to gt the feeling of cold noddles out of my mouth.

"You know, Phoebe would find it ironic that we are sitting here right now," Alexander says, turning around from the microwave.. "Never would anyone have thought we would sit together alone."

"She always was 10 steps ahead of us," I answered.

"Sometimes I think that maybe Phoebe knew this was going to happen. Maybe she knew when she died that her not being there would bring us together," Alexander smiled.

"She knew what she was doing bringing the two of us together," I said. "She knew that if she wasn't going to be there, she wanted the two people who meant most to have each other."

"Well, then I propose a toast to Phoebe Conners," Alexander says, holding up the steaming box of noddles.

I grabbed a soy sauce bottle next to me, lifting it in the air as Alexander begins.

"To Phoebe Conners, she's the reason the both of us are here today, and we miss her more than anything else in the world."

We clinked the articles in our hands together before setting them down and going back to eating. We sat there together, laughing as we talked about the various memories of Phoebe and the times we wished she could have seen. For the first time today, I was able to laugh about these memories. It was true that I would never get them back. Those memories would remain just that, memories, but this is what Phoebe would have wanted.

Phoebe would want Alexander and I to sit here laughing about the times we had with her. She would want us to be able to create new memories with each other. If all I had left of Phoebe Conners was those memories, I was going to make new ones around those I already had.

All felt right in the world as Alexander and I sat talking. The pain had settled in my stomach. It was still there. That pain was never going away, but it felt much better knowing the two of us both knew what it was like lose her. Both of us knew what it was like to live with the pain of after.

Before

Phoebe fell asleep in my arms that night. She was so close, and yet, I had never felt farther away from her. We hadn't spoken about what she said earlier. Deep down I knew it was true. After everything, my love wouldn't be enough to make her stay. My love wouldn't erase all of the pain she endured. I myself wasn't enough for her to want to stay.

I held her throughout the night, terrified that if I fell asleep she wouldn't be there when I woke up. I watched her as she slept, running my fingers through her hair, pressing kisses to the top of her head. The only time she moved was to turn around, placing her head in my neck. Her skin was warm against me, a constant reminder that she was still here. She was still alive. I hadn't lost her.

I engrained the look of her sleeping form into my brain. The way her muscles relaxed. The curve of her spine as she leaned into me. The look of peace on her face. Peace. For the first time since Autumn died, Phoebe looked as though she didn't have a care in the world. I had never seen that look before.

She was always on fire. Blazing through the road in front of her, never stopping for a break. Everyone knew it was only a matter of time before that fire burned out. Before the fuel ran out and the flame burned out forever. She didn't know when to stop. Phoebe never knew when to stop. She would always keep going. No matter how much it hurt or how little was left of her, she would never take a break. Because to take a break was to give up, and to give up was to accept defeat. To accept defeat would be death.

When the two of us weren't together, it didn't feel like this. Before I fell in love with her, it never pained me to watch her suffer like this. I was led to believe she deserved whatever was coming to her. Now, every second of my day was spent wishing things were different.

Maybe in some other life things were different. Phoebe and Sydney, two girls who were in love with each other. Our lives were normal. Her father had never touched her or her sister. She had Autumn still and loved everyone they were not fighting me on every little thing. For the rest of our lives, it would only be Phoebe and Sydney.

That life wasn't the one we were living though. There was nothing I could do that would erase what had happened to her. I couldn't take away the years of pain and suffering just because I loved her. My love wasn't enough. My love would never be enough.

She shifted slightly in my arms and settles back down. I held my breath, terrified that she had woken up. I didn't want this moment to be over. I didn't want her to wake up and have to continue that fight.

"I know you're awake Sydney," I hear her voice call up. "I'm not going anywhere. Go to sleep."

If only it was that easy. If only I was able to close my eyes and fall asleep with not a care in the world. When I closed my eyes, all I saw was death. The nightmares that followed were even worse. I lost Phoebe in every single one. I would be running, trying as hard as I could to get to her but no matter how far I ran, it was never enough. She was always the same distance away. I was always too late.

"I'll try," I whispered, pressing my lips to the top of her head.

NOT A NOISE SPREAD across the house the whole morning. I knew my parents were awake. I knew my siblings would be downstairs having breakfast, but not a single sound escaped the dining room. Every so often Phoebe would anxiously look at the door as if expecting someone to come barging in but no one ever did. It was just completely silent.

"It isn't always like this," I said to her as we laid in bed together.

She looked up at me from under her eyelashes, giving me a soft smile.

"I know."

Neither of us say anything to each other as we lay there. Her hand rested on my stomach, tracing shapes up and down. My chin rested on her head, holding her as close to me as possible.

"I didn't expect you to stay after last night," I hear her whisper. "I would have thought that would have been a breaking point for you."

There wasn't anything I could tell her that I hadn't told her a thousand times over. When you loved someone you didn't leave at the slightest inconvenience. You didn't leave because things got hard. You stayed with them. No matter what happens, you always stay with them.

"You ask me to be here anytime, Phoebe Conners, and I am here."

Phoebe pushes herself onto her elbows, pressing her lips to mine. It didn't start gentle like her kisses usually started out as. Her kiss felt urgent as if this was the last time she would ever get to kiss me. I tried to slow her down and kiss her slowly to let her know everything was going to be okay, but she kept going. Kept going as if this was the last time she would be able to kiss me.

I held her to me. I kissed her with just as much force as she was kissing me. I kissed her like it was going to be my last time as well because when you loved someone as much as I loved Phoebe

Conners, you treat every day as if it is going to be the last one you have together.

PHOEBE CLOSED OFF AGAIN after that day. The day following was the worst. I would have to call her name multiple times so that she would answer my question. She looked around every corner, constantly checked over her shoulder, and walked faster than usual throughout the school. It was like she was trying to run away from something. I knew not to ask. She wouldn't have told me if I had asked.

The day after that, she was gone. No phone calls, no texts and no notes. That same as it was before. Just disappeared. I texted her every hour. Begging her to at least give me a two letter answer. I got nothing but her reading my texts.

I wanted to drive over there. I wanted to barge in through the door and ensure everything was alright. I wanted to be able to save her. I wanted to fucking kill him. I wanted to take away all of her pain. Wring his neck to make sure his death wasn't a slow one. Make sure he felt just as much pain as he had caused her. Only then would I be able to make sure she was completely safe.

I picked her up at the house that next morning. I was expecting at least some form of greeting. Maybe an apology. She gave me nothing. She was silent throughout the entire drive. I kept looking over at her, trying desperately to catch her eye, but she would look away and out the window. I parked the car in my spot and turned over to her, resting my arm on her shoulder so she would turn and look at me.

"Phoebs," I asked. "Are you okay?"

She turned over to look at me for the first time throughout that entire car ride. Her smile was forced. I didn't even need to look in her eyes to know there was nothing about that smile that meant anything.

"I'm okay, Syd," she answered.

I wanted to believe her. I wanted to be able to take her answer at face value and leave it at that. I couldn't. With her, you couldn't do that.

I went out of my way to walk her to her classes. I sat with her my car duing lunch. Her hand was in mine as I drove her home. Not a word was spoken. I pressed a kiss on her forehead before she left the car. I wanted to force her back into the car. I wanted to drive her far away from this place, but the look on her face told me to step away. Told me only danger resided within those four walls. Danger that I couldn't protect her from.

I drove back home, promising myself that everything was going to be okay. That wasn't Phoebe. That was a shell of Phoebe. She had a rough day yesterday. That was the only problem. Maybe she had overslept. Maybe things just hadn't been going wrong. I ignored the nagging at the back of my mind that told me something worse had happened.

I spent the night shadowing my father at the department. It was the first time he had invited me back in over a month. For the first time in a while, everything seemed almost normal. The officers struck up casual conversation. My father would have me stand outside the interrogation room and tell him questions to ask when he came back inside. It was just like how it had been before Phoebe. That was until 11:30 that night. That was until a call came through needing backup for possible underage drinking and public intoxication. A name came through next. Phoebe Conners.

Phoebe. Something had happened. A look of unbridled anger filled my fathers face. He grabs my arm, dragging me out to the car.

He was waiting for me to say something as he drove. He wanted me to admit he was right. Wanted me to say I should have listened to him when he told me she was more trouble than she was worth. I wouldn't say it. I stared out the window, trying to pretend like I didn't see the flashing of the lights coming from the top of the car. Trying to pretend that I wasn't currently on the way to take Phoebe into custody after she had relapsed.

My heart plummeted as my father pulled into the school parking lot. Distantly I saw a figure sitting against the wall, a bottle pressed to it's lips. Phoebe. She was right there. I wanted to scream at her to stop. I wanted to get everyone out of here. She wouldn't want anyone seeing this. She wouldn't even want me seeing this.

Another officer knocked on the window, my father immediately rolling it down to get the needed information. I grabbed the door handle, opening the door to race towards Phoebe. I heard my father shout from behind me and felt an arm latch onto mine. I fight against the weight holding me there, delirious to everything else other than Phoebe. She needed me. I needed to get to her. I needed to help her.

"What the hell do you think you're doing, Garcia?" I distantly hear my father demand.

I try to pull away, but he grips my arm tighter.

"I have to get to her. Let me go," I growl.

He doesn't let go. He pushes me behind him before walking towards Phoebe, his hand resting on the gun at his belt.

"Phoebe Conners," he calls out. "Come on; we've talked about this."

I had never seen that look on her face before. The look of drunk amusement. The look of someone who would not remember this the next morning.

"Ah, Mr. Garcia, it's such a pleasure to see you again." she laughs. "Bet you were just waiting for this moment."

"Ms. Conners, we have talked about the law. You can't drink on school property. Let alone drink as a minor," he tells her.

Phoebe snorts, taking the bottle and a long swig, not even wincing as it went down.

"I bet you can't wait to put me behind bars, Garcia. You know, with me corrupting your daughter and everything. Turning your favorite daughter against you."

Phoebe laughs at the look of astonishment on his face.

"It's not much of a secret that you hate me Garcia. Don't think I hear about how you talk about me. Don't think I don't know what everyone thinks I have been doing to Sydney. That I'm secretly brainwashing her. That I'm holding her hostage and she is suffering stockholm syndrome. I've heard it all."

She slowly stands up, stumbling as she stalks towards him.

"You are part of the problem in this world, Mr. Garcia," her voice raises.

My father starts to unlock the hold that keeps his gun in place. I fought against the arms holding me in place. I needed to get her away. My father was going to kill her. If she came closer he was going to fucking kill her. She continues closer. My father reaches down and grabs his gun, holding it in his hands as he trained it on her. She didn't even stop. Just kept getting closer, as if she didn't even see the gun.

"You were given a position of power and now you believe you can do anything you want. Like train a gun on me. You have no true reason to shoot me. I am not doing anything that puts you in a position of harm, and yet here you are, shoving a gun in my face. Do you think that if you pull the trigger you can convince everyone here that I was delirious and trying to kill you? That I myself had a gun pointed at you? Maybe your other officrs might, but you are going to have to try a lot harder to try and convince Sydney."

I saw the vein in my fathers neck pulse as she said my name. Phoebe laughed as she saw it, looking past my father towards me.

Her eyes go dark as they meet the officer holding me back. She stares at us for a second before looking back towards my father.

"I think you know you won't be able to convince her. You know that if you kill me she will never forgive you. She would spend the rest of her life hating you. But is it worth it? Is the years of hate and resentment worth saving her from me?"

I feel the hands holding me loosen the smallest bit. I twist around, breaking free. Phoebe's eyes glance over towards me, a smile breaking out on her face as she sees me running towards her. My father drops his gun, using her moment of distraction to pin her arms behind her back and place the cuffs on her wrists. She doesn't try and fight against him. I watch as she begins to walk towards the direction of the car, but my father stops her, turning her around so she is looking him in the eyes.

"You are lucky I didn't fucking shoot you right then and there. You have no idea what I am capable of girl. This is the last fucking time you understand. Your father isn't going to be able to do anything about it."

"What the fuck is the matter with you?" I screamed. I could feel my heart in my throat. My hands were shaking at my side. He had held her at gun point. He would have shot her. He would have shot her if I hadn't been standing right there.

"Sydney Garcia, move out of my way," he demands. I moved myself in front of the car, preventing him from putting her anywere.

"You didn't answer my question. What the fuck is the matter with you?"

"She was delirious. I did what I had to do to protect myself and my fellow officers."

"She wasn't fucking delirous."

"Sydney Garcia move out of the way of this car, or I will arrest you for obstruction of justice."

My eyes meet Phoebes as she choked down laughter. She didn't think he would actually arrest me. To her this was just an empty threat. I knew my father. There was nothing about this was an empty threat.

"Fine," I said, holding my hands out in front of me. "Arrest me."

Fear fills her eyes as my father grabs another pair of cuffs and wraps them around my wrists.

"Don't do this Sydney. Don't fucking do this," she screams.

My father didn't even spare her a second glance before locking the cuffs around my wrists. No words were spoken as she shoved both of us into the car and sat in the front seat. Miranda Rights. He never once read the Miranda Rights.

"You didn't read any Miranda Rights," I yelled to him. "You are the goddamn police chief, and you didn't read the Miranda Rights. Fuck you."

PHOEBE'S HEAD RESTED on my shoulder as we sat on the floor of the holding cell. I could feel everyone's eyes on us as we sat there. There had been moments of pandemonium since we were brought in. Officers tried getting my father to explain what had happened. My mother was called in by my father. She had stood in front of the holding cell demanding to know what I had done. I didn't say a word. Didn't even look in her direction. This was just as much her fault as it was my fathers.

My hand was wrapped around her's as her face was tucked into my shoulder. I didn't want her to have to see the seering bright of the flourescents when she woke up. We hadn't spoken a word about what had happened. I knew the full effect of the night hadn't hit her yet. Her relapse hadn't hit her yet, but it would. I knew when she woke up, there would be many pieces that would have to be picked up.

My father hadn't stopped staring at me since my mother had come into his office. I had watched as she cried into his shoulder as he stared out at me. Our last level of trust had been broken tonight. He had pointed a gun at her. He had threatend to shoot her. He wold have killed her. If I had not been standing there he would have fucking shot her. Nothing would have happened to him. The other officer would have lied about what had happened. Body cam footage would have mysteriously gone missing.

Phoebe shifts, raising her head, groaning as the light hits her eyes.

"Jesus fucking Christ, I have a headache," she mutters.

My hand snakes around her waist, holding her closer towards me. I didn't know what to say. I didn't want to have to be the one to explain it to her. To promise her that everything was going to be okay. I couldn't promise her everything was going to be okay. I didn't even know if I could form the words.

"Do you remember anything of what happened?" I whispered.

I feel her shake my head into my shoulder. "Everything before your father pointed that gun at me is a complete blur."

A lump appeared in my throat as Phoebe turned towards me. Her eyes filled with fear.

"There was a vodka bottle. I remember smelling smoke."

Tears filled her eyes. Her grip on my hands tightened.

"Tell me I didn't Sydney."

When I didn't answer, she stands up, her hands gripping her hair.

"Tell me I fucking didn't Sydney," she screams.

"I'm so sorry," I whispered.

She didn't even try to stop the tears from spilling down her face. Her hands tore at the base of her hair, slumping against the wall. That was when she started screaming. Her head was slamming into the wall, the tears mixing with screams.

Over her screams, I heard the opening of a door and the pounding of feet against the floor but I was too worried about getting her to stop. She was going to hurt herself. She would get a concussion if she kept going.

"Sydney, what the hell is happening?" I hear my father yell from the other side of the bars. I didn't answer.

I placed my hand against the wall so she couldn't pound her head against the wall. My heart pounded in my chest as her screams quieted into quiet whimpers.

"It's going to be okay Phoebs," I whispered.

I was lying. We both knew it wasn't going to be okay. Phoebe didn't answer. She just sat there, her eyes vacant of all emotions.

"Sydney, what is happening?" my father demands.

Phoebe looks past me at my father, her eyes slightly darkening when she sees him before turning back towards me.

"You have to get out of here Sydney," she whispers.

I shook my head, reaching to grab her hand put she pulls away.

"Get out of here Sydney."

I reach out to grab her hand again but she flinches.

"Get the fuck out Sydney," she screams.

I rear back, my heart pounding in my chest. She watches me, her eyes darker than I had ever seen them as I slowly picked myself up off the floor and walks towards the bars of the cell. My mother grabs the keys from my father, fumbling with them before unlocking the cell and grabbing my arm to pull me out.

She holds me at an arms length as if checking to see if there were any bruises before wrapping me in a hug.

"We will talk about this when we get home Sydney," she whispers. "For now, let's get out of here."

I look back towards the cell where Phoebe sits, her head in her hands, her shoulders shaking.

"Sydney," my father calls, beckoning towards the door.

"I'm sorry, Phoebe," I whispered just loud enough for her to hear before following my parents out the door.

The three of us walked out to the car, my parents whispering to each other as I followed distantly behind them. My mother opened the back door to the car, waiting for me to get in before closing it behind me.

None of us said a word as we drove. I could feel my mothers eyes on me as my father drove. My head was resting on the cool window, trying desperately not to let the tears escape. I had just left her. She needed me and I had left her. I didn't know what would happen to her. For the first time she had had something to fight for. Now that she relapsed, she would feel she didn't have anything left. I couldn't lose her. Not like this.

The clock read 11:30 pm as we pulled into the driveway. I couldn't bring myself to get out of the seat. It felt as though my entire body was made of cement. My mother and father began whispering in the front seat again, but I couldn't bring myself to make out what they were saying.

"Sydney, we have to get inside," my mothers whispers, reaching back and grabbing my hand.

I couldn't bring myself to do anything but nod my head. I wanted to move. I wanted to get out of this seat and move. To get up and walk away from this and be okay. To know that Phoebe was going to be okay. I couldn't bring myself to though. I couldn't bring myself to move.

My father walks out before my mother does. He leaves the car, unlocking the door closing it behind him. My mother walks towards my side of the car, opening the door and beckoning me out.

"Come on Sydney," she whispers, grabbing my hand, beginning to pull me out. "It's time to get inside."

She walked me inside the house, taking me up the stairs and into my room. She sits me down on my bed, stepping away as I sit there.

"We need to get ready for bed," she tells me.

I followed her into the bathroom, my body not feeling like my own. Everything felt distant, as if I was watching from a distance. I felt her wiping off my face before handing me a toothbrush. I took it from her, silently pleading her to leave. Her being here only made it worse. My mother grabs pajamas as I brush my teeth, putting them down on my bed before walking back into the bathroom.

"Get changed before you go to bed. We will talk about this in the morning," she whispers.

She hesitates a minute, pausing in the doorway. She turns around to face me, tears filling her eyes.

"You better have a plan mija. I won't be able to hold your father back for much longer. You might think you love her, but is she worth losing your family over? Is one person worth losing all of us?"

She stood for a second more, as if waiting for a response, before turning on her heel and walking out of the room. The world around me was silent. The door was open just enough that I could see a light shining underneath my parents door. I watched until that light went out, the only light source now gone. The darkness consusmed the world, but I didn't shy away. For the first time, I found comfort in the darkness. In the darkness I couldn't see my world falling down around me.

After

I feel asleep on Alexander's couch that night. I told myself I needed to pull myself together. I would wake up the next morning and be expected to act as though all was normal. You didn't get an excuse for the next day. The days after would hurt less. I had made it through six years. Six years without her. I could make it in the days after. I could make it through the next year.

I couldn't remember the day after Phoebe died. I could remember small snippets overtime but was never able to piece together an entire day. I could remember small bits of my parents bringing food up to my room. Cindy had run up and cried into my shoulder, my parents chasing after her to try and get her out of the room. My mother had come and sit on the side of my bed at one point, but I couldn't remember anything past that.

Alexander had agreed it was the same way. He could remember taking his car and driving around. He didn't remember where he went or how long it had taken him to get there, but he does remember a lake. He told me he had sat in front of a lake until his parents came looking for him the next day.

We might never be able to piece together every part of that day, and mauve it was best that way. Maybe it was best we didn't remember what had happened in the weeks following. Maybe it was a way of our own brains protecting us. Protecting us against the pain it knew we wouldn't be able to handle.

In the weeks after Phoebe died, there had been calling hours. Neither Alexander or I could bring ourselves to go. We couldn't go and apologize to her family. Tell them with honesty that we were sorry for their loss. They weren't the ones who had lost anything. They were the reason she was gone. My parents didn't urge me to go. Never even asked the question. Alexander had come over to the house. We had sat there in silence together, neither of us having enough strength to say anything.

The funeral was the day after. Neither Alexander or I could get out of it. My mother watched as I got dressed in the black dress she had handed me only seconds before. After she had stood me in front of the mirror, flattening my dress. I didn't recoginie the girl staring back at me. That wasn't me. I didn't have the dark circles under my eyes. My hair was never this flat. This wasn't me.

Her casket had been closed. She had never wanted it too be open. I felt the eyes on me as I walked up towards the front, my parents following close behind. My hands were shaking as my eyes settled on the picture set right next to her casket. The thought came into my head that I would never see that smile again. I would never feel her hair between my hands again. I would never trace the wrinkles that appeared by her eyes when she smiled.

A scream had escaped my lips. A scream that I had been holding back for so long. My father held me as I collapsed, the tears that hadn't been shed in a week finally coming pouring out. My mother and father had walked me to the back of the church. They sat me next to Alexander, his hand reaching out and grabbing mine. When I had looked up I had seen tears trailing down his cheeks. He tried to force a smile on his face, but it didn't hold the weight he wanted it to.

We had sat there and listened to what her family had to say about her. Her mother saying she was the only thing she had left after Autumn died. That she couldn't believe she had lost the only two daughters she had. Her father had talked about the joy she brought him. That he didn't know what he was going to do with his life now that she was gone.

My mother had wrapped her hand around my shoulder, holding me to her chest as he spoke. I wanted to fight against her. I wanted to make him pay. Make him hurt for what he had done. Make him hrt int he same way Phoebe had hurt, but I didn't have the strength. I couldn't get myself out of that pew. Couldn't move.

Phoebe was buried the next day. I stood in the back of the crowd, holding an umbrella as watched that wooden box being set gently in the ground. It had moved so slowly, as if just prolongng in inevitable. Alexander was no where to be seen on that day.

I was the only one who remained after the dirt had been shoveled over and the temporary marker set into the ground. The rain was pouring down around me, but I couldn't determine the difference between my tears and the rain. I stood there in the same black dress I had worn the night before, staring at the space on the ground that now contained Phoebe Conners.

I was alone after that. Lindsey stopped coming around. Alexander started pulling away. My parents, no matter how sympathetic they were, were happy their daughter would have her life back. They were thankful their child would never see Phoebe Conners again. She was alone in her grief.

Alexander was the only one who knew what it could possibly feel like and even then, he could never truly understand. He had lost his best friend. He had lost the only person he had for four years. I had lost my future. I had lost the person I had revolved all of my plans around. I lost my entire world.

Looking back on it now, I know how immature it was to think this way, but one never truly is thinking straight when they have just lost someone. I was never the only one. I had Alexander the entire time. I had just never wanted to reach out. Never wanted to make that relalization to myself that I wasn't okay. When you lose someone that you loved, you feel as though you are the only one going through this pain. That you are the only one who loved this person. It doesn't matter how many people have lost someone. You will always feel as though you are the only one.

I had a normal life before Phoebe. I had a family I was close with. I had my future entirely planned out. Our relationship wasn't healthy. Nothing about it was good for either of us, but I would not trade what I learned from it. I gained pain. I learned what it was like to lose someone like this. But I also learned I was stronger than that pain. I hadn't let myself be swallowed by the pain throughout any other this. I learned just how much I could take. Just what it took for me to break.

Neither of us could ever go back to who we were before Phoebe. We had lost a part of ourselves with her, but we could move on. We could find better parts of ourselves. We could be there for each other when we hurt. Those first few years hadn't been ideal. We had too much pride. We were to scared to admit to ourselves or each other that we might not be in the way.

When I fell asleep that night, I dreamed of her. I dreamed of holding her in my arms one last time and telling her how much I loved her. She smiled at me, pressing her lips to mine. It didn't feel like goodbye this time. If felt like a promise. A promise that we would find each other again. It wasn't goodbye. It was a promise of a future that was never to come.

ALEXANDER WAS STILL sleeping on the floor of his bedroom when I woke up that morning. I winced as I set my feet on the hardwood floor, the cold sending a shock through me. The takeout containers were still on the container where we had left them the night before. I grabbed my phone from the charger, ignoring the thousands of messages I received from my mother the night before and pressing call next to Reno's name. It didn't take him more than 10 seconds to pick up the phone, his voice sounding awake and alert despite the early hour.

"Good morning Sydney," he says from the other end of the phone.

"It was a needed day yesterday, but I'm ready to get back at it. Can we meet for breakfast this morning? I'm calling Carson after this. I think it's time we finally finish what needs to be done with this case."

I heard a chuckle before Reno speaks. "I was thinking the same thing Ms. Garcia. Can you meet at Literary Tea in 10 minutes? I'm already there."

"I'm on my way."

IT TOOK A GOOD MINUTE to get Alexander out of bed. He wasn't fully impressed that I had already called Reno and was meeting him at 7:15, but after some pleading he agreed. As he was getting ready, I called Carson. She was just as alert as Reno had been. When I asked her if she was willing to meet, she agreed instantly.

Before we left, I called my father, asking him to get something ready for me so I could pick it up on the way there. I had spent so long avoiding the memories. Stepping away from them because I knew I was never going to make anymore. I couldn't keep picking and choosing what I wanted to remember. If I truly wanted to remember everything, then I needed to look back on the things I had tried so hard to forget.

Alexander was confused as we pulled into my driveway. I promised him that it would just be a few seconds. I just needed to grab something. My father was waiting by the doorway as I knocked. A smile covered his face as he stood there, holding the box out in front of him.

"I was wondering when you would want this," he laughs.

I don't answer, but pull him into a hug.

"Thank you for never giving up on me," I whispered, feeling the tears prick at the back of my eyes.

He wraps his arms around me, resting his chin on the top fo my head.

"I always knew you would come back. You just neeed some time."

I hugged him one last time, promising I would be back after the meeting before opening the door, clutching the box to my chest.

"What is that?" Alexander asks as I approach the car.

"Phoebe Conners," I muttered. "Everything she ever told me. Everything we ever did together. Everything is right here."

ALEXANDER FOLLOWED Reno inside. I promised him I would come in when Carson got here. He knew I was stalling but said nothing. I sat on the hood of the car, the box feeling heavy in my hands. I hadn't opened it since I had first come back from New York. After meeting with Jonathan Conners I had shut it away Closed off that part of my mind. I didn't want to think about what these memories signified. Didn't want to have to go through everything Phoebe had ever told me and relive those times. It had been easier to shut it off. Forget it had ever happened.

This box could be what saved us. It could hold all of the answers to everything we had been searching for. I couldn't tuck away the memories anymore. This was what I needed. This is what my team needed. This is what Phoebe Conners needed.

I heard wheels upon the pavement. I looked up, Carson moving to stand in front of me.

"Are you okay?" she asks.

I feel her squeeze my hand, giving me a reassuring smile.

"I'm okay," I whispered. "Just so ready for this to all be done."

"Then lets go finish this. For Phoebe. For Autumn."

Alexander and Reno already had drinks waiting as we walked in. I take my seat next to Alexander, setting the box down on the table.

"Six years ago I wrote down everything Phoebe Conners had ever told me. Every little detail about her life she had deemed necessary to say. I never told her I did any of this. She doesn't know this exists. After she died, I took all of the pictures the two of us had together and this document and shoved it into a box. It's all right here. This is what will win us this case."

A smile covers Reno's features as he takes off the lid of the box, reaching in and grabbing the stack of papers stapled together.

"Let's get going then."

THE FOUR OF US SAT there for three hours. Reading through every last word I had written. Looking through every picture I had taken of the two of us. It felt as though a part of me had been ripped open. I had shoved these memories back for so long, it was as though I was reliving them. Every little moment I had forgotten over the years was now right here. Right in front of me. Staring me down. Pleading with me to remember. I hadn't realized how many of these memories had slipped my mind. I had wanted to keep these memories. I was so terrified of losing them, but they hurt. These memories were the only things left of Phoebe that I had, but remembering them hurt as much as forgetting them would.

Remembering the good times meant I had to recognize that I wouldn't have any more of those moments. Forgetting them meant she was gone forever. I never realized how little I remembered of her until I opened this box. All of this. All of these memories were the memories of the woman I loved. I couldn't pick and choose what I wanted to remember. I couldn't choose to remember the moments when the two of us were happy. When there was nothing plaguing our minds over the times when I held her while she cried. The times when she laid in my bed, curled into my side because the world was too much to handle.

Reno and Alexander sat next to each other at one end of the table, flipping through page by page of Phoebe's life. Carson and I sat there looking through all of the pictures. Each and every one brought back I memory I didn't know I had forgotten.

She was smiling in every single one. That smile I used to tell myself I would do anything to see again. Her smile that I hadn't seen in six years was right there. Her hair was the same shade of red I remembered it being. The bright red as if it was on fire. I could feel it in my hands. Could feel the soft strands between my fingers.

"She always looked so happy," I hear Carson say.

I move my eyes to the picture Carson was holding. Phoebe's hair was flush against the ground, her eyes closed tight. Her hands were resting on the ground, her fingers spread apart as if to feel the morning dew in between her fingers. A smile lightly played at her lips.

"Autumn always looked like this. Was always smiling. I would always ask her why she was always so positive. Told her always being happy was slightly unsettling. I never stopped to appreciate it until I realized what was going on in her life. Even with all of the shit she went through, she was always happy. No matter what, she was grateful for what she did have," Carson whispers, tears pricking her eyes.

"Phoebe didn't believe she was worth anything after Autumn died. She never saw herself ever being older than Autumn. Never saw a life after 18. When she turned 19, I thought maybe she would finally understand. She had made it. She could keep going if she had made it a year. It was different than just not seeing a future. She didn'mt understand how someone like her could live when someone like Autumn didn't. I saw pieces of Autumn in her everyday. I never met Autumn, but I listened when she described her.

She was so full of light. She shined brighter than anyone else I have ever met. She cared. When she loved you, she cared more than you could ever believe one person could care. She saw the good in the world. Despite the shitty life she had been given, she saw the good in the world. She believed there was good out there. She was patient. She was good.

I know other's didn't see her the way I did. I only saw her like this because I was in love with her. That love blinded me from a lot. That relationship wasn't healthy for any of us. I went into it with the mentality that I could change her. I would be able to fix her. She went in looking for a distraction. Anything to take her mind off of what was happening in her life. In no way was it healthy for either of us but we fell in love with each other. We looked past why we had gotten into the relationship in the first place and truly fell in love with each other's souls."

Carson sets the picture down, grabbing my hand, tears trailing down her cheek.

"She would be so proud of you Sydney. So beyond proud."

I nodded my head, the words feeling stuck in my throat.

"Sydney, this is the best piece of evidence we have in the case so far," Reno says, looking up from the stapled document. "This proves he assaulted both her and Autumn. Do you have anything else? Anything she might have written in her own handwriting? Something we can say was directly from her.

The thought came into my mind before I could block it out. I had shoved that so far back in my mind. Hidden the paper because

I never wanted to see it again. Never wanted to have to read those words again.

"Her suicide note," I whispered, my voice sounding foreign to my ears.

"Do you still have it? Could you get it to us before the trial?" Reno asks.

I nodded my head, my entire body feeling as though it weighed a ton.

"Good, that's good. I need you to get it. I need you to bring it to me. We have a date for the trial. We go into court on the 31st."

I snap up, my heart pounding in my chest. The 31st. In less than a month, we were going to be finishing this. In less than a month I would finally see him in that courtroom. In less than a month, the end would begin. In less than a month, everything I have spent the last six years fighting for would finally be happening.

"I'll get it to you tomorrow," I told Reno.

Reno smiles, placing the document in the bottom of the box.

"Good, because we are meeting Mr. Conners tomorrow. If I were to suggest something, I would say you bring it tomorrow. Maybe read it to him. It would do him good to remember the evidence against him in this trial."

Alexander and I met Reno at the prison the next day. I was highly aware of the paper in my pocket. Of the weight it would hold against him.

"Do you have it?" Reno asks as he stands in front of the gated door.

I nodded, reaching into my pocket and holding out the letter. "It's here."

He nods his head, turning back towards the door.

"Read it to him if you can. If you can't just tell him you have it. Make him fear that you

have it."

Alexander reaches down to grab my hand.

"Don't read it," he whispers. "Don't do that to yourself. Reading it to him will elicit no emotion. He won't feel bad for what he has done. He won't feel anything. Just let him know you have it."

He was right, and I knew that, but some part of me still wanted to read it to him. To force him to listen to the words his daughter had written. To make him listen to what her last thoughts were before she took her own life. It wouldn't do anything. He wouldn't feel anything. They were just words. He would never feel sorry. Would never feel remorse for what he did. He was incapable.

I followed two steps behind Reno as we walked through the hallway. I held my head high. Didn't let anyone see the emotions running through my body. The thoughts spilling into my head. This was the last chance I had to make Conners believe I wasn't worried. That I knew we would win this trial, no matter what he brought against us.

I didn't wait outside the room. I didn't stop to look in on him. I knew that if I looked in there and he wasn't dead, I was just going to make myself more angry. No matter what condition he was in, as long as he was alive, it was still more than he deserved.

"Hello, Jonathan," I declared, sitting down in front of her and opening the file in front of me.

A smile covered his face as he looked over at me.

"Well you are in a rare form today Sydney Garcia. Tell me, what brings that smile to your face?"

"Well, Johnathan, I realized today that this will be the last time I will ever have to see you outside a courtroom. That's why I'm smiling. I'm sitting here smiling because I know that when I walk into that courtroom, and when I look the jury in the eyes and tell them everything, everything you did to your children. I get to sit there and watch as you burn, and I will do nothing but smile."

Alexander, follows me in, taking a seat next to me.

"I see you brought your lakey in with you. Tell me Alexander Chadwick, how do you feel about this case going to trial?"

"I am enjoying the thought of watching you crash and burn in front of me," he answers.

Jonathan's face twists into a smile.

"This may not be the last time Ms. Garcia. I don't plan on pleading guilty because, as far as anyone on that jury knows, I am not guilty. I may have to stay here because of abuse towards my children and my wife, and I can deal with that because it's only a matter of time before I get out. But I never touched Autumn or Pheobe. I never did that to them," Jonathan says.

"You can't deny that you raped Carson Keller. If you assaulted Carson Keller, then her statement also says that you raped Autumn. With all of the evidence presented, including a confession by Phoebe Conners and her suicide note, I am confident a jury will convict you. It doesn't matter if you plead guilty Jonathan. Every piece of evidence towards you being guilty is stacked against you.

I stalked closer towards him. He doesn't shy away, just continuing to stare me down.

"See, Johnathan, that's the problem with people like you. You don't believe anything bad could ever happen to you. You are so filled with your ego that you don't think anything bad will ever happen to you. I've been told multiple times you are a narcissist and a psychopath. I was told you physically couldn't feel remorse for your actions. That doesn't mean you didn't do them.

The two of us were around Phoebe Conners when you did everything to her. We were the ones who held her when she cried. You may have been able to pay your way out of something initially but not anymore. No coroner, jury, or judge will take a penny of your money. And that, Jonathan Conners, is why I am smiling. Because I know that you will finally get what you deserve."

I wanted to see fear in his eyes. Wanted to see emotion in his cold, dead self for once. His smile takes a dark turn, his eyes darkening.

"This interview is over. I want you out of this room," he answered. He sounded as though he was ready to lose every bit of composure he had left.

"Try and kick us out, but you know the truth Jonathan. You know there is nothing you will be able to do to convince the jury that you are innocent," I yelled out as Reno shepherded us towards the door. "Start counting your days Jonathan, because after the 31st you are going to spend the rest of your life, wasting away in this hellhole."

THE COUNTDOWN TO THE trial had started. We had 17 days to get anything else into court. 17 days to collect anything else that would get him to stay behind bars. I submitted Phoebe's suicide note, not reading it before I did. I couldn't read those words again. Couldn't sit there and hear her voice in my head, telling me that she was out of pain. That it didn't hurt anymore.

Reno encouraged us to find whatever we could. Go through our own homes again. Look through our phones. Try and find something at the Conners house. The Conners house.

We hadn't searched the Conners house for anything after Phoebe died. Her mother would never have allowed it. Her mother had closed off the house, tried to sell it for years. It never sold. No one wanted to live with the ghosts that haunted that home.

Neither Alexander nor I would ever be able to convince her to let us search through it. Never would give us the time of day to even begin to ask. She had stopped answering calls from our numbers long ago.

When Alexander first approached me about the idea, I told him it was insane. In no world would it work, but the more I thought about it, the more it made sense. The more it seemed like the proper thing to do.

When we told Reno our idea, he told us we were fucking crazy. There was absolutly no way either of us had the money to buy the Conners house, and even if we did, it wouldn't look good in the press. It would make us look like we were trying to hide something.

It took five days of Alexander and I constantly bringing it up, until he finally agreed. It was the only way we would be able to get the important information that we needed. He made us agree that one of us would live there. One of us would spend at least a year before trying to sell it again. Alexander already had an apartment, and I was still living in my childhood bedroom. It wasn't even up for debate. I was the one who was going to be living in the Conners house.

Reno put in the work to make sure the press wouldn't know Alexander and I bought the house. At this point in the case, any bit of bad press could go against us. And we only had 10 days left.

Everything was set in motion. The two of us put in an offer, making sure our names stayed anonymous. Mrs. Conners had accepted that offer immediately but had one request. The house purchase was contingent on a meeting between the new and current owners.

Alexander was convinced we were completely fucked. Once she learned it was us that put in the offer, she would never allow us to buy the house. She wanted to stay out of the case. Stay as far away from the reminders of what her life was like as she possibly could. Having us buy the house would only bring those memories right to the surface.

Reno told us to stay anonymous during the entire process. Up until the point where we met her, she couldn't know who we were. We strictly communicated through emails. She sounded excited in each one. Telling us how wonderful the house was and how excited she was to be getting rid of it.

We met on day 7. One week. One week for us to get enough evidence to put him behind bars forever. I laid awake the night before, my mind tossing and turning over ever scenario of what could happen. There was still a chance we could be turned away. She could tell us the same thing she told us six years ago. She could demand we never speak to her again. That we don't involve in any further in the case.

I couldn't stop the glimmer of hope that stuck in the back of my brain. What if it worked? What if she sold us the house? What if we found something? What if this last piece of evidence would be just the thing we needed to be able to cement our case? There was still a chance. We weren't down and out yet.

Alexander didn't have a shred of confidence when I picked him up the next morning. His leg bounced up in down in the passenger seat, his hands wringing in his lap. I knew there wasn't any use of consoling him. He wouldn't believe me even if I did. He knew Mrs. Conners better than I did. I could almost see the thoughts running through his head. The doubt that this would work. The fear of what would happen if it didn't.

My heart rate quickened as we pulled into the all familiar driveway. I felt a sense of deja-vu, having to stop myself from looking over at the passenger seat. She wasn't going to be sitting there. Phoebe was never going to be there.

The two of us sat in the car for a moment, trying to muster the courage to actually go up to the house. Mrs. Conners wasn't here yet. We had made sure we came early. This was our first time seeing the house since Phoebe died. This was the place where Phoebe died. Six years ago I sat on these steps, her suicide note clutched in my hand as I watched the flashing lights of the ambulance drift off into the distance.

The feeling of the wood on the banister was familiar. I felt a pull in my chest as I saw the front door. There was still a dent from where I had rammed myself into it. I hear the creak of the steps and turn around, Alexander following me onto the porch. He stops when he sees the door, his hands shaking at his sides. He moves to lean against the railing of the porch, his had going to his hands.

"What the fuck are we doing Sydney?" he whispers? "I mean this is her house. She died in this house and now we want to buy it? Her father raped her in this house. Autumn took her own life in this house. What the actual fuck are we doing?"

I move to stand next to him, leaning against that railing. The feeling of the peeling paint and splitering wood dug into my elbows.

"We are doing this because we need to find whatever Phoebe left in this house. You and I have both known for a long time she wouldn't have just given us everything. She left something in here. Autumn had to have left something in here. Something that if we find, could win us this case," I answer, reaching out and grabbing his hand. "Would she have wanted this house to stay in the hands of her parents? This house that she holds her favorite memories of Autumn? The house that holds memories of the times you were there for her when no one else was. She would want someone to reclaim it. Someone to remember all the good that happened in that house. The memories she cherished up until the very end."

The sound of tires against gravel pulled us out of our thoughts. Alexander's grip on my hand tightened as the car slowed and we watched as the door to the drivers side opened. My heart pounded in my ears as our eyes met. Mrs. Conners didn't move. She just stared, her eyes filling with anger.

"Mrs. Conners," I finally say, my voice coming out choked.

Before I could take a step towards her she is sitting back down in the car. We hear the sounds of a cars engine being turned on. Taht was it. That was our last chance and we blew it.

I fell Alexander's hand tear out of mine and see him running towards the car, throwing himself in front of it so she couldn't turn the car around.

"Please, Genevieve. Just hear us out," he pleads.

The door to the car slams opens, Phoebe's mother stalking out, her eyes filled with rage.

"What gives you the right? How could you possibly think I would ever sell the house to you two. You two are the reason I am even selling the thing in the first place. You just couldn't get enough. Couldn't stop at taking my husband away from me. Couldn't stop at making me wake up every single morning and remember that I don't have children because of you. That wasn't enough was it? You just needed to keep going. You needed to keep ruining the Conners name. You just needed to keep taking piece by piece away from us until there is nothing left?" she screams.

"Mrs. Conners, your husband raped your chidren," I shouted. I regret the words as soon as they leave my mouth but I couldn't take them back. She couldn't keep pretending that her husband had never done anything wrong. She had confessed he had hit her. That he had hit her children. He was the reason there was nothing left of the Conners. He was the only one who could be blamed.

"Your husband is the reason you no longer have your children. He raped them and hit them until they believed there was no way out other than death."

Tears shine in her eyes as she glares at me.

"You knew this. You knew what he did to your children but you were to scared to say anything. To scared that he would come and find you if you ever tried to run. What would he have done then? Would he have killed you all? Would he have forced you to come back and pretned nothing was wrong until it was just you all in the house? Would he have hit you then? Would he have hit your daughters? Would he have hurt them in the way he hurt you?"

Her purse slips from her hand, landing on the rocky ground. She braces herself against her car as I continue.

"It's not your fault you couldn't take them away. Keeping them there was the safest choice no matter what you tell yourself. It's not your fault your daughters are gone. It's his. You know this. You've known this for a while. You know what he did to them. You know how he hurt them. I know you want to stay far away from this and Alexander and I will respect your decision, but please, just let us buy the house. Let us find whatever is in there to provide some kind of reparation for what your husband did to your children," I pleaded with her.

Alexander takes a few steps towards her, hesitate as if she would walk away.

"It's not your fault Genevieve. You and I both know this. Sydney knows this. The jury will know this, but we need something. Anything that will make him pay for what he did. Anything that will finally give her payment for what he did to Autumn and Phoebe."

Tears fall down her eyes as Alexander wraps his arms around her.

"Its my fault," she whispers, her voice sounding weak. "They were my daughters. I should have done something. I should have protected them from him, but I was too scared. I was too scared for my own life that I couldn't even protect my own children. My girls. My sweet girls."

"It's not your fault Genevieve," Alexander whispers, his hands moving up and down her back in a soothing motion. "He would have just hurt the three of you more. You did all that you could."

"My sweet girls. They didn't deserve any of this. They deserved a life. A better life than the one I had, but I couldn't give that to them. It's too late for them to have it. My girls are gone. There is nothing I can do now. Nothing I can do now to save them."

Alexander pulls back, grabbing both of her hands and holding them out in front of her.

"You can help us Genevieve. You can let us buy the house. Let us go through and find anything that Phoebe or Autumn might have left for us. You can make your husband pay for everything he has done to your family. To Autumn and Phoebe."

She nods her head, reaching down to grab her purse from the ground. Her hands dig through her bag until she finds what she is looking for. I watch as she pulls out a set of keys, holding them out to me.

"Take the house, but please, do not call. Please do not ask for anything else. I did what you asked. I have done everything I can. Please just let me move on with my life."

Alexander reaches and grabs the keys from her hand, pulling her in for another hug before turning back towards me.

"We promise Genevieve. You have helped us so much. I can't eve begin to thank you for everything you have done."

She nods one last time before sitting back down in the car. Alexander moves out of the way so she can pull out. She begins to move before stopping and rolling down her window.

"Do me one last favor," she calls out.

"Anything," Alexander answers.

"Let him know that I'll see him in hell, and that I will be waiting right there, to finally give him what he deserves. Something no court system could provide."

THE HOUSE HAD BECOME a mess over the years. Anything Mrs. Conners hadn't wanted to deal with after her husband was put in prison was shoved into the house. There was one path throughout the entire house, taking you up the stairs and through all of the hallways.

"This is a fucking mess," Alexander grumbles, opening the box closest to him. He takes one look inside the box before slamming it shut. "And of course, the first fucking box I open just happens to be one from the older Conners bedroom."

I wince, blocking off the mental image.

"We need to get a dumpster out here. Something that we can throw all of this shit in."

Alexander nods, walking towards the stairs.

"Let's leave all of this here and go to Phoebe's bedroom. I can't imagine her mother would have ever touched it."

He was right. The door was closed as we walked up to it. I reached out, lightly twisting the knob, trying to calm my mind as more of the room was revealed. Nothing inside of the room had been touched. I dragged my finger against the top of the dresser as I slowly walked through the room. When I pulled my finger away there was a coating of dust. The shades were open, light pouring in from behind the trees.

I reached for the desk, grabbing the thin white remote that sat on it. Tears threatened to spill as I clicked the fairy lights on. The light from the walls illuminated what I couldn't see a moment ago. Her crystals were still there, sitting on every flat surface she could find. Her tapestries depicting constellations and the tree of life. Strings of fake leaves clung to the ceiling, trailing down the walls.

I hear Alexander's footsteps as he walks slowly through the room. His reaches out to touch a picture of the two of them, but retracts it, as if the memory would burn him.

"She really didn't touch a single thing," he whispers.

I didn't answer. We both saw the proof right in front of us.

"I almost don't want to go through it. It feels as though if I touch any of this she will just disappear," he chokes out, sitting next to me on the bed.

"I would have thought he would have come in here. He would have looked around for anything that might incriminate him. It's untouched though. He never came in here after she died. Never took a single thing," I muttered.

"That's good for us right?" Alexander asks. "That means that more will be left behind."

He stands up, moving toward the dresser. "Let's just start from here. Go from the most basic place. There has to be something in here that we can find."

Alexander and I spent hours going through her room. Looking behind furniture, ripping open drawers. Taking items off of shelves and posters off the wall. There was nothing. Alexander suggested searching through Autumn's room. We picked apart those pastel walls piece by piece. There was nothing.

We made our way back to Phoebe's room, sinking to the floor as it dawned on us that there might not be anything in this house. That maybe we had bought this house for nothing.

"There has to be something here," Alexander mutters. "I know Phoebe. Phoebe wouldn't just leave like this. She would have hid something somewhere."

I wanted to believe him. I wanted to believe there was something here that we were just missing, but deep down, I knew there wasn't anything. We had scoured the two rooms. Neither Phoebe nor Autumn would have put something this important anywhere else in the house. It could have been found by anyone. If it was something this important, it would have been in these two rooms, and these two walls held nothing.

Alexander placed his hands on the ground, pulling himself up. I heard a creak in the floor as he did. His eyes shift towards where his hands were.

"I knew it. I fucking knew it. That tricky bitch," he laughs under his breath.

I quickly jumped out of the way as Alexander throws himself towards the floor, his fingers prying at the floorboards.

"Alexander what the fuck are you doing?" I call out.

He pries up a floorboard, throwing it behind him.

Alexander pulls out a leatherbound notebook.

"I knew it," Alexander mutters under his breath, a smile covering his face. "I fucking knew it."

He begins unwrapping the journal as I race to his side, looking over his shoulder at the first page of writing. His hands hover over the sides where small tabs stick out from pages. He turns to the page with the first tab and begins reading.

"August 10th

Father always said writing in diaries was weak. It was a childs activity that only taught children it was okay to hide things from adults. This isn't a diary. I'm not some insecure teenager writing about her feelings for a boy who will never reciprocate them. This is physical evidence. A first hand account of what happened to me. This is something that will protect Phoebe from what happened to me. This will keep her safe from him.

I, Autumn Conners, was touched for the first time by my father when I was 4. I found him inside Phoebe's room, trying to take off her onesie. I demanded to know what he was doing. I demanded that he let go of my sister. He tried telling me he was just changing her. I demanded to know why he wasn't changing her on the changing table. He told me it wasn't any of my business.

I was terrified. This was my little sister. My baby sister. I needed to keep her safe like I vowed I would. I told him to do whatever he was going to do to her to me. He told me he wouldn't. Tried to force me out of the room, but I planted my feet. I threatened to scream for my mother if he forced me out. He finally agreed. Sometimes I wished I never did that. I should have just screamed for my mother.

I used to wonder what would have happened if I had just ignored him with Phoebe. If I didn't, maybe Phoebe wouldn't be here, though. As I got older and finally started to understand what was happening, I pleaded with him to take me instead of Phoebe. He only ever wanted Phoebe. Even as an infant, he wanted Phoebe. He barely tolerated me, even when I was a child. When Phoebe was born, I thought Mother and I would see another side to him. He seemed so happy, just so in love with the new baby. I thought I was going to get a father. I realize now why he was like that.

It disgusts me that I share DNA with that man. It disgusts me that the man I thought of as my father had done all this for so long. That before me there were others. I only stay here to keep Phoebe safe, but I don't know how much longer I can handle this. I promised Phoebe that when she could move out, we would go to the police and tell them everything. He had never touched her like that before. He only hit her. He would get upset, and that would be it. He would hit. He would apologize after. He would beg for her forgiveness and promise that he loved her, and she would believe him. I knew he wasn't sorry. He never acted sorry. He would only apologize out of feelings of necessity. Apologizing never stopped him from hitting her the next time he got angry.

I tried as much as I could to keep him at bay. I did everything I could to stop him from touching Phoebe. I never wanted her to have to go through that. But all he ever wanted was Phoebe. That was the only thing he had ever wanted in this world. I will never leave Phoebe until she can leave herself. She is my responsibility now. She is mine to take care of."

Alexander turns towards me, his eyes glistening with tears.

"We found it."

I sent a silent thank you to Autumn. I sent a promise to Phoebe as well. I knew the two of them were together. This was what we needed. No jury could say that he never hurt his children. No jury would be able to take one look at this and say he had never raped his children. We were winning this case, and it was thanks to Autumn.

Autumn who wanted nothing more than to protect her sister. Autumn who wrote all of this down in case someone like Alexander and I came along and found it.

"We found it Autumn," I whispered. "You can rest now."

Before

I didn't see Phoebe for another week. I told myself that she needed time. She needed to figure out whatever had happened, but she would come back. She could come back to me.

The tensions at home didn't lighten throughout the week. My siblings could sense something was wrong. They noticed my father not even looking in my direction. They noticed the door taken off of it's hinges. They noticed the silence that echoed throughout the entire house.

I knew my mother wanted to talk to me. She wanted to make sense of whatever had happened, but I didn't have an answer for her. I didn't have an answer myself. I knew she was right. I knew I needed to have a plan. I needed to know how I could make all of this right, but there wasn't a way I could make all of this right anymore. That chance had dissipated long ago.

I broke into the new routine. Alexander would come and get me every morning. I would crane my neck out of the window to see if Phoebe was riding shotgun and try to control the fear that crawled through me when I saw that she wasn't. My fathers eyes would follow me out of the door. I would look back once to see him staring at me through the window and then we would leave.

I walked the route to all of Phoebe's classes. Looked in every single one to see if she was in one of them. She never was. I ignored the stares and the whispers in the hallway. Ignored the rumors that spread like wildfires about what happened that night. It was easier when Alexander was right there with me.

I would wait at the car after school for Alexander to come outside. I would pretend to be busy doing something. Anything to keep the whispers out of my head. Alexander would drive me home, waiting outside until I flashed the hallway lights three times before pulling away.

My parents would ignore me. My siblings would cast me side long glances at dinner, but would never say anything. I would get up before all of them, making up some kind of excuse as to why I needed to go upstairs.

I would sit against my door, my phone pressed against my ear as the rest of my family laughed downstairs. All of my calls went to voicemail, but my family never stopped. I was a part of that laughter a few months ago. I was the one cracking jokes that would leave my father waving his hand as if that would stop all of us from laughing and his water from shooting out of his nose.

I was the one dancing around the kitchen with my mother as we did the dishes together. I was the one choosing the show we would be watching that night. I was the one helping tuck my siblings into bed. I had lost my family. Had lost the very thing I swore I would never. I let the one person I swore never would come in between my family.

I would lean against the door with tears flowing down my cheeks as I heard Dean Martin being played downstairs. It was if this wasn't my family anymore. I was just a person passing through. A boarder who would leave once they found a way out.

My family was supposed to be the one group of people I could go to no matter what. For years they had held me while I cried over girls. When I got a bad grade on my math test. When I scrapped my knee. But here I was. Crying alone in my room, longing for a relationship that just kept slipping farther and farther with every decision made.

I would hear my mother whispering to my father in the hallway every night. She was worried about me. She had never seen her daughter like this. I needed to talk to someone. Someone who wasn't involved with the Conners. My father told her I was too far gone. They had tried to talk some sense into me, and I wouldn't listen. Whatever happened to me after that, was my own fault. The tears only came harder then.

On the weekend, I waited for my family to leave for their various activities. I drove to Phoebe's house, praying she would be there. I couldn't bring myself to knock on the door. I parked father down the driveway, walking through the woods until I found the log. I texted her, telling her I was there. I called her, begging her to come out and see me. I just needed to make sure she was okay.

She never came out. On Monday, Alexander drove up and Phoebe still wasn't there. I went to her house that weekend again. Nothing. No Phoebe Conners. Monday came around again, and she still wasn't there. I had stopped trying to curb the fear. I didn't know where she was. She could be dead somewhere and I wouldn't know it. She had worked so hard for her sobriety. Tried to hard to quit all of it. It had kept her going. Now she didn't have it. The only thing she thought she had to fight for was gone.

I risked talking to my father about it. He claimed there was nothing he could. She went missing all the time. She ran away. It was none of the police departments concern. That was the first conversation we had had in two weeks, and it ended with him telling me he refused to do anything.

I called her more often. Begged her to just answer me. I needed something. Anything to show me that she was still alive. Proof of life in anyway. It never came.

That Thursday morning, my entire body felt heavy. All of the hope in me was extinguished. I stopped trying to assure myself that she was okay. I knew Alexander did as well. We didn't talk about it. We didn't bring up the fact Phoebe had been gone for two weeks. We didn't mention that this was the longest we had ever gone without hearing from her.

It had been two weeks of hell. Two weeks of not knowing if she was dead or alive. Two weeks of trying to maintain hope that somewhere out there, Phoebe was okay. We were almost at week three. Three weeks of no contact. Three weeks of Phoebe being missing.

We didn't want to acknowledge what would happen if she didn't come back. My father wouldn't do anything. Her parents would never want to admit that she was gone. That something was out of their control. That Phoebe was out of their control.

So Alexander and I stuck to our routine. He drove me to school. Neither of us spoke a word. We didn't need to. All of the words that went unsaid were the thoughts we didn't want to say out loud. As if because we talked about them, it would come true.

The whispers hadn't stopped. But now they just begged the same question I had been wondering for two weeks. I didn't have an answer. I didn't know where she was. Didn't know if I ever would again.

The day went on in a blur like the past ones. A blur of my phone letting me know the call was sent to voicemail and the messages going unanswered. Alexander walked me to my last class. We must have looked like an odd pair. Two sluggish individuals moving their way through the hallways as if they hadn't slept in weeks.

That was until we looked into the classroom. That was until she was right there. I watched as Alexander's face lit up, his eyes filling with tears. Phoebe looked up from where she was sitting, waving at Alexander before looking back down at her phone. She had her fucking phone. She knew I had sent every single one of those messages but never answered. Never bothered to say anything.

Alexander doesn't walk into the classroom. He wipes his tears, promising to meet me at the car after before speeding away, his steps filled with energy.

I tried to avoid her eye contact as I sat down at the desk next to her. Tried to ignore the swell of relief that she was here. That she was okay. I felt her lean over, pressing a kiss to my cheek. I looked up, Phoebe's face coated in a sickenly sweet smile. I had never seen her smile like that before.

"Hello, Sydney Garcia, and how are you on this fine Thursday morning?"

Her voice send shivers down my spine. She was actually here. She was in front of me. She was okay. She was alive.

"It would be a lot better if I knew where you have been these past two weeks," I answered her.

I watched as anger flickered through her eyes, quickly replaced with the same childlike joy she had a second before.

"I took a vacation. Thought I could use some time to myself," she responded.

I grabbed her hand, pulling her towards me. A smirk appears on her face as she stares down at me.

"If you wanted to make out in front of everyone, Miss Garcia, you could have just said so."

"It's been two and a half fucking weeks, Phoebe. It's been two and a half fucking weeks of me texting and calling and driving past your house so that I could see if you were anywhere in there. You never thought to call? Respond to at least one of my texts? I thought you were dead Phoebe. I thought I had fucking lost you."

She doesn't try and stop the anger in her eyes this time. She pulls her arm out of my hand, jerking away from me. If she saw me flinch, she didn't say anything. She just kept staring down at me.

"You want to do this here, Garcia? Let's fucking do it," she says between gritted teeth. "You have built our entire relationship on being honest with each other, but when was the last time you were honest with me? You have me talk. You have me spill everything, and then what do you do? You hide everything away. You say nothing as to what is happening with you.

It's not being honest with each other, no. It's Phoebe Conners on a pedestal time. Let little old Phoebe Conners spill everything about her life while I sit here and internalize everything. Well, I won't do it anymore. I won't let you sit here and act as though you care when you just want to hear what happened to me. I won't sit here and let you act as though you care about me just to get the truth."

I don't have time to say anything before she storms out of the classroom, knocking papers from Mercer's hands. I could hear whispers from around the classroom, words like bitch and psycho being thrown around. Mercer bent down to pick up the papers, and I usually would go to help her, but my entire body felt numb.

This was the first time I had seen her in two and a half weeks and I fucking yelled at her. It was my fault. My fault that she had stormed out. My fault that she was upset. Out of the corner of my eye I see Lindsey rolling her eyes. I didn't turn to look at her, my cheeks flaimg red.

Mercer was in the front of the classroom now, her papers that had fallen out of her hands strewn everywhere on her desk.

"Thanks to that little interruption, I will be giving everyone the first 5 minutes of class so I can get everything in order," Mercer tells us.

I heard the whispers. Felt the stares on the back of my head. My fingers itched to grab my phone. To just text her. To get her to talk to me. Make sure we could talk through it all, but I couldn't. She needed space. I knew that. She wasn't expecting to get into a fight with me. It caught her off guard. She needed some time to collect her thoughts after that.

I tried paying attention in class. I stared straight ahead at the board, ensuring I answered every possible question. I felt like the old me again for a moment. The me who had her entire life figured out. The me who was confident. The me who had everything together. The me everyone still loved.

When the bell rang, I ran out of the classroom before any of the whispers began. I shut myself in the bathroom, trying to keep the tears from ripping out of me. I had promised Phoebe I would never leave her and intended to stick to that promise. I told her it didn't matter what she did, I would always be there with her, but sometimes it was hard. On days like this, it was extremely hard to stay there.

If I stayed, would it be like this for the rest of my life? Would there be those days when I would be yelled at and have to sit there and take it because it would pass at some point? Would she always lash at and then storm away? Would there always be those times when she disappeared?

Is what they say about ignorance being bliss correct? Would it have been easier to live my entire life in the dark than open my eyes and see through the lies I had always known to be true? I can't know now. I will never be able to go back to not knowing. I knew now, and there was nothing I could do about it.

I hated myself for having these thoughts. I hated myself for even thinking of leaving. I made a promise, and that promise was one I intended to keep. Phoebe Conners held all parts of me in her hands, and I would never let her go. I would ruin myself ten times over for her. I would let her break me down into a million pieces because I was her's to break. She had all of me.

I GOT HOME LATE THAT night. It was almost dark between waiting at the school and walking home. I couldn't face Phoebe in that car. Couldn't face the rest of the world outside of that bathroom.

I just wanted to get to sleep. I wanted to crawl into my bed and try and forget everything that had happened today. My family hadn't even noticed I wasn't home. It wasn't like they wanted to see me anyway. I walked up the stairs and into my room, not even paying attention to where I was going.

I opened the door to my room, moving to close it behind me before I noticed someone lying down facing the wall. I recognized the hair. I knew those flames that were covering the pillow.

"Phoebe," I whispered, trying to stay quiet, so my parents didn't hear me. "What are you doing here?"

She didn't move for a moment, just lay there in bed. When I called out her name, she slowly turned to me, rubbing the sleep out of her eyes. She didn't say anything for a moment, staring at me from the bed as if I was just some hallucination her brain had conjured up.

"Phoebe," I asked her. "Is everything okay?"

She shook her head, stumbling out of bed and walking towards me.

"No, it's not okay. I blew up at you today in front of everyone," she said, rushing towards me. "I knew it was wrong as I was doing it, but I couldn't bring myself to stop now. I couldn't stop myself."

Her voice sounded weak as she finished that last sentence.

"Pheobe, it's not your fault," I whispered, reaching over and wrapping her in my arms. She didn't say anything; she just held onto me. She had never held me like this before. It was like I was the last thing on this earth.

"It's okay, Phoebe," I whispered. "It's okay. I know. I know things are hard sometimes. I'm not going anywhere. I am going to be here through those hard days and the bad ones. You can yell at me. You can push me away as much as you want, and I will return to you every time.

She pulled away, resting her forehead on mine.

"I know I'm not perfect, and I can't promise you that this will never happen again. There are going to be things that I do without thinking about it. What I can promise you is that I will always try as hard as possible. I can tell you that I will always come back no matter what. I can promise this will happen again, but I will also promise you, Sydney Garcia, that I will work through this. I won't answer you anymore. I will let you be there for me," she tells me.

"That's all I want, Phoebe. I meant that I will always love every version of you," I whispered, slowly pressing her lips to mine.

"I don't know how Syd," she whispers after she pulls away. "I still don't know why you fell in love with me Sydney Garcia. I will never stop questioning but don't think for a second that I will ever take that love for granted. I will continue to thank you for that for the rest of my eternity."

After

ugust 15th

A   *"Everything was cold when I woke up that morning. This was not out of the ordinary, as the house was so big that sometimes the heat didn't get through the entire house, but this morning, it felt different. This felt like a sigh. An omen that cold times were to come. Father always said it was always a coincidence. He said that the universe did not give signs. That was why I started to believe in those signs, all because he said he didn't.*

Phoebe was already downstairs when I had finally gotten ready. She had just started high school two weeks ago. Sometimes it shocked me to look at her and realizing she was only four years younger. Four years ago, I was in the same position. Four years ago, I walked into that school for the first time and started in this whole new world. Now it was Phoebe's turn.

She smiled at me, not saying anything as she shoved cereal into her mouth. I smiled, kissing the top of her head and grabbing my keys from off the counter. I sat there and waited for her to finish before she jumped up, grabbed her bag, and ran out the door toward the car. I followed behind her.

There was a melancholy feeling today. I wasn't sure what it was that was making me feel this way. I couldn't shake the feeling of sadness me I drove to school. I hugged Phoebe before sending her on her way, watching as she ran towards the school and through the doors. I got back into the car and drove away, an unsettling feeling in my stomach preventing me from going inside.

I should have just fucking went in. I should have just fucking gone back inside. Maybe I wouldn't be here right now if I had gone inside. If I had just fucking gone inside, then none of this would have happened. I should have just fucking went inside.

"AUGUST 29TH

When people tell you that everything happens for a reason, do you believe them? Do you just sit there and think it makes sense, so there is no reason not to believe in it? I used to. I used to tell myself when he would touch me or when I would beg that he take me instead of Phoebe that this was all happening for a reason. There was a reason for all of this.

I don't believe that anymore. How am I supposed to be able to wake up in the morning and think that all of this is happening for a reason? How am I supposed to close my eyes and think all this is happening for some messed up reason? I'm not my mother. I'm not a spineless animal that just lets herself get kicked around.

Nothing in my life has ever happened for a reason, and it never will."

"September 10th

I did everything I could to save Phoebe, and there were times when I still wondered if it would be enough. When I was gone, would I still be able to protect her? After I was gone, there was nothing I could do to save her from him.

I tried to stay strong and brave throughout my entire life. I was four years old when I first demanded he does what he was going to do to Phoebe to me. Maybe if I hadn't done that, I would not be here. Maybe if I had not done that, I would not have decided to die.

I was determined to spend my last few weeks with Phoebe. I wanted to give her memories to last forever. I wanted her to remember me as her sister, who loved her more than anything in the world, as her weak older sister who killed herself to escape their father.

I did everything she wanted. I drove her to school every morning. I would make her breakfast. I would let her sleep in my room some nights. Nights when I was sure father wouldn't come into my room. I did absolutely everything I could, so when someone said the name Autumn Conners. Phoebe did not think of her weak older sister, who killed herself."

"October 31st

I spent Halloween with Phoebe. She insisted she was too old for trick or treating, so we bought candy and watched movies together. She fell asleep on my shoulder that night about halfway through the third movie. I didn't have the heart to wake her up, so I picked her up and carried her to her room. After putting her to bed, I returned to the living room, sitting back on the couch. For the first time, it didn't hurt to know that this would be the last Halloween I had. It was almost relieving."

"November 14th

These last two weeks have been the worst two weeks of my life. Every night father would come into my room. For the first time, I begged him not to. I felt so weak in those moments. I had never asked him not to touch me like that. I would rather he did it to me than Phoebe, but I couldn't handle it anymore. I cried. I cried the entire time. He yelled. He told me I had never cried before so why had I started now. He apologized but hadn't said he would never do it again. We both knew that would be a complete lie.

I refused to let Phoebe see me like this. I tried to act like everything was normal because Phoebe didn't need to know what he had done to me, but it got harder and harder every day. I stopped going to school. I would drive away from the house and get as far away as possible. I just didn't want to be there anymore. I just wanted to fucking die."

"DECEMBER 24TH

While writing this, I realized that maybe Phoebe would find this. If this is Phoebe reading this, please know I was sorry. I wanted to stay for you, Phoebe. I made so many promises. I only wish I was staying so we could fulfill them. I can't take this anymore, Phoebe, and I apologize. You are stronger than me; you always have been and always will be. You will be able to make it through this without me. You will survive through this and longer than I did. You will be able to do what I promised you I would do so many years ago.

I can't fulfill every promise I made to you. I can't make them come true, and I can't take back what I am about to do. I just hope someone finds me before you do. If you are reading this, I will assume you will know why this is happening. You will know what I can't handle anymore. I know you know the word already for what he has done to me. I just don't like saying it. I don't like even thinking about it. I don't like thinking of the meaning behind the word.

I used to think I could live and say I had survived one of my worst experiences. I would think that I would live and when people asked what I was, I would say that I was a survivor, but I can't even say that now. I can't say that I survived this because, after tonight, I won't. I know this is what he wants. He wants me out of the way so he can have access to you, but right now, Phoebe, I can't force myself to stay.

If anything happens to you, you can blame it on me. You can say I wasn't strong enough. You can sit there and tell everyone you were hurt because your sister was weak and couldn't handle it anymore, and you wouldn't be lying. It's my fault, Phoebe. Everything that will happen to you is my fault.

You will make it through this, though. I know you will. You will be able to stand up someday and say the things I can't bring me to because you, Phoebe Conners, are the strongest person in my life.

I will never forget when you fell in the woods and broke your arm. You didn't cry; you just walked back to the house and told the mother that it was broken in the calmest voice I had ever heard. A little ten-year-old girl, your voice not wavering at all. You didn't cry when they had to set it. You didn't cry when they had to set it or even cry when you had surgery. It was like nothing had ever happened.

That's how I know you will make it through this, Phoebe. This is how I know that no matter what, you will live longer than me. You will live on to tell people about what he did to us. So go ahead and tell people that if I had been a little bit stronger, you would never have had to go through the things you had to through. Go ahead and tell everyone that I was the one who was fucked up inside the head, but I need you to know that I did everything in my life for you. I never want you to forget that, Phoebe. I did all of this for you.

I love you more than anything, Phoebe. I love you more than you could ever possibly understand, and I am sorry I couldn't be stronger than this. I'm sorry for what happened to you. I wish I could take this. I wish I could be stronger, but I just can't.

Forever loving
Autumn"
"February 13th

I wish I could tell you that I was good, Autumn. I wish I could tell you that I was stronger than you and could handle this, but I couldn't. You weren't strong enough to stay for me, and I wasn't strong enough to stay for Sydney.

You would know Sydney. You went to school at the same time as her older brother. Her father is the police chief. Never once did I think I would end up with the daughter of the police chief. You would like her Autumn. She's level-headed. She thinks about everything she does before she does it. Most importantly, I love her. And I know she loves me.

That seems like a sentence I haven't said since you left. I feel like I haven't felt truly happy since you left Autumn, but Sydney makes me feel happy. Sydney makes me feel like I have a future outside of Aurora. She makes me feel as though I could be something other than the daughter of Jonathan Conners.

I tell you, I tried Autumn. I tried being strong. I tried closing my eyes and pretending it wasn't happening, but I couldn't do it anymore. Sydney is the one thing in this world that made me feel I could make something of myself, but I can't do this anymore.

I know there is a good chance Sydney will read this at some point, so I want to say the same thing Autumn said to me four years ago. I wish I were stronger for you, Sydney. I wish I could stay with you. It's not even that you are not good enough to hold me here because you are. I know that if I stay, I will have a future, but I know you won't stay with me.

If I stay here, it will only delay the inevitable. Everyone who loves me leaves. You say you love every part of me, but Sydney, I know I will become too much after some time. I know it would only be a matter of time before you realize just how fucked up I am. I fucked up your life. I ruined your relationship with your best friend and your entire family. You have no one left but me, and I can't have that anymore. I can't be the reason you don't have anyone else. I can't be the person you leave everyone for.

Move on from me, Sydney. Fix your relationship with your parents, and please don't hate me for leaving. Please understand that this was what was best for both of us. I love you, Sydney Garcia. Go and make something of yourself like you always wanted to. Become the police chief if that is what you truly want. Become a writer. Go to college. Do everything you can because you won't have me there to hold you back."

Before

She fell asleep in my arms that night. Her weight was heavy in my arms. I held her close to me all night. For the past three weeks I was so terrified that I would never see her again. So terrified that she had died. I held her to me because these past few weeks, I didn't know if I was ever going to be able to do it again.

I tried to fight off the sleep as long as I could, but it took over. When I woke up the next morning, Phoebe was gone. She showed up to school the next few days, but she was a shell of herself. I could feel her leaving me again. I could feel her retreating into herself. It seemed like nothing I could do would make all of this better. I would talk to her, and she would nod, not entirely listening. She stopped coming by the house. I stopped getting rides to and from school. Some days, she just stopped showing up.

I had fought to get her back. I wanted nothing more than to have her back in these past weeks, and now she was gone again. She was physically there, but she wasn't. This wasn't Phoebe. This wasn't the Phoebe Conners I had fallen in love with.

Phoebe Conners wasn't herself anymore. She was a shell of herself and what hurt the most was that there was nothing I could do to help. There was nothing I could do to fix it. I just had to sit and wait it out. I didn't want to wait. I had waited before. I couldn't wait again.

I came home one night from the station to find Phoebe sitting in the driveway. I slowly got out of the car. She pulled her head up, tears covering her cheeks. She didn't even give me a chance to take a few steps towards her before she ran towards me and threw her arms around me.

"I'm so sorry," she whispers.

I wrap my arms around her, holding her to me. This was the first time I had held her in almost four weeks. Three weeks since I had felt her against me. It had felt like an eternity.

"It's okay, Phoebe. It's okay, I understand."

"Can I just stay here tonight?" she asks, her voice sounding almost tired as I felt. "I can't go back there. Not tonight."

I held her against me, fighting off the tears.

"Of course," I answered.

The two of us lay in my bed that night. She had her arms wrapped around my waist, holding me impossibly close. She would kiss the side of my head every so often. She kept whispering that she was sorry. I thought she was apologizing for being away for so long. I would never have thought that she would be apologizing for.

She fell asleep before me that night, practically laying on top of me. When I woke up the next morning, she wasn't there. All that was left of her was a single ring, pressed onto my bedside table. No note with it, but the ring.

I couldn't care less about her being gone. I had my girl back. I went about my day as normal, knowing I would see her next week at school and I could text her throughout the day. She would always respond with more effort than before. It seemed like things were looking up. It seemed as though she was coming out of her longest episode.

I went to the station with my father that afternoon. He offered to drive me. He talked to me on the car ride over. For the first time in over a month, I had everything I could have wanted. I had Phoebe. I had my family back.

My father had me sit in his office during a team meeting. He started referring to me as his daughter again. My chest swelled with pride everytime he mentioned the intern, his daughter would be around shadowing in the next couple weeks. That was me. His daughter. It was like I was getting my father back.

I was sitting in my father's office during the last 10 minutes of my shift when my phone rang. My father looked up from his desk, narrowing my eyes as I clicked to decline the call. A slight smile appeared on his face as I went to put it back in my pocket, but it continued ringing. This time, I looked down at my phone. I saw Phoebe's name. It came back to me what had happened beforehand. I pressed my phone to my ear and answered as quietly as I could.

"Phoebe, what's going on?"

There was only breathing on the other end for a little while before I heard a small voice whisper, "I'm sorry. I hope you can forgive me."

Those words made everything inside of me stop. I kept screaming at myself to think of something to say, but I couldn't. My words were choked up in my throat.

"You don't have to be sorry, Pheebs. You haven't done anything. You haven't done anything yet, right?" I said. My voice came out in a whisper. I couldn't add anything more.

"It's already done," I heard her mutter before the line went dead.

"Phoebe," I screamed into the other end of my phone, but I couldn't hear anything than the dead dial tone on the other line. I wanted to scream. I wanted to sob. I wanted to throw my phone down on the ground and run to her. There were no thoughts other than getting to Phoebe as quickly as possible.

I forced myself to move, even though I couldn't feel any part of my body. I didn't even run in to grab the rest of my things; I just ran. Everything felt like it was running too slowly. I couldn't unlock the car fast enough. I couldn't put the car in drive fast enough. I couldn't pull out of the parking spot fast enough. I didn't follow the speed limit a single mile there. No speed in existence was fast enough at this moment.

"Fuck, fuck fuck," I screamed, speeding through her driveway's winding road. At that moment, I had never cursed her winding driveway as much as I had at this moment. I slammed the car into the park right in front of the door. My seatbelt felt like it wasn't coming undone quickly enough. I fumbled with it, my hands shaking before getting it undone and opening the door. I didn't even close, I just raced towards her front door.

The door broke open, slamming into hundreds of pieces as I ran in. I turned the doorknob, trying to burst in, but it was locked. Tears of frustration and pain filled my eyes as I slammed my shoulder into that door. My body didn't even register the pain in my shoulder as I slammed into the house.

I can never forget what I saw as I walked into her kitchen. I could never forget the pool of blood on the ground. The blood staining her hair, coloring it an even deeper color of red. I was frozen, staring at her, dying on the ground. I didn't know what to do.

"For fucks sake Sydney, move," my mind screamed, but I couldn't. I was frozen. I couldn't move. I was stuck there staring.

When I finally could move, I felt sluggish, almost as if my body was moving in slow motion. This wasn't happening. This wasn't happening. At some point, I would wake up, and she would be sleeping there right next to me, and I would wake her up and tell her I had a nightmare, and she would hold me and tell me everything would be alright.

I sat down next to her, tears freely streaming down my face.

"Phoebe, no," I cried, picking her up and bringing her head on my lap. "Phoebe, Phoebe, no," I cried.

I placed my fingers on her pulse point, trying to find any feeling. Any remainder of life that remained. It was faint, but it was there. I grabbed her wrist to stop the bleeding, but the blood continued pouring through my fingers.

Something in my mind told me I was doing all of this in vain, but I pushed that far back in my mind. She was going to be okay. Phoebe Conners would be okay, and the two of us would get through this together.

"No, Phoebe, please," I whispered, trying to do anything to wake her up.

I fumbled with my phone, hurriedly typing in the number before pressing a shaking hand to my face.

"911, what's your emergency?" someone on the other end of the line asked.

"My girlfriend," I sobbed. "My girlfriend slit her wrists. She's bleeding out. I need help immediately."

"Okay, okay," the woman on the other end said. I could hear the keys clacking from the other end. "What is the address?"

I took a deep breath, trying to remember Phoebe's address.

"679 Callaway Dr," I answered, my heart bursting in my chest.

"Someone is coming, ma'am," the person on the other end said. My hand was shaking so much, my phone fell out of my hand. I heard a shatter but nothing inside of me cared. Phoebe was right here. I couldn't lose her. Not like this.

Deep down, I knew it was too late. Deep down, I knew I had lost her. Holding my hands to try and stop the bleeding wasn't going to do anything. Pleading with her and holding her to me wasn't going to help her stay, but I sat there. I sat there holding her and trying to keep her there.

When the ambulance arrived, they had to drag me away from her, not letting me see her. I screamed and tried to run toward her, but I was held back by police officers. I heard shouting and turned to see my dad running out of a police car and grabbing me, hugging and kissing my head. He didn't say anything. He just held me. I watched as they loaded her into the ambulance and drove her away, watching the lights until I couldn't see them anymore.

A police officer would come to hand me a folded piece of paper before my dad walked inside to look around. I sat on the front steps, holding the paper in my hand as I stared into the distance. Lights appeared in the distance, and I watched as a car tore into the driveway before stopping, yanking the keys out of the ignition, and racing over to me. Alexander just stared at me. I looked at my blood-stained clothes and the piece of paper I was holding in my hands before tossing me the keys to his car.

"Are you good to drive?" He asked. "I would crash the car if I were to drive right now."

I shook my head, unsure of what to say. There was no way I was going to be able to drive. I was shaking, my entire body cold and yet burning simultaneously.

"Phoebe," he kneels in front of me. "We need to get to that hospital. You haven't done this before, but I have. Get someone to drive us and meet us there. After that, we will wait for her to wake up and then make sure the doctors do everything right until she goes home. It's okay. Phoebe is going to be okay. It's never worked before, and it will not work this time."

He was wrong. Nothing would ever be alright. She had almost fucking died. I almost lost her. I could still lose her. Things would not be all right.

IT'S IMPOSSIBLE TO forget the sound of a flatline. Hearing the consistent beeping as people rush around trying to get that person back, even though you know that person is gone deep down. Hearing as they announce the time of death as you sit there looking at that person, their eyes closed as though they are just sleeping. But this time, they won't wake up from this sleep.

I finally understood why Phoebe said she didn't cry. As they announced the time of death and left for the room to give her parents a minute with her, I didn't feel anything. I was completely numb. She wasn't dead; she wasn't gone. She would come back, and someday we would laugh about this. Maybe after getting over the shock of this ridiculous prank, but I would laugh about it someday. It wasn't until her parents walked out of the room, and I watched as they pulled that sheet over her body, that she was gone slowly started to sink in.

They sent me out of the room and asked if they could call anyone. I nodded, showed them my father's phone number, and then dialed it. I was asked if I wanted to explain it to him, but there wasn't anything I could say. I shook my head and went to sit in the corner chair in the lobby. Putting my head in my hands.

I'm not 100% sure how long I sat there, but I was there until my parents put their arms around me, guided me out to the car, and drove me home.

I didn't sleep that night. I just lay in bed, staring straight at the wall. Nothing made sense; nothing mattered anymore. She had been here last night. She laid in my arms last night. Her ring still sat on my nightstand. A stark reminder of what I had just lost.

I remember my parents coming in and trying to get me to talk, but I just stared straight ahead. At one point, Tyler walks in and sits on my bed.

"Do you want to talk about it?" he asks.

I shake my head but don't answer the question. Tyler nods and continues sitting there, not moving.

"I think we should just sit here tonight. Just sit here, and watch whatever you want. We don't have to talk; it would be much better if we sat together."

I didn't even bother to say anything. I just nodded my head again, and he moved closer to me. I rested my head against his shoulder, not sleeping but sitting there.

The day after that was Phoebe Conners calling hours. My parents tried to get me to go, but the minute I put on the black dress, I felt like I couldn't breathe. My mother found me crying in the corner of my room. The dress stripped from my body. I couldn't give condolences to people who didn't care about her in the first place. I couldn't bring myself to face them like that. My parents told me I couldn't go to the calling hours. My mother slept in a chair in my room that night.

I knew she wanted me to sleep, but I lay there again. It had been three days of no sleep but I couldn't bring myself to close my eyes because when I did, all I saw was Phoebe lying in that kitchen. It was easier just not to sleep than have to see that in my mind.

The day after that was the funeral. My mom stayed in my room and watched as I got dressed. I didn't recognize the face that stared back at me as my mother brushed my hair. The sunken in eyes. Skin a tone of gray. The dark circles. That wasn't me. I didn't know who was staring back at me, but it wasn't me.

HER CASKET WAS CLOSED. I hadn't wanted to walk up there. Whatever was up there wasn't Phoebe Conners. Whoever was underneath that wooden cover, wasn't her. She wasn't dead. Phoebe wasn't gone.

My mother and father insisted I go up there. Give myself a moment of time to say goodbye. They told me I had to go up there and say goodbye. That is why we were there. To say goodbye to Phoebe Conners.

I followed them up to the front, every step feeling heavier than the last. My mother had her hand on my back and I walked up to the casket, staring at the picture of her they had sitting next to the casket. That wasn't her. That picture of her staring straight ahead, not a single smile on her face wasn't her.

I rested my hand on the top of the casket, my knees giving out from underneath me. I wasn't supposed to be here. Phoebe wasn't gone. This entire funeral wasn't supposed to happen. She wasn't dead. She wasn't fucking dead.

My mother kneeled beside me, whispering that I needed to get off of the floor. I needed to move. I needed to get up and move. My body wouldn't let me. It was like I was frozen. That wasn't Phoebe Conners. Phoebe Conners was not the one lying in that casket. That wasn't her.

My father pulled me up to help me stand, ushering us back to our seats in the back. I sank into the seat, my body feelings as though it weighed a thousand pounds. My parents were on either side of me while the rest of my siblings sat outside of them. Cindy was the only one who was crying. Cindy, little Cindy, was sitting in the pew and sobbing.

I sat through that entire sermon, listening to everyone speak about Phoebe. Alexander sat there, in the pew across the way from me. Not once was he asked up to say anything about Phoebe. Neither was I. The two people who knew her the most. The only two people in this room who knew the true Phoebe Conners, and neither of us said a thing.

I wasn't crying. It was like I couldn't cry. I sat there, and I listened to everything that was said about Phoebe. I listened to the speeches by her mother, her parent's friends and even her father. I thought I would feel something when I heard her father talking about her, but I didn't. It was like I couldn't feel anything.

After the service ended, everyone was told that Phoebe would be buried immediately following the ceremony, open to anyone in attendance. My mother encouraged me to go home. I could tell my parents wanted nothing more than to forget this ever happened. Still, after the service, I let them drive me back to the house before grabbing my car and driving toward the cemetery.

I was slightly late when I got there, but I stood there, watching as a priest talked about Phoebe and said scripture, then lowered her into the ground. It was raining as I watched what was left of Pheobe being lowered into the ground, but after everything, I stayed there. I stood there as everyone else was leaving, holding my umbrella close.

I stood there, watching dirt gets shoveled onto her casket. I watched as she was left 6 feet on the ground—my Phoebe Conners. The light of my life is now gone and buried.

I STOOD THERE UNTIL the water had soaked my shoes, the world had grown dark around me. I couldn't bring myself to move. I couldn't leave her. I had promised I wouldn't leave her.

At some point, I felt arms wrap around my shoulders and start guiding me toward the parking lot. I looked over to realize it was my father walking me toward the parking lot. Neither of us said anything as he put me in the car.

"Don't worry," he whispers. "I'll make sure we come and get the car tomorrow morning."

I wasn't worried about that. My car was the last thing on my mind. I sat with him in the car, looking out the window at the surrounding area. I could tell my father wanted to talk. He wanted to say something, but I just couldn't. I can't talk about it right now. I couldn't handle that.

Lindsey came over the next day. She set down a 7/11 bag on my bed and watched as I slowly opened the bag. Taking a few bites of the tater tots. For the first time since Phoebe died, I tried talking to her and answering her questions the way she wanted me to, but I couldn't muster more than one-word answers. Just speaking felt like it took so much out of me. She finally did exactly what Tyler did and just sat there with me.

She grabbed my hand and held it in her lap, gently tracing the back of my hand. When she left, she kissed the top of my head and pulled me in for a hug. That was the first time we had talked with each other in over six months. I didn't care about that now, though. I didn't care. We had been friends until that point. I couldn't care less that she had hated me all these months. I couldn't care that she made absolutely no effort towards helping All I cared about was Phoebe, and she was now gone.

I could hear the worried whispers from my family outside my door as they stood outside my door. I pretended like I didn't hear them. At this point, I had gotten good at tuning out everyone and everything. When they finally came in, they sat on the bed and tried talking to me. They told me my siblings were worried about me and that they would give me all the time I needed for me to be able to heal. I did the same thing for Lindsey, only giving one-word answers. There was nothing left in me.

Alexander came the next day. He walked through the door to my room, and the first thing I noticed was the pronounced dark circles under his eyes. One look at him, and it all came pouring out at once. I sobbed, grabbing my pillow to muffle the sounds of my cries. Every emotion from the last week came out at once. Every feeling I hadn't felt was there present at that moment. Alexander came over to sit next to me, crying silent tears.

"I'm so sorry," he whispers.

I could answer something with a full sentence for the first time in a week.

"She was your best friend. You lost her as well."

He nodded, looking away from me and at the surroundings around him.

"It's good you haven't been to school. I've heard all this bullshit from people who didn't even know her. There was a 5-minute moment of silence to remember her. People were laughing like it was a joke the entire time. It's not a joke," he murmurs.

His voice sounded as weak as I felt. Just so tired. So exhausted. So done with everything.

I couldn't even bring myself to be angry with those people. I knew what they thought of her. I would expect nothing less.

Neither of us says anything else. We just sit there together. What is there to say in a moment like this? I'm sorry it doesn't cut it. Prayers don't do shit; my deepest condolences mean nothing to the people receiving them. Nothing anyone says would be able to bring her back. Nothing will take away the pain you feel when that one person leaves. People tell you to remember the good times and be grateful for that time, but how can I look at those times and not think I won't have them again? Those times we had together are over, and there will be no more.

The memories will fade over time, and Phoebe Conners will become a distant memory. Memories that 30 years later, I will look back and remember the hurt, remember the pain. I never want to forget the pain. I don't want it ever to go away because it is the only thing reassuring me that I am still alive. I don't want a day to go by where Phoebe Conners isn't in the front of my mind, almost close enough to grab and hold onto but just out of reach.

Part 3

After

Every eye was on me. The room was silent. My hands were tucked into my lap, trying not to let anyone see them shaking. I looked out at Alexander. His hands were clutching the ends of the table. Water coated his cheeks. Carson had her hands clenched into fists, her leg bouncing up and down.

After six years of trying so desperately trying. Fighting tooth and nail for someone to just listen to me, I was here. I wasn't here to judge anymore. My opinions on the Jonathan Conners were irrelevant now. All that mattered were the facts

"No more questions, your honor," I hear Reno say, but I don't look at him.

For the first time since Phoebe died, I told the entire story. No one would ever be able to know the pain that I felt after she died. Alexander's pain would never be the same as my own. Her mothers would never be the same as mine. Mine was individual. Mine was what led me here.

Mine was the story of a girl who fell too hard and fast. Mine was the testimony of a girl who dedicated eight months of her life to a girl she thought she would be with forever, only for it to end at those eight months. Mine was the tale of a girl who learned the consequences of falling hard and fast the hard way, but because she loved that girl, she would stop at nothing to fulfill a promise to that girl.

"I have some questions I would like to ask your honor," Jonathan Conner's lawyer said. Reno sits down, sending me a reassuring smile before turning to talk with Alexander.

"Now, Sydney Garica, how long have you been writing this?" she asked me.

"Phoebe Conners and I began dating seven years ago. I began writing everything down just after," I answered.

She nods, beginning to pace.

"So, you could have gotten some details wrong if you just heard it from her mouth."

" One does not forget something like that. I wrote down whatever Phoebe Conners told me. Whatever she deemed necessary for me to know," I responded.

"Miss Garica, this is not a first-hand account from Phoebe Conners herself. If this were something she had personally written, that would be different, but..." she starts.

"Oh, you want a first-hand account like the suicide note Phoebe left. What about the journal that Autumn wrote in and then Phoebe did? Or the voice notes that she gave Atlas in his toy. She did that before she died, ma'am; no one else would have had a voice recording like that. I may have written this myself, but everything I wrote came directly from Phoebe Conners herself," I cut her off.

Alexander looked at me as if to say, "keep it going." Reno kept a straight face.

"Miss. Garica, I do not deny that there were some main sources, but you are a biased witness. You had a closer relationship with Phoebe Conners than anyone in this room other than Alexander Chadwick. You, the both of you, are bringing this case to trial. You would never admit that Phoebe Conners might have written something down wrong. You would never say anything against Phoebe Conners. How are we to believe anything you say?"

"You are correct, ma'am. Alexander and I are the most biased in this room. We are the ones who have known her the longest, but take into consideration why we are here. The two of us are here now because we loved her more than life itself and want not to let her die in vain."

"And Miss Garcia, would you say you would do anything not to let her die in vain?"

"I would do what she would want me to do. I will do this the correct way, the way Phoebe wanted this to happen."

Johnathan's lawyer turns back to the judge, her shoulders held high. "No further questions, your honor,"

"We will reconvene tomorrow at 9 am. Everyone is dismissed," the judge says, banging their gavel against the stand.

That was it. Alexander and Reno gathered all their things as I returned from the stand. I grabbed my bag, stood up, and walked out of the courtroom, not paying attention to all the stares around me.

Alexander followed me out, walking right behind me to the car. We got inside, both of us silent as we just sat in the car.

"Are you okay?" he whispers finally.

I didn't know what to say. I wasn't okay. Nothing about this would ever be okay. I wanted Phoebe to be here. I wanted her to be the one sitting on that stand talking about what happened to her, but instead, it was me. Instead, I was the one who was up on that stand, talking about what happened to Phoebe. Not her. It would never be her.

"I used to think I would miss her less after this was over. I would feel better about myself and know I finally did something right. It's not like that, though. We are not even halfway through this, but it hurts. It hurts because it is real that she isn't here right now. She will never be here again. I am doing everything I promised her I would do. I promised her we would do this together, but now it's just us. It's not Phoebe. Only you and I." I whispered,

"I won't say I know how hard this is for you because I don't know. I can tell you what it feels like to wake up every day and know she isn't here. I know what that feels like. I miss her more than life, and we are allowed to miss her. But at the same time, we must do what we set out today. I am here. You are here. Reno is here for us. We can do this. All of us together can do this. So let's do what we set out to do. Let's go out and finish what we set out to do. Let's send that fucker to hell," he answers.

I wipe the tears from my eyes, smiling.

"Let's send the fucker to hell."

THE JURY WAS SETTLING down as we walked in the next morning. Carson sits down next to me, her hand reaching for mine. Reno begins to distribute the files from his briefcase. I hear the click of the back door opening. My body tightened. I heard the shuffling of chains as Jonathan Conners walks towards his seat in the front. I tried to focus on anything but the feeling of his eyes boring into the back of my head.

"Don't look," Reno muttered. "Stare straight ahead and act like he is not even there."

Carson squeezed my hand. I took a deep breath in, my heart hammering in my chest. He wasn't there. I didn't need to pay him any mind. I didn't move until the judge walked in. I couldn't block out the rattling of the chains as Jonathan Conners stood up. He was right there. Right fucking there.

Carson squeezes my hand once more. I look up at her, a smile coating her features. She cocks her head towards the front of the courtroom where the judge bangs her gavel, signaling the court was in session. Reno stands up, pacing towards the front of the courtroom.

"I would like to call Alexander Chadwick to the stand."

I cast Alexander a look, hoping it will convey everything I wanted to say. He smiles, as if assuring me he understood before walking up to the stand. I watch as he places his hand over the bible.

"Do you solemnly swear to tell the whole truth and nothing but the truth, so help your God?" the judge asks.

"I do."

Reno walks towards the other end of the courtroom.

"Mr. Chadwick, it is to the understanding of this court that you were friends with Phoebe Conners; is that correct?"

"Yes."

"How did this friendship come about?"

Alexander looked stiff in his seat. His hands that were originally resting on the stand were now shoved below. He didn't want anyone to be able to tell how nervous he was.

"My parents were talking about Autumn Conners at the dinner table. We lived on the property next door, so they were some of the first to know what happened. I heard that and wanted to do something for her. I had seen her at school. She had withdrawn, and I knew she needed someone to be there. I went over to her house. I talked to her. I got her to trust me. I never left after that. It was just her and me."

Reno nods his head.

"Mr. Chadwick, did Phoebe Conners tell you anything about what occurred in her household?"

"She didn't originally. She tried as though nothing was the matter, but over time, I saw something was wrong. When I asked her about it, she told me but demanded I not tell anyone. She said she could handle it on her own. I knew she couldn't, but I didn't want her not to trust me. I had enough trouble with getting her to admit to me something was happening in the first place."

"How was Phoebe Conners acting the last time you talked to her?"

Alexander freezes. He opened his mouth a few times, but no sound came out. He knew this question was coming but there is no amount of preparation that will allow you to talk about watching someone slit their wrists. While I had received a phone call, he got a video call. He watched as the life slowly bled out of her. He had the worse end of it.

"She was sitting in the middle of her kitchen, holding a blade from a box cutter. She was almost whispering as if someone was around her. She apologized and told me I had spent the past four years trying to fix something permanently broken. She told me she never meant for me to get this involved, but she couldn't handle it anymore.

I told her she didn't have to do anything. I told her I was on my way and could be there on time. I begged her to put down the knife. She answered, and it told me it was too late. I watched as she dragged that knife against her wrists as I screamed at her to stop. I begged and pleaded, but she sat there looking down at her wrists as blood poured from them. I had never seen someone look that at peace. And she was at peace while she was dying. She told me she loved me. Apologized and said she would always love me."

"And why did you get to her house after Sydney?"

"She called Sydney first. Sydney was already on the way. Phoebe's property is over 2 miles wide. My car wouldn't start, and the battery was dead, so I didn't know what to do. I didn't think to run. I called my father, begging him to come home so we could jumpstart the car. He did, and right after, I drove away. When I got there, they were loading her into the ambulance, and Phoebe was sitting on the steps," Alexander responds.

I know how lucky I was only to get a call. I know that having to watch as she killed herself broke Alexander. All I got was a phone call. The last time I saw her alive was in the hospital, but she was alive. The last time Alexander saw her alive was when she dragged a knife against her skin.

"I have obtained records of that video call. If it is okay with the court, I would like to play it."

Alexander looks over at me, fear in his eyes. I glanced at Reno, silently begging him not to play it. It didn't matter what either of us wanted. It was crucial. It needed to be played. No matter what it would do to the two of us.

I wanted to look away. I couldn't watch as she died. Couldn't watch as the life slowly bled out of her, but I knew what it would look like if I didn't. I knew what the jury would think. They would think of me the same way they though of Jonathan.

I didn't look away, just stared straight ahead at the screen as I watched Phoebe Conners drag that knife against her skin and blood fell onto the ground. I didn't once cover my eyes. I kept them open. I kept watching that video. I watched as the knife met skin. I watched as blood pooled on the floor.

That blood had once covered my own skin. After I had left the hospital, I tried to scrub myself clean for hours. I had bled myself from trying to get all her blood's remnants off me. I had stood there in that shower, watching as the red stains poured down the drain.

Sitting there, it felt as though I had it on me again. I could feel the wash cloth I had scrubbed myself raw with. I wanted it off of me. I wanted the feeling to go away. It took everything inside of me not to try and itch my arms.

I didn't look at the jury as Reno ended the video. I just kept staring ahead. I couldn't see the sympathy in their eyes. The minute I saw their face. I saw their reactions to the same thing I had witnessed six years ago, I would break.

"Now, Mr. Chadwick, how long did it take you to get Phoebe Conners's house?" Reno asked.

"It took me about half an hour to get over there."

"What happened when you did get there?"

"Sydney was sitting on the steps of the Conners' house. I had passed an ambulance, so I

knew Pheobe wouldn't be there. I asked Sydney if she would be able to drive. We drove to the hospital and stayed there until Phoebe died," Alexander answered.

"Mr. Chadwick, when did you leave Indiana and move to Washington, DC?"

"I left Indiana about eight months after Phoebe Conners died and did not return until three years later."

"Why did you leave?"

Alexander looks down at me from the stand. I could feel my heart in my throat.

"I couldn't handle the stress of everything. I couldn't live with the constant reminder of what had happened. I had spent so much of my life with her, but after she died, I couldn't bring myself to stay."

"Why did you decide to come back?"

"The case followed me. Wanting to get away from it wasn't possible, no matter where I was. I saw Sydney and everything that she was doing. I couldn't stand to see Sydney doing it by herself. I loved Phoebe. She had been everything to me, and yet I had left. I came back because I knew leaving wasn't right. I came back because I loved Phoebe and was not about to let the man who hurt her get off free."

"No further questions, your honor," Reno says, moving to sit.

The silence was deafening. Every eye was trained on Jonathan's lawyer, just waiting for her to cross examine. Jonathan leaned into her, whispering something into her ear. She doesn't answer. She doesn't say anything.

"We will take a 90-minute recess, everyone gathering back inside the courtroom at 2:00 pm."

The gavel hit the desk. The chains attached to Jonathan rattle as he is escorted out of the courtroom. I look back towards Alexander, my heart in my throat. He shared the same expression. Silently the two of us agreed. We needed to get out of this courtroom. We needed to get the image of what we were shown out of our heads.

I feel Reno's hand grab my elbow, ushering me away from the courtroom.

We wait at the doors for Alexander. Carson's hand reaches and grabs my own. She gripped my hand tightly, providing a steady pressure as we continued. The flashes of cameras hit my eyes as we left the courtroom. I heard the shouts from reporters, desperately trying to get one of us to answer anything.

I kept my head down. I focused on the feeling of Carson's hand clutching mine. Reno opened the car door for us, usering us in before closing the door behind us. Reno moves and sits in the front seat, leaning back to talk to us.

"I know it wasn't expected. I didn't tell you all for a reason. I needed those reactions to be genuine. I needed everyone to see how it affected you without the reactions being rehearsed."

The four of us sat in silence as we drove. Carson never once let go of my hand. She kept it there, squeezing and providing extra pressure every few minutes. I leaned towards her, resting my head on her shoulder.

"I know," I hear her whisper. "I know."

Reno pulls into a coffee shop parking lot 20 minutes later. He instructs us to meet him inside in 10 minutes max. He would be sitting at a table in the very back.

We sit there for a moment, enveloped in the silence. I had long since stopped trying to find something to say for these moments. There was absolutely nothing one could say that would provide a glimpse of comfort.

I knew Reno was right. I knew he needed our reactions to be genuine and real or else his plan would not have worked. I couldn't get the image out of my head. I couldnt't unhear the screams from Alexander as he begged her to stop. He wanted to get a genuine reaction, well he sure as hell got one.

"I never wanted to see that again," Alexander whispers.

I turn to look towards him. His hands were folded together in his lap, tears streaming down his cheeks.

"I wasn't able to sleep for a two weeks after she died. The minute I closed my eyes I would see that. I would see her right there. I had blocked it out. Tried to forget it for so long. He brought it back. He got a video. He made us watch as she died again. Made us watch just for a genuine reaction."

I didn't reach out. Didn't grab his hand. Didn't utter those words of encouragement I had done so many times before. He was right. We had to sit there and watch as she died just so we could give the jury what they wanted. We had the evidence we needed. We had the testimony's. We had everything we needed to win, and he decided to bring one more thing. One more thing he knew would bring this reaction. One more thing.

"There isn't any forgiving for someone for this," Carson answers. "This isn't something you can just shake off and pretend as though it never happened. We don't have time for this though. We can't sit here and let this distract us from the rest of the case. It sucks. It was shitty thing to do without telling you. You can go home and cry about it as much as you want to. You can scream into the abyss that it isn't fair and he was a dick for doing it, but right now we need to act as though we are still in session. Don't let them see how badly this hurts. Let no one know how much it hurts.

We need to go in there, and shove it to the back of our minds. Pretend as though it didn't happen. You can unbury it and drop the act the minute you walk through your front door, but right now, there are three people who need justice to be served."

Carson reaches out her other hand, grabbing Alexanders.

"We go in there, and we pretend. We pretend as though you didn't have to watch her again. We go in there, fighting for the same thing we have been fighting for the past year."

The words felt lodged in my throat. I wanted to be able to nod my head and walk in there doing just as Carson said. Pretending. I had been doing that for six years now hadn't I? Why would it be so hard for me to do it now? I had been waking up every morning and pretending my life had been normal since she had died. This wasn't any different. Why did it feel as though it would be so different?

I didn't voice my concerns. I didn't say wat I was thinking. I just nodded, releasing Carson's hand and following them inside. Reno was right where he said he was, with three drinks placed at the seats around the table.

I followed the rest of them, sitting down in the seat right next to Carson. Reno looks up at me, slightly nodding his head as if to ask me if I was okay. As if to ask if I was ready to keep going.

I wasn't okay. That much was true, but I nodded my head, assuring him that I was ready.

Reno reaches into his bag, grabbing the manuscript and Phoebe's suicide note, placing them in front of us.

"You're next Carson. The jury will want to hear what happened leading up to the assault, during and after. Expect quesitons along the lines of why it took you so long to report, and if you knew anything about the Conners life behind closed doors. You have told all of this before, just reiterate everything.

After Carson, I will submit the suicide note and the manuscript as readings. After that we will have one more witness before I close the case on my end.:

My heart thunders to a stop. One more person. Someone else that hadn't been brought in front of us before.

"Who is this other person?" Alexander questions.

"They have wished to remain anonymous until called to the stand," Reno responds.

Anger flares in my chest, but I try to bury it down. Pretend. We have to pretend. Everything was just the same as it has been everytime before. This new witness didn't change anything. It was the same as it was before. Nothing was different.

"Sydney," I hear someone call.

I look up, everyone's eyes trained on me.

"Sydney," Carson says again. "Are you okay?"

I wasn't. We were supposed to be in this together. It was supposed to be the four of us agreeing on everything that would be brought before the court. Instead, Reno got another witness and obtained the video call between Phoebe and Alexander. These were the things we were supposed to be doing together. Decisions we should have been making as a team.

"I'm fine," I answered.

I meet Alexander's eyes across the table, a look of understanding covering his features. He knew how I felt. He knew how all of this was supposed to happen. Neither of us had wanted to have to sit through that. Neither of us wanted to have to watch that video call. Neither of us knew abot this other witness. It was just a shock to me as it was for him.

"Why didn't you tell us about this other witness," Alexander asks, tearing his eyes away from my own.

Reno looks up from the papers in front of him, meeting Alexander's eyes over his glasses.

"I didn't know until today if we would be able to get them here in time for the trial. This witness could very well win the case for us. I didn't want anyone to start believing we had won and stop trying."

Alexander glances over at me, doubt flickering through his eyes.

"If this witness agreed to work with us, why would they want to remain anonymous. They will have to reveal themselves on the stand, so why waste the time of staying nameless until then?

"This is a precaution built on protecting you all. You could be accused of knowing more than you do. You knowing who the witness is could compromise this entire case and your credibility to the jury. It's much easier for this person to remain anonymous until the date comes when their identity will be revealed."

He ended with a note of finality. There were no more questions that would be asked. No more information would be obtained. That was the end of the conversation.

We had to trust him. Trust that Reno knew what he was doing. Trust that this case wouldn't be run into the ground with the information that remained unknown to us.

After

"The prosecution would like to call to the stand Carson Keller" Reno calls.

Carson walks up to the stand, her head lifted high. She sat at the stand, her hand reaching out and resting on the bible placed in front of her. Her eyes met mine as she repeated after the judge, swearing herself to the law of the court.

"Ms. Keller, you say you were raped by Jonathan Conners 15 years ago, is that statement correct?" Reno asks.

Her eyes shift from mine, locking on Jonathan. Hatred fills her face as she stares at him. Years of terror and regret, burrowing it's way to the surface.

"Yes, that is correct."

"In your statement, you said 15 years ago you were at a sleepover at the Conner residence when both you and Autumn were raped. What led up to that night?"

"Autumn had been resisting on having a sleepover at her house for years. I had never understood it. I thought she was being selfish. She had this massive house and didn't want to share any of it. It wasn't until I told her my parents would be out of town and there was no way we could have a sleepover at my house that she agreed to let me stay over at her house."

"Did Autumn Conneers ever once look fearful? Was she looking over her shoulder? Checking behind corners? Anything that would tell you that she was at all scared?"

"She spent her entire night checking over her shoulder. She kept us away from the main parts of the house. We spent most of the time in her room. Anytime I said that I was hungry or wanted a drink, she would insist that I stayed in the room while she got it. She told me to lock the door everytime she left, and not open it again until I heard a series of three consecutive knocks.

I thought she was just playing a game. I never understood why she had me lock the door or wait until she knocked in a certain way, but I played along. It was an innocent little game. Nothing too serious."

"What happened after you two went to bed? When did the assault begin?"

Carson's eyes shifted back towards mine, shining with unshed tears. I nodded towards her. I had told her long ago that the pain wouldn't go away. Telling this story. Sending him to prison wouldn't do anything to erase the pain it brought, but it would bring a sense of comfort. Comfort that you had finally done everything you could to make sure that person paid for what they had done.

"We went to sleep at 10:30 that night. Autumn had told me to start getting ready for bed while she put Phoebe to bed. I locked the door behind me just as she told me and began to set up the blankets on the floor. She came back with that series of three knocks after half an hour.

Autumn didn't say anything as she laid down on the blankets right next to me. All she did was flick off the lights. I fell asleep right after that. Around 12:45 I heard whispering. When I opened my eyes, Jonathan Conners was gripping Autumn by her shirt, pressing her against the wall. I opened my mouth to scream but Autumn met my eyes, shaking her head.

Jonathan looked behind him to see me sitting there and dropped Autumn. I heard her begging him not to touch me. Told him to take her instead and do nothing to hurt me. He didn't listen.

I tried to fight against him. Tried to fight my way out of his grasp but he was stronger than me. He told me if I screamed he would kill me. So I stayed silent. I went limp. I closed my eyes. I pretended I wasn't there. I shut out Autumn's pleas. I closed my mind off to the sound of Jonathan Conners. I waited until he was done, trying desperately no to cry. When he was done, he turned towards Autumn.

I was lying on the floor as she lowered herself to the ground. I tried telling her to run. He was going to hurt her. He was going to do the same thing to me as he had done to her. She didn't listen as I screamed. She just laid there. She didn't even put up a fight.

When he was done he straightened his shirt and made both of us promise not to tell anyone. He said that if we told anyone he would kill the both of us and everyone we loved. Autumn just nodded as though she had heard this speech a million times before.

He left us after that, pressing the lock on the inside of the door. I will never forget what he said. He looked us in the eyes as he was locking the door whispering 'you wouldn't want any monsters to find their way in here now would you?'"

Carson's eyes overflowed with tears. I heard the rattle of Jonathan Conners as he looked around the courtroom before setting his eyes on Carson.

"He shut the door behind him, leaving us there. I asked Autumn if he meant what he said. If he really would kill us if we told anyone. She assured me he would. He would do whatever he could to never be caught.

Jonathan drove me home that next morning, his hand resting on Autumn's thigh as I sat in the backseat. When he parked in my driveway he turned his head, dragging his fingers over his lips as if to tell me to keep them sealed. I promised him again I wouldn't say anything. Would never tell anyone what he had done to me. I went inside and cried. My mother tried asking me what had happened but I didn't tell her. I was terrified that he would kill me. That he would do something to hurt me and my family."

Carson's eyes drift over again towards Jonathan Conners. I watched as their eyes met, her's flaring with a fire I had never seen before.

"I never told anyone what had happened that night. My parents refused to allow me to be around Autumn anymore. They didn't understand what had happened, but they knew enough to never allow me over there again. When I went to school Monday morning, I didn't even need to tell Autumn that we were not allowed to talk to each other again, she just knew. She didn't try and talk to me. Asked to be moved to another seat as soon as she saw me sit down at our table.

My parents moved us away from Aurora a few years later. We had gone to New York for a fresh start. I lost all contact I had with the Conners. It wasn't until Sydney Garcia started doing interviews that I learned both Autumn and Phoebe Conenrs had died.

Jonathan Conners took my entire life away from me. He took my innocence away from me because he couldn't control himself. He took Autumn and Phoebe's futures away from them. When he wanted something, he took it. He took whatever he wanted because it made him feel better. Made him feel stronger. Made him feel more like a man.

He took away other's lives because he wanted more from his own. He kept taking and taking from his own children, they felt the only way they could escape was to kill themselves. They felt that was the only bit of power they had left in their lives."

"I have no further questions your honor."

I keep my eyes trained on Carson as Jonathan Conners lawyer stands up, asking to begin her cross examination.

"Ms. Keller, if I might ask, what kept you from coming forward after you moved? Surely my client could not have hurt you if you were out of state," she questions.

"My family left for New York three years later. I lived those three years in fear. After we left, I was too scared to tell anyone. I was terrified that he would find a way to hurt my family if I did."

"Ms. Keller, what made you come forward?"

"I saw Ms. Garcia doing interviews. I saw she was fighting against the same man that had raped me. He was already in prison for domestic abuse. Both of his daughters were dead. I came forward because I had loved both of them. He couldn't hurt me when he was put away. I finally felt that it was safe for me to come forward."

"Ms. Keller, why were you so scared? Jonathan Conners is nothing but a man. Why were you so scared that he would do anything?"

Anger fills Carson's features. She turns, anger taking over her body as she stares down at Jonathan's lawyer.

"I was a child. I was a child who was terrified of losing my life. Terrified of something happening to my family. We are here because this person you called 'just a man' assaulted three children. His own children killed themselves because they felt as though they couldn't escape him. He is not just a man. He is a monster who stole the childhood and innocence away from three young girls.

So I didn't come forward because I was terrified. I didn't come forward because I knew he would do something. If I had come forward I would not be here today. I would be laying in the ground somewhere, just as his own children. It doesn't matter that it took me 15 years to come forward. It doesn't matter that I stayed silent for 15 years. I came forward because I was safe. I came forward because nothing could happen to me or the one's I loved.

Go ahead and blame me for Phoebe and Autumn's deaths. Go ahead and say that if I had done anything they would not be dead. You can pick apart my story a thousand times but I it will remain the same. The facts will remain the same. Jonathan Conners raped me 15 years ago, and right after, he raped his own child Autumn Conners. That is the truth. Those are the facts."

"I have no further questions your honor."

Reno gives Carson a nod and she leaves the stand, tears streaming down her face, but her head held high. She sat there and retold the worst experience of her childhood, and yet here she was, holding her head high.

That would have been Phoebe. If she was standing here today, she would have held her head high. Would never have let her father, or those on her fathers team rip that confidence away from her. This was all she had ever wanted. Right here was the only placed she had ever dreamed about. She had that dream ripped away from her by Jonathan. Had her entire life torn away from her.

The four of us were here, fulfilling the dream that she had always wanted. I liked to think she was looking down at us, smiling as she realized that Phoebe Conners had made an impact on this world. She hadn't disappeared. She hadn't faded with time. She was still here. She was still with us.

After

"The court would like to enter the diary of Autumn Conners into evidence."

Reno grabbed the diary from the corner of the desk, bringing it up to the judge. The judge opens up the pages, marked by Reno and begins reading.

"I wish I could tell you that you were good, Autumn. I wish I could tell you that I was stronger than you and could handle this, but I couldn't. I wasn't strong enough to stay for you, and I wasn't strong enough to stay for Sydney.

You would know Sydney. You went to school at the same time as her older brother. Her father is the police chief. Never once did I think I would end up with the daughter of the police chief. You would like her Autumn. She's level-headed. She thinks about everything she does before she does it. Most importantly, I love her. And I know she loves me.

That seems like a sentence I haven't said since you left. I haven't felt truly happy since you left Autumn, but Sydney makes me happy. Sydney makes me feel like I have a future outside of Aurora. She makes me feel as though I could be something other than the daughter of Jonathan Conners.

I tried Autumn. I promise you I tried. I tried being strong. I tried closing my eyes and pretending it wasn't happening, but I couldn't do it anymore. Sydney is the one thing in this world that made me feel I could make something of myself, but I can't do this anymore. She isn't enough for me to stay. She can't take away the years I have spent pretending. She can't take away the pain of losing you and the truth. The truth that I will never be anything other than the troublesome daughter of Jonathan Conners.

    I know there is a good chance Sydney will read this at some point, so I want to say the same thing Autumn said to me four years ago. I wish I were stronger for you, Sydney. I wish I could stay with you. It's not even that you are not good enough to hold me here because you are. I will have a future if I stay, but you won't stay with me.

    Everyone who loves me leaves. If I stay here, it will only delay the inevitable. You say you love every part of me, but Sydney, I know I would become too much after some time. I know it would only be a matter of time before you realize just how fucked up I am. I fucked up your life. Our relationship isn't healthy. You shouldn't have to be there for me, no matter what. You shouldn't have to shove everything you feel back just because you feel as though the person you love isn't strong enough to handle it. You need someone who is stronger. Someone who will listen. Someone who isn't broken.

    Move on from me, Sydney. Fix your relationship with your parents, and please don't hate me for leaving. Please understand that this was what was best for both of us. I love you, Sydney Garcia, and make something of yourself. Do everything you can because you won't have me there to hold you back."

My hands shook in my lap. Phoebe's final letter to Autumn. Everything she had wanted to say in those last four years. The judge kept reading through the diary entries left by Autumn. My mind felt numb.

For so long I had wanted nothing more than to hear one last time that she loved me. That was all I wanted, and here it was. She had written it down. That I loved her and she loved me. She had always loved me, but I was never enough. Maybe in soe other time I could have been enough. Maybe in another universe it would be her sitting here next to me, grabbing my hand and holding it in her laps.

"The court is dismissed. They will reconvene at 10 am tomorrow."

Alexander drove me to the Conners house. He watched as I walked inside and turned on the light in the foyer before pulling away. I watched out the window as his car pulled out of the driveway, the silence of the house enveloping me.

I stood by the window, staring out at the forest just beyond the gravel. How many times had I followed Phoebe into those woods? How many times had we both sit there and watched the sun pass through the pines?

This entire house was filled with memories. It felt as though every inch had been touched by Phoebe. There wasn't a place I could go here that would be free of Phoebe Conners. She had touched every inch of my life.

I stood in that foyer until I couldn't feel my feet underneath me. I let myself walk up the stairs, feeling the smooth wood of the banister underneath my hands. I didn't stop myself until I had walked up to the last floor. Phoebe's door was open just slightly. I followed the light from the moon shining through the window into her room, the tears finally breaking through.

My knees gave out from underneath me. I collapsed on the floor in Phoebe's room, the floor feeling cold underneath me. Sobs broke through, ripping out of my body.

I don't remember anything after I went into Phoebe's room that night. I woke up the next morning in her bed, wearing one of her old sweatshirts. The clock read 7am. I didn't feel as though I had slept at all. I was just as tired as I was the night before.

My head pounded as I stumbled down the stairs. I stood and watched as the coffee dripped into the pot, praying the ibuprofen took effect. The house felt emptier than it had the night before. Just as devoid as the first day after Phoebe died.

I didn't start getting ready until 8:45 that morning, and even then, it felt as though putting on clothes was draining all of my energy.

I drove to the court that morning, trying to straighten myself up. I walked into the courtroom by myself that day. I saw all the eyes on me, but I stood up straighter and walked toward Alexander and Reno. I had a job to do, and I would be damned if I let my emotions get in the way.

After

The court was antsy. The trial was going on longer than they had been expecting. Jonathan's lawyer had been cross examining everyone she could. Reno asked more and more diary entries be entered.

My head was pounding. I felt as though I had been run over by a truck. Every second I spent in that courtroom felt as though another part of me was gone. The court was dismissed early. No one could focus on anything that was being brought up to the stand.

Reno insisted on driving me home that night. Alexander made me promise that I was okay. That I was going to be okay when I came in the next morning. I promised. Told him I just needed the night.

I couldn't bring myself to leave the car when Reno pulled into the driveway. I didn't want to have to sit in that empty house and remember what was there once.

"Sydney, we're here."

I looked up at Reno. His hands were resting on the steering wheel, the lights from the car reflecting off of the house and shining on his face.

"I can't do it," I whispered.

He reaches over, wrapping his arms around me.

"I can't go in that house. I can't stay there by myself. I can't do it."

"Then we don't go in. I'll drive you back to your parents house. You don't have to go in there."

I nodded my head, pulling away from Reno's grasp and staring out at the driveway. The wind was blowing, the trees swaying in the sky. Reno stepped out of the car, his phone pressed up against his head. I heard blips of the conversation. He was telling my father I would be coming home to them tonight. He assured my father everything was okay, I just needed to stay at the house for a the night.

The drive to my parents house was silent. I stared out of the window. The headlights shone off the trees as we passed, illuminating a small bit of the forest at a time. Phoebe used to find solace in this forest. She used to go there when everything became too much. It provided her a place to relax. Somewhere she didn't need to pretend that she was okay. That she wasn't dying inside.

Reno watched as I walked up the steps to the house. He made me promise that I would call him in the morning. Check in just to make sure I was okay for the trial that day.

The second I opened the door to my house, my mother was hugging me, wrapping me in her arms.

"Hey, baby."

"Hey, mama."

She walked over to me and sat on the couch, letting me lay my head on her thigh. We said nothing; we just sat there together. She ran her fingers through my hair as I sat there, my eyes closed.

"You shouldn't have to deal with this," she whispers.

I didn't answer. I knew I shouldn't have to either, but I was here. This is where my life had led me. This was the path I chose for myself.

I fell asleep lying there with her. It was the best night of sleep I had gotten since the trial had begun. I woke up in my bed the next morning, the blaring of my alarm disrupting me from my sleep. I wanted nothing more than to snooze that alarm and go back to sleep, but I knew I had another day in court. I slinked out of bed, my eyes feeling heavy as I walked downstairs.

My entire family was sitting around the kitchen table, laughing and talking. I sat in my old seat next to my brother. He smiled, shoving a cup of coffee into my eagerly awaiting hands.

"Good Morning Syd," my dad says.

I looked over to see him in a suit and tie. He had been called in to testify today. He was our second to last witness. We had called everyone we could, every responding officer that ever came to the Conners' house, every previous teacher of Autumn and Phoebes, her grandparents, and her extended family. Anyone who could give us anything about the life of Phoebe and Autumn. After my father, we had the anonymous witness Reno had called.

After Phoebe died, my father and anyone else who had been involved with the Conners had been fired. The public was never told why. My father wouldn't speak of it. He would give the same answer the police force told anyone who asked. Actions could have been taken to protect the Conners, but they weren't.

I had known for years he could have taken action. That he could have done something to protect Phoebe but never did. There were times when I hated him for it. Times when I wanted to scream at him for the pain I had gone through for the past six years. He could have done something. He could have done anything to protect Phoebe but never did.

But he was my father. He had been there for me when I lost her. He shoved aside every feeling he had about her and held when when I cried. He had been there for me when no one else had. Despite what he thought, he was there, and I couldn't discredit that

I looked around the table at my family. Christine and Carlise, now grown adults, came home from college for a weekend because they repeatedly told us that the dining hall food was not as good as our moms' and that they needed to do their laundry, but that was unrelated. Tyler was there with his wife and kids, my niece and nephew throwing pancakes back and forth at each other. Adam was sitting there on his phone and Cindy desperately tried to get my niece from throwing the pancakes at her chocolate milk glass.

These were the people that had been there for through all of this. The people that had shoved aside their own opinions to promise me that everything was going to be okay. These were the people that cared about me enough to put their entire lives on hold for this trial.

I was fighting for Phoebe, but a small part of me was fighting for this family. This family that had been there for me through everything. The family that loved me enough to put aside our differences and come together. The family that had forgiven me.

MY FATHER AND I MET Reno outside of the courtroom. Reno had told us to meet early so we could miss the cameras and reporters. It was what was best for my father. Reno came and pulled my father aside, discussing what would be said during the trial. Alexander met me inside of the car.

"Do you ever hate him?" he asks. "I know he's your father but do you ever hate him for not doing something when he could? Do you ever blame him for what happened?"

"I do," I answered. "There are times when I blame him for everything that happened. He could have done something in his position of power to help her if he wasn't too blind to see it, but I think the same of myself at times. I try not to blame anyone for what happened other than Jonathan. He is the real reason we are all here. He is the real reason Phoebe isn't here with us now."

He leans back in the seat, the heels of his hands resting on his eyes.

"I went to the station so many times to bail her out. Everytime he told me the same, that I needed to gain better control of my friend. I promised him everytime that I would try. He would unlock the holding cell and I would help Phoebe into the car. On the way home she would cry. She would apologize for putting me in that position. She would promise me that she would never do it again. I should have known better than to believe her, but I did. I did everytime."

He opens his eyes, turning his head to look at me.

"I thought this trial was going to help. I thought as we progressed it would make me feel better, but in truth, it's made me feel worse. I know this is what Phoebe would have wanted, but it's not fair that she is not here to do it herself. It's not fair that there are people who are out there that could have done something to help her but didn't. It's not fair that Jonathan Conners gets to sit there while she is six feet in the ground."

"None of it is fair Alexander," I answered. "No one has ever claimed for any of this to be fair. You and I both know Phoebe should be here. Every single person inside of that courtroom knows that she should be the one testifying, but she's gone Alexander. She's not here. She's not here to testify. She's not here to watch him get his life sentence.

We are doing this because she isn't here. That doesn't make it hurt any less that she isn't. We are doing this because we loved her. Because she was the only thing that mattered in our lives for so long. We have sacrificed everything for this trial. Six years of our lives have gone to this moment. We will never get those years back. We will never be able to change the path we have set ourselves on. We need to make the most of this.

We don't get forever for this trial. We don't get to bullshit our way through it with pointless information. We get this one chance One chance to do everything Phoebe would have done if she were here. So we do it. We do it just as she would have and we don't blame others for what happened. We blame the person who is truly at fault. We blame the person Phoebe would blame if she were here today."

A knock on the window sounds as I finish. Reno is standing outside of the window, my father close behind.

"We go in there. We go in there and we finish this the way she would want us too. The way she would have done it herself."

"Let's finish this," Alexander whispers.

379

After

My father sat behind the four of us in the courtroom. It was silent for a moment before everyone started pouring in. Hundreds of eyes trained on us. I heard the familiar sound of the door opening, and the rattling of chains. Reno had told us many times before to never look at him as he is walking into the courtroom. It's just adding fuel to the fire. But this time, I trained my eyes on him. I watched as the sick son of a bitch was dragged in by handcuffs. I watched as he sat down in his seat, and I met his gaze as he stared right back at me. I didn't break eye contact. I was not about to be the first one to look away.

In my mind, I wanted nothing more than to watch as every ounce of life bled out from him, just as I had Phoebe. In my mind, I wanted to kill him myself. He was the reason she wasn't here. He was the reason the last six years of my life were gone. He was the reason I lost her. I wanted the mother fucker dead.

"NOW, MR. GARCIA, IT is to our understanding that you were one of the responding officers to many of the cases involving Phoebe Conners. Why was she never detained and given a trial?"

"I will be the first person to admit there was corruption within this police department. We were paid off by Johnathan Conners and his wife every time she was arrested. We found some way to erase the records and act as though it never happened," my father answered.

"Why would you accept that money from Jonathan Conners?"

"The department was underfunded. Some of my deputies and officers raised concerns, but I told them not to do anything. I didn't want anyone to know about the money. I made it look as though I had been donating. It was just easier that way," my father answered.

"What was Phoebe arrested for the times you did arrest her?"

I could see the nervousness all over my father's features. He sat there, his hands wringing on top of the stand. I could imagine my mother sitting at home watching the trial any way she could. My siblings would be gathered around her, and they would all be sitting there, holding onto my mother's hands as she recited the lord's prayer under her breath.

"She was arrested for indecent exposure, a Class 1 misdemeanor, drug possession without intent to distribute, and public intoxication. I would tell the judge what happened and give whoever it was a portion of the bribe. She was never tried, and the record was immediately expunged." he answered.

"Exactly how many records were expunged? Reno asked.

"I don't remember off the top of my head. If I had to guess, I would assume it was about 15."

"Mr. Garcia, are you aware that your actions are against the law, and you could be incarcerated?" Reno asked him.

My father looks towards me, a sad smile on his face. I looked away, not able to look him in the eyes. I didn't know what I would do if I met his eyes.

"I am aware. I regret what I did. I regret taking bribes, but I regret how my actions influenced my daughter and her life. I would be willing to go before any judge or jury and be tried for my crimes because my actions caused my daughter to be in this position. I played a direct hand in Phoebe Conner's death, and she is no longer with us because of my actions."

"No further questions, your honor," Reno says, sitting back down next to us.

The three of us sat together as Johnathan's lawyer came and tried to ask more questions, but I wasn't paying attention. My father had accepted bribes. He had known what was happening the entire time and yet did nothing. He did nothing.

Reno stands up once more, turning towards the back of the courtroom.

"The prosecution would like to call Phoebe Conners to the stand."

My heart stops in my chest. My head spins around as I see a woman stand up from the crowd of thousands in the courtroom. It was her. It was Phoebe. I watch as she walks up towards the stand, her eyes meeting mine as she walks past.

I didn't know how this was possible. This shouldn't be possible. I watched her die. I watched the sheet be drawn over her body. She was supposed to be dead. She was supposed to be dead, yet she was standing right in front of me. She was supposed to be dead.

"Do you swear to tell the truth, the whole truth, and nothing but the truth?" the judge asks, but everything sounds faint.

I had mourned her death for six years. For six years, I had sobbed at the memories of us. For six years, I had fought to bring her the justice I had promised her when she was alive, yet here she was. For six fucking years, I had cried myself to sleep when she was alive and well.

"May you please state your name for the court," Reno tells her.

Phoebe's eyes meet mine as she speaks.

"My name is Phoebe Andrea Conners, and my father sexually assaulted me for five years."

I looked away from her. I couldn't bare to see her sitting there.

"Miss. Conners, I understand the court may be confused about the nature of your appearance, so could you please disclose the events of the last seven years?" Reno asks her.

I knew she was trying to meet my eyes again, but I couldn't bring myself to look at her. Instead, I looked over at Alexander for the first time since Phoebe had appeared. His cheeks were stained with tears as his mouth was hanging open in shock. For a moment I thought that those tears were those of shock and anger but I quickly realized they were tears of happiness. Alexander didn't even care that she had made us all believe she had been dead for six years. He didn't care about the pain he had suffered for those years. All he cared about was that Phoebe was right here.

"When I was 19 years old, I tried committing suicide. Sydney Garcia had found me and I was brought to the hospital. It was there I flatlined. I was revived by the staff, and told they told Sydney Garcia and Alexander Chadwick that I had died. According to them, there was no one who knew that I was alive except for the doctors. I was told my sister Autumn Conners had been in contact with a lawyer before she died. A man named Reno. Reno had been tasked with keeping track of my fathers wrongs committed against me if anything were to happen to her.

It was then that I met Reno. He told me the hospital staff, social workers and himself made the effective decision to fake my own death to protect my safety and the safety of those around me. He told me when the time came I would be able to be integrated into my old life but it was safest if I changed my name and left the country."

When I finally look up at her, Phoebe is staring down at me, tears filling her eyes.

"I have been living in Denmark for the past six years. I was in constant contact with Reno and was given monthly updates about the life and case back in Indiana. It wasn't until a week ago Reno told me there was enough evidence to take the case to trial. I packed a bag and booked a flight as quickly as I possibly could."

Reno knew. Reno fucking knew this entire time and didn't say anything. He let me believe for 3 fucking years that she was dead and he knew the entire time.

"Miss Conners, would you please tell the court the details of the abuse you suffered at Mr. Conners hand?"

Everything inside of me was telling me to look at her. Meet her in the eyes, but I couldn't bring myself to look at her.

"Mr. Conners first raped me two days after Autumn Conners funeral. He opened the door to my room and made me promise not to tell my mother anything he did. He said Autumn had done a good job at keeping the promise and he expected me to do the same," she says.

"How often would be touch you?" Reno asks.

"It started with only around twice a month. As the years progressed it became once a

week and then became almost every day of the week."

She said he raped her. That was the first time I had ever heard her say that before. She hated the word. Hated the way it conjured up an image in your head no matter what context it was said in. She despised the way it made her sound weak.

"Would you say Jonathan Conners touched you or raped you?" Reno asks.

For the first time since the trial started, Phoebe looks over towards Jonathan. Before she died she had always avoided his gaze and when he looked at her, she shrunk away, trying to avoid his gaze a much as possible, but here she was, staring him right in the eye. Looking down on him as if he was nothing.

"Jonathan Conners raped me for five years," she says. "Touch doesn't encapsulate what he did to me."

"The prosecution rests."

The judge announced the end of the day and everyone started packing up. I saw Phoebe staring at me from the corner of her eye but I couldn't bring myself to move towards her. Alexander tears from my side and runs to her, wrapping his arms around her and sobbing into her shoulder.

"It's you," I hear him say. "It's really you."

Phoebe wraps her arms around him, whispering into the side of his head. "It's me Alexander. It's really me."

Tears threaten to spill from my eyes as I watch them. I wanted to be able to run up there and hug her and cry because she was alive, but I couldn't. They had lied to me for years. Reno knew she was alive. He took this case because he knew she was alive.

"Sydney could we talk about this?" I hear Reno ask from behind me.

He sets his hand on my shoulder, but I shove him off. I wheel around to stare at him, the tears filling my eyes.

"You've known this entire time. You have known she was alive this entire time and you didn't even think about telling me," I muttered. My voice didn't sound like my own.

I knew I needed to keep my voice down. News sources would eat this shit up if they heard me screaming at Reno but I couldn't stop myself.

"Sydney you have to understand we did this to protect Phoebe. All of it was done to keep her safe and away from harm," Reno assures.

He was right and I knew that. I knew what he had done kept her safe. She wasn't hurt by her father during these past seven years. But her being safe had meant she needed to leave. I needed to believe she had died. Everyone needed to believe she had died. I had grieved over her for seven years. I had cried at her headstone. I had cleaned up all of the dead flowers and spray paint off of her headstone because I believed I was doing it to keep the best part of her alive in some way and yet she had been alive this entire time.

"I know you might be upset with me but we did this for Phoebe. You have grieved her death for six years and that is a lot for someone to go through, but you were not the only person who was effected. You get the chance that almost no one else has. You have that person back. You have the chance to go and redo what you have wanted to redo for seven years. Don't let that go just because you are upset," Reno tells me, patting my shoulder before walking over towards where Alexander was standing.

I angrily wipe tears from my face and turn to see Phoebe standing in front of me.

"Sydney," she breathes.

My heart pounded in my chest as she said my name. There it was. I had been wanting to hear that for years and there it was.

"Can we talk?" she asks.

I shook my head, backing away from her. She moves to place her hand on my arm but I jerk away.

"You're dead. You're supposed to be dead."

She takes another step towards me.

"Sydney, please just give me a second to explain."

I shook my head again, backing away from her.

"You lied for six fucking years. You let me stay in this godforsaken town, mourning your death for six years. Six years that I could have spent having a life. Having a future."

She reaches her hand out again as if to stop me.

"Don't fucking touch me," I whisper.

From the corner of my eye I see Alexander starting to walk towards Phoebe. I couldn't stay here. I couldn't be in this room with a woman who was supposed to be dead. I couldn't be here with my father and I couldn't be here with Alexander.

So I ran. I didn't care about the whispers or the flash of the cameras, I just ran. Ran away from the case. Ran away from Phoebe. Ran away from that courtroom. I ran, praying my life would leave me behind. That when I finally stopped, it would all have just been my imagination.

After

I unplugged the house phone from the wall after Phoebe's tenth message. I stopped opening the door after hearing Phoebe's voice on the other side 5 times. I shut off my phone after Reno texted me three times to ask if we could talk. I kept the every door locked after Alexander found his way in through the back door.

I didn't leave the fourth floor other than to get food. All of the lights were shut off. I couldn't bring myself to see those dark corners of the house. The corners that I had looked through over and over again for something that would keep Phoebe's memorie alive. I hadn't needed it the entire time.

I had shut the door to Phoebe's bedroom after coming home. That room that was filled with dust. The room that I had ripped apart looking for anything that would prove he was guilty. Anything that would prove without a shadow of a doubt that he was the reason she was gone.

She wasn't gone. She had never been. She had been living in Denmark. Living across the country this entire time. I had spent six years destroying myself over her. For six years I had let myself be consumed by Phoebe. For six years I lived with the fear of forgetting her. The fear that if even one memory would slip that all of them would start leaving. I tortured myself with the memories because I felt that was the only way I could keep her alive.

And yet, here she was. Alive and well. Looking healthier and happier than I had ever seen her before.

She wasn't supposed to be alive. She wasn't supposed to be back here. I had mourned her for six years. Had cried myself to sleep for a year after she died. I had cut off every single person in my life that did not have a direct corelation to the case. She had been in contact with Reno the entire time. Reno had known for six years. He had been in contact with her. He had seen everything I had done to ruin myself, and never said anything. Never once let me know that she was okay, or that she was at least alive somewhere. He let me believe that she was dead. That I was never going to be able to see her again. He let me torture myself, when he knew she was alive the entire time.

I had three days. Three days to pull myself together and walk into that courtroom as if this was the plan all along. Three days before I had to pretend that my life hadn't been turned upside down in a matter of minutes.

"WE WOULD LIKE TO CALL Phoebe Conners to the stand."

I see Phoebe out of the corner of my eye. She is sitting next to me, her hands clenched into fists in her lap. Alexander reaches over grabbing a hand and giving it a reassuring squeeze. She stands up, adjusting her blazer before walking to the stand. Her hand reaches out mechanically, placing it on top of the bible gingerly, as if it would burn her if she touched it too quickly.

She mutters through her promise of truth, jerking it away the moment they begin to move it away. Her eyes turn to her father, cold malice filling her gaze. Jonathan isn't effected. He stares back, equal amounts of anger filling his eyes.

"Phoebe Conners, you and Sydney Garcia were involved romantically am I correct?"

Phoebe fixs her stare on Jonathan's lawyer.

"Yes, we were," she answers.

"So you are in fact a homosexual?"

Her hands uncurl from fists, pressing down onto the stand. I watched her lips tighten into a thin line. Red began to creep up onto her cheeks.

"I have a romantic interest in women. That is why Sydney and I were togther," she answers, her voice coming out clipped.

"What about sexually?"

"Excuse me?" she demands. Anger fills me. They were trying to say what her father did was justified. Trying to make the jury believe she just needed to be saved. To be protected.

"Were you and Sydney Garcia ever sexually involved? Has you ever been sexually involved with anyone?"

"I do not experience sexual attraction. No, I was not sexually involved. I have never been sexually involved with anyone."

"I believe you mean to say you were never sexually involved with anyone other than my client Jonathan Conners. Let us not forget that you did have a sexual relationship."

"Excuse me," Phoebe whispers, her voice taking a dangerous tone.

Reno leans forward, his jaw clenching. She was getting out of control. She was going to start screaming. They would paint her to be emotional. Psycotic. Out of line. Any of those words could sway the jury in a second.

"My father raped me. He would pin me down and tell me if I made a noise he would gut me. He would put his hand over my throat so if I even thought about moving I would be choking. Nothing about that is a sexual relationship. He was my father. He was in a position of power over me and he abused that time and time again."

"Miss Conners, you can not deny that no matter if it was a case of rape or a case of sexual assault, there was still a sexual aspect to your lives together."

Phoebe stands up, her hands quivering as they braced her onto the stand.

"Women have to spend their entire lives wondering what may happen to them daily. We have to look over our shoulders every second of the day and wonder what may happen if we walk home alone at night. We are taught to put our keys between our fingers, so if we need to defend ourselves from someone, we have a defense right there. We are taught to keep a man in our lives who can protect us if we need to. That man should never be able to take advantage of someone who has spent nothing, but their entire life worried about what may happen to them. Johnathan Conners was in that position to be that man, and he took advantage of that.

Never should a child have to worry about what may happen to them if they go home one night. Never should a child worry if their father will hurt them one night. A father should be there for their children and protect them from those bad things. They should not become that bad thing. Time and time again, Johnathan Conners took advantage of the position he was in and hurt his own children and others.

You can not even think that using the fact that I am queer as an excuse for his assault. I didn't need fixing. I didn't need to be converted and he knew that. My father will use any excuse in the book to try and make what he did okay. He hurt me. He hurt Autumn. He hurt Carson. He took our innocence from us. Carson had to move just to get away. Autumn had to die just so she could get out of the situation she was in.

Sitting here, trying to say that because I was queer, I just neede fixing is some of the biggest bullshit I have ever heard. There is no excuse for what Johnathan Conners has done to his children, and to try and blame it on the fact that I am queer, is nothing but lazy and offensive."

No one speaks a word when as Phoebe finishes. It was quiet all around me. Phoebe's eyes stray over towards mine, meeting my gaze head on. Despite myself, I smile. Her eyes turn glassy as she chokes down a laugh.

"This is not a case to determine whether or not I am queer. This is not the case to determine the validity of queerness. This is a case to show that I, Phoebe Conners, my sister Autumn Conners and Autumn's best friend Carson Keller were sexually assaulted and raped by my father. This is a case to prove that Johnathan Conners is a psychopath who hurt his children. Those will be the only questions I will be willing to answer now."

Phoebe turns back towards Jonathan's lawyer, anger in her movements.

"Are we done here?"

"No further questions, your honor."

"I have some questions, your honor," Reno says, standing up and walking towards the stand.

"You may proceed," the judge tells him.

"Now, Miss Conners, when did you first realize you were queer?" Reno asks.

"I've always known. It was just one of those things that I never had to question.."

"Did you ever feel ostracized because you are queer?" he asks me.

"My mother listens to whatever my father says. My father is a bigot. They hated that I am queer. They hated that Autumn was queer. I was never safe there."

"I've read about your struggles with religion. You have said it was just another way for your father to control you. If it was as bad as you say, then why did you never leave? Why not just report him and put the past behind you?" Reno asks.

"I was terrified. He made me terrified. He had convinced me from the time I was born that if I said anything against him I wouldn't be believed. He told me he had eyes everywhere. He knew what I was doing at all moments of the day. I was never given any reason to doubt that."

She pauses, turning to look towards me. Her eyes well with tears as she meets my eyes.

"I was scared. Scared of what would happen if I told anyone what he did to me. He had threatened to kill me. He told me he would drive me to the edge just as he done to Autumn. I had no where to go. No where that was going to protect me from him. I believed him when he said he could find me anywhere. That there was no where in the world I could go that he couldn't reach me. After being told that for so long, it isn't one of those things that you can just forget.

The only person who made me believe I could truly leave was Sydney. She made me doubt everything he had ever told me. With her, it didn't matter that none of the police would ever believe a word that came out of my mouth. It didn't matter that this town was the only place I had ever known. It didn't matter that he was rich and had every single person in the town under his command. With her I truly believed I could leave it all behind. Start a new life where I wasn't haunted by my past."

"I have no further questions your honor."

"This court will reconvene tomorrow at 9 am. Court dismissed."

The bang of the gavel tears my eyes away from hers. I itched to run to her. To hold her to me and tell her I was always going to be there. To press my lips to her's and make up for six years of lost time.

In this distance I heard Alexander call my name. I look up, Phoebe standing by Alexander, tears pouring down her face.

"Phoebe just want's to talk," I hear him say.

They all sounded so far away.

"Please, just give me a chance to explain everything," she begs.

I don't. I run.

I heard them calling my name as I fled the courtroom, pushing past everyone who was in my way. I needed to get out of there. I couldn't be in the same room with her. I couldn't see her again tomorrow. I couldn't see her again at all.

THE COLD OF THE DOOR grounded me. My head was in between my legs, as I tried to gasp down breaths. My heart was racing. She shouldn't be here. I couldn't see her everyday. I couldn't let myself be pulled into her again. She wasn't supposed to be here. She was supposed to be dead. Why was she not dead?

Trails of tears covered my cheeks. My hands shook from where they laid on the ground. I tried picking my head up, letting it rest on the door behind me.

5 things I could see.

4 things I could feel.

3 things I could smell.

2 things I could hear

1 thing I could taste.

I repepeated the cycle. Trying desperately to find anything to calm my racing mind. At some point, Atlas had come lay at my feet, his head resting on the floor, his eyes peering up at me. I reached out, resting my hand on his head. I took another deep breath. Then another one after that. Then another one after that.

A pounding at the door interrupted me. The hand that rested on Atlas's head shook as I closed my eyes. I wasn't going to answer it. Answering it was only going to cause more problems.

I felt Atlas leave from underneath my hand. His tail was wacking against mine, a bark working it's way through his small body. I opened my eyes, looking over at Atlas.

He was pawing at the door, his entire body shaking. A smile covered his small face, this tail creating a strong breeze.

In heard a knock again.

"Sydney, I know you are in there. Can we please just talk this through? Just give me time to explain."

She was here.

Atlas turns to look at me, his face lighting up. He knew it was her. It been six years since he had last seen her and here she was as if no time had passed. Atlas deserved to see her. She deserved to see Atlas.

I picked myself off the floor, resting my shaking hand on the doorknob. Atlas stared at me expectantly, waiting for me to just turn the knob and open the door. Waiting until he could see Phoebe again.

I turned the knob, the light from the porch pouring in.

Phoebe stands at the door, her

hand raised as if to knock. I open my mouth to say something. Anything, but the words can't make their way out of my throat.

Atlas brushes past my legs, jumping up to see Phoebe. His entire body shook as he jumped onto Phoebe. I watch as she bends down, wrapping her arms around him and pulling him into her chest. He attacks her face with kisses as she holds him, his entire lower half shaking from the force of his tail.

Her words come out choked as she holds him, tears welling in her eyes.

'Hi, buddy," she whispers, pressing a teary kiss to the top of his head.

She looks back up at me, a smile covering her face.

"Thank you," she mouths before pressing another kiss to Atlas's head.

I watch as she makes her way inside, her hands carresing the banister in the same way

I had watched her do hundereds of times before. She starts to make her way up the stairs, remembering each and every step up to her room. I follow her, my heart pounding in my chest.

Her hand presses against her door as she reaches sit. I watch as she inhales in a deep breath before pushing the door open. Atlas rushes past her, jumping onto his designated spot on the bed. She walks around the room, her fingers brushing against every single iten I had left untouched.

"I never thought I would see this place again," she whispers. She turns to face me, the tears filling her eyes.

"I never thought I would see you again," she whispers.

"I never thought you would be here," I admit.

She smiles reaching out and grabbing my hand. I don't pull away this time. I let her

grab my other hand before wrapping her arms around me. She feels just the same as she did six years ago. Her smell is still the same. I still found the same comfort in them as I once did. I let the tears fall. I let myself cry into her shoulder. Her hand rests on my head, holding my head onto her shoulder.

"I'm so sorry," she whispers. "So fucking sorry for everything."

The juxtaposition of our situation strikes me. Six years ago, it was me holding her like this. It was me wrapping my arms around her's and promising her everything was going to be alright, when both of us knew there was a good chance it wouldn't be. She had changed in these six years. She was stronger. More secure.

She is happy, I realized. That's what the difference is. She isn't fearing for her life everything steps foot into her house. She's happy, because she is safe from what her old life used to bring her.

"I'm so sorry Sydney," she whispers into my hair. "I never wanted to disappear. Never wanted all of this to go this far. I have missed you more than anything else in this entire world."

"I know," I answered. For the first time since she came back, I actually believed her. "I know."

After

"I don't remember much from the first year. I vaguely remember waking up in the hospital. One of the doctors told me it hadn't worked. I was so convinced it would this time. I thought that was going to be the end.

The next thing I remember was being on a plane headed to Denmark. That's where I first met Reno. He told me who he was and why he was there. Autumn had hired him years ago right before she had died. He had stayed on this entire time. He told me I was going to Denmark. There I was going to live my life just as I would have in Aurora but I wasn't allowed to have contact with anyone from my old life.

After that he dropped me off at an apartment and told me he was going to be in contact. After that, it was a blur. I didn't go out much in that first year. I stayed in the house, getting my groceries from a scheduled delivery set up by Reno. I hated living there. Hated that this was my life now. Hated that I couldn't call my mother. Hated that I couldn't talk to Alexander anymore. More than anything, I hated that I wasn't there with you.

I attempted twice in that year. They never worked. After the second time, Reno finally came down. I remember him sitting in the chair in the hospital room as I woke up. He didn't waste a second before going into his lecture. He told me I had been given chance after chance at life and I still took it for granted. Now I had been given even more of a chance at life. I had been given a better life. A life far away from the one I had been born into. He told me

I needed to take the opportunity I had been given. To take what few people had. I would go back to Indiana at some point. I would see you again, but I needed to be patient. I needed to trust that you knew what you were doing. I would have the chance to give my father what he deserved, but I can't do that yet. I needed to have faith in you. Faith that you would do this. That you would make it possible for me to come back.

I spent the next five years preparing. Preparing my testimony. Figuring out just what to say that would put him away for the rest of his life. Reno would come my every so often and make me promise that I would go out more. That I would meet people. I promised him everytime and never did until he dragged me out of the house.

And it actually worked Sydney. I have friends in Denmark. I have the life I never thought I could have. It never felt complete though. It always felt as though I was missing something. I was always missing you. You were the only thing I thought about for the past five years. The only thing that kept me going. It was you. It's always been you Sydney Garcia."

"I went to NYU like I said I would. I tried leaving you behind. Leaving your memory behind. I thought that if I could pretend that I never met you. That if I just acted like I hadn't lost you, the pain would go away. It didn't. It never did. I would dream of you. I would see you when I closed my eyes. I would see around the corner of a hallway. You were everywhere. I couldn't get you out of my head."

My hands are shaking as I sit across from her in her bed.

"I have missed you more than you could now," I whispered.

She smiles, grabbing my hand and holding it between her's.

"I think I have a pretty good idea Sydney Garcia."

A laugh breaks free as I wrap my arms around her, holding her to my chest.

"What you and I wasn't healthy," I whispered.

She looks up at me, hurt flickering through her eyes.

"I'm not saying I don't love you but you and I both know neither of us were in a place where we could have been in a relationship like that. We moved quickly. Faster than we normally woud have if we weren't terrified we wouldnt't have had that time."

"I've missed you more than anything else in this entire world. I've wanted nothing more than to be here with you for the past six years Sydney."

I pull away, grabbing her hands in mine.

"I've missed you more than anything too Phoebe. I want this to work. I want us to work, but to do that, we need to do what we didn't do six years ago. We start over. We need to take this slow and do whatever we didn't do all of the years ago."

She smiles, turning towards where Atlas was laying on the bed. She takes her hands from mine, grabbing Atlas and holding him to her chest before sticking out a hand.

"Hello Sydney Garcia. My name is Phoebe Conners and this is Atlas the most amazing corgi in the entire world," she says.

I laugh, holding out my hand to shake her's.

"Why hello Phoebe Conners."

"Is it too forward Miss Garcia to say that I am completely in love with you and would nothing more than to kiss you right now?" she asks.

"I can't of anything that is less forward," I laugh.

She cuts me off, pressing her lips to mine. Her hands find the back of my neck as she holds together. When she pulls away she rests her head on mine, a smile covering her face.

"I love you Sydney Garcia."

"I love you Phoebe Conners."

This was not just her fight, and it was not just mine. This was a fight for us. A fight so there would be a world for us. A world that we could live together and be happy. Fight to bring back the dreams we once had together. It was her and I again. It was Phoebe and I, just like it was supposed to be all those years ago.